STORMRISE

STORMRISE

JILLIAN BOEHME

TOR
TEEN

A TOM DOHERTY ASSOCIATES BOOK
NEW YORK

STORMRISE

Copyright © 2019 by Jill Schafer Boehme

Design by Mary A. Wirth

A Tor Teen Book
Published by Tom Doherty Associates
120 Broadway
New York, NY 10271

www.tor-forge.com

Tor® is a registered trademark of Macmillan Publishing Group, LLC.

The Library of Congress Cataloging-in-Publication Data
is available upon request.

ISBN 978-1-250-29888-1 (hardcover)
ISBN 978-1-250-29889-8 (ebook)

Our books may be purchased in bulk for promotional, educational, or business use. Please contact your local bookseller or the Macmillan Corporate and Premium Sales Department at 1-800-221-7945, extension 5442, or by email at MacmillanSpecialMarkets@macmillan.com.

First Edition: September 2019

Printed in the United States of America

0 9 8 7 6 5 4 3 2 1

For Maggie,
who never stopped believing

Fiery red, the pride of heaven,
Fierce T'Gonnen.
Bowing to her lord and master,
Loyal, brave Nuaga.

—THE LAMENT OF NUAGA

STORMRISE

1

I assumed the second stance—legs spread, knees bent, back sword-straight—and wondered for the thousandth time if I looked anything like the son I should have been.

"Quiet your breathing, Rain." Papa's voice was a murmur, a rumble of sound that calmed me like distant thunder. "Don't let me see your chest heaving."

Of course my chest was heaving. We were on the third round of the third set, and my too-late night had stolen the edge from my strength. I closed my mouth and forced air in through my nose, long and slow. Like a snake.

"Better." Papa matched me, his form graceful and balanced. He was every bit the grandmaster I wished I could someday be.

But could never be.

He moved a half-breath before I expected him to—more evidence that I was short on sleep. I arced my knife arm and matched him anyway, thinking through my paces as my feet danced on the packed earth. Papa's face was serene, as if this were effortless. That's what I was supposed to do with my face, too, and most days, Papa's praise for my "centeredness" was high.

"Masterful control," he would say. "From a distance, no one would guess you were a girl."

That was the highest compliment—to fight like a boy. Because being a girl was never quite enough.

Papa had just gained the advantage when he stumbled and lost his center. I stepped back, hesitant to claim victory when I saw that he'd slipped on one of my writing pens. He righted himself and gave the Great Cry before slicing forward with a double palm strike that I barely had time to block. I lost my balance and landed hard on my backside.

"Never lose an opportunity!" The hard edge in Papa's voice had more to do with his own shame than my weakness. "The hesitation of an enemy should be the moment of your victory."

"I know, Papa." I drew up my knees and rested my arms on them. "But it was my fault. My writing pen—"

"Was no reason for you to show mercy." He offered his hand. "We are not promised a path without obstacles."

It was like him not to mention that I shouldn't have been so careless with the pen. I took his hand. "I have the best teacher."

"Papa, you won!" My twin brother Storm shuffled toward us, eager for Papa's attention.

I tightened my grip on Papa's hand and pulled myself to standing, not missing the warmth in his eyes—my compliment had gone deep. "Only because I stayed up too late writing."

Storm giggled—a throaty sound that didn't match his stature or the deepness of his voice. "My turn now." His words were slow and slurred and better suited for a five-year-old.

Papa smiled broadly, but his eyes were sad as Storm approached. The sickness we'd had when we were barely a year old had left him forever scathed—half the son he should have been. It was hard, sometimes, to be the one left untouched.

I turned to Papa and bowed, arms crossed over my chest. "As the sun rises."

He bowed in return. "So it sets."

Storm swung his arm around my shoulders and squeezed. "Will you spot me?"

"Of course." Our sister Willow was waiting for me, but this was more important.

I sat cross-legged while Papa helped Storm assume the first stance, reminding him to relax his arms and straighten his legs. Storm nodded with each word of instruction and clapped his hands when Papa said it was time to begin the round.

I scuffled through the dirt, now in a crouch, now on my knees, following Storm and calling reminders to him. Never once did I interfere with anything Papa said—no instructor could have been finer. But Storm's exuberance always got the better of him, and he needed me to keep him focused.

"Eyes on Papa!" I cupped my hands around my mouth to amplify my voice. "Eyes on Papa, Storm!"

Storm lunged awkwardly to the left, and I rolled out of his way moments before he stumbled and fell. I rushed to his side and sat beside him.

"Are you hurt?"

"Not hurt, Rain." But his eyes swam with tears.

I kissed the face that looked more like mine than a brother's should. Eyes, nose, the height of our brows—until Storm's facial hair had begun to darken, even Mama sometimes confused us. Especially since I often wore pants instead of my sister's cast-off skirts.

"For reasons unknown, I almost always find you sitting in the dirt."

Willow crossed her arms as she approached, her perfect hair, tied at the nape of her neck, framing her perfect, heart-shaped face.

"I was spotting Storm." I rose while Papa reached for Storm's hand.

"You're a mess." Willow grabbed my wrist, her pale olive hand in stark contrast to my darker, sun-goldened skin. She eyed the ink stains on my second and third fingers and wrinkled her nose. "I knew I smelled oil last night. You should go to bed earlier."

"Sleeping is overrated."

"I've been ready for almost half an hour," Willow said. "Might we go to town before all the shops close?"

"It's barely past morning tea." I turned to Papa. "He was a little quicker that time, don't you think?"

"A little, yes." It was the same game we always played—seeing improvement that wasn't there.

Willow stepped between us. "Rain. Honestly."

"Give me five minutes." I ran toward the house, pretending not to hear her as she called out a reminder to wash my face.

Fifteen minutes later, with a clean face and a fresh linen skirt and blouse, I met Willow at the gate of our modest yard. A rehearsed apology was on my lips, but the irritation I had expected didn't seem to be there. She smiled in a sort of not-quite-there way and opened the gate, stepping aside to let me pass through.

Ever since her betrothal, there hadn't been much to lower her spirits. As if finding a husband were the single most important thing in the universe.

"How much are you spending?" I asked as we made our way down the flower-lined footpath.

"As much as I need to." She must have seen the skepticism on my face, because she added, "It's just a few basics. Materials for my bridal trunk, a new dress for dinner with his family. Not more than a couple of *tak*."

I stared. "That could buy enough food to feed us for days."

"Well, it's not grocery money," Willow said, her voice edged with defensiveness. "Papa and Mama set it aside for me, along with my dowry."

"I know that." I gentled my voice. "You deserve it. Truly."

Papa hadn't been able to afford Willow's dowry by the time she turned eighteen, and it had been a source of shame for her. Now, at nineteen, she was delighted to be at the receiving end of Papa's recent good fortune.

"I'm so eager to meet him," Willow said, her voice airy again. "He's from Thorn Village, just over the rise."

"Yes, you told me." Six hundred times.

"Do you think he will mind an older wife?"

I held back a laugh. "Seriously, Willow. You're nineteen, not forty-nine."

"You know what I mean."

"He's eighteen," I said. "I don't think a year makes so much difference."

"Most girls my age are married already."

I frowned. "Are you going to start that again?"

"No." Willow grabbed my hand and squeezed it. "We're going to pick out the most beautiful, seductive nightgown we can find."

"*We?*"

"Yes. And you're going to pay close attention, because your turn is next."

My stomach did the same flip it always did whenever someone

brought up my own betrothal. "I don't mind waiting until I'm nine-teen."

"You won't have to, silly duckling! Papa already has half your dowry put away. You're in much better shape than I was at your age."

I bit back my normal retort—that I'd rather die a toothless hag in the gutter than be married off to a boy I'd never met. Willow was the daughter any parents would dream of—lovely, obedient, eager to serve the high king by becoming a wife and siring fine soldiers. Even if it meant marrying a boy who, for whatever reason, was willing to accept a girl past the traditional age of betrothal.

"I don't think I'll find a boy who won't mind if I greet him at the door wearing my Neshu robe."

"Once you're betrothed, you won't waste your time on that any-more," Willow said. "You'll realize what's really important."

"I already know what's important."

Her face clouded with scorn. "Neshu is for boys, Rain. And no matter how good Papa says you are, that's not going to make things any better for Storm. And you know it."

I wanted to say the words that burned on my heart every time we had this argument—that if I hadn't been born, Storm would be the Neshu fighter I aspired to be. But I remained silent, certain she knew the truth as well as I did.

She softened her voice. "You'll bring Papa and Mama honor in your own time. Besides, you—"

"Move!" I pushed her out of the way as several fine black steeds made their way across our path. As expected, I lowered my eyes and bowed my head, not daring to look even though I longed to cast a disdainful glance at them.

Willow peered after the riders. "Didn't they see us?"

But we both knew the answer. It was up to us to move out of the way or be trampled. To the noble, a girl upon a country road had as much value as a flea in a horse's ear.

I glanced at the backs of the riders, their bright red and green liv-ery indicative of the underking of Tenema, our province. My stomach twitched, nudging me that something wasn't right.

"Stupid riders," I said, threading my arm through Willow's. "Let's get your shopping done before they line the streets with dung, *s'da?*"

Willow nodded, and I watched the riders grow smaller as they headed toward town. For several delicious seconds, I imagined knocking one of them off his horse and riding it to the sea.

If Willow saw my smile, she ignored it.

Nandel sat nestled among the rolling fields of *avila,* a cultivated flower known for its medicinal properties and its use as both a flavoring in local dishes and a liqueur that was known to be the best in the province of Tenema—possibly all of Ylanda. The medicine, derived from the roots of the *avila* plant, was a potent antidote for everything from festering wounds to heart ailments; even many who didn't sell spices or spirits had small fields for their own use. Our town was a popular place for visitors, not only because of the beautiful *avila* fields and local liqueur, but also because of the rich selection of shops and eateries.

Willow loved the bustling streets and crowded shops. I was happier at home, where I could write poetry and practice Neshu away from the gazes of those who wouldn't approve.

I was also happier near Storm, whose world existed at home. He was our barely whispered secret—the damaged child who had stolen my parents' honor. If our small property and the roof over our heads was good enough for him, it was good enough for me.

Also I hated shopping.

Hours later, my arms ached with the wrapped bundles I carried—a fine bathing pitcher, embroidery floss, scented oils, lace, and yards of silk and linen for bedclothes, table covers, and undergarments. We'd be doing much sewing in the weeks ahead. I groaned inwardly and tried not to think about it.

Willow hugged her newfound treasure—an embarrassingly transparent nightgown that trailed to the floor and dragged behind her like an oversized broom. I couldn't believe she'd actually tried it on and made me look at her. I'd requested an extra layer of paper wrapping to make sure nobody could see it.

"One more stop," Willow said, leading me down a narrow, winding street I wasn't familiar with.

"Why so far off the main square?" I tried not to sound irritable, but I was hungry as well as tired.

"Because Madam S'dora's shop isn't on the main square."

"Madam S'dora?" I stopped short. "Are you joking?"

Willow spun around, a mischievous glint in her eyes. "I hear she sells things for the wedding night." She turned and kept walking.

"Things?" I hurried to keep up, the packages shifting and rolling in my arms. "What things?"

But she didn't answer. I wasn't even sure which shop was Madam S'dora's, but I knew enough from local tongues to know what was in it—potions, powders, and, for all I knew, poisons, none of which would find their way onto any respectable apothecary's shelves.

Her old-days name made it no secret that she was born in the province of Ytel, where people supposedly adhered to a belief in the old tales—and in magic. Some people laughed and rolled their eyes at the mention of her name; others scoffed and said she was evil. I wasn't sure if it was because she believed in dragons or because she looked like one; I'd only seen her from a distance, once. I was five, and a sudden wind had blown a handkerchief from my hand. I ran to fetch it, and the tallest, thinnest woman I'd ever seen stepped from an alleyway, picked up the handkerchief, and held it out to me. I stared for several seconds before running away.

"It's good you ran," Mama had told me later. "Madam S'dora doesn't walk on the light side of the moon."

I sighed and hastened after my sister, bracing myself to walk into darkness.

2

Willow waited for me by the substantial wooden door of Madam S'dora's shop, its surface thick with layers of paint, its leaded glass panes grimy. From the awning, a sign creaked on its iron rings: *Tinctures and Cures.*

Willow reached for the door's handle, but I stepped in front of her.

"What would Mama say if she saw us here?"

"She won't see us," Willow said. "And you won't tell her." She cupped her hand around my cheek in a distinctly older-sister way. "It's fine, Rain. She's just an old woman selling things that nobody gives her credit for. And Mama said to buy whatever would make me happy."

I sighed. "You don't even *know* this boy."

"When you're betrothed, you'll understand." She pushed the door open and gestured with her head. "Go on."

The air in the shop was heavy with scents I didn't recognize, pungent and musty and sickeningly sweet all at the same time. In the dimness, I stumbled over a basket of—something—on the floor when I stepped aside to let Willow enter. Long, big-knuckled fingers caught me by the forearm and kept me from falling.

"I told Current to find another place for the basket. Looks like I'll have to move it myself."

"I—thank you."

One of the packs of embroidery floss slipped from my pile, and Madam S'dora bent to pick it up. She had to have been older than mud—stories of her little shop stretched back to my grandparents' day—but her hair was as solidly black as my own, hanging to the small of her back. When she stood again, she towered over me by a head at least. Taller than Papa.

"There's a place here," Madam S'dora said, patting a rough wooden table that sat in front of the curtained shop window. "Lay your things down and give your arms a rest."

Gratefully, I dumped Willow's goodies onto the table and thanked Madam S'dora again. Willow cleared her throat.

"You're Madam S'dora?" The squeak in her voice told me she wasn't feeling as confident as she had a moment ago.

"Well, I'm not the queen of Ylanda." Madam S'dora turned toward the counter at the back, her gait slow but not stiff. "One of you is clearly getting married." She slipped behind the counter, then turned to face us, her eyebrows arched, her eyes on me. "Is it you?"

My face grew warm. "No. My sister."

Willow sidled through a narrow aisle between shelves of merchandise. "I'm looking for something for my wedding night."

"You'll have to be more specific," Madam S'dora said.

I spied a short, round stool near the other end of the table, so I sat and made myself as small as possible. Hopefully, Madam S'dora would figure things out and we could leave. I didn't want to listen to Willow talking about her wedding night for longer than I had to.

"Well . . ." Willow cleared her throat again. "Two things, really. I've heard . . . I mean, friends have told me . . . that you have something to take care of . . . of unwanted bleeding?"

I closed my eyes and sank lower onto the stool.

"Ahh." Madam S'dora sounded all-knowing. Empathetic. "No bride wants to be surprised by her monthly bleed on her wedding night."

"Yes," Willow said. "That's it exactly."

"Easily remedied," Madam S'dora said, "though I am admittedly low on supply right now. That will affect the price."

"Any price is fine."

I opened my mouth to contradict her, thought better of it, and clamped my mouth shut.

Madam S'dora pulled something out of a jar—a small bag of some sort. "I've found that the most effective way to administer the tincture is through a simple tea. Drink three cups during the day your bleeding starts, and by the next morning, it will stop."

Willow took the bag. "How does it work?"

Even in the dim shop, Madam S'dora's smile was bright. "Dragon magic, of course. That's all you really want to know, isn't it?"

"Yes." Willow's laugh was nervous. "If you say so."

"Whether I say so or not hardly matters." Madam S'dora took the bag from Willow's hand and placed it on the counter.

"Three cups of tea, then," Willow said. "And you're sure it will work?"

"I wouldn't sell something I wasn't sure of." She gestured to the bag. "Extract of dragonmilk never goes bad. So if luck goes your way on your wedding night, you can save it for another time. Is there anything else I can help you with?"

"Well, yes. I was wondering . . . I mean, some of my friends told me you have . . ."

She lowered her voice so that I couldn't understand her words. I considered sneaking up the closest aisle and eavesdropping, but that would have been like admitting to Madam S'dora that my own sister didn't want me to hear what she was ordering. I folded my arms and wished they'd hurry.

"One *tak*, thirty," Madam S'dora said when they'd finished whispering.

My head shot up as Willow sucked in an audible breath. "Two hundred thirty coin?"

"It's a full *tak* for the tea," Madam S'dora said. "Creating extracts is a long, complicated process."

I waited for Willow to look over her shoulder and ask for my advice with a raise of her eyebrow, but she only sighed and reached into her leather pocket-purse. Two dull *plunk*s sounded through the dust—a *tak* and a half-*tak* hitting the counter.

Madam S'dora scooped them up, then counted the change into Willow's hand. "May every blessing be upon your wedding night."

"Thank you." Willow placed the small package on top of her embarrassing nightgown and picked them both up. "Ready, Rain?"

I gathered her purchases from the table, balancing them carefully before following her out the door. As soon as the door closed behind us, I turned to her.

"What were you thinking, spending that kind of money on back-alley tinctures?"

Willow bit her lip. "I didn't know the tea would be so expensive."

"And for what? To avoid bleeding on your wedding night? Why would it even matter? You're going to be married the rest of your lives—he can surely wait a few days if he has to."

"A successful wedding night ensures the blessing of future sons," Willow said. "You know that."

I didn't know any such thing. But if it were true, then Papa and Mama must have had an unsuccessful wedding night.

"You're going to have a successful marriage no matter what," I said. "I wish you'd stop worrying."

Willow kissed my cheek. "Once you meet him and approve, *then* I'll stop worrying."

"Why then?"

"Because if you like him, you won't attack him in his sleep."

I laughed. "Let's go home. I'm starving."

We passed two of the horsemen as we turned onto the main street. As always, I lowered my eyes and continued along my way. But as soon as they were some distance, I turned and gawked.

"I wonder why they're here."

Willow shrugged, her mind too full of wedding plans to be bothered about the horsemen. We continued in silence until we passed another horse and rider. Something in my stomach tightened.

"What do you think is going on?" I said after the rider had passed.

"It could be anything," Willow said absently. "Or nothing."

By now, we were at the mouth of the Central Square. A fourth rider made his way through a growing crowd that had clustered around a wooden signpost.

"Some sort of edict has gone out," I said.

"Or an invitation?" That was Willow—always hopeful.

"We're not close to any holiday. Come on."

Worry gnawed at my stomach as I tried to read the faces of those who had already seen the sign. Concern. Introspection. Anger.

One girl shoved her way through the crowd, her face wet with tears.

"Rain, let's not push," Willow said.

But I was beyond worrying about stepping on anyone's toes. My arms burned with Willow's tower of purchases, and I used their bulk to my advantage as I wedged my way between unyielding people. It was either move aside or be squashed by wedding clobber.

Finally I reached the sign, nailed firm and embellished with the seal of the high king's secretary. The words dropped like stones into my heart.

> By order of His Majesty the high king of Ylanda: Every household within the borders of our kingdom shall submit unto His Majesty's national army one able-bodied male, whether father or son, nephew or brother, according to the census and in accordance with the Law of Mandatory Conscription. Soldiers must report to the camp at Grigsbane by Bri 20 to receive immediate assignment or training.

Willow pushed up beside me as I stared at the words, her breathing rapid in my ear. "What does this mean? What's going on?"

My mouth could barely form the words. "It means we're at war."

I didn't say what I also knew to be true—that Storm was bound by law to go, because he bore no physical disability.

And he would be among the first to die.

3

I turned away from the notice and shoved my way past people trying to move in closer. Willow's voice floated on the periphery of my hearing, her words lost to me.

Storm.

It was enough that his intellect had been stolen. Would he now lose his life on the front lines of battle—and never know the injustice of his sacrifice?

"Rain, stop." Willow's fingers dug into my arm.

I dropped my armload of her things, remembering at the last moment to let the bathing pitcher land lightly. "You'll have to take some of these."

Willow picked up the nearest package. "Storm is a simpleton. Surely they don't mean for him to go."

"One male from every household. It's Storm's place to honor his family."

"But that's not fair. Why can't—oh!" Her face contorted into something close to horror. "My betrothed. He's an only son."

"And he will go and fight, as an only son would."

"No, Rain! No!" She hugged the package to her breast, pacing. "This can't be happening."

Before my eyes, Willow's world began to fall apart. I draped my arm around her shoulders. "All brides must prepare for this sort of thing, yes?"

"I haven't even met him! I've waited so long for this, and now I'm going to lose him before I ever see him."

I wanted to point out that her concern should be for Storm, and not for some boy she might end up hating. But I pinched the words back and instead said, "Let's go home."

We divided the bundles more evenly, though I still took the bathing pitcher, figuring it was safer with me. I knew I was walking faster than Willow could handle—she spent most of her time sewing and painting, after all—but my need to see Papa and bring him this news grew more urgent with every step. When we came into view of our gate, I started off at a run, only to come up short when I saw Papa standing outside the low wall with a visitor. I slowed then, catching my breath and hoping to look at least somewhat presentable.

Papa turned to me, his face lighting. "Ah, Rain. May I present General Tamar?"

I curtsyed, my face pressing into my armload. "Sir."

"Your father and I once fought together," General Tamar said. "I was in the area, and I thought I would pay him a visit."

My mouth felt dry, as though I might choke if I kept talking. I could detect no hint on Papa's face that he had already received the news I'd rushed home to bring him myself.

At the last moment, I remembered my manners. "Will you stay for lunch?"

"Thank you," General Tamar said, "but I have many miles to travel before nightfall." He gestured to the black steed tethered to our fence.

Willow finally caught up, breathless. "Papa!" she said in the midst of her curtsy to the general. "Papa, we've such news."

Papa exchanged a glance with the general, but his face remained placid. Unreadable.

The perfect Neshu grandmaster.

"I will leave you to your family." The general patted Papa's shoulder. "It was good to see you again."

"And you, Branch," Papa said. "Thank you for your visit."

We waited respectfully while the general mounted his horse and gave us a final wave. Then, as soon as he had passed beyond our property, I cut off Willow's attempt to speak.

"He's already told you, hasn't he?" I said.

"It was kind of him to come," Papa said.

"What did he say?" Willow asked. "What did he tell you?"

We had reached the door to our house. Papa turned to face us, his eyes gentle. "Clearly the high king's notices have already gone up in town. It spares me the sorrow of telling you about it."

Willow stifled a soblike sound. "But, Papa . . ."

He held up his hand. "Your mother is inside waiting to serve our meal. Calm yourselves, and allow me to tell her myself."

We followed him silently into the quiet warmth of our home, its low ceilings and exposed beams hugging me with a welcome I didn't feel. Everything was tidy as always—clean-swept floors, cinderless hearth, freshly plumped pillows on every seat. The family table, round and worn and filled with memories, sat laden with a meal fit for an underking.

Mama's face was wreathed in steam from a large bowl of quail cakes as she placed it on the table. She smiled at us, her eyes fixed on Papa. As always.

"I'm sorry for the delay," Papa said, sitting at his place and dipping his hands in the water bowl to wash them.

"Who was that?" Mama asked.

"Branch Tamar. An old army friend." Papa passed the water bowl to me.

I dipped my hands into the warm water without taking my eyes from him. He dried his hands as though nothing were the matter.

"And?" Mama's normally calm voice had an edge to it.

"He's been called out of retirement to return to his post as a general in the high king's army," Papa said. "There is a conscription."

Mama's hand went to her mouth, pressing against it with such force that I thought her teeth might break. She said nothing, holding back her words with the strength of her will. Her eyes were large, waiting.

"Branch tells me the threat is greater than any we have known. They're asking for one able-bodied male from every household."

"Me," Storm said. "I'm a able boy. I can fight."

Papa met Storm's gaze. "You are an able boy. And I will go with you to Grigsbane."

Storm's eyes widened, his expression like a sunrise. "Together?"

"Yes, together," Papa said.

"But, Papa," I said. "The battlefield is no place for Storm."

"Branch assured me there'll be noncombat work for him. Honorable work."

Like digging latrines and disposing of severed limbs. "It's too much for him."

Storm frowned. "It's not too much. I'm a Neshu fighter."

"Yes, you are," Papa said. "But the high king may need you for other things."

"He's my little boy." Mama had found her voice. "My forever-child."

"And yet we must send him," Papa said gently. "If it's not enough, I will be there to take his place."

"You can't go," I said, though I was out of turn. "We need you here."

"*Rain.*" Mama shaped my name into a sharp hiss. A slap. "Do not dishonor your father."

Papa reached across the table and laid his hand on Mama's. "She means no dishonor."

"It's bad enough they would take Storm." Mama's bottom lip quivered. "You would let them take you, too?"

"He cannot go alone."

"Surely there's no way for them to know that he exists."

Papa's words were calm, like warm tea. "His name is on the census."

"Yes. Of course." Mama squeezed her eyes shut and swallowed hard. When she opened them, they were bright. "They might turn you away, though."

"Branch assured me they won't. Stonewall has been breached—they will take every man they can get."

Fear swam through my stomach. "How is that even possible?"

Stonewall was our greatest defense—a hefty wall that had proven impenetrable for generations. Its sheer height and breadth were deterrent enough, but Ylanda warriors stood guard on its broad walkways as well. The nomads of the barren northern plains, though covetous of our fertile provinces—and especially Tenema's prized *avila* crops—had always fought among themselves more often than they attempted to breach our wall. No more than two or three tribes had ever been known to unite against us, such as during the skirmishes on the seaward border. Where Papa had been wounded.

"General Tamar says one of the chieftains—Tan Vey—has conquered all the other chieftains and united the nomads into a single people. A single army."

"Bigger than ours?" I asked.

"Bigger by far," Papa said. "That's why the conscription has been called."

"And they're marching for Ylanda City?"

"Most likely." Papa wrapped his hands around his tankard of ale. "We must protect our high king at all costs. If he falls, so falls the kingdom."

I knew the ancient law, set in place long before Stonewall existed. In the land stretching from the western mountains to the eastern sea, a kingdom with no ruler belonged to whoever claimed it. Ylanda sat within these boundaries, fair and prosperous since the first high king took the throne centuries ago.

This was why our high kings throughout history were never seen on the field of battle. The death of our ruler and his heirs would mean the loss of everything we held dear—our traditions, our safety. So the royal family lived ensconced in the castle in Ylanda City, ensuring that not even the greatest invasion would put us in jeopardy of losing everything.

Surely the nomads, the only ones who ever sought to claim us, would never reach the capital. Perhaps they were great in number, but this was our land, and they couldn't know it as we did. The *avila* they coveted might've been theirs through fair trade, but always the various tribes had tried to take what they wanted through raids and border skirmishes that they almost never won. It was about more than the medicinal plant, I was certain. But I had no idea what.

"I'm a grandmaster, like you, Papa." Storm looked at me. "I'm your favorite grandmaster, right, Rain?"

My heart twisted. "Yes. You're my favorite."

"So, then," Papa said. "It's settled."

Oh, Papa.

He had served his time, fighting faithfully in the border skirmishes when I still had my baby teeth. I remembered the papa that left us—strong, quick, ready to toss me into the air or race me along the hedgerow. And I remembered the papa that came back—broken, barely making it down the lane on a rough-hewn crutch, his chest and shoulder heavily bandaged.

He hadn't given his life for the high king, but he might as well have, because, for several years, he couldn't work at all. We almost starved. When he had healed enough to resume teaching Neshu students, it took a while for word to spread. Finally, last year, he had achieved the position of grandmaster, and our fortunes turned. Papa had regained the life and the honor he once had.

And now the high king was taking him again—all because his only son wasn't able to do it alone.

I'm sorry, Storm. Things would be different if I hadn't been born.

Willow sighed. "It's not fair."

"We live to serve our high king, voice of the Great God," Papa said. "It's not ours to say whether or not something is fair."

"But, Papa—" A sharp sound from Mama's throat arrested me.

"My son and I will serve the high king," Papa said. "There's nothing more to discuss."

I saw the pride in Papa's jaw and heard it in his voice. But I saw the sorrow in his eyes, too. And the shame. It shouldn't have been necessary for him to accompany his son to the army camp. If Storm had recovered from the fever, we would all have been proudly sending him off. Then Papa could have stayed home, where he belonged, and provided for his wife and daughters. My eyes filled with angry tears that I brushed away.

"We will manage until you return." Mama's words shook like petals in the wind.

Papa took a great breath. "And if we do not—"

"Don't say that, Papa!" I couldn't restrain myself. "Of course you'll come home."

Papa glanced at Mama and said nothing.

"Besides," I said, "you're the greatest grandmaster in Tenema. Your students need you as much as we do."

"Most of my students will go and fight, Rain," Papa said softly.

I pressed my lips together and lowered my eyes. Saying more would only make Papa's shame greater.

"Me and Papa are brave soldiers," Storm said through a mouthful of quail cake. "Don't worry, Rain."

"Papa." Willow's voice was not quite a whisper. "How will this affect . . . my dowry?"

"The Chance family will hold it in good faith until their son returns," Papa said.

"But what if . . . what if . . ." Her words crumbled into a silent sob.

"There is no *what if,* Willow L'nahn," Mama said gently. "A woman knows that her place is to wait quietly and trust the Great God to take care of things." She must've missed my grimace, because she continued without reproving me. "When your time comes to marry, nothing will hinder it."

"I know," Willow said. "It's just that I've waited so long."

"You're nineteen," Mama said. "You do not yet know what it means to wait long."

I took Mama's meaning, and Willow's expression told me that she did, too. Papa and Mama had been married for fourteen years before Willow was born. A huge disgrace, those years of childlessness. Willow had been welcomed with as much joy as if she had been a son. When Storm and I had come along two years later, they would have been content with only my brother.

They would never have admitted that. But any second daughter in Ylanda knew it to be true.

"Remember, too, that you had an additional suitor," Papa said. "To my knowledge, he has still not found a wife."

Willow's mouth opened, a huge O. "But he's old. And widowed."

"He's not *that* old," Papa said dryly.

"He walks with a *cane.* Surely you wouldn't turn my dowry over to him, Papa."

"If Storm and I do not come back, there will be three mouths in this house that need feeding. Do you think, perhaps, it might be better to marry an old widower so that he could take care of you— and your mother?"

I chewed my quail cake while Willow retreated into silence. Papa hadn't mentioned who would take care of me if he didn't come back. I would rather live on the riverbank and hand-catch my daily meals than marry an old man with money.

"Rain."

Papa's voice filtered through the layers of my thoughts as I scribbled words I knew I'd only have to discard later. I looked up from my bed to see him framed in my doorway, his features soft in the lamplight.

"Yes?" I stuck my pen behind my ear.

He raised an eyebrow at my stained fingers. "Am I interrupting your poetry?"

"It's not going well, anyway," I said. "Do you need something?"

"Since we'll be leaving the day after tomorrow, I thought this might be a good time to give this to you." He walked to my bedside and handed me a thin wooden box.

It was heavy in my hands, and something inside it shifted. "What's this?"

"Half of your dowry."

I stared at him for a moment before opening the box. More *tak* than I had ever seen at once lay piled inside.

"Papa."

"Fifty *tak* isn't enough to secure you a husband, but when I come home, I will provide the rest."

The weight on my heart came from words unspoken. If he didn't come home, I would at least have half a dowry to build upon. After a few years of laboring in the fields, I could, perhaps, make up the difference.

"Why give this to me now?" I asked. "Why not leave it in Mama's care?"

His smile was sad. "Somehow, I think you will do just fine, Rain L'nahn. Even if you marry at thirty, I don't fear for you."

Something half laugh, half sob came out of my throat. "Thank you, Papa."

He kissed the top of my head. "We will weather this storm, my daughter."

But I had no intention of weathering the storm. I would face it head-on—and take it down. Like the Neshu fighter Papa had trained me to be.

I hugged the coin chest for a long time after he'd left. And for even longer, I sat in the dark, unable to sleep.

"Rain." Storm's whisper was husky at my door.

I pulled my blanket over the money box. "Come in."

"I had a bad dream."

"Tell me about it."

He sat on the bed and rubbed his eyes. "I can't remember. But there were soldiers. And monsters."

"Did you kill the monsters?"

"I don't remember."

I took his hand. "Are you afraid to go to war?"

"No. I'm a brave soldier."

"Being brave doesn't mean you're never afraid."

He sighed, long and deep. "Can I sleep in here?"

"No, Storm. Papa and Mama want you to sleep in your own bed." I kissed his hand. "I love you."

He stayed a while longer, sitting quietly, probably hoping I'd change my mind. Finally I gave him a gentle nudge, and he rose and shuffled out, already half asleep.

It should have been me, waking in the dark with the dreams of a child. When Storm and I were sick, the healer had only enough medicine for one of us and said he'd come back the next day with more. Of course my parents had told him to give the medicine to their son, but he had given it to me instead. Overnight, I improved, and Storm grew worse. And never fully recovered.

I couldn't let him go to war. The likelihood that he and Papa would return was lower than I could bear to admit. But the only alternative would be for someone else to step up in his place.

A nephew or cousin, second male in their own families. A second son, sound in mind and body.

We had none of those options. There were only Papa and Storm and Mama and Willow.

And me.

I should have been a son.

I could be a son.

At first, the idea terrified me. True, I was quick on my feet and not curvy—and I looked so much like Storm. With a military hairstyle and armor, maybe I could create the illusion. But how long would it take for me to be discovered? Would the first words out of my mouth betray my true sex?

And what would I do during my monthly bleed?

Discovery would mean death. If I were caught, my punishment would be swift and sure.

But.

What if there were some way to strengthen my disguise?

Madam S'dora's shelves were filled with mixtures and powders and potions beyond my imaginings. And she had sold Willow a tea that would make her bleeding stop for her wedding night. Surely she had something similar that I could use to stop my bleed indefinitely?

My heart battered my chest, forcing my breaths to come fast and shallow. If my disguise were good enough, no one would know. The possibility of meeting someone who would recognize me was small; I spent most of my time at home and had no friends from town. And because we'd kept Storm quietly hidden away since he was six or seven, there was little chance anyone would recognize him by sight, either.

If I left at night, while everyone else slept, I could make my escape without worry.

A hundred things could go wrong, but in my heart it was settled.

I would go in the morning to Madam S'dora's. If she had what I needed, then nothing would stop me.

I would become the son my father needed.

My hands curled around the money box, guilt prickling the edges of my heart. This was dowry money, entrusted to me in good faith. Even if I only spent a quarter of it at Madam S'dora's, that was a lot.

But if I went in Storm's place, then Papa could stay home, too. He wouldn't have to worry about never returning. And if I died, I wouldn't need a dowry, anyway.

"I'm doing this for you and Storm, Papa," I whispered. Then I slid the box beneath my pillow and willed myself to sleep.

4

The money bag was heavy in my satchel. At first, I had intended to only bring half of the coins. But then I realized that if Madam S'dora had what I needed, I should buy as much as possible and not have to worry about running out. So I'd taken all fifty *tak* from the box and slid them into a bag that barely contained them. Then I stuck the bag into a satchel, hiding them beneath the linens from my bed, which I claimed I needed to wash.

"I've warned you about writing in bed," Mama had said as I left.

It was only a partial lie. There was no ink spill on my sheets, but I did intend to wash them and lay them out on the grassy bank to dry. That part, at least, would be true. I pulled my straw hat low over my eyes and set off.

It was hard, at first, to remember which street to turn down. Yesterday, I mostly had been following Willow and trying not to drop everything I was carrying. After a moment or so of near-panic, I recognized the building at the corner of the street I was looking for. I ducked my head and hurried into the obscurity of Madam S'dora's street and into her shop.

She looked up as soon as I opened the door and watched me as I made my way to her counter. I meant to say hello, but my heart was beating too fast for talking to seem easy. So I forced a smile instead.

"Has your sister sent you, or are you here on your own business?"

She remembered me. "My own business." I dropped my satchel—carefully—at my feet.

Madam S'dora nodded as if she weren't at all surprised that I'd come. "So. What does Little Sister need that she didn't want to ask for while Big Sister was present?"

Heat rushed to my face, and it occurred to me that there was no way for me to explain why I needed what I needed. "I need something to stop the bleeding."

"Bleeding?" She leaned in, her hands splayed on the counter. "Monthly bleeding, or something else?"

"No," I said. "Yes. Monthly."

A smile played at the corners of her mouth. "An elopement?"

If my face were any hotter, it might spontaneously combust. "No. Nothing like that."

"Well, you'll have to be clearer about what you want."

"I want"—I took a deep breath—"to stop the bleeding. Permanently."

I could hear the dust settling as Madam S'dora stared at me. It wasn't a stare of judgment or even surprise. It was, simply, a stare. Like she was trying to read the thoughts behind my brow bone.

"Permanently?" she asked.

"For a long time, anyway," I said. "As long as possible."

"Hmm." She turned her back and disappeared through a small, curtained doorway.

I drummed my fingers on the counter in an effort to make myself feel casual. Inside, though, I was tight as a bowstring, ready to snap if someone so much as touched me on the shoulder. I peered around the shop, making sure the scuttle I'd heard was only a mouse and not the soft shoes of someone else waiting to buy a potion.

It seemed an entire day before Madam S'dora emerged, bearing an amber jar with a thick cork stopper. The glass was too dark for me to see inside, and I tried not to stare as she set the jar before me.

"How much are you willing to risk?"

I opened my mouth but closed it when I realized she hadn't said "pay." A creeping sensation played along the edges of my hair and down the back of my neck.

"Silence tells me you're unsure," Madam S'dora said.

"I don't know what you mean by 'risk,'" I said.

Her voice trailed lower, almost reverent. "This is an ancient magic, and powerful. Not to be dealt with lightly."

I swallowed. "What is it?"

She pried the stopper from the bottle and took a slow, gentle sniff. Euphoria spread over her face like sunlight. "This." She pushed the jar toward me and gestured to her nose.

I didn't want to smell it. I wanted to change my mind and run from the shop. But I leaned over and took a tentative sniff.

And gagged.

Whatever was in the jar smelled sharp and dull and fresh and old at the same time. Mostly it smelled like dead feet, or the inside of a fish barrel that had been left in the sun.

Madam S'dora grinned. "It's an acquired taste."

"What is it?" I asked again.

"A strong powder from the remains of T'Gonnen himself," she said. "One pinch a day beneath your tongue will keep your womanly time from coming. But you may find it has other effects as well." She cocked her head, waiting for my question, but I was too busy trying to imagine placing a pinch of dead feet under my tongue every day. So she continued, "It may increase your facial hair or deepen your voice. Or it may not."

My heart jumped. Either of those effects would help with my disguise. "Is that all?"

Madam S'dora coiled cold fingers around my hand. "You understand what I mean when I say dragon magic?"

I bit back a retort. Dragons were nothing but myth, dragon magic a child's tale. If Madam S'dora believed in that, it was no wonder she sold her wares in a dark shop off the beaten path. Anyone making claims like that in the Tenema marketplace would have been ridiculed.

Still, I didn't want to jeopardize the sale. So I kept my expression neutral and said, "I know nothing about dragon magic, Madam S'dora."

She nodded soberly and her grasp on my hand tightened. "T'Gonnen was high king of dragons! When you swallow this powder, his magic becomes a part of you."

"I don't care what's in it, as long as it works." Which, at this point, I was beginning to doubt. T'Gonnen was a name from the dragon mythology. A story told to scare children into obedience.

Madam S'dora shrugged and wrapped her hands around the jar.

"If you buy it, you can choose to care or not about what you are swallowing." She cocked her head. "It might awaken things. You could have dreams."

I frowned. "Dreams?"

"The power of T'Gonnen is strong," Madam S'dora said. "His final gift to us. There's no telling how it may affect you."

"I just need to know that it works."

"Everything in my shop . . . *works*." She raised an eyebrow. "Do you want to buy some or not?"

I hesitated. Madam S'dora studied me, and for a moment I was five again, and she was holding out the handkerchief, smiling.

Kind. For two heartbeats, that's what my heart had said. But then childish fear had taken over, squashing my heart's impression.

"You're afraid," she said softly. "But it's not the powder you fear."

"I'm only afraid of doing the wrong thing."

"Of breaking the law by pretending you're a boy?"

I cringed. "I know it's against the law."

On the surface, it made sense—since men owned all property in Ylanda, a woman caught impersonating a man was branded a thief, under the assumption that it was her intent to claim ownership that wasn't legally hers. The penalty was death without trial.

"If you're discovered, they will show you no mercy. But the magic in this powder is . . ." Madam S'dora lowered her voice to a whisper. "Immeasurable."

"I hope you're right."

Madam S'dora smiled. "How much do you need?"

It was a good question. How long would I have to keep up this deception? How many weeks would I last until I was found out—or fell in battle?

"A year's worth," I said.

"Dragon magic is powerful. Are you sure?"

"I need enough for a year."

She nodded. "That will be eighty *tak*."

"Eighty!" It flew from my lips before I could stop it.

"This particular magic of T'Gonnen is not replenishable," Madam S'dora said. "When the powder is gone, there will be nothing to replace it."

The rarity of the powder made no difference—I didn't have eighty *tak*. "I'll take six months' worth, then," I said.

"Forty *tak*."

So much money. Too much. Almost the entire half of the dowry Papa had given me in good faith. What would he think if he saw me right now?

I swallowed the tightness in my throat. "*S'da*."

"Very well. This will take me a few minutes."

She retrieved a small, wide bowl from the shelf beneath the counter, along with a tiny, long-handled spoon. With a steady, graceful hand, she began to scoop the dark powder into the bowl, pinch by pinch.

"One . . . two . . . three . . ."

I turned away, desperate to find something—anything—to distract me while she painstakingly measured the powder. A box of cylindrical metal amulets set with tiny, uncut jewels caught my attention. Their beauty was negligible, but there was something compelling about them. I had just picked one up to examine it more closely when the shop door creaked open.

A young man entered, and I lowered my head and studied the amulet as though nothing else in the world were so important.

"Madam S'dora?" The boy's words were brusque, as though he had no time for politeness.

"I will be right with you," Madam S'dora said, and returned to her muttered counting.

"I don't have much time."

She ignored him, and he let out a short burst of air before beginning to pace. I peeked between baskets of empty bottles and rabbits' feet and stole a glance. He was short and stocky with a prominent jaw and a nose that looked as though it had once been broken.

I pulled my hat lower and made my way back to the counter, so he would see that Madam S'dora's attention was mine right now. More than anything, I wanted to leave. She counted so slowly.

"Seventy-one . . . seventy-two . . ."

"You know mine will only take a moment," the boy said.

"You'll have your moment next."

He made another exasperated sound and began to pace again. I bit back the rebuke that sizzled on my tongue. What mother had raised a son to be so rude?

Endless minutes later, Madam S'dora tapped the contents of the bowl into a soft leather pouch. I lifted my satchel onto the counter and withdrew the money bag.

I'm sorry, Papa.

I counted out the forty *tak* and placed the leather pouch in my satchel. Then I slung the satchel over my shoulder.

"One pinch every night before sleeping," Madam S'dora said. "No more or less. And don't skip a single night."

"Thank you." The words felt like gravel.

Then, suddenly, Madam S'dora reached across the counter and patted my cheek. "Whatever happens, don't be afraid."

My nod felt awkward. I was going to thank her again, but Rude Boy had returned to the counter.

"Will you help me now, old lady?"

Ire rose in me like sparks at a blacksmith's. I clenched my teeth to keep hot words from spilling out, and instead purposely shoved my satchel into the boy as I turned around. Our eyes met, and his face shifted into a leer. As I moved away, I felt his hand groping at my bottom.

I swung in an instant, bringing up my knee and knocking his arm back while hitting his chest with my knife hand. He staggered backward, catching himself on the counter, his face red.

"Your tongue should have been cut out at birth," I spat.

"Who do you think you are, little bitch?"

"Someone who thinks men should know how to treat women." I looked at Madam S'dora. "If he gives you any trouble, poison him."

Her eyes twinkled at me—I was sure they did—before I spun and exited. If I stayed another moment, I would be tempted to pummel that poor excuse for a son to the floor.

I worked out my trembling as I washed my bedding in the stream, scrubbing beyond what I needed to. After I had spread the sheets onto the grass to dry, I waded back into the water to catch some fish for that night's meal. A surprise for Mama. Or perhaps a guilt offering.

Papa had taught me to fish by hand as soon as my hands were big enough. "The patience of fishing lends itself well to the centeredness of a Neshu fighter," he would tell me. I'd never forget the first fish I caught—slippery, chaotic, exploding from between my fingers. A proud moment of my girlhood.

I took a Neshu cleansing breath, stilling myself in the water even as my mind turned over and over again the thought of swallowing Madam S'dora's powder. One pinch under my tongue at bedtime. How bad could that be? The worst of it was having spent forty *tak* of my dowry and not even knowing if the powder would work. But even if it worked, then what? Would I be able to train with the others? Would my speed and agility in Neshu make up for my lack of brawny muscle and male swagger?

It would have to. I'd made a choice that I couldn't unmake. And didn't want to.

The flick of a fish tail caught my eye, and I poised to grab it. On the first try, I swept it from the water and threw it onto the bank, where it flopped in mute protest. Then I returned my attention once more to the water.

After my third catch, I scooped the fish into my bag and left the linens to dry. I took a shorter route home, walking quickly. Even so, Mama met me in the mudroom as I was slipping off my shoes.

"What took you so long?" she asked.

"I caught you some fish." I opened the bag to show her my still-twitching catch.

She nodded, pleased. "Well, come and help me harvest the crimson squash. I can hardly keep up—such an abundance this year."

"I'll be right out."

I hastened to my room and placed the remaining ten *tak* in the box beneath my pillow, along with the pouch of powder. As I passed my parents' room on my way out, I glimpsed Papa inside, polishing his sword. My heart banged against my chest like a trapped bird as I hesitated, unsure whether to knock or to keep moving silently by.

He looked up, sparing me the choice. "The sadness of a hundred winters is in your eyes."

I stepped just past the doorway. "Not sadness, Papa. Just anger at the injustice."

"I'm honored to serve our high king."

"I know." I moved closer. "But Storm isn't fit for this. He had nightmares last night."

"I will be with him," Papa said. "I'll calm his fears."

"But you shouldn't have to go. You should have a son capable of fighting, instead of a second daughter."

Papa laid the sword on the bed and turned to me, placing his hands on my shoulders. "You are worth more to me than twenty capable sons. Surely you know that."

"I—" No, I didn't know that. I had never asked, had never let Papa's words and actions speak for themselves. Always, it was my own inner voice whispering that I was a disappointment. That Storm should have been the one to recover from the fever instead of me.

How many times had I heard Mama say, "If only the healer had given Storm the medicine!" when she thought I wasn't listening? Yet now, as the warmth from Papa's hands sank into my skin, I realized that Papa himself had never said that.

"Thank you, Papa." Tears puddled in my eyes as he drew me into a hug. "I'll miss you."

"And I will miss you," he said into my hair. "More than I can say."

I nestled into his chest, flooded with the satisfaction of knowing I would save his life. Both their lives.

In this moment, nothing else mattered.

———————

Willow sat at the table, slicing cucumbers. I grabbed a knife and sat beside her, grateful to finally have her to myself.

She eyed me sideways. "This doesn't bode well."

"I thought I'd help you." I grabbed the nearest cucumber.

"Please don't cut any fingers off, little sister."

I wrinkled my nose at her and tried to think of a casual way to bring up what I wanted to say. "Where are Mama and Papa?"

"Walking by the stream," Willow said. "I . . . wanted to give them some time together."

I heard the tremble in her voice but chose to ignore it. "I was wondering." I waited while she sniffed and wiped her eyes with the back of her hand. "What was the other thing you bought at Madam S'dora's?"

"Oh. That." She broke into a smile that hinted at embarrassment, then leaned close and lowered her voice. "For ease of the loss of maidenhood."

"What—" But I didn't really want to know. "Don't you worry that these things might be dangerous?"

"No."

"Because?"

"Because, Rain, if people died from Madam S'dora's wares, she wouldn't have stayed in business this long."

She had a point. "And you have friends who've drunk the tea?"

"Yes," Willow said. "And it's not only them. A lot of people have purchased from Madam S'dora over the years. They just don't talk about it."

"Really?" I wanted to lay this fear to rest.

"Really." She placed her hand on my wrist. "Still. Don't tell Mama and Papa about it, please?"

"I won't say a word."

"She's from Province Ytel, you know. Madam S'dora."

I frowned. "Yes, I know. But her belief in the stories about dragon magic doesn't make them true."

"It's hard not to believe them when everything she sells works so well."

"You don't know that, Willow."

"I've never heard a single tale of something going wrong." She sighed. "Do you remember *The Lament of Nuaga*? They say Madam S'dora can recite it from memory."

I barely remembered; the *Lament* was another piece of the childhood stories that had kept me up at night. "You don't have to keep defending her. If you trust her, then I trust you."

Willow's lower lip trembled. "I need to keep believing I'll actually need those things. That I won't lose him before I even have him."

"You deserve to be happy," I said. "I don't think the Great God will steal that from you."

"I hope you're right." Willow reached for her next cucumber. "And please don't think I'm not worried about Papa and Storm. I can't bear the thought of losing either of them."

"Don't worry about them."

I had Papa and Storm covered.

By the pale light of the moon, I made my way to the barn, where I had hidden a hastily altered pair of pants and a shirt from Storm's clothing chest, and the rest of what I needed for my journey. I crept past the half-sleeping donkeys into the empty stall at the back. A single candle cast its glow as I slipped out of my nightgown and into the pants, which were slightly too big. I fumbled with the belt, cinching it tightly. Then I took the strips of linen I'd carefully cut from an old sheet and bound my chest.

It took me three tries to get it right; the first time, it was too loose, the second, too tight. When I knotted off my third attempt and ran my hands over my breasts, I felt satisfied. I wasn't well-endowed to begin with, and the binding did its work well. I slipped a shirt over the strips and belted it with a length of braided rope. A pair of Storm's socks and Papa's old boots—with rags stuffed into the toes—completed my outfit. Fortunately I'd be doing more riding than walking, so the boots would be sufficient until I was outfitted at camp.

Next, I set up a hand mirror near the candle and set to work on my hair. Papa had worn his in the military style ever since returning from his days of battle; it would be easy to imitate. After combing the tangles from my long hair, I cut it to boy-length, an inch or two below my shoulders. When I was satisfied that it was even, I swept it back and pulled it into a knot at the crown of my head, securing it with a length of twine.

Then I stepped back and peered at my reflection.

In the play of shadow and light, if I squinted, I looked like a boy. Like Storm, whole and bright. I studied my face, recalling the many times I'd worn his clothing and fooled my family. When we were babies, Mama had relied on the traditional "son's cap" to tell us apart—a white silken bonnet signifying the honor of being a male child. There was no such cap for infant daughters, but tonight I passed for the son I might've been. Or that Storm might've been.

The smoothness of my cheeks bothered me, but it wasn't unusual for some boys to mature later. The matchmaker's grandson was sixteen, and he didn't look a minute older than twelve.

With some luck, I could do this.

I opened the leather pouch from Madam S'dora and took a pinch of the powder between my thumb and finger. Without breathing, I tucked the pinch beneath my tongue and closed my mouth.

The initial bitterness that crept along the edges of my tongue gave way to a warm tingling, followed by a hint of earth and a distinct muskiness that made it hard to swallow. The powder itself dissolved quickly beneath my tongue, as though it were sugar. I shuddered as the bitter, earthy musk trailed down my throat. Then I took a long swallow of water from the jug I'd brought to the barn.

Heart pounding, I stood in the quiet warmth, wondering what sudden transformation I might experience. I felt nothing different, though. Only the lingering tingle beneath my tongue hinted that I'd swallowed anything at all.

Time would tell. I was probably three quarters of the way to my next monthly bleed. I would know soon enough if the powder was working.

I folded a heavy blanket and laid it across the nearest donkey's back—Sweetpea, I'd always called her. It wouldn't be fair to take Papa's saddle, and I could sell Sweetpea and send the money home so that Papa could replace her. He'd always claimed Sweetpea was lazy, anyway.

My satchel contained a few things I needed—extra socks, some food, a few sheets of parchment with a writing pen and inkstick. Beneath it all lay several carefully folded rags, should my monthly bleed decide to show up despite the powder. I threw the satchel crosswise over my shoulders and led Sweetpea from her stall. She balked, not wanting to leave comfort behind in the middle of the night. I stroked her shaggy neck.

"Come on, Sweetpea," I said. "It'll be an easy ride. I promise."

Once I'd coaxed her from her stall, I affixed a carefully written letter on the uppermost crossbeam of the door to the stall:

Papa,

You deserve a son who can go to war and bring you honor. If I hadn't been given the medicine meant for him, Storm would be that son today. He is the dearest brother I could ask for, and his place is at home, where he will be safe.

You spent so many years unable to provide for us, and now you are living honorably and have the life you deserve. Mama has no one else to provide for her, and there is a great chance that Willow's betrothed will not return from the war, despite what Mama says. They both need you. I'm glad that I'm your daughter—but now it is my turn to be your son.

Please do not send anyone after me; by the time you read this, I will already be a long way from home. Forgive me for taking Sweetpea without asking. I will sell her and send you the money so that you can replace her.

I love you and Mama to the moon and beyond. I will make you proud.

Your affectionate daughter,
Rain

My hand trembled as I took Sweetpea's lead and walked her out of the barn. She was unusually quiet, and I was grateful. Probably it was because I hadn't saddled her—she was always happier to be bare-backed. After I'd eased the barn door closed, I walked her to the gate, which swung soundlessly open when I pushed it.

I turned one last time to gaze at my home, its low, curved roof nestled gently over the four people I loved best in the world. Then I mounted Sweetpea, urged her with a single whispered command, and started out.

I did not look back again.

5

The sun's first light was barely kissing the sky when I tethered Sweetpea to the low branch of a tree and found a deep, smooth hollow between two protruding roots where I could catch a few hours of sleep. I'd made good time through the night—Sweetpea seemed eager to be out and about without a saddle, and there had been just enough moonlight to help us both see where we were going.

Now, though, I was feeling the effects of being awake all night, the heightened sense of excitement having long since worn off. It would take the rest of today and the best part of tomorrow to arrive at Grigsbane. A few hours of sleep were mandatory.

I emptied my bladder a few trees over, struck by yet another thing I'd have to hide and suddenly wondering how difficult it might be to find the privacy I'd need to take care of my personal business.

"One thing at a time, Rain," I said.

Then I settled between the roots while Sweetpea quietly munched on the tender undergrowth. It took a while to get comfortable—I couldn't remember the last time I'd slept on anything hard and bumpy—but soon exhaustion claimed me, and not even the strident calls of early birds could keep me from falling soundly asleep.

I woke suddenly to a sharp crack and the sound of Sweetpea braying. I sat up, heart ramming into my chest, eyes scanning my surroundings.

Less than a cat's throw away, a boy stood peeing by a tree.

Every bone in my body froze, as though I couldn't have moved if I tried. I averted my eyes and debated whether I should pretend to be asleep. Sweetpea was still braying, though, and nobody could sleep through that.

I had the thought, sharp as a knife's edge, that this was the perfect time for me to start being the boy I claimed to be. No boy would avert his eyes. No boy would pretend to be asleep simply to avoid being confronted by another boy in the woods.

So I stood up, stretched broadly, and walked over to Sweetpea as noisily as I could, my back to the boy.

"Hush, Sw—" I cleared my throat and began again, forcing my voice a bit lower. "Hush, Sweetpea. Let's move along now."

I was trying to remember if boys actually said "hush" when I heard the distinct *swish-crunch* of boots in the undergrowth behind me. It was easier to pretend not to hear, rather than turn around and show my not-exactly-male face to whoever was approaching.

"You on your way to Grigsbane?"

Clearly a boy's voice—deep, but young. I squared my shoulders and turned around, my heart pattering so fast I could scarcely draw breath.

"Yes," I said.

The boy surveyed me. He was tall, but not too much, so that he only had to peer down at me a little bit. His face was pleasant, and he wore his wavy-brown hair in a low, loose tail. I held my breath, wondering if my entire ruse would end with his next words.

He placed his right hand, fingers splayed, over his heart. "I'm Forest. I'm heading there, too."

I returned the gesture, feeling awkwardly female. If Forest had noticed anything amiss, though, he didn't show it. I flashed what I hoped was a boyish grin.

Forest raised an eyebrow. "You have a name?"

"Storm."

He nodded. "Where do you come from?"

"Nandel," I said.

"We're neighbors, then," Forest said. "I'm from Thorn Village."

Of course. Anyone traveling this way to Grigsbane would be coming from one of the inner villages. Probably the only reason I hadn't met anyone yet was because I'd traveled at night.

"You must have left before sunup." My voice sounded squeaky in my ears. Did it sound that way to Forest?

"You must've, too."

"I—" No. I couldn't tell him that I'd left in the middle of the night. That would require some sort of explanation. "Yes."

"Well, I'd be happy to travel with you," Forest said. "It's a long journey to take alone."

I wasn't ready for this. I'd been dressed as a boy for less than half a day, and I had no idea if the powder was going to work. Truly, I had been looking forward to the solitary ride, to allow myself time to gradually get used to my disguise.

But to say no to Forest would be rude.

"A pleasure," I said.

He didn't ask questions as I untethered Sweetpea and led her back to the road, where Forest's donkey stood calmly chewing on some weeds. It was the shaggiest, most haphazard beast I'd ever seen, and I stifled a laugh.

"Appalling, isn't he?" Forest said.

"No, I—" *Stop being apologetic. Act like a boy.* "He's a nightmare."

Forest laughed. "If I told you how old he is, you wouldn't believe me." He mounted. "I have an uncle just outside Grigsbane; I'll drop him off there. If he lasts the journey."

I mounted Sweetpea. "He seems sturdy enough."

"You're riding without a saddle?"

"I've preferred it, ever since I was a g—" I turned the unfortunate consonant into a cough. "Since I was a boy."

"I'd probably fall off."

I smiled. "It's not so hard."

For the first time, Forest looked at me more pointedly. An assessment. "How old are you?"

"Seventeen."

"Ah. You look younger."

Already I was stumbling my way through all the plans I'd made. I had meant to tell everyone I was sixteen, to make my smooth face and smaller stature more believable. Too late.

I shrugged as though his comment were no big deal. "Everyone says that."

"Don't worry about it," Forest said. "I was almost seventeen before I had to shave."

We lapsed into silence. The midmorning sun was warm and higher in the sky than I had wanted it to be. Clearly I'd slept too long. I sighed, wrestling between the elation of having successfully deceived the first person I'd met and the dread of making some sort of mistake. For now, it was easy—Forest seemed happy to ride without chatting much, and it was almost impossible to make a mistake while riding Sweetpea.

But when we stopped a few hours later to rest our beasts and take a bit of food, my bladder was full. I took an extra-long time to tether Sweetpea by a narrow stream while Forest relieved himself beside a nearby tree.

Beside. Not behind. Because he had no reason to hide from me. No need for modesty.

Forest had already pulled some food from his saddlebag and was sitting in the grass by the time I stopped fiddling with the tether. If I didn't relieve myself soon, I would soil the only pair of pants I owned.

"I'm, uh . . ." I glanced across the stream, where a small thicket basked in sunlight. "I'm going to go see if I can find some tinberries."

Without waiting for Forest's response, I hopped across the stream and made my way between the two nearest trees to the thicket beyond. A quick glance told me I wouldn't find any tinberries there, but I'd deal with that in a moment.

When I was sure I'd moved far enough away, I slipped out of my pants and squatted behind a tree, terrified that at any moment Forest would come lumbering up. He didn't, though, and I pulled myself together quickly and dove back into the thicket, desperate to find something to bring back.

It was past the season for wild berries, though—even the late ones, like tinberries. So I checked my belt once more and made my way back to Forest and the donkeys.

"Any luck?" Forest asked through a mouthful of something.

"No," I said.

"It's too late for tinberries, really."

Right. And I would have to come up with a new excuse the next time I needed to pee.

The day was long, a constant unfolding of *avila* bushes in neat rows, well past their flowering but still bearing the leaves that would be dried and powdered for medicinal tea. Empty rows signified where plants had been dug up for their roots—these would lie fallow for a year before replanting. Sometimes, distillery workers passed us on their way to the steeping vats to check the temperature and perhaps add the right infusion of whatever ingredient distinguished their proprietor's flavor from the next. To the west, the Fingerling Forest rose in the distance, a dark smudge against the horizon. In the warmth of the afternoon sun, I wished for its shade.

We rode until long past sunset, when there was just enough light in the sky to make out the tired, orderly outline of a small town. As we drew nearer, lanterns flickered to life, illuminating the daubed walls and worn wooden doors of shops and homes standing in pressed-together rows, like fish in a basket. Forest turned his donkey toward the main street at the same moment I led Sweetpea to the right. We both stopped, and Forest gestured toward the town with his head.

"I thought I'd stay at the local hostelry," he said. "Want to share a room and split the cost?"

"Uh . . ." Suddenly my tongue was incompetent. "Thanks, but I won't have money until I reach Grigsbane and sell my donkey."

"Ah. Well, share the room, anyway. A gift."

"N-no, thank you," I said. "I don't wish to be in anyone's debt."

I braced myself for insistence, but none came. Instead, Forest shrugged. "I'll see you in the morning, then."

Relieved, I gave him a short wave and made my way to the outskirts of the town and a thin stand of trees, where I soon discovered others, like myself, were settling in to camp for the night.

More recruits for the high king's army. Suddenly, sharing a room with Forest seemed less daunting.

They were better prepared than I—bedding rolls, a tent or two, and food to cook over their fires. At least a dozen men milled around or sat near one of the fires. Most of them were older—husbands and fathers with no sons, or with sons too young to fight. One or two looked closer to my age. An easy sense of community seemed to have come to life among them, as though their common destiny drew them together.

I stayed in the shadows and observed. This was a perfect opportunity to study the men's behavior and adopt whatever would help me appear more masculine. I slipped from Sweetpea's back and rubbed the side of her face so that she would stay calm. The scent of roasting meat moistened my tongue and drew protest from my stomach. If I were brave enough, I could saunter into the men's midst and end up with a portion of whatever was cooking.

But I wasn't quite ready. Especially since I was certain that ale was beginning to flow. I stayed a while longer, listening to the inflections of their words and watching the way they moved. Then I gave Sweetpea's rein a tug and led her deeper into the trees, away from the welcoming light and the warmth of laughter. After tethering her to a branch, I dug into my satchel and fished out the dried apricots and quail cake I'd saved for tonight's supper. Then, stomach full, I flopped beside Sweetpea, flat on the ground.

"I don't know if I can do this, Sweetpea."

She made a soft donkey-sound in her throat, as though she knew exactly what I meant.

I lay for some time while she rolled languidly in the grass, thinking of Storm and how hard a trip like this would've been for him. Then I sat up, reached into my satchel, and pulled out the pouch of powder.

It sat warm in my palm, and when I dipped my fingers inside, the powder felt light and gritty, a cross between salt and sand. Not like something I wanted to eat.

I swallowed the dank bitterness as it dissolved beneath my tongue and washed it away with a mouthful of water. The tingling in my mouth gave way to a warmth that spread down my neck, across my shoulders, and into my chest. I pressed my hand to my heart.

The sensation faded. In its wake, I felt an incredible sense of calm—a connectedness to the earth that made me feel almost invincible. As though nothing could touch me. It flowed through my limbs and nestled deep in my belly, lingering long after my eyes grew heavy with sleep.

I awoke in the paleness of dawn with a crick in my neck and a hungry stomach. Sweetpea was grazing nearby, and my heartbeat hitched when I remembered that today I would be selling her.

I smoothed the blanket onto Sweetpea's back and led her in a wide arc around the dispersing camp, toward town. I hadn't made specific plans to meet Forest in the morning, but it would have been rude to simply leave without him. So I munched on my last dried apricot and dallied at the town entrance, where we had parted. Already the streets were alive with the early business of the townspeople—sweeping front stoops, opening shop windows, heading toward the well with buckets and jugs. Among them, Grigsbane-bound men and boys walked, the final leg of their journey already begun.

"Storm!"

I didn't respond at first—the name didn't yet feel like my own. But when Forest called me a second time, I snapped to attention, scanning the street until I saw him waving.

"Join me for breakfast!" he called.

Shouting that I had no money wasn't a good idea—I was having enough trouble keeping my speaking voice low enough to be believable—so I crossed the street to meet him.

"I already told you I don't—"

"I want to buy it for you, *s'da*? It's been nice having someone to travel with."

My stomach begged me not to argue. "Thank you."

I followed Forest to a tiny eatery sandwiched between the hostelry and a public house. He held the door with his foot, and I walked in.

"I smelled the cooking as soon as I woke up this morning," Forest said.

My hunger doubled as I breathed in the warm aroma of sugar-eggs and *t'gallah*—fried biscuits filled with meat and vegetables. I squeezed among crowded tables to the only remaining one.

Forest sat across from me. "Order whatever you'd like."

I opted for two duck-and-eggplant *t'gallahs* with potatoes and warm fruit salad. While we waited for our food, the serving girl, who looked younger than me, brought us white tea in an earthenware pot. I poured myself a cup and laced it with a dollop of goat cream and a swirl of spiced honey.

"You drink your tea like a girl," Forest said, sipping his own plain tea.

Ugh. Was I going to get every little thing wrong? I regrouped and pretended his comment didn't bother me.

"My sister drinks it this way," I said. "I like it."

He grinned. "Drink it however you like. I don't think they'll give us cream and honey in the army, though."

I smiled back. "Guess I'd better have a few cups now, then."

Our banter felt natural. Normal. Whether it was the cleverness of my disguise or the fact that Forest would never have expected me to be a girl in the first place, he seemed to accept me at face value. Storm, a boy on his way to serve the high king. Nothing more.

The sweetness of the warm fruit was still on my tongue as we mounted our donkeys and joined the throng headed north. This was the final stretch to Grigsbane from the south, and tomorrow was the last day to show up. I'd done well enough as a boy so far, riding and talking and eating. But living and training with the other soldiers was nothing short of terrifying. For me, the final stretch couldn't be long enough.

The day was warm, one of the final hurrahs of late summer as it melted into the falling season. At first, Forest talked now and again about things that didn't matter much—the crowd, the migrating butterflies, the dead dog by the side of the road. But soon he lapsed into silence, and I did nothing to break it.

The mood on the road in general was somber. Dogged. Men and boys on their way to fight for the high king had little to keep them lighthearted. Or perhaps it was the not knowing that was worst. Papa had told us about the breach of Stonewall because General Tamar had told him first. It was unlikely that many others knew the details behind the sudden and urgent call for men-at-arms.

I tried to imagine killing a nomad. Then I realized I didn't know what a nomad looked like.

By noon, Grigsbane was visible in the distance, a smear of low buildings that stretched across the horizon like a sleeping beast. My stomach dropped over and over as we drew nearer, until I was certain it would fall right through me.

"I hear the food's bad," Forest said.

"I'm sure it is." I didn't plan on eating anytime soon. Maybe never.

"But the ale is supposed to be good," he went on. "They say that's how they keep the soldiers happy."

I grunted agreement, which felt like the right thing to do. But girls weren't supposed to drink ale, and so I never had. Well, I'd stolen a sip from Papa's tankard once when he'd left it sitting on the table. It had gone up my nose and burned my throat, and I'd coughed so long and loudly that Mama came running.

"I thought it would taste like oats," I'd said, because Papa had told me that was what it was made from.

"Ale is a man's drink," Mama had said. "It's bad luck for women to drink it."

I couldn't afford to believe that anymore. Storm was a boy, and he would have to drink ale with the others.

———————

Sweetpea fetched the fair price of four and a half *tak* from a trader making his way toward town. A smattering of merchants' stalls dotted the road to the left and right; I found the message courier in the shade of a twisted tree. Three horses stood tethered behind it, their saddlebags already bulging.

An old man slapped a small wooden box, a piece of parchment, and a pen onto a rickety table. "Fifteen coin for the box, seven coin to send."

I placed four *tak* into the box and wrote my father's name and "Nandel" on the parchment. No letter would be necessary—I had already let him know that I would send the money. I slid the remaining half-*tak* onto the table and waited while the man counted three fifths and eighteen coin into my hand.

I tucked the money into my satchel while I waited by a stone marker for Forest to return from his uncle's farm. It seemed a long time before he arrived, and his smile warmed me. Already he felt familiar. Safe. My gaze lingered for a moment on the deep crescent on one side of his mouth, until I caught myself and looked away.

What did it matter that he had a dimple? No boy would notice something so insignificant.

With each heartbeat, I'd have to remind myself not only to act like a boy, but also to think like one. Regardless of dimples.

Grigsbane was a military town. As soon as we reached the entrance, I felt the difference—a gate that locked at night, tall watchtowers, and a large open market that already tickled my nose with its tantalizing scents of fried and roasted foods. A perfect lure for a soldier's meager pay, considering the rumors of bad army food.

A large sign was posted just past the gate: *Experienced soldiers to Station A at the west gate. New recruits to Station B at the east gate.* An arrow indicated that Station B was to the right.

My insides in a thousand knots, I shifted the satchel on my shoulder and headed to the right along with Forest. Immediately, someone cut in front of me as though I weren't there, pushing his way through the crowd heading to Station B.

"This way, River," he said.

Something in his voice arrested me—a vague familiarity that loosed unease in my stomach. A tall boy joined him, and they began play-sparring as they made their way to the line. The first boy grabbed his friend's water skin and threw it; I raised my hand with the speed of my Neshu training, catching the skin before it hit me in the face. The boy turned toward me, his eyes meeting mine as I offered the skin.

It was the rude boy from Madam S'dora's shop.

6

My breath froze in my throat as I waited for him to take the skin.

He took it, his eyes boring into me. "Good catch, midget."

I didn't trust myself to speak. I threw back my shoulders and gave him a short nod, as though he didn't interest me much.

"Where have I seen you before?"

If my heart had beat any faster, it would've jumped from my mouth and into his face. "I don't know you."

He narrowed his eyes. "Dragon's blood, if I haven't seen you somewhere before."

The other boy sauntered up. He was tall with a pointed chin and high-arched eyebrows—like something from a fairy tale, overgrown. "We'd better get in line, Sedge."

"Looks like we'll be training with a midget."

"My name is Storm." I'd hit him once. I could do it again.

Forest stepped from behind Sedge. "We getting in line?"

"I'm River, and this is Sedge," the tall boy said.

"Forest." He nodded at River and didn't acknowledge Sedge at all. "Storm and I met on the road two days ago."

"Sedge and I are from Thistle Spring in S'dona Province."

I hid my surprise; Thistle Spring was a two-day journey from Nandel, and Sedge had made it sound like Madam S'dora was used to his business. Willow was right—many people bought things from Tinctures and Cures.

"Isn't that where the famous Grandmaster Marfen was from?" I hoped to deflect any questions about where I lived; Sedge might suddenly remember where he'd seen me before.

"Yes," River said. "Our master was one of his last students."

My heart quickened to know I was in the company of Neshu fighters. "You have no grandmaster in Thistle Spring?"

"He died this past winter," River said.

"It's not fair, the way the good ones go first," Sedge said. "I'd have traded my father for Grandmaster Denerek in a swift second."

I felt my jaw drop a little, but River didn't seem to mind that Sedge had said something so horrible. They turned to make their way to the line.

Forest raised an eyebrow. "Midget?"

"Apparently I'm too short."

"You're the only one shorter than him."

He shook his head and turned to join the queue, and I smiled at his back and waited for the line to move forward.

"Town?" The recruiter's hair was pulled back so tightly that his eyes appeared stretched.

I shoved my voice as low as it would go. "Nandel."

"Family name?"

"L'nahn."

He flipped through a thick-paged book, then ran his finger down one side, reading. "Name?"

"Storm." It came out effortlessly, though my lips tingled.

After the recruiter wrote my name, he gestured to the wooden stall where Forest already stood in line. "Head over there for your gear."

I nodded and strode as confidently as I could to the line of boys. Forest bantered with the boy in front of him, who wore a thick braid in his hair.

That's when it occurred to me that none of the other boys had arrived with army hair. I was the only one.

"This is Dalen," Forest said.

Dalen, whose old-days name marked him as having come from Province Ytel, offered an awkward smile. His face was round, and so was his torso—like a barrel, only soft. I figured I could down him on a first Neshu round.

"Storm," I said.

"Forest says you're from Nandel," Dalen said.

I nodded, wondering if perhaps I should have kept quiet about my hometown.

"A lot of people travel there to buy magic tinctures," Dalen continued.

My heart flew into my throat, but I held my face still. "I don't know about that."

"Some little shop or other? My brother's wife says she went there to buy something for their wedding night. Took her four days to get there."

I shrugged as though none of this meant anything. "There's a shop in some dark alley that people have mentioned. My mother would never let us go there."

"Well, my brother talked about his wedding night for weeks afterward," Dalen said. "I guess that's worth a four-day trip for anyone."

I cringed. Of course boys were going to talk about things like this. I tried hard to laugh with the others.

"So, your brother's here somewhere?" I said, hoping to change the subject.

"He's already a soldier," Dalen said. "He was called to duty a week ago. His wife's living with my parents while he's gone." He grinned. "Guess her bed feels empty these days."

Fortunately, it was Dalen's turn to receive his gear, so I was spared having to think of something else to say. I looked at Forest, relieved to see that he wasn't sharing Dalen's fascination with wedding nights.

"Good thing we don't have to worry about any of that," I said.

Forest's brow tightened. "I'm betrothed."

Immediately, I wanted to suck my words back into my mouth. "I'm sorry. I shouldn't have said anything."

Forest shrugged. "You didn't know. Anyway, I haven't even met her yet."

"Ah. It's the same for my sister," I said, glad to be able to offer empathy. "It's bad timing for anyone recently matched."

"It's easier than being recently married, I'm sure," Forest said. "Assuming you actually like whoever you're stuck with."

The bitterness in his words caught me off guard. "Not all brides and grooms dislike each other."

"No," Forest said. "But, honestly, what are the odds that you're going to actually want to be together?"

"My parents are happy." It sounded like a flimsy defense.

"Maybe that's what happens when you realize nothing's going to change. You learn to be happy."

"Well, my sister was really upset," I said. "She wants to be married more than anything."

Forest snorted. "Most girls are like that."

My jaw tightened. *Most girls, maybe. But not the one standing behind you.*

"Next!" The voice was sharp as a blade, and Forest stepped forward quickly.

When it was my turn, I stepped up before anyone had to shout for me. I signed my name on a gear roster and, after being quickly eyeballed, was handed pants, two linen shirts, a leather belt and scabbard, and a neatly folded blanket.

"Next roll call is at sundown, and two men per tent," the rough-voiced soldier said. "You're with the man in front of you."

I looked over at Forest, who held a slip of parchment in his hand along with his pile of supplies. Then I nodded at the soldier. "Thank you."

He had already started to shout "Next!" to whoever was behind me, even before the words were fully out of my mouth. Reminder number three hundred: be careful not to use too many manners.

Forest held up the slip of parchment. "Tent seventy-seven."

I didn't want to share a tent. Not with Forest, not with any boy. But it could've been worse. It could've been Sedge.

"Let's go," I said.

Long rows of sand-colored tents stretched before us on the trampled field. I cupped my hand over my eyes, assessing.

"Looks like twenty tents per row," I said.

Forest pointed. "That's our row."

We made our way to the tent with the number seventy-seven

painted roughly on one side. The peak of the tent reached my nose, and its width seemed barely enough for two to sleep side by side.

This was going to be more challenging than I'd allowed myself to imagine.

"Storm L'nahn!" The recruiter's voice clipped my name like a scythe to grass.

"Here!"

Over a hundred fifty new soldiers stood in a haphazard line, answering the roll call. Others had arrived at the camp after me, but tomorrow would see the final influx. When the last names had been called, the recruiter stepped forward.

"Welcome to the high king's army. Tomorrow the last of you will arrive, and formal training will start the following morning." He stepped aside, and a tall, broad-shouldered man was suddenly visible. His skin was sun-darkened, his hair almost as black as mine.

The recruiter gestured to him. "This is Commander Jasper Dane."

Everyone bowed, hands spread on their hearts, as the commander stepped forward—I was half a second late, but I bowed, too. When I rose, the recruiter had retreated, and Commander Dane stood alone on the low platform in front of us, shoulders straight, hands behind his back. I stared.

He was a boy. Fully grown, to be sure, but he had definitely seen fewer than twenty summers. His smooth brow and long lashes gave him a look that was so boyish I almost laughed.

How could he possibly be a commander?

"New recruits!"

I jumped at his voice, which was deep and fierce, with a raw edge that didn't match his youthful appearance. I held my breath, and it seemed that the others held theirs, too.

Commander Dane took a step forward. "Tomorrow our ranks will be filled, and I will address you as a unit. Even so, you are from this moment a soldier in the high king's army. Once training begins, you may not leave the camp. You will obey all orders. You will serve the high king with life and limb, and your families will receive your honor."

Everyone waited for more, but Commander Dane stood there, surveying us and saying nothing. When his eyes swept in my direction, I shrank inwardly, even as I stood taller. Fear coiled tightly in my stomach as I waited for him to sense that I wasn't what I pretended to be.

Nothing happened. He regarded me no differently from everyone else in the line of soldiers.

"Your evening meal will be served shortly," he said. "Dismissed!"

I watched him as he turned to talk for a moment with the recruiter. He frowned, which made him look like a petulant child. Even if he had been recently promoted, he seemed so young. Maybe I was wrong, though. Maybe he was one of those men whose faces belied their age.

"Want to get our places in the food line?" Forest asked. "Maybe it'll taste better if we get it nice and hot."

I grinned. "Doubt it."

I was right. The barley was hot but dry and overcooked, the cabbage mushy. My stomach was hollow from having missed lunch, though, so I ate every morsel in my bowl. I couldn't bring myself to taste the ale—not yet—so instead I filled my tin mug with water from a leaking barrel and sat beside Forest in the meal tent. The ground was hard and packed beneath the long, low tables—it felt strange not to have a bench to sit upon or a water bowl with which to rinse my hands.

Dalen slapped his third ale on the table and sat across from me. "No second helpings on the food, but at least the drink flows freely."

I sipped my water and refrained from commenting that Dalen could stand to skip the second helpings. When I put my cup down, he looked at it and frowned.

"What are you drinking?"

I regarded him with what I hoped was a bored expression. "Water."

"*Water?*"

"You know, the clear stuff that falls from the sky sometimes," Forest said.

Dalen shook his head as though I were a complete mystery. "I've never seen anyone turn down a good ale." He drank deeply.

I glanced at Forest and gave him a tiny nod of thanks. He nodded back, then tipped his own cup to his mouth.

Already, he felt like a friend. It was the last thing I had expected.

———————

I sat in the grass by one of the campfires, watching the men return
from bathing somewhere beyond a thick grove of trees, until I summoned my courage. My breasts ached from the tightness of my binding, and I stank. Probably there would be a lot more stinking in my
future, but tonight it would feel good to wash the several days of soot
from my body.

I slipped through the trees, following the sound of water and aided
by the light of the almost-full moon reflecting on the water. Subtle
sounds of splashing came from somewhere up ahead; I averted my
eyes when I suddenly stepped into a clearing and saw three men in
water that reached only to their thighs.

*Oh, Great God. May my eyes never fall on anything I don't wish to
see.*

I crept around a bend in the small lake, close to where it was fed
by a burbling stream. No one was near, and I was neatly hidden from
view by the bend and the trees.

Heart pounding, I peeled off my shirt and untwisted the strips of
cloth from my chest, breathing deeply of the cool night air as my
breasts spilled free. The dull ache I'd been enduring left immediately,
and a smile crept across my face.

There was something satisfying about the exquisite danger of being discovered. And also terrifying.

Hastily, I wriggled from my pants and undergarment and stepped
into the water, my toes sinking in squishy mud. I waded quickly, my
stride as wide as I could make it, until I reached water that came up
to my waist. It was delightfully cool, the water—holding still a hint
of the sun's warmth, but freshened by its own depths and the spring
water feeding it. I unknotted my hair and ducked beneath the surface, then came up for breath, my face streaming.

I scrubbed the grime from my hair as best I could without the
benefit of soap. After retwisting my bun, I swam into deeper water,
relishing the freedom of bathing in my own skin, naked beneath the

moon. Three more minutes, I told myself. Only three, and I would
return.

Rain.

I froze in midstroke, terror lacing through me like a heated lance.
Then I ducked beneath the water until only my head wasn't submerged, my heartbeat pounding in my ears. And I listened.

Even the splashes from around the bend had ceased. I was alone
in the lake. But who was on the shore? Where had the voice come
from?

Who knew my real name?

I stayed in the lake until I began to shiver, my eyes darting back
and forth from trees to brush to the surface of the water. No one was
there.

After allowing fear to immobilize me far too long, I talked myself into coming out. I bound my breasts as quickly as I could and
pulled my clothing over my damp skin, all the while looking around
in every direction, eyes spread wide to the night.

Whoever had said my name was nowhere to be seen.

Perhaps I'd imagined it.

I walked back to the campfires, easing my breaths and willing my
heart to stop racing. By the time I found Forest, I'd convinced myself that my own fear of being caught had played with my imagination. I sat beside him, careful to emulate the way his legs were spread
and bent at the knees, forearms resting upon them. I didn't want to
be accused of sitting like a girl.

Forest had just acknowledged me with a nod when a long, low
horn sounded, signaling curfew. Men at adjacent fires stood immediately and began to douse the flames, so I stood, too.

Two other boys took care of the fire. I walked with Forest to our
tent, fighting the awkwardness that welled up as I thought about sleeping beside him all night. I reminded myself once again that I was the
only one who knew I was a girl. Nothing would feel strange to Forest.

I pulled off my boots and stood them in my corner of the tent.
While Forest busied himself with spreading his blanket over the grass,
I pulled the small pouch from my satchel and took a pinch of the
powder. Too late, I realized I didn't have any water to wash away the
taste. I would have to deal with it.

The same warmth coursed through me, and I closed my eyes and savored it. Whatever was in that powder was certainly doing *something* each time I dissolved it under my tongue. I only hoped it would do what it was supposed to.

"What's that?" Forest asked.

I tucked the pouch hastily into my satchel, scrambling for an answer. "Just a tincture."

"Are you ill?"

"No." I had to change the subject—quickly. "Do you miss home?"

"I haven't been gone long enough to miss it." He settled onto his back; I could barely see him in the darkness. "What about you?"

I swallowed the emptiness that curled through my heart. "I guess so."

"My mother was more disappointed about having to postpone the wedding than seeing me off to war, I think."

"Surely not."

He half-chuckled. "Maybe equally disappointed."

"She's pleased with the match?" I lay down, careful not to brush against him.

"We've never met her," Forest said. "We were supposed to meet a week or so from now. My mother was sewing a new dress and everything."

I smiled sadly, thinking of Willow and Mama. "Weddings are more exciting for the women."

"Especially for my betrothed," Forest said. "Apparently her father wasn't able to afford her dowry when she was eighteen. So she's actually a year older than me."

A slow prickling sensation gathered in my stomach and began to spread. "Is she?"

"Yes. And I'm told she's pleasing to the eye, as well. Although that's what every bridegroom is told before he meets his bride." He shifted onto his side. "Maybe you know her. She's from Nandel, like you."

"There are a lot of girls in Nandel."

But there was no denying what was clearly the truth. Forest was betrothed to my sister.

7

I might know who you mean." I fought to keep my voice calm. "There's a girl in Nandel who wasn't betrothed when she turned eighteen. Some people whispered about it." That much was true, though I'd never told Willow.

It was too dark to see Forest's expression. "I'm not supposed to know anything about her until we meet, but . . ." He sighed. "Never mind. I don't need to know."

"She's beautiful," I said. "Only an idiot wouldn't think so."

"There's more to life than beauty."

His answer surprised me. "I guess that's true."

"Doesn't it bother you?" Forest asked. "The way our wives are chosen for us?"

"Yes," I said. "I'd rather not get married."

"It's not that I don't want to get married. I'd just rather not get married *now*."

"Well, who knows if we'll even make it home." I clamped my mouth shut, realizing how negative I sounded.

If it bothered Forest, I couldn't tell. "It's better that we never met. If we ended up liking each other, it would've been harder."

I wanted to tell him how hard it already was for Willow. I wanted to tell him he *had* to come home, that my sister's dreams hinged on it, and that she would be unbearable if he didn't. But I'd already said too much.

"At least you don't have to worry about it for a while."

"Plenty of other things to worry about instead." He shifted on his blanket. "Good night, Storm."

I wished him good night and breathed a prayer to the Great God that Forest would live to be my brother-in-law. For as much as Willow loved me, I was certain she would be happier knowing that her future with Forest was secure.

Words, dovetailing one another, rising and falling, but making no sense. And in the middle of them, my name, clear as the first trill of the lark.

Rain.

Swirls of light and color without form, and a sweet-scented wind stealing my breath and nudging at me from every corner. And still the words came, whispers and statements and singsong phrases, but I couldn't understand any of them, except one.

My name.

Over and over, near, then far away. Gentle, coaxing, sometimes admonishing.

Rain. Rain. Rain.

I sat up in the dark, my breaths coming sharp and short. Forest lay sleeping beside me, unbothered. I pressed my hand against my bound chest and willed my heart to calm itself.

It was only a dream—a jumbled confusion of thought that could have meant something but probably didn't. I lay down again, telling myself that the latter was true—that the dream meant nothing. That it was merely the nightmare of a girl-turned-soldier during her first night in training camp.

But my words rang false. Because the voice that had spoken my name in the dream was the same voice I'd heard in the lake.

The final swell of new recruits arrived throughout the next day, so that by sundown our ranks had topped four hundred. We were all measured for boots and helmets—which was easy, except for the fact that my feet were apparently "small for a man's"—and for leather breastplates, which was terrifying.

Fortunately, the recruiter in charge of chest measurements seemed only half engaged with his work, as though he had measured the girth of so many chests that he'd long since stopped actually looking at anyone. He did pause to double-check my measurement before writing it, but other than that one moment, there was no difficulty.

We'd have to wait for the breastplates, but the boots were already available, piled by size into baskets. I took mine thankfully; the rags inside Papa's boots didn't keep my feet from sliding, and I was certain I couldn't train in them without tripping. My new pair was strong and supple and fit me so much better than Papa's, though it was still a size too big.

Once I was wearing my armor, I would blend in better with the rest of the soldiers. Perhaps I wouldn't even have to bind my breasts so tightly, which made me ache and restricted my motion. I would have to experiment with that until I got it right.

We stood at attention after dinner, rows of untrained soldiers from all over Ylanda. Commander Dane stood in full armor, the purple braid of his rank stitched onto the left side of a fine, canary-yellow military cloak. He placed his hands behind his back and scanned the ranks once from left to right before tilting his head back and addressing us in the same confident voice he'd used the night before.

"Soldiers of Ylanda!" Once again, his tone didn't match his boyish face. "Tomorrow your training begins. The horn will sound at sunup, and you will have ten minutes to report to the eastern field."

Ten minutes? I would have to be sure to get up before the horn so that I could take care of my morning business. The latrine would be quickly overrun with men who would question why I wasn't standing with everyone else.

"You honor your families by being here," he went on. "You honor your towns, your underkings, your kingdom, and your high king. And you honor yourselves. Always, we will expect ten times more from you than you think you can give. In this way, we will train you into the kind of soldiers that are worthy of representing His Majesty in battle."

Uneasiness crept up and down my spine like a shifty rodent. The reality of training for battle was foreign from everyday life, something to talk idly about in the comfort of home. But now, standing with my fellow recruits in tense lines, the reality settled on me like sudden rain.

We would fight. We would die. Not for ourselves, but for our high king. For our families at home.

More than anything, I was thankful to have saved Storm from this fate. The crowd and the yelling commanders would have terrified him. Even digging latrines would have been too much. I stuffed the rising terror deeply inside myself. For Storm, I would face death. I wouldn't let anyone see that I was afraid.

"You may have heard that the nomads have breached the wall," Commander Dane said. "You may not have believed it, because for generations Stonewall has kept us safe from the nomads of the north. But at long last, our greatest defense has given way."

A low murmur went through the crowd. I bit my bottom lip and kept my eyes pasted on the commander.

"For several years, the M'loh tribe has been conquering the other nomadic tribes one by one and bringing them all under the leadership of Tan Vey, the M'loh chieftain who now sets those combined forces against our wall and our kingdom. Separately, the nomadic tribes posed little threat. United, they are a formidable foe."

I side-eyed the soldiers in my row, and a small, sinking feeling grew in my heart. We did not look very formidable.

"Ylanda's *avila* fields, abundant resources, and natural defenses to the south and west have been coveted by our nomadic neighbors for generations. By joining together they clearly believe that the time has come for them to claim what they've always wanted." Commander Dane raised a fist in the air, punctuating his words with it. "We. Will. Destroy. Them."

Perhaps we were supposed to cheer, but silence met the commander instead, an uneasy, awkward silence so thick that sounds wafting from the other camp—the one with the experienced soldiers—seemed suddenly intrusive. I tried to swallow the dryness in my mouth.

Commander Dane stood a while longer, his arm slowly lowering to his side. Then, without another word, he turned and stepped off the platform, joining two older soldiers off to the side. One of them said something to him, and he nodded, his hand rubbing his jaw. The second soldier patted him on the back.

Their faces showed affection—and respect. Whoever this boy-man was, his elders thought highly of him. I couldn't help but wonder why.

The dreams came again that night—words I couldn't understand, except for my own name. I woke several times, heart pounding, the last vestiges of the dreams dancing in my ears as though I could still hear the shapeless words. In the pale light of dawn, I woke again, the sound of my name still ringing in that same, unfathomable voice.

Rain.

As though the speaker knew me. As though the weight of my name carried the weight of the world.

Rain.

I sat up, my breath catching as I remembered Madam S'dora's words: *It might awaken things. You could have dreams.*

Was it the powder? I wrapped my arms tightly around my bent knees. Forest's breathing was soft and even in contrast to my own, and I focused on the sound of it to help center myself. What had Madam S'dora called it? The magic of T'Gonnen. It was a name from childhood, a mighty dragon from tales I barely remembered. Our ancestors believed the dragons were real, worshipping and revering them like gods. But the dragons were fierce, wreaking destruction and death, and when the powerful dragon T'Gonnen fell, it was the end of an era.

Something like that. It was all a fairy tale, anyway, regardless of whether or not Madam S'dora thought it was true. How could a few pinches of powder beneath my tongue produce dreams?

My heart squeezed tighter. The first time I'd heard my name, I was alone in the lake. Not dreaming. I'd thought someone along the shoreline had called me.

But, no. The voice was inside my head.

I lowered my face onto my knees. It was too soon to know if the powder was actually working—my monthly bleed was due to arrive in a few days. If it didn't, I would have to decide if the results of taking the powder were worth the risks of being driven slowly mad.

And if my monthly bleed came on schedule, I would curse myself for wasting Papa's precious coin and throw the remaining powder away.

I crawled quietly from the tent and made my way through the still-sleeping camp. By the time the horn blew, I'd finished my personal business and was making my way to the eastern field.

Off to the side, someone stood alone, his body perfectly aligned in the second stance of Neshu. I slowed, then stopped altogether as he moved fluidly through a drill I knew well. His knife arm was swift and sure, his kicks fluid and precise. Aside from Papa, I had never seen such grace and perfection. I stood with my mouth hanging open, my heart hammering in admiration, and watched him finish. He turned swiftly and met my gaze.

It was Commander Dane.

I shut my mouth and pressed my lips together, heat crawling across my face. He gave me a sharp nod and walked across the field, his stride wide and smooth. If he was out of breath, it didn't show. *Masterful control,* Papa would have said.

This was a Neshu grandmaster if ever I had seen one.

As Rain, I would never have had the opportunity to train with someone like this—highly skilled in Neshu and in a position of command with the high king's army. As Storm, I now had six weeks to learn everything I could from someone whose skill surpassed my own.

I reached the field as a different commander—taller, broader—stepped forward and called for our attention. Silence fell, and when he spoke, his voice was like a thousand spikes, shredding my ears.

"I am Commander Beldan," he thundered. "Every morning will begin with warm-ups. No resting, no stopping. On my mark."

Commander Dane stood nearby, his arms folded behind his back. I was in the middle of wondering why he wasn't leading us when Commander Beldan thundered his first order.

I spent the next hour gasping for air. "Warm-ups," the commander had called them. It was more running and jumping than I'd ever crammed into sixty minutes. Even with my intense Neshu training, I was pushed to my limits. When the drills had ended, I looked around and saw that many of my fellow soldiers had dropped out. Some had hobbled off to the side to catch their breath, while others simply lay in the grass where they'd dropped.

I was one of only about thirty left standing—including Sedge, who was close enough for me to see the satisfied expression on his face. He was also panting, though, and sweat dripped down his temples. He'd seemed like one of those boys who was all bluster without much physical substance. Apparently he had more substance than I'd given him credit for.

"Those of you who are still standing may go first for breakfast," Commander Beldan called. "The rest of you will stay here until you're dismissed."

That was probably a good thing, since at least two of them were retching into the grass. I did a quick scan for Forest and was relieved to see him walking across the field, chest heaving. Reluctantly, I moved toward the meal tent with the others. My body wasn't ready for food yet.

I hung back, taking the last place in the food line. By the time I sat beside Forest with my bowl of porridge and dried figs, the food had started to smell appetizing. I scooped the first spoonful into my mouth and grimaced. Tasteless. So I began pulling the figs into bits and tossing them into the porridge. Their sweetness would surely make the porridge more palatable.

"Figs too big for your mouth, midget?" Sedge called from one table over, where he sat with several other soldiers.

I smiled and lifted my spoon to him as though I found him amusing. Secretly, I imagined what it would be like to whip the contents of my bowl into his face.

"I'm impressed," he said. "If I'd placed a bet, I wouldn't have said you'd still be standing after that workout."

That sounded too close to a compliment for Sedge. I couldn't trust it. "I would have said the same about you," I said.

He took several gulps of water, his eyes watching me over the rim of the cup. Then he placed the cup on the table and wiped his mouth on his sleeve. "Bet you won't last a day of field training."

I decided to ignore him, though it would have been decidedly more satisfying to walk over and flip him onto his back.

The rest of the morning passed in a blur of sweat and sharp words. After lunch, Commander Dane lined us up in several sets of rows facing one another. I stood across from a boy with a pockmarked face and a mouth that hung open like a tent flap.

"Some of you may know nothing about the art of Neshu," Commander Dane began. "Many of you have had training from boyhood, and some of you have taken that training to a respectable level. Today, I'm looking for those among you who excel."

My heart swelled within me—this was one skill I knew I had. In this, I would not embarrass myself. I raised my chin as Commander Dane walked by.

"Everyone will assume the first stance and face their opponent. As I walk through your ranks, I will dismiss those of you who are failing and will repartner those who remain. We will move swiftly through Neshu rounds until only the best remain for the final rounds."

I sized up the boy across from me. The expression on his face told me he had no confidence in his skill.

"On my mark," Commander Dane said.

My opponent didn't stand a chance. He raised his arm in a defensive posture that had nothing to do with Neshu, and I flattened him with a cut and a swift kick.

I moved from partner to partner as incompetent fighters were weeded out and my opponents became worthier of attention. Without missing a step, I engaged each one with the poise and agility Papa had ingrained in me. I lost all sense of time; I only knew what my next move would be.

When Forest appeared in front of me, I stifled my moment of surprise and prepared to engage him. Within the first few exchanges, I could see how good he was. Move for move, he matched my skill and pacing, until finally I outmaneuvered him.

He bowed, his brow beaded with sweat. "As the sun rises."

"So it sets." I couldn't help smiling.

Soon no more than three dozen of us were left standing. Commander Dane paired us and watched us spar, calling out when he'd seen enough or if he wanted to see us fight someone different. My stomach twisted as I caught sight of Sedge still standing among us, and I itched for a chance to outperform him. Moments later, Commander

Dane ended the sparring round and dismissed all but about twenty of us.

Sedge remained. So did Forest. Scanning the rest of the boys, I saw that River and, to my surprise, Dalen were also standing.

"You've all shown great skill," Commander Dane said. "Now I want to test that skill myself."

Commander Dane engaged his first opponent, and a sense of awe settled over the field. As I had glimpsed that morning, his skill was immeasurable. He dismissed the first two boys after one round. Sedge stepped forward next and fought better than I had expected. Commander Dane bested him in the second round, but I could tell he was pleased with Sedge's fighting. He did not dismiss him.

Several more fighters were dismissed, and then it was Forest's turn. I watched, mesmerized, until suddenly I gasped as the commander's knife arm arced into Forest's shoulder. He lost the round, but Commander Dane praised his sense of balance and mindful control and allowed him to stay.

He gestured for me to step forward.

"What is your greatest weakness?" he asked.

"My father tells me it's not taking advantage of my enemy's hesitation."

"You studied with your father?"

"Yes."

He assumed the first stance. "Clearly none of your opponents here have drawn out your weakness. Let's see if it exists."

I knew the fire in his eyes—it was the same fire in Papa's, and the same one Papa always pointed out in my own. I assumed the first stance, willing my heart to settle.

It was like dancing. Every cut, every feint, every twist and kick followed a flowing pattern that made me feel as though I were sparring with my own shadow. Neither of us had the upper hand; neither of us fell behind. Move for move, we were matched. Never had I felt so completely centered—and so utterly breathless.

Then a moment came where somehow, in the smallest way, he seemed to lag. An emotion crossed his face that I couldn't read, and as he hesitated, I pulled back, slowing my dance.

With a swiftness beyond comprehension, he hooked my shoulder and flipped me onto my back, his Great Cry ringing across the field. I lay stunned, staring at the sky, breathing in jagged gulps of air.

He leaned over me, his nose inches from mine. "Your father's right."

I accepted the hand he offered, allowing him to pull me to my feet. Then I crossed my arms and bowed.

"As the sun rises," I said.

"So it sets." As I made my way back to the group, he said, "Well fought, soldier."

His words filled me like a sunrise.

Well fought.

Soldier.

I gathered the honor in my heart and lifted it to Papa and Storm. "For you," I whispered.

8

Fifteen recruits remained standing with Commander Dane. I glanced at Forest, who gave me a slight shrug. An officer handed Commander Dane a sheet of parchment nailed to a thick slab of leather, which he held aloft.

"Write your name on here and report to my tent at warm-up time in the morning."

That's all he said. No explanation, no further instructions. I waited while the parchment was passed around, then wrote my name in bold strokes: *Storm L'nahn*.

I turned to pass the parchment to the person behind me, who happened to be Dalen. My expression must have revealed how hard it was to believe he'd made it this far, because he offered a sheepish grin. I found myself wishing I could spar with him, just to see what he could do.

Sedge and River were also among us. No huge surprise, since they had spoken of their Neshu training, and I could tell they took it seriously. There was no time for anything beyond exchanged glances, though; orders were being called for the next drills. I threw back my shoulders and headed toward the main group, feeling as though I'd accomplished something without knowing what it was.

◆

The evening meal of fried sausage and lentils lay heavy in my stomach as Forest and I sat in front of our tent scraping mud from our boots. Sedge was wrong—I'd made it through the first day.

Barely.

"How's your arm?" Forest asked.

"Fine." It ached a bit, but I'd felt worse. Hopefully tomorrow's sword-fight training would go better than today's.

"Sorry about that."

"Sorry, nothing," I said. "I went for the block a moment too late. The practice swords are heavy."

"They'll make our combat weapons feel lighter," Forest said. "I think that's the idea."

I nodded. "I'm sure it is."

"You've done quite a bit of Neshu, haven't you?" Forest asked.

"Yes, with my father."

"It shows." He knocked the toe of his boot against his palm. "Your form is close to perfect."

Warmth swelled in my chest. "Yours isn't so bad, either."

"I'll have to step up if I'm to keep up with you."

I laughed—too high and girlish, but Forest didn't seem to notice. "I'll go easy."

"What do you think Dane wants with us?"

I'd been thinking of little else all day. "I don't know. Training others, maybe?"

"I doubt it," Forest said. "Just because you're a good fighter doesn't mean you're a good teacher."

"True."

Talking with Forest made me feel safe in my role. He was steady and honorable, the kind of boy that a mother would want her son to befriend. He smiled—and my spirit fluttered. It was over in a heartbeat, but it left me on edge. Nothing like that had ever happened before.

I couldn't let it happen now.

If we both survived this, we would laugh about the days when I'd fought beside him in my boy clothes, never letting on that I would one day be his sister-in-law.

That is, if he could forgive me for deceiving him.

⸻

In the morning, while the rest of the camp lined up for warm-ups, I stood with the fourteen others, waiting for Commander Dane outside his tent. He appeared from behind it, his face the unread-able mask I'd already gotten used to. His eyes assessed us—counted us—and then he placed his hands behind his back.

"Your skill in Neshu sets you apart from everyone else," he said, "and the high king's army has a great need for you. For the next several days, I'll be working exclusively with you, marking your stamina, your strength, and your ability to make quick decisions. If at any point you fail to meet my standards, you'll be released from consideration for this unit. Any questions?"

I added my "No, sir" to the others that rang out. Commander Dane nodded, as though not having questions were the right thing.

"Meet me at the northern edge of the field for warm-ups," he said. "You have three minutes to get there."

———————

The next three days were brutal—warm-ups before breakfast, hours of weapons drills and combat practice. Each day, one boy was removed from the group. I remained.

The practice sword was heavy and unwieldy in my hand, and the calisthenics were inhuman. I felt unequal to every task except Neshu training, which was effortless. In addition to being invigorated by the sparring, I was inspired by Commander Dane. It was hard to imagine surpassing his level of skill.

Though I intended to.

In addition to our drills, we were also given chores on a rotation. On the third afternoon, I was assigned to dish out the food at lunchtime. It was hard to miss the dismissive glances and outright smirks that flew my way as I spooned carrot broth into tin bowls and counted out slices of brown bread—three per person.

"He looks ten years old," I heard one soldier say as he walked away with his soup.

I would've liked to flatten him in an impromptu Neshu match, to show him how little he knew of me.

The food line trickled to nothing, and I was trying to figure out what I was supposed to do with the remaining soup when Commander Dane approached. I immediately stood at attention, my heart in my teeth.

"I'd like some soup, soldier," he said.

My face burned hot. Of course he wanted soup; why would I stand at attention when I was supposed to be serving food?

"Yes, sir," I said, spooning the soup into a bowl and grateful that I didn't have to look at him.

He took the soup and bread. "How long have you studied Neshu?"

I forced my voice extra-low. "Since I was seven."

"Your name is Storm, yes?"

"Yes, sir."

"Storm." He studied me with those piercing eyes, and I felt as though he could see right through my shirt and the layers of binding that hid my femaleness. "You have the makings of a Neshu grand-master."

A compliment?

Warmth blossomed deep inside me. "Thank you, sir."

"In fact, your skill surpasses anything I've seen here." He regarded me for several more seconds. "Work harder to build your upper-body strength, *s'da*?"

"I will, sir. Thank you."

He nodded once, then took his food and went to find somewhere to sit. I stood behind the soup pot, caught in the afterglow of his kind words. I'd watched him move with the grace of a mountain cat and the speed of wind during Neshu drills. I'd sparred with him, matching him move for move until his superior skill found my weakness. It would be an honor to improve myself under the command of one of the finest Neshu fighters I'd ever seen.

Not just improve—*excel*. Commander Dane's praise fed me as though it were solid food. I wanted to become more in his eyes, to be the soldier he wouldn't expect me to be.

To be his equal.

If I succeeded, it would, perhaps, make up for the fact that I could never be the grandmaster I longed to be.

⸻

I crawled into the tent bone-weary, as I had every night. Forest was already sprawled on his blanket, so still I thought he was already asleep.

"Your feet stink," he said.

I kicked him. "So do yours."

Sometimes it was ridiculously easy to be a boy.

The dreams had come each night, wordless syllables interspersed with my name, and I rolled onto my side and braced myself for more of the same. If I hadn't been so exhausted, I probably would have stayed awake, fighting sleep. But my eyelids were heavy and my body was already in a state of complete rest. And if I were honest, I'd have to admit that the dreams didn't frighten me anymore. I was drawn to the voice, desperate to understand it. It didn't feel threatening or fearsome, though I didn't quite have a word to describe it.

I sank into sleep before I could finish figuring it out.

The words came, shapeless and meaningless as always. Something was different this time, though. I could hear distinct vowels and con-sonants, forming words I didn't know. When my eyes shot open some time later, the last trace of the final word rang in my ears:

T'Gonnen.

I lay in the dark, savoring the word even as I feared it. T'Gonnen, the dragon. His magic, Madam S'dora had said, was in the powder. But dragons weren't real. And if they were, we would be living in terror.

Why was this ancient dragon name showing up in my dreams?

It took me a long while to fall back to sleep. I considered drag-ging out my parchment and pen and scratching down some poetry; it had been forever since I'd written anything. But I had no light, and even if I did, it would have been rude to bother Forest simply to quench my longing for words. So I lay still and willed myself to settle.

For the rest of the night, I dreamed and woke, dreamed and woke. By the time the horn blew, I was convinced that someone—or something—was trying to speak to me in another language in my dreams. I jumped up, still groggy, and hurried to the secret place I'd scouted out for mornings when I wasn't able to beat the horn.

As I emerged from the tangle of bushes, a series of horn blasts, high and short, cracked through the morning air. I joined the throng of my fellow recruits as we made our way to the east field; their heads were all turning toward the northeast.

I found Dalen and matched his stride. "What's going on?"

"I think they're marching," Dalen said.

Marching. The word carried a weight that I wasn't ready to bear.

From the east field, I could clearly see the seasoned soldiers in formation—hundreds upon hundreds in rows of straight backs and shining helmets. Instead of shouting us into motion as they usually did, Commanders Dane and Beldan allowed us a few minutes to stand and watch the troops head out. From somewhere among us, cheering began, and soon I was joining in, my voice lost in the deep tumult of voices around me, a thin thread of sound in the commotion.

But my heart swelled, and my eyes stung with tears. Fathers, brothers, husbands, sons, marching to the call of their high king. It was no girlish response, though, and I did not wipe away the wetness that spilled down my cheek.

I was proud of them. I was proud of myself for being one of them. *Papa, I want to bring you honor. I want you to be proud of me, too.*

Late in the afternoon, the twelve of us stood in a wide semicircle facing a high wooden crossbeam supported by stout posts on either side and in the middle. From the crossbeam hung four ropes, two on each side of the middle post. The ropes were knotted on the bottom and thicker than any rope I'd ever seen.

Commander Dane stood to one side, his arms behind his back. "Four lines, one for each rope," he called. "Three men in each line, on my mark!"

Already, we had learned to respond quickly and without hesitation. On his mark, we moved into four lines faster than, a week ago, I would have thought possible. I hung back, securing the last spot in the line on the far right.

"This test won't be given to the other recruits for another week," Commander Dane said, "but I'm using it today to determine that each of you are ready to embark on the mission I've chosen you for. If you fail, you'll return to the main company of recruits."

He paused, sweeping his eyes across us as though gauging our response. I fought hard to keep my expression neutral.

"Your goal is to climb to the top, remove a strip of silk, climb down, and hand it to me. If you slide backward or fall from the rope, you'll go back to the end of your line and take another turn. Every soldier who hands me a silk strip will have the privilege of calling me Jasper."

My own surprise was reflected in the faces of some of the soldiers I could see, though no one made a sound. It seemed obvious that Commander Dane would be leading this special unit, but sharing his given name was a sign of equality on the battlefield. If I could achieve that, surely I could achieve equality as a Neshu fighter as well.

"On my mark." He waited a few heartbeats, then blew into his thin silver pipe.

The first four stepped forward and began climbing. I took notice of the way they grabbed the rope between their boots and used their legs to propel themselves upward. Sedge was on the first rope; he and the next two made it look effortless. The fourth soldier, whose name, I thought, was Cedar, visibly struggled, and when he was about half-way up, he slid down almost to the knot. I cringed at the thought of the rope burning his hands.

"To the back!" Commander Dane yelled.

I tried to swallow the dryness in my mouth.

Cedar took his place behind me, breathing heavily. At first I thought it would be better to keep my back to him. But then I turned around.

"You'll make it next time," I said.

"Thanks." Sprays of curly red hair had jumped free from his army bun, and his sweaty face made his freckles glisten. He brushed the back of his hand across his brow. "It's harder than I thought."

Our lines moved forward. Dalen fell and was sent to the back of his line; Rock, all huge limbs and gentle spirit, made it slowly and steadily to the top. A wiry boy named Mandrake made it almost to the top before losing his grip and sliding down. Briar, the boy in front of me, was tall and muscular, and I watched him scale the rope as though he had done so hundreds of times. He landed lightly on his feet and brought his silk strip to Commander Dane.

I stepped forward. My turn.

I wiped my hands on my britches and approached the rope as if it were a Neshu opponent. It was thick, making me conscious of how small my hands were. I wrapped them around the rope and gave it a little pull, testing its strength.

Squeezing the knot between my boots, I tightened my grip and tried to move my legs up the way I'd watched the others do it. Nothing moved. I clenched my teeth and pinched the rope between my knees while I pulled up a second time. This awarded me about three inches. I reached higher and tried to scoot up more.

The rope slipped like fire through my hands as I slid down and landed hard on my feet.

"To the back, soldier!" Commander Dane's eyes had obviously never left me.

I bowed my head so no one would see the angry tears blurring my vision and returned to the end of my line. I took my place behind Cedar, who gave me an encouraging nod before heading forward for his second turn. This time, he climbed all the way up without falling.

I was the only one left. Twelve pairs of eyes were on me; I felt them burning into me even though I wasn't looking. My gaze was on the remaining strip of silk.

I gave myself an extra moment to prepare. Boots up, knees closed, hands ready. I scooted and pulled, thrilled when I made a good first stride. The rope swung crazily, and I waited for it to still. Then I redoubled my efforts and went for the next bit of distance up the rope. I made it.

My arms were already aching, and when I went for the third pull, I lost a little ground. Panicked, I squeezed my feet and knees tightly to the rope and closed my eyes, waiting for Commander Dane to yell at me. He must have missed the slide, though, because no call came. I opened my eyes, fixed them on the crossbeam above my head, and went for the next bit of rope.

Before I knew what was happening, I had slid back down again, this time landing hard on my tailbone. I was too angry to cry when Commander Dane yelled at me to try again.

I stood and wrapped my hands around the rope as the first drops of rain slapped my cheeks. Ignoring them, I caught the knot between my boots and started my third climb.

And fell.

The rain came faster and harder as I made my fourth attempt. After I landed hard in the dirt that was quickly turning to mud, Commander Dane addressed the unit.

"Well done, men. To your tents until the supper horn!" He turned to me. "Upper-body strength, soldier."

I watched him walk away, deeply feeling the shame of his unspoken words—that I had failed and would not be a part of the special unit. Thunder rolled in the distance, and the rain splattered in my eyes as I stared at the one remaining strip of silk on the crossbeam.

I rose and wrapped my hands around the rope, my eyes still on the silk. Then I clenched the knot between my boots and began to climb. My breaths came in sharp gasps as I pulled and scooted, pulled and scooted. I was halfway up when my arms gave out and I half slid, half fell to the mud, hands burning.

I stood up and climbed again. The rain began to soak the rope, making it easier, somehow, to keep my grasp on it. The crossbeam inched closer.

Alone in the rain, without the critical eyes of Commander Dane and the others, I was able to concentrate. By the time I was three-quarters of the way up, the pain in my arms was so sharp that I had to keep alternating which arm held my weight, while squeezing the rope between my thighs so that I wouldn't fall.

Inch by inch. Hand over hand.

When I reached the top, I hung for a moment, resting first one arm and then the other. The strip of silk was looped over a metal ring on the top of the crossbeam. When I was sure my left arm was rested enough to hold me, I reached up with my right and worked at the loop of silk. It was soaking wet, and the rain fell so hard that I had to squint to keep it from blinding me.

The silk finally came free, and I held it in my teeth as I eased my way down the rope. When I reached the bottom, I allowed myself to fall. I lay on my back, legs splayed, mud squelching between my fingers. The rain pelted my face and neck and every part of me, scouring away the exhaustion and the heat of shame from my face. When my breathing was normal again, I got up, wiped my hands on my britches, and made my way to Commander Dane's tent.

I stood outside the full-sized, flag-festooned tent, unsure how to proceed. There was no way to knock, and I couldn't even be sure that he was inside. The rain was starting to make me shiver, and the longer I stood there, the more foolish—and chilled—I felt.

"Commander Dane." Thunder rolled over my words. I sighed and tried again, more loudly. "Commander Dane."

The tent flap moved to the side, and Commander Dane appeared in the opening. He stared at me, his mouth open. I wasn't even sure if he recognized me, though my failure had been so profound that I couldn't see how he'd forget my face.

"Storm?"

I wanted to tell him that I'd kept trying. I wanted to thank him for reminding me that I needed to build arm strength, and to let him know that, once everyone had left, I was able to find my inner strength and climb the rope. Instead, I said nothing and handed him the wet strip of silk.

"Sir," I said.

He took the silk, understanding dawning on his face as he continued to stare at me. Slowly, the understanding melted into something that looked more like approval.

I bowed my head. "Commander Dane." As I began to turn away, he placed his hand firmly on my shoulder.

"Call me Jasper."

9

The rain had tapered off during supper, and we now sat in the mud around our campfires celebrating the completion of six days of training. Tomorrow was Oradon, the Day of Resting. There would never truly be complete rest for us—our morning warm-ups would go on as scheduled, for one thing. But everything else would be deferred until the next day.

Jasper hadn't addressed the twelve of us again, and I imagined he was waiting until morning to tell us what was next. I wrapped my hands around the mug of ale I'd been holding for at least half an hour. Forest bumped my leg with his foot, which sent a strange thrill through me.

"Are you going to drink that, or are you just catching bugs in it?"

I smiled. "A few."

Dalen sat on my other side. "I'll drink it if you don't want it."

"Oh, no," Forest said. "Storm said he'd give the ale a try tonight. I'm waiting for him to make good on his word."

It still felt odd being referred to as "he." I raised the mug. "I'm always true to my word."

I touched my lips to the rim of the mug and held my breath. Perhaps I could take a swallow without actually tasting it. I tipped the mug, and the warm, tangy ale filled my mouth.

The warmth remained after I'd swallowed, and a rich, nutty flavor lingered on my tongue. I took another mouthful.

Forest and the others nearby raised their own mugs and cheered. I wanted to exclaim about the surprising nuttiness and pleasant fizz of the ale, but I reminded myself that fewer words were preferable to more.

"Better than I expected."

"Guess you're a real man now," River said.

If only he knew.

"Here's to Storm, for not giving up until he made it up the rope—in the rain," Forest said.

Shouts of my name were interspersed with laughter, and I raised my mug again and felt the warmth of their praise.

"I've been drinking ale since I've worn a son's cap," Dalen said. "I was going to call you 'Grandmother' if you didn't like it."

"Why?"

"My grandmother tried it once," Dalen said. "Spat it out and called it dragon's piss."

"She knows what that tastes like, does she?"

"Apparently." Dalen took a long swig from his own mug. "She once bought something from that little shop in Nandel—the one I mentioned before. Some sort of tincture to smear on a sore inside her mouth. The woman told her it was made from dragon's piss."

I raised an eyebrow and tried to act as though my heart weren't pattering relentlessly against my ribs. "Did your grandmother believe her?"

Dalen hesitated, furtively eyeing the others. They seemed to have lost interest in the conversation. "We're from Springton Village in Ytel. Of course she believed her."

I tightened my fingers around my mug and tried not to sound too eager. "So, you believe it, too?"

"What, dragon piss?"

"All of it."

Dalen took a long swig of ale and lowered his voice. "If you're asking me if I believe in the dragons, then . . . yes. I do. And I believe they'll return. But that's not something I like to talk about outside of Ytel."

"So, you believe T'Gonnen was real."

"Yes," Dalen said. "Always have."

"But what do you base that belief on?"

"You've never read *The Lament of Nuaga*?" He sounded a bit incredulous.

"Probably in school, I did." Not that I had any idea what school was like, since my tutoring in reading and household skills had happened at home, like it did for all girls. And of course my brother had never seen the inside of a school, either. "But it was just a story. Something to scare children with."

"There's nothing frightening about the *Lament*," Dalen said. "It's the story of T'Gonnen's sacrifice and the promise of the dragons' return."

"The stories I grew up with were about flesh-searing dragons rampaging through the land. Dark fairy tales."

Dalen smirked. "Then you didn't grow up with the truth."

A little over a week ago, I would have had to hold back laughter. Now I wanted to ask a dozen questions. I'd never known anyone from Ytel, though I had heard of their beliefs. Even the names they gave their children displayed a connection with an ancient, forgotten world that was so long gone that fact and myth seemed inextricably woven together.

"If the people of Ytel believe in dragon magic, why did your grandmother come all the way to Nandel to buy a tincture?" I asked.

"Selling dragon magic is a family business," Dalen said, "and the families who sell it don't share what they have. It's all very . . . proprietary. Handed down from father to son, mother to daughter."

"Like secret recipes?"

"It's the actual content," Dalen said, "depending on which desiccated dragon parts belong to their family."

Desiccated dragon parts? I must have looked dumbfounded, because Dalen went on to explain.

"Let's say your family owns three teeth and a thigh bone. You can't produce the same things as the family who owns the stomach. And you're not going to share your secrets once you find out the best way to extract the magic from the teeth, or to stretch the thigh bone into several generations' worth of powder mixed with other things."

"*S'da . . .*"

"Well, T'Gonnen had a lot of teeth, for instance, so some of these sellers went to other provinces to sell their wares, because the demand in Ytel wasn't great enough. But the shop in Nandel? It's known in Ytel for selling things made from relics no one else has."

"Such as . . . ?"

"T'Gonnen's heart. And his manhood, so to speak."

"His—" I almost gagged, thinking about what I'd been swallowing every night. "And these teas and tinctures work because they're made with . . . bits of dragon?"

"Yes. Or extracts. No one in my family is in the business, so I don't know much about how it all works." Dalen rubbed his forehead with the heel of his hand. "That's probably more than you wanted to know."

"No," I said. "It's interesting. Thank you."

"You're the first person from outside Ytel I've met who actually listened."

I had so much more to ask, but Mandrake chose that moment to throw an empty mug at Dalen. Laughter erupted as he retrieved it.

"You owe me a fill-up," Mandrake called.

Dalen rose good-naturedly, obviously willing to fulfill whatever promise he'd made. No matter—I'd corner him some other time, preferably when no one else was around. If my dreams were related to the powder I swallowed every night, Dalen might know.

My mug was empty by the time the horn sounded, and my bladder was full. I knew I'd need to hurry in order to relieve myself and get back to my tent, so I ran off before anyone could slow me with conversation.

I made it to my secret spot without being seen. By now, I had become proficient at not peeing on myself, and I finished quickly. The clouds were still thick, hiding the moon, and I focused on the thin light from the lanterns at the edge of the camp as I made my way back.

Rain.

I froze, every inch of my skin tingling. Not since the first time I'd heard the voice, when I was bathing in the lake, had I heard it outside my dreams. I only had about a minute before being late for evening curfew, but I didn't want to lose this opportunity.

"Who are you?" I whispered.

I am Nuaga.

My bones, my breath, my very heart tightened. "What do you want?"

Silence.

Then: *Release me.*

The words were urgent—they vibrated deep in my breastbone. The dryness in my mouth made my own words feel sticky.

"From what?"

I waited, but no answer came.

I closed my eyes, willing the voice to speak again. But the final good-night calls and sounds of settling in the camp tugged at my concentration. I opened my eyes and moved quickly across the dark field as the lanterns winked out one by one.

The morning was cool, as though yesterday's rain had washed away the last hold of summer's heat. It made warm-ups slightly less exhausting, which left me with more of an appetite for breakfast. I had made a habit by now of tearing my dried fruit into bits and stirring it into my porridge; I smiled as I watched Forest pulling a prune apart, his strong hands making easy work of it.

He caught my gaze and shrugged. "It makes it more edible."

"I'm a genius," I said. "Admit it."

"Sounds like you swallowed a frog, though," Forest said. "Maybe it was the ale?"

"What do you mean?" And then I heard it. My voice sounded lower, like I'd caught a cold. Except, I wasn't sick.

"You sound a bit rough, that's all."

I wanted to dance on the table and shout at the top of my new voice. Instead, I popped a bit of prune into my mouth. "Tired, I guess."

Since the day I'd met Forest on the road, I'd trained myself to force my voice slightly lower. If the powder had lowered my voice, as Madam S'dora said it might, maybe I would be able to speak normally now, without forcing it. The contents of the powder were disgusting—but discovery meant death, so I had no choice.

Sedge slapped his bowl onto the table on the other side of Forest. I frowned and averted my eyes, closing myself off. Since being singled out, the twelve of us had been eating meals together, at the table nearest the front of the tent. Sitting as far from Sedge as possible had become a habit.

"I'll admit it," he said, pulling apart a prune. "This really works. Whoever came up with it deserves second helpings."

"It was Storm's idea," Forest said.

"Is that right?" Sedge sucked a bit of prune from his thumb.

"That's right."

"How about that." Sedge looked at me. "I hear Commander *Jasper* gave you another chance to climb the rope."

I sucked on my cheeks and met his gaze. "Commander Jasper didn't give me another chance. I stayed out there until I climbed it."

"That's it? You try again and it makes you good enough?"

"It's called stamina," Forest said.

"It's called not fair," Sedge said. "What's Jasper going to do when Storm's aim is so bad he throws a knife into someone's neck instead of into a target? Give him another chance?"

I plucked a prune from my bowl and flicked it at Sedge's face, hitting him squarely in the forehead and drawing immediate laughter around the table. "What were you saying about my aim?"

Sedge rose to his knees and leaned on the table, his face ruddy with anger. "You won't be laughing when Jasper throws you out of this group because you're such a *girl*."

"Twenty laps around the meal tent, soldier." Jasper stood, bowl in hand, at the head of our table, his expression a thundercloud. "Not one of you is to speak ill of the other eleven. Ever."

Sedge's face fell. "Sir. I—"

"Now," Jasper said. "Or I'll make it thirty."

Sedge rose slowly, squaring his shoulders as though it were an honor to be called out by the commander. "Yes, sir."

Everyone at our table was silent. Jasper watched Sedge make his way out of the tent and begin running. Then his gaze fell on me.

"Perseverance like yours will go a long way," he said.

"Thank you, sir."

Jasper raised his eyes to the entire table. "As soon as you've finished breakfast, meet me on the opposite side of the meal tent." He turned and walked away.

"Sedge was only kidding," River said. "He's like that."

I rolled my eyes. "Tell that to Commander Jasper."

After we'd eaten, we waited for Jasper while the rest of the camp dispersed to go about whatever business they meant to accomplish on this Day of Rest. When he appeared around the corner of the tent, I straightened my shoulders, determined to always appear strong and ready.

"It's time to strike your tents. We'll be moving to a camp three miles north of here, where we'll prepare to carry out our mission."

A three-mile march didn't seem like a restful way to spend Oradon. But what restfulness would there truly be anymore, for any of us?

"We need to become hardened without the convenience of a military town," Jasper continued. "We'll be in the wilderness, which will be home from now on. And I'm going to do everything I can to make sure you're not soft. Once we've set up camp, I'll reveal our mission."

"Sir," Mandrake cut in. "What about our tentmates?"

"They'll be reassigned," Jasper said. "Be ready to march in twenty minutes."

He stepped away without waiting for further questions. Not that any would come—we knew by now to accept orders and to obey at all times. I caught Forest's glance and raised an eyebrow. Then we quietly made our way to our tent.

A new camp meant creating privacy for myself all over again. I didn't even want to think about how difficult that might be.

We were ready before the twenty minutes were up. Everything was muddy—especially my shirt from yesterday, as well as the pants I was still wearing today, since they were my only pair. Forest offered to carry our rolled tent for the first half of the march, and I didn't object. We lined up in three rows of four—a tiny army—and waited for Jasper's signal to march.

The sun fought its way through thin clouds as we headed north. The trees thinned almost immediately, giving way to a rock-strewn expanse of wild grass gone to seed. For about an hour, Jasper marched in front of us, never once looking back or calling a single command. Then, unexpectedly, he broke stride and moved back to march beside me.

"There's contention between you and Sedge," Jasper said.

"Yes, sir."

"See that it stops."

I opened my mouth, the force of the protest within me almost too strong to squelch. But I gathered myself and swallowed words that would have condemned Sedge and made me look small. "I'll do my best."

"Thank you," Jasper said. He marched for a while longer by my side before returning to his position at the front.

We marched in silence for a time. Forest stretched his neck to the left and right, working out a kink.

"Let me take the tent," I said.

He shook his head. "It's fine. I've found my stride."

"I wish I were riding Sweetpea right now."

Forest looked at me sideways. "This from the soldier who climbed a rope in the *rain?*"

"It was cooler."

Forest laughed—loud, rich laughter that came straight from his heart. I found myself drowning in its warmth, in the way I had made him laugh. Heat fluttered through my stomach and I forced my gaze away from his.

In moments like this, I felt too much like a girl. And it was the last thing I needed to feel like.

Commander Jasper called a halt just over a ridge that opened into an expanse of flat, rocky ground. A supply wagon already sat there, having been sent ahead. My heart sank when I saw that the nearest tree line was quite a distance to the east. Privacy would be even harder to find here.

The weight of worry slid from my shoulders when Jasper directed us to a flat expanse closer to the line of trees. It was still more than an easy distance away, but I was sure I could make it there and back quickly if I needed to. Forest dropped the tent and motioned to me.

"Let's get it up," he said.

It was easy enough to find a large stone to knock our tent stakes into the ground, and not so easy to clear out enough stones so that we could properly secure the tent. Others were having similar trouble.

"Can I borrow that when you're finished?" Commander Jasper gestured to the stone in Forest's hands.

Forest offered the stone. "Take it now, Commander. We're still digging out rocks."

"No, thank you—just finish what you're doing," Commander Jasper said. "I've got to clear some rocks, too."

I stared as he turned and walked to a pile of tents and belongings beside ours. I'd expected him to pitch his tent apart from the rest of us, the way he had marched. He went onto his hands and knees, dug a rock from the dirt, and tossed it. His eyes caught mine, and I felt my face burn hot.

"We're equals," he said. "No special treatment."

I opened my mouth to point out the obvious—that he was our commander. But I funneled the words back into my mouth before they spilled out. "Yes, sir."

Face still burning, I turned back to Forest and the tent, wishing I hadn't let Commander Jasper catch me staring. Standing in amazement of him wasn't going to help me gain his approval or rise to his level of competence.

Next time, I would regard him as the equal he'd named himself.

There was no meal tent, no tables to sit at or shade for eating beneath. The only convenience was a makeshift latrine, which was set up a comfortable distance from the tents. Commander Jasper worked alongside us, digging holes, unpacking supplies, creating order. I watched the easy way he interacted with everyone—the way he commanded respect with a mere gesture or a well-timed word. It was obvious I wasn't the only one who admired him. Even Sedge, who seemed not to respect anyone, held him in the regard his rank deserved. Especially since having to run laps around the meal tent.

It was late afternoon by the time the camp was set up. My stomach was rolling in on itself with hunger; we hadn't had any lunch. To my relief, Jasper assigned Cedar and Coast, our best swordsmen, to prepare an early supper, while the rest of us lined up to retrieve practice swords from the wagon, which we were instructed to store inside our tents.

"Eat," Jasper said, "and then we'll talk."

Supper was simple—cold salted pork and ale. We took our food and sat around a fire that had yet to be lit. Some lay on their sides, their mugs sitting beside them in the trampled grass. Others sat back-to-back, leaning on each other while they ate their pork. I took advantage of what might have been my only opportunity to sneak away to the latrine.

"Hold these," I said, handing Forest my slabs of pork.

Then I jogged lightly toward the latrine, afraid of what I'd find when I got there.

It was worse than I'd expected—three holes in the ground in a row, a haphazard tent strung above them to offer some protection from wind or rain. Unlike the latrine in the first camp, there was nothing to divide the spaces or create any sense of privacy. It was all men together.

Relieving myself was going to be one of my worst challenges. I practiced squatting in such a way that nothing showed, and prayed to the Great God that no one else would show up.

I was going to have to spend more time scheduling my private business than anything else. But at least my monthly bleed hadn't come. It was still too early to know whether the dragon powder had worked, or if the bleeding was a few days late. Mama had once explained to me that anxiousness might do that to a girl.

But in my heart, I knew. The words, my name, the warmth and tingling—and now the lower voice. It was hard to look at everything and say that it was merely coincidence. I was certain that the powder was working, and that my monthly bleed was one thing I would not have to worry about. Not as long as the dragon powder lasted.

I had taken no more than a dozen steps across the field when, from everywhere and nowhere, words so warm and clear I could almost *feel* them sounded in my ears:

Release me, Rain L'nahn.

My head swam and I closed my eyes. When I opened them, everything around me had shifted, so that nothing felt real—a waking dream. The air seemed shadowed and misty.

Then, from the tangled branches of the trees, a creature emerged, its sleek form murky in the fading light. It drew itself forward on six leathery legs, twice as high and five times as long as a horse, majestic and terrifying.

A dragon. Looking directly at me.

10

The world tilted. I closed my eyes and opened them again—the dragon remained, her mere size squeezing me with terror.

Release me.

Her voice came from near and far away. Or perhaps from deep inside me.

I staggered backward, wracked with the certainty that, if she came any closer, I would die. For several frantic seconds, I glanced to my right and left, to see if anyone else was there to witness what I hardly believed myself.

But it was only me . . . and the dragon.

She moved from the shadows, barely making a sound. A great head with hooded eyes and a long snout rested on a serpentine neck, slick with coppery scales and softened with long, dun-colored hair.

I couldn't breathe. Couldn't swallow the dryness in my throat.

"Am I dreaming?" My words were broken pebbles.

You are awake, but I come to you in a dream, where no one else can see. Release me so I can leave my nest.

"But . . ." I didn't know what to ask next.

A dragon will not come unbidden. Release me.

"How? Why?"

Spill your blood upon the ground that I may find you. Then release me.

I opened my mouth, but a violent trembling seized me, stealing my voice. I folded my arms tightly in an effort to steady myself. "But . . . why?"

Silence, profound and disappointing, met me. In the next heartbeat, she turned and vanished like mist. The shadows lifted, and the
world around me felt real again, as though I had awakened from
sleep.

I stared at the place where she had stood, my pulse rattling in my
teeth, the cry of terror I'd never uttered threatening to choke me.
Afraid to move, afraid to make a sound, I scanned the tree line, looking for any hint of movement. But there was none.

Releasing a long breath, I let my arms fall to my sides. Normal
sounds encroached once more upon my ears—a bird's call, the rise
and fall of voices across the field.

The dragon's words rang in my skull—*Spill your blood upon the
ground that I may find you.* Finding me would mean finding everyone
I was with. I imagined the panicked outcry from my unit, weapons
drawn before I could stop them. Dragonbreath, wielded in self-
defense, would surely melt the skin from their bodies where they
stood. Or perhaps she would come at night, trampling our tents and
crushing us into the damp earth while we slept.

I thought of Jasper's strength, River's kindness, Forest's steadfast-
ness. Did the dragon expect me to lead her here, putting everyone at
such great risk?

There was no way I could do that.

I walked quickly to rejoin the others, balling my fists to control
the trembling. I had about a hundred paces to shake the terror and
make sure it didn't show on my face.

No one would believe me if I told them I'd spoken to a dragon.

Forest waved my salted pork at me, and I made my way to his
side, determined to act normal.

"I almost ate this," he said, handing it to me.

"You would have lived to regret that." I plopped beside him, my
heart still racing.

"Now that we're all together, it's time to talk." Jasper stood several paces from me; his glance told me he'd been waiting for me.

He sat on a flat rock, and the rest of us shifted so we could see
and hear him easily around the crackling fire. I rested my forearms
on my knees and locked my gaze on him, forcing myself not to look
over my shoulder at the tree line.

"The first thing you need to know is that Tan Vey's army outnumbers our own. Our main forces are on a mission to intercept them before they reach Ylanda City to the north, but there is little chance of stopping them. They want our farms, our storehouses, our *avila* fields. That's what they've come for."

The sinking of my stomach mirrored the silence that followed Jasper's words.

"Why would they invade us for . . . crops?" Mandrake asked.

"For too long, we've had what they could never have," Jasper said. "*Avila* can't thrive in the north, and our land in general is more fertile than theirs." He gauged our response before continuing. "The nomads, and particularly the M'loh tribe, value land over life. Nothing is safe in their path—no village, no farm, no unwitting child. They do not wish to conquer us in order to rule us. They wish to destroy us and take everything that is ours."

"So there's no hope." Coast was more proficient with a sword than with words; I was surprised to hear him speak. His large hand was rolled into a fist and pressed against his chin, which was so prone to hair that he shaved morning and night.

"*You* are our hope," Jasper said. "You've been chosen because of your skill as Neshu fighters and because you've shown me that you have the stamina required for this mission. Your main task will be to enter Ylanda City and remove the high king from his palace."

It was hard not to exchange glances with anyone—it made no sense to remove the high king. Someone cleared his throat, and a loud snap from the fire made me jump.

"With due respect," Mandrake said, "I don't understand why the high king should be moved. Ylanda City is the safest fortress in our kingdom."

"Its safety has been untested for ages, because Stonewall has kept our enemies out," Jasper said. "And as I've already told you, we're outnumbered. Tan Vey's men will kill everyone in their path. That includes the high king and his family. If they die, Tan Vey will claim our kingdom and declare himself ruler."

"An army without a king can still fight," Mandrake said.

"An army without a king has no kingdom," Dalen said. "The law says, 'In the land stretching from the western mountains to the eastern sea, a kingdom with no ruler belongs to whoever claims it.'"

Sedge spat. "It's a myth, not a law."

"It's a truth that's older than Ylanda," Jasper said. "If the high king and his family fall, our kingdom will belong to our conquerors. The Great God himself decrees it." He sat taller. "We will save our king."

"Why us?" Rock's gentle voice belied his huge girth.

A moment of hesitancy flickered across Jasper's face. "You are skilled Neshu fighters. Some of the best I've seen."

"But we're untested in battle," Rock said. "Why choose us over more experienced men?"

"Our original Neshu unit was training near Stonewall when Tan Vey invaded. They were lost. Thirty of the kingdom's finest Neshu fighters." The heaviness of his words was reflected in his eyes. "Every other active soldier was needed on the battlefield."

I didn't know whether I felt large or small. Honored or terrified.

"But why us?" Forest pressed. "Why not choose Neshu fighters from the experienced soldiers in the next camp?" His gaze remained fixed on Jasper—a challenge.

"Because the Neshu has been trained right out of them." Jasper crossed his arms. "Field combat isn't anything like a Neshu round. You have to think like a unit, fight collectively. A Neshu warrior will always have more agility, quicker responses, but it's the field training that makes a man into a soldier. It would take me twice as long to train an experienced unit for this mission—because I'd have to *un*train them first."

Forest nodded slowly; he seemed unconvinced. "We have what it takes, then."

"We wouldn't be having this conversation if you didn't."

"Once we rescue the high king, where are we taking him?" Dalen asked.

"A secret place, hidden from the common man. In the age before the wall, the high king was always taken there when he needed protection."

"Where?" Sedge asked.

"I'll disclose that when the time comes," Jasper said. "The reason I tested you on the ropes was because we may be required to climb over the city or palace wall, or both. We'll use our time here to strengthen our upper bodies and sharpen our combat skills."

"I still don't understand why Tan Vey would focus on killing our high king, especially if his forces are as great as you say," Cedar said. "Ancient law or not, defeating the high king's army is the same as defeating the high king himself."

"True," Jasper said. "But Tan Vey and his nomads believe the ancient stories of the dragons and their loyalty to the kingdom of Ylanda."

My heart tumbled within my breast and I twisted the fabric of my shirt in my fingers, waiting for him to say more. Feet shuffled and somebody coughed.

"I don't pretend to understand those stories," Jasper continued. "But it's believed that Tan Vey thinks the dragons of Ylanda will switch their loyalty to him if he kills the high king."

"There aren't any dragons," Sedge said.

"I know," Jasper said. "But it matters little. If Tan Vey intends to kill the high king, it's our job to make sure he doesn't succeed." He reached behind the rock and withdrew a pile of curled parchments. "These are crude maps of the region between here and the capital. Study them until the light has failed. Tomorrow we'll get to work."

I took a map and spread it on my lap, holding the edges down while I perused the smudged markings of road and hillock, town and stream. Before, I would have delighted in tracing my finger across reaches of the kingdom I never thought I'd see. Now I imagined only death and destruction in the wake of an army beyond my imaginings. And dragons lurking in the shadows, whispering my name.

I stared at the map until the darkening sky forced me close to the fire's light, the pork in my hand largely forgotten.

"You going to eat that?" Dalen asked.

I took a bigger-than-usual bite. "Yes."

"Nice try, Dalen," Forest said.

"I don't know how you can move at all, with the way you eat," I said through the mouthful of meat.

He shrugged. "I'm slower than I should be. But faster than I used to be."

I looked around, checking to see how many others were close by. Except for River giving Sedge rapt attention as he highlighted details of one of his female conquests, the three of us were fairly isolated on the opposite side of the fire. I turned to Dalen.

"What do you know about Nuaga and T'Gonnen?"

Dalen gave me an odd look. "Why?"

"You believe in them," I said, "and apparently so does Tan Vey. I'm interested."

"Don't you remember anything from *The Lament of Nuaga*?"

"A little, maybe." Nothing, mostly. "Tell me about T'Gonnen."

"High king of the dragon clan," Dalen said. "He sacrificed himself for the other dragons."

I picked up my mug of ale and set it in my lap. "Why?"

"So they could sleep in peace and have a chance to reawaken someday. Sacrifice was always required to accomplish great magic like that."

"Even if they did exist, why would anyone want them to wake up?" Forest said. "Dragons are supposed to be fierce. Melting people's faces and things like that."

"That's not how it was," Dalen said softly. "The mark of the dragon was a symbol of honor."

"But it's just legend," Forest said. "None of it's actually true, right?"

"Dalen believes the dragons will return," I said.

Forest frowned and said nothing.

"'Ylanda' means 'dragon' in the Old Tongue," Dalen said. "You could say we're the kingdom of dragons."

"If they wake up, then what?" I asked.

"I only know what's in the *Lament*," Dalen said. "I have some of it memorized."

Curiosity burned inside me. "Only some?"

"Yes." He paused, seeming to gauge my level of interest. When I raised my eyebrows, he began:

> "From the Great God, ever breathing,
>   Came the Dragons.
>   Heat of sun and strength of thousands,
>   Came the Mighty Dragons.

"Fiery red, the pride of heaven,
Fierce T'Gonnen.
Bowing to her lord and master,
Loyal, brave Nuaga.

"By his side and never failing,
Never shirking.
She-king to the Clan of Dragons,
Lovely, strong Nuaga.

"Long their vigilant protection,
Through the ages.
Faithful to their charge and calling—
Faithful to the faithless."

Dalen flashed a sheepish smile. "That's all I know by heart."

"Faithful dragons?" Sedge's voice cut into the conversation like an unwelcome guest. "They were killers. Monsters."

"That's not what the *Lament* says." As if I knew.

Sedge snorted. "That was written by some dragon-lover from Ytel. Everyone knows an army was sent to destroy the dragons rampaging the land. T'Gonnen was killed at Stonewall and the rest of the dragons disappeared. End of story."

"That's not how it was," Dalen said again, his gaze lowered.

"I remember the story of T'Gonnen," River offered. "But didn't he save the dragons or something?"

"Yes," Dalen said.

"All lies," Sedge said. "The dragons may have existed, but the rest is a fairy tale."

I remembered Jasper's admonition and smothered the words that wanted to lash out at Sedge.

"I wonder where Tan Vey got his story about stealing the dragons' loyalty by killing the high king," Forest said.

Dalen shrugged. "I don't know."

"That's not in the *Lament*?" I asked.

"No," Dalen said. "It only says that T'Gonnen's magic will wake Nuaga."

Sedge threw his head back and downed the last of his ale. "Believe what you want, dragon boy. I think we've got worse things to worry about than dragons." He rose and sauntered away to refill his mug.

I barely heard him. Dalen's words were echoing in my brain: *T'Gonnen's magic will wake Nuaga.*

"He believes more than he lets on," River said. "At least, he believes in the magic."

My scalp tingled. Hadn't I first met Sedge in Madam S'dora's shop? Perhaps River knew what he'd bought there.

"My sister bought something from a shop in Nandel," I blurted. "Something to stop the bleeding on her wedding night."

"That's some apothecary," Forest said.

"Not an apothecary," I said.

River raised an eyebrow. "Did it work?"

"She hasn't had a wedding night yet."

Forest laughed. "That proves a lot."

"I know which shop you mean," River said. "I'm pretty sure Sedge made a stop there on our way through Nandel. Not sure if he bought anything, but I know he gives as much credit to those potions as I do."

Whatever Sedge had purchased from Madam S'dora was clearly something he was keeping to himself. Not that I was one to talk.

"I wonder what he bought," I said.

"Why are you so worried about dragons and old hags' tales?" Forest asked.

I took a long drink of ale, then wiped my mouth on the back of my hand. "If Tan Vey believes them, I think we should pay attention."

———◆———

The light from the dying fire was barely enough to help me see as I picked my way from the latrine to Forest's and my tent. I saluted to Jasper, who had taken first watch, before ducking through the tent flap.

"I thought maybe you'd deserted," Forest said.

"Not a chance. The food's too good." I sat down and pulled off my boots.

"So, are you going to tell me why you're so interested in dragons?"

Prickles skittered across my skin. "I'm not, really."

"You're more obvious than you think you are."

I unknotted my hair and rubbed my fingers through it. "It's like I said. If Tan Vey believes in them, we should pay attention."

"That stuff you swallow every night," Forest pressed. "Did it come from the shop you and River were talking about?"

Words clustered in my mouth, getting stuck there. Hadn't I been subtle, grabbing moments alone in the tent when I could, turning my back in the dark when Forest was there? "Yes."

"What's it for?"

I had prepared the lie ahead of time, but now that I was ready to tell it, it felt unbelievable on my tongue. "It's to keep my feet from turning in."

"You're pigeon-toed?"

"I was, a little." Each word buzzed across my lips, annoying untruths.

"But now you're not?"

"Do you think I could fight Neshu pigeon-toed?"

"Guess not." He shifted onto his side while I lay back—I still wasn't used to being this close to a boy all night. Especially a boy with an endearing dimple. "So now you're wondering if it's really dragon magic? Is that it?"

"It's hard not to question it." This part was true, and easier to say. "I saw changes only a few days after starting the powder. What healer could do that? And what herb or oil do you know of that could fix something like this?"

"I don't know," Forest said. "But calling it magic is a bit of a stretch."

"You'd have to experience it to understand."

"Maybe." He was silent for a moment. "What did your sister buy for her wedding night?"

My cheeks burned; I wished I hadn't mentioned it earlier. "A tea. She says she has friends who used it."

"Is that dragon magic, too?"

"I don't know."

He sighed. "Did you know that most of the towns in S'dona allow men to choose their own wives?"

"Really?" A strange heat settled in my stomach. "How did you learn that?"

"River told me. He's from Thistle Spring, and he says he's betrothed to a girl he fell in love with on his own." Forest scratched his head. "Can you imagine kissing a girl who really wanted to kiss you, and not because your families were watching?"

My breath caught in my throat as I tried to come up with a clever answer. But no words came—there was only the intense closeness of Forest in the dark and an alarming moment of wondering what his lips might feel like against mine.

Great God.

I scooted imperceptibly away from him, desperate not to brush against him and heighten the storm in my breast. "I suppose," I said.

"Hah. You're like me, then," Forest said. "You'd rather wait a long time before you get married."

"Yes," I said. "Definitely." But the word shook as I spoke it.

He stretched in the dark, rolling onto his back. "Morning will be here too soon. Good night."

"Forest?"

"Mmm?"

"Don't tell anyone about the dragon powder."

"I won't say a word."

I rolled away from him, as always, only this time I made sure the space between us was as large as possible.

Forest is promised to my sister. Whether I'm a boy or a girl, nothing will change that.

I closed my eyes and willed myself to grow drowsy. But my mind was wide awake, reliving the terror of Nuaga's face and the insistence of her words: *Release me.* When I slept tonight, would I see her?

Almost, I opened my mouth to tell Forest about her—but his breathing had already deepened, soft and steady with slumber. I fell asleep wondering if he'd believe me . . . and when I'd see Nuaga again.

11

Oraclava, the first day of the week, dawned fair and clear. After breakfast, Jasper gave us time to take our dirty clothing to the stream that meandered behind the tree line. "Once we've broken camp, we'll live rough," he said, "but for now, I want disciplined soldiers." I hung back, kneeling in the tent with yesterday's soiled shirt balled in my hands, thinking.

"You coming, Storm?" Forest called from outside.

"Go on," I called back. "I'll meet you there."

I had to figure something out—fast. The other men would strip to their undergarments, and sometimes further, in order to wash all their clothes at once. At breakfast, Dalen and Flint had joked about naked Neshu, and it was hard not to take them seriously, though Flint was already well known for his dry humor.

Quickly, I peeled off my second, almost equally dirty shirt and rolled it with the first one. I lifted the tent flap and peeked out to make sure Forest had walked away before hastily unwrapping my bindings. They could have used a washing, too, but that was a luxury I couldn't risk. I rebound them as quickly as I could. Then I pulled out the shirt I'd arrived in—Storm's shirt—and put it on. I wrapped myself, and the shirt, in a brief hug.

I remembered the time Storm and I had to wait out a sudden hailstorm in the barn. He had squeezed me into a lung-crushing embrace and told me, over and over, that he would keep me safe, as though the hailstones meant certain death.

I miss you, twin.

I caught up with Forest and River near the tree line. Dalen was a few paces in front of them, talking with—or rather, listening to—Sedge. I lengthened my stride to keep up.

"Upstream's best," River said. "We won't get the runoff from everyone else's dirt."

He was right, but apparently most of the others had already thought the same thing. We meandered along the bank for a while until we found an open clearing. Sedge pushed ahead, and Dalen slowed his pace to join us—gratefully, I thought.

As soon as we'd claimed our spot, the others peeled off their shirts and, after pulling off their boots and socks, stepped out of their pants as well. I pulled off my own boots and socks and stepped out of my pants. Luckily, men's undergarments were thickly padded in the front, creating an illusion of maleness. The shirt hung almost to my knees, giving me enough coverage to feel safe.

Almost safe. As soon as my legs were exposed, they felt slender and vulnerable. Girls' legs.

Not for the first time, I scanned the tree line for any sign of a dragon—a glimpse of long neck wreathed in dun-colored fur or hulking, scaled body—but saw nothing. Then I grabbed the bucket of soft oil soap that River had carried from the camp and brought it near the water's edge. Without making eye contact with anyone, I carried my muddiest shirt—the one I was wearing when I fell numerous times off the rope—into the water until I was in up to my knees, and plunged it in.

"You going to wash that shirt while you're wearing it?" Dalen asked.

"No, this is my extra." I trailed the soaking shirt behind me in the water as I walked back to the bucket and scooped up a squishy handful of soap.

"You afraid someone will notice your lack of chest hair?" Dalen teased.

"Something like that."

"We're all in this together, Storm," Forest said, scrubbing his own shirt not far from me. "It doesn't matter."

I shrugged, trying desperately to act like I wasn't fazed. "It matters to me."

"Looks like the water's too cold for the midget," Sedge called from his spot slightly upstream. "Maybe he needs a good dunking to help him get used to it."

He laughed, and Coast and Flint, who were near him, laughed, too. I ignored them, scrubbing the mud from my shirt and rinsing it well before bringing it up to the bank. After finding a clean place for it, I reached for the second shirt.

I had just returned to the knee-deep water with another handful of soap when someone shoved me hard from behind, knocking me off-balance. I fell sideways into the water and went under. When I came up, Sedge's laughter was the first thing to greet me.

The water streaming into my eyes did nothing to cool my rage. I rose slowly, forcing myself to look Sedge in the eye. My face was as still and expressionless as I could make it.

"That shirt keep you warm in the water?" he said.

"Go wash your clothes," Forest said behind him.

Sedge gave him a sideways glance. "He deserved it. Besides, if he can't take a little dunking, how's he going to carry his weight on the mission?"

"That's not for you to say."

"You're right." Sedge returned his attention to me. "The midget should speak for himself."

With my toes curled into the rocks on the bottom of the stream, I assumed the second stance—legs spread, knees bent. I moved subtly, letting my arms hang free and relaxed. "Back off."

"You're the one who threw the prune at my face in front of Commander Jasper."

Slow breaths. Stay centered. "You questioned my aim."

"Your aim cost me twenty laps." He took a step toward me. "Have another bath, midget."

His arm shot out to push me, but I was faster, blocking his arm and sending the heel of my knife hand into his forehead. He staggered, and I twisted onto my left leg and kicked him in the chest, just hard enough to send him sprawling backward, his arms flailing as he hit the water.

Sedge didn't share the laughter that assaulted him. He rose, his eyes hard coals that bored into me as he waded toward me, each step deliberate. I returned to the second stance, ready for whatever Sedge would try next.

He crossed his arms over his chest and offered a stiff bow. "As the sun rises." The words felt like coiled springs squeezing past his jaw.

"So it sets." I stayed ready, unwilling to believe that he would be so quick to honor a Neshu defeat.

He glared at me for too many breaths. Then he grabbed his floating shirt from the water, his gaze still pulling on mine.

"I'll give you this one, midget." He turned away and waded back to his spot upstream.

"Good move, Storm," River said.

I tried to brush it off. "He's an oaf."

"You caught him unaware," Forest said. "I was watching you the whole time, and I didn't see it coming, either."

"Why does he call you 'midget,' anyway?" Dalen asked. "He's shorter than all the rest of us."

I rolled my eyes. "But taller than I am."

"You move like a grandmaster," Dalen said. "Even in the water."

Their praise warmed me, and for a moment I stopped worrying about my shirt and the very real girl parts underneath it. "Thanks."

I glanced at Forest, who nodded. Admiration shone from his eyes, and a wave of delicious warmth crept through my middle, despite the weight that always tugged at me—the undeniable truth that, if he knew I was a girl, the admiration would turn to scorn.

"We're going to push ourselves to the edge of endurance until the order comes for us to march north," Jasper said.

We stood, the twelve of us, in a ring around him—a barely dressed, shirtless unit, save for me, in my too-long shirt. He turned slowly as he spoke, addressing us around the circle, making eye contact with each of us.

"First order of business, rebuilding the rope climb," Jasper said. "When it's done, we'll start our drills, including knife-throwing for hunting. There's limited food in the wagon, which means we'll soon get used to living off the land. Now's the time to prepare your bodies and minds for what lies ahead."

True to his word, Jasper pushed us hard all day. For the first hour, surrounded by shirtless men in their undergarments, I felt I would melt from embarrassment, but I soon grew accustomed to their near-nakedness. Which was rather disconcerting.

It was nearing dusk by the time we were able to return for our now-dry clothing, spread in the grass near the creek bank. It felt good to gather up my sun-warmed shirts and pants and socks, though it was a reminder that a young soldier's modesty would only last so long. Probably Forest and the others expected that I'd soon be tossing my clothes off with the rest of them.

But I wouldn't be. And at that point, I didn't know how I would keep their suspicions at bay.

We cooked salted pork and beetroot on skewers over the fire while Jasper told us everything he knew about Tan Vey and his army of united nomads.

"As soon as we get our orders, we'll head to the military outpost at Chancory, south of Ylanda City. You should recognize it from the maps I gave you."

"Wasn't the outpost abandoned generations ago?" Cedar asked.

"Once Stonewall was completed, yes," Jasper said. "But since Tan Vey's invasion, the army's first priority was to establish the outpost as a command base. It's from there that our intelligence will come."

"Aren't we wasting time here?" Flint was our best swordsman and the only one in the unit who still intimidated me.

Jasper's face grew hard. "I will not send you untested."

He drilled us on our map study as we ate, though exhaustion made it seem impossible to think. After, I drew lines and circles in the dirt with my empty stick, trying without success to create a map.

Forest made an exasperated sound. When I looked up, his expression was dark, his mouth clenched. He threw a stone at the fire.

"Forest?"

He glanced at me before lowering his gaze to the map half-crumpled in his hand. "I can't keep it straight."

"It'll come." I smiled, but he shook his head, and my smile melted. "Are you always this hard on yourself?"

He shrugged and said nothing. I stared at the play of light and shadow on his face, wishing I could rub my palm against his cheek and feel the strength of his jaw, the scratch of day-old stubble against my skin.

Then, appalled, I looked away, determined to wrench those thoughts from my brain.

From my heart.

Conversation was sparse as the fire crackled low. Cedar carved a chunk of wood into the shape of a chipmunk, the wood curls falling onto his lap like snow. Dalen stretched out his legs and lowered himself onto his side, as though he might fall asleep right there.

"We're just east of the commune, eh, Kendel?" he said, eyes closed.

"Several miles east." Kendel was from Province Ytel, like Dalen.

"What commune?" I asked.

"The Commune of Mennek the Lesser," Kendel said.

Something around his neck caught the light of the fire, and I frowned, thinking at first I'd imagined it. "What's that?" I asked, gesturing with my chin.

"Oh. An amulet from home." He seemed embarrassed as he tucked it hastily inside his shirt.

I caught a glimpse of it as it disappeared beneath the fabric; it reminded me of the amulets I had seen in Madam S'dora's shop.

"Dragon's blood," Dalen said, his eyes still closed. "That's what's inside it."

"Inside what?" Apparently I was missing something.

"The amulet," he said. "It's good luck."

"Leave it, Dalen, *s'da?*" Kendel folded his arms across his chest.

"So, where's the commune, exactly?" I asked, hoping to ease Kendel's embarrassment.

"In the finger of Ytel that cuts through Tenema from the west," he said. "Just a few miles, and we'd be in our own province, Dalen."

"Still far from home," Dalen said.

Home wasn't something I allowed myself to dwell on. I tossed my stick into the fire and decided I would catch Dalen alone as soon as possible and ask him to tell me everything he knew about the *Lament*. And dragons in general.

I caught up with Dalen after our morning warm-ups. We were both out of breath, so I walked alongside him for several paces, until speaking became easier.

"Can I talk with you?"

"I need to piss."

I was so used to boy talk that I didn't even blush. "I'll walk with you."

We headed toward the latrine, and I tried to think of a way to bring up the dragons without making myself sound insane. A bit of casual chatter might be a better way to start the conversation, but I couldn't think of any.

"What do you want to talk about?" Dalen asked.

"Remember when we were talking about dragons? *The Lament of Nuaga* and all that?"

"Yes."

"I was wondering if you could teach it to me. The *Lament*."

Dalen narrowed his eyes. "Why?"

"I'm not ridiculing you," I said quickly. "It's just . . . I've been having some bad dreams."

"About dragons?"

Time to choose my words carefully. "Sometimes. I'm sure they're just nightmares, but . . ."

"Just nightmares." Mild disbelief danced in his eyes.

"Yes. Maybe if I learn a little more about the dragons, the nightmares will stop."

Dalen stopped by a tree behind the latrine; I averted my eyes. "Or maybe you've had a taste of dragon magic. Otherwise you wouldn't be so worried about bad dreams."

His words brushed too close to the truth. With great effort, I gave a sort of half-laugh, hoping I sounded casual. I scrambled for something to say while he finished peeing, but words stumbled against each other, afraid to come out. I couldn't let him know about the dragon powder.

"I'm not worried," I said at last. "I'd just rather sleep well."

Dalen finished his business, then dug deep into his pocket and pulled out a small, tightly wound scroll. He held it out to me.

"Read it for yourself."

My heart caught. "You carry it with you?"

He nodded. "Keep it as long as you want, *s'da*? Just don't lose it."

"Thank you." I curled the scroll into my palm, strands of excitement weaving through my stomach.

"It's just a copy, of course," he went on. "One of hundreds, I'm sure."

"Where's the original?" Or perhaps it no longer existed.

"In the Commune of Mennek." Dalen's words became more animated. Passionate, even. "Kendel and I were talking about it last night."

"Yes. I remember."

"They're faithful to the dragons, and they keep a library of dragon lore," Dalen went on. "The Archives, it's called."

"They believe in Nuaga's return?"

"Yes. Same as Kendel and I do. They're said to be very protective of their Archives." He gazed in the direction of the commune. "I wish I could see it. The original *Lament*."

His reverence wrapped around me, warm and real. "This is important to you."

"It's important to everyone in Ylanda," he said. "But most folks don't realize it."

"I think I'm starting to."

Dalen looked, for a moment, as though he didn't quite believe me. But then his expression relaxed, and a slight nod of his head told me, in a way I had no words for, that he had accepted me as an ally.

"It's no small thing, dreaming about dragons," he said.

"I'm sure it's nothing. But . . . don't tell anyone just the same, *s'da*?"

"*S'da*." He turned to walk back toward camp. "I'll give you my ale ration if you think an extra mug would help you sleep."

I smiled—Dalen had keenly felt the tightening of our ale supply. "I'll be fine."

It wasn't until almost dusk that I had a private moment to read the scroll. I slipped away from the others and sat behind my tent, shielded from view. Pulse fluttering, I unrolled the parchment and read *The Lament of Nuaga,* my lips moving silently as I savored each word.

> From the Great God, ever breathing,
> Came the Dragons.
> Heat of sun and strength of thousands,
> Came the Mighty Dragons.

> Fiery red, the pride of heaven,
> Fierce T'Gonnen.
> Bowing to her lord and master,
> Loyal, brave Nuaga.

> By his side and never failing,
> Never shirking.
> She-king to the Clan of Dragons,
> Lovely, strong Nuaga.

> Long their vigilant protection,
> Through the ages.
> Faithful to their charge and calling—
> Faithful to the faithless.

> From the north, in tribes disjointed,
> Came the nomads
> Lusting for the strength and magic
> Of the mighty Dragons.

> "Build no walls; create no borders!"
> Cried the Dragons.
> "Ours, this land, and yours, our power,
> Ever to protect you."

> Foolish people of Ylanda,
> Self-important.
> "By our might and with your blessing,
> We shall build defenses."

Clan of Dragons, ever faithful,
Gave no blessing.
Seeds of enmity thus planted,
Tearing them asunder.

By the sweat of brows and bosoms
Over decades,
Miles of stone, the wall assembled,
Solid, vast, defiant.

Soft, the Dragons crept, retreating
To their caverns.
Thus betrayed by those they honored,
Sent to endless slumber.

"Join them in their resting places,
Dear Nuaga.
"Flesh and bone I now must offer,"
Spoke the bold T'Gonnen.

Grave of heart and torn in spirit,
Wailed Nuaga,
"Sleep with us in rest eternal—
Suffer not this torture!"

Yet despite impassioned pleading,
Fierce T'Gonnen
Gave himself for all Ylanda
And the Clan of Dragons.

Took he neither food nor water,
So to languish.
On the eighteenth day, his spirit
Finally departed.

Tears of Nuaga flowing, pouring,
Grief unending,

As she watched his body plundered,
Bone and flesh together.

Now dispersed, the great one's power,
To the peoples.
Satisfied, the mourning she-king
Joined the sleeping Dragons.

By his sacrifice, the power
Of the Dragons,
Wends its way through dale and village
Calling to his people.

Fair Nuaga waits in slumber
Intermittent.
When T'Gonnen's magic wakes her,
She will speak and beckon.

Where is Onen?

Each breath was loud in my ears as I reread the final verse, its meaning unmistakable. T'Gonnen's magic would wake Nuaga, and she would beckon.

But why? And who was Onen?

Nuaga had said the *Lament* contained the words I would need to wake the dragons. Did she mean that I needed to know the entire thing? Be able to recite it? I could certainly do that. But I still didn't understand how that would help me wake any dragons.

Not that I wanted to.

I read the *Lament* several more times, and the conviction that every word was true burned deep in my belly. There was no plausible reason for feeling this way—I simply felt it. Knew it.

Perhaps it was the dragon powder, coursing through my veins. Or the simple fact that I had spoken with Nuaga before I had ever read the *Lament*.

There wasn't anything about having to spill my blood so she could find me, though. It only said that she would speak and beckon.

I ran my fingertip over the final line: *Where is Onen?* I'd studied and written poetry almost since I could hold a pen. The more I thought about it, the more it sounded incomplete.

But why would Dalen have an incomplete version? It made no sense.

If only I could slip away to the Archives, to see if the original *Lament* really did reside there. Or perhaps I was thinking too hard about this—perhaps the *Lament* ended exactly the way it was intended.

I rerolled the scroll and tucked it deep inside my pocket, the words still tingling on my lips. "Help me understand," I whispered to Nuaga.

She didn't answer.

———————

I rolled gratefully onto my side that night, exhausted from the day's training. Forest's good-night faded into the distance as I fell quickly into dream-vivid sleep. Throughout the dreams, my name, clear and strident, rang in my ears, until I sat upright, fully awake, sweat dampening my face.

Release me, Rain.

I pressed my fist against my mouth and closed my eyes, reminding myself that Nuaga only came in dreams.

I'm waiting.

Though my eyes were closed, she loomed before me, as though I had been transported into someone else's dream—and in the dream, my eyes were wide open. I felt the heat of her breath and smelled her musky scent as she dipped her head toward me. Her eyes were luminous, and she held me in her gaze until I felt I would explode.

She was terrible. And beautiful.

Release me. You can then receive my mark and wake the dragons.

Nuaga's eyes, shades of vibrant blue mixed with honey and topaz, regarded me with such intensity that, for a moment, I closed my own eyes.

I feared she would consume me, though she wasn't really there.

"Why do you want me to wake the dragons?" I asked, my words scratching their way out.

Because the dragons are Ylanda's only hope. Look into my eyes, Rain L'nahn.

I looked, and her eyes grew large and transparent, drawing me into them as though I were mere breath. I cried out as darkness closed around me. Immediately, light and a thousand colors sliced into my eyes, and I sank to my knees and pressed my hands over my face.

Behold. A single word, whispered into my soul.

Birdsong and the warmth of sunlight on my neck both calmed and confused me. Had she taken me somewhere else? I lowered my hands and gasped—I knelt in the shade of a sprawling tree, my knees sunk into the dirt. Not far away, the grass sloped gradually downward, and a strange keening wafted on the breeze.

"Where is this place?" I asked.

But I was alone.

I rose and followed the sound of the keening, the ground's dip becoming steeper until it widened into a hollow. By the time I neared the bottom, the keening had stopped. In the middle of the hollow lay a freshly born dragon, the slime of birth still glistening upon its neck and back. Nearby, its mother rolled toward it and lowered her head, nuzzling it with affection so great that my heart ached.

The cries of men pierced the air. Startled, I looked up to see them hurtling down the hollow on the opposite side—fifteen, twenty men in braided armor, swords aloft. Panic tore through me as I realized I had nowhere to escape their advance.

But they seemed not to see me. I stood rooted to the grass as their weapons bore down upon the mother dragon, swords slashing. Blood arced from the dragon's neck and breast, and I screamed as three of the soldiers descended on the baby, throwing a thick-roped net over it and cinching a cord around its neck until it could barely breathe.

I backed away, stumbling over myself on the way up, unable to tear my eyes from the horror before me. Cold wind rushed at my skin as darkness once more swept over me, and then all was still. Nuaga stood before me in the shadows of the waking dream.

That is the legacy of the northern tribes, she said. *They must be stopped.*

The horror of what I'd seen stole my words. I folded my arms across my chest to try to stop the shivering.

"H . . . how?"

She blinked. *Only the dragons can stop Tan Vey and his army from destroying your people. Release me and receive my mark so you can wake the dragons.*

I stared, words failing me.

The mark of my breath, she said. *Only the worthy survive it—but T'Gonnen is strong within you. I believe you are worthy.*

Fear crept through my body. "Why me?"

Because you have awakened me, Rain. And the other will not listen.

The other?

Will you release me?

"You've asked me to spill my blood."

Yes. The scent of faithful blood will show me where to find you.

I couldn't reconcile it. My heart was drawn to Nuaga, but what of the men in my unit? Could I willingly invite such a creature into their midst?

"I'm not ready," I whispered.

Her face reflected a thousand sorrows before she faded into black. I opened my eyes in the darkness of my tent, my breathing loud and ragged. Forest lay sleeping; I was careful not to wake him as I lay down, bathed in sweat, my heart banging against my ribs. The throaty warmth of Nuaga's voice echoed in my mind.

The mark of my breath. Only the worthy survive it.

Dear Great God, did she think I was mad?

And who was "the other"?

The *Lament* said nothing about dragonbreath or receiving Nuaga's mark. What else was missing? For the first time, I wished I had grown up believing in dragons. Surely this would be easier if it weren't all so terrifyingly new.

———◆———

I slept little for what remained of the night, which was long. My sporadic dozing deepened into actual sleep some time before dawn, and when Jasper yelled us from our tents, I could barely raise my head from the ground.

"Are you alive?" Forest hovered like a rain cloud.

I groaned and rolled onto my back. "Barely."

"You'd better get moving." His boots were already on; he ducked out of the tent.

I jammed my feet into my boots and started running toward the latrine, twisting my hair back as I went. Several boys were relieving themselves along the outskirts of the tree line that hugged the stream. I hoped that meant the latrine itself might not be full, but as soon as I ducked inside, I saw that all three holes were taken up.

I groaned inwardly, then made my way to the private place I'd found just behind the latrine, in a not-quite-big-enough cluster of holly bushes. I considered skipping it altogether, but my bladder was full, and I knew I wouldn't make it through warm-ups without relieving myself.

I stood for a few moments in the holly bushes, pantomiming. Moments later, Cedar squatted behind a tree, obviously having forgone the latrine for other business. It seemed reasonable that I might get away with it, too.

I had just finished when someone squatted on the other side of the bush. I froze, feeling too exposed to pull myself together. I continued to squat until my legs began to fall asleep, and then I summoned the nerve to stand up. When I did, I got a clear view of the boy on the other side. It was Sedge.

He didn't see me, and as soon as my pants were up, I cut a wide arc around the bush, hoping he was too intent on his business to notice me. I was a few steps away from moving outside his range of vision when I saw him shake something from a small bottle into the palm of one hand. He rubbed whatever it was into his neck, first on one side, then on the other.

I should have kept moving, but I knew in the pit of my stomach that whatever he was rubbing on his neck was his purchase from Madam S'dora's shop. In the next instant, he looked up, as though he had sensed me watching him.

He narrowed his eyes, like the time we'd first met and he thought he'd recognized me. Was he thinking the same thing now? Straining through layers of memory to figure out why my face looked familiar?

"What are you staring at?" he said.

I frowned and walked away, embarrassment coursing through me like a boiling river. I hated to think how this would incite further abuse from him. I was supposed to be working to make things better, not worse.

And then it struck me, like a blow to the skull—Sedge could be "the other." Whatever he rubbed into his skin was surely imbued with dragon magic, similar to the powder I swallowed. Perhaps it wasn't as strong, or Sedge wasn't having dreams.

Nuaga may have been drawn to the magic in Sedge's oil, but I was the one she reached out to.

Asked to wake dragons.

I headed toward the open field, hoping I'd find the courage to say yes.

12

By the end of the week, our weapons and breastplates had been delivered from the main camp, though without the helmets we would have worn into battle. The breastplates were specially crafted—thin and supple, made from tightly stitched braids of leather, so that we could engage in Neshu without being encumbered. Not as protective as a full breastplate, but better suited for our unit. Intense training with a weighty practice sword made my real sword feel lighter, though the added bulk of the breastplate, despite its lightness, made me feel slow.

Jasper pushed us to our limits, demanding stamina when we flagged while sparring and speed when we faltered from exhaustion. Over and over, he drilled us on the details of the high king's rescue and the layout of Ylanda City. We practiced walking silently through the grass and slipping into shadows; we took turns launching surprise attacks on each other to heighten our reflexes. And we stood quietly when twice runners came with word from the north, speaking privately with Jasper before spurring their steeds for the return journey.

My dreams were laden with Nuaga's unseen presence and with visions of the slaughtered dragon and her captured dragonling. I was certain Nuaga had imprinted the scene in my sleeping mind, and the horror of it hung thick in my heart every day when I awoke. It was hard to ignore the fact that, despite her beautiful eyes, Nuaga was the embodiment of the violence she'd shown me. Huge, scaled, serpentine. Surely that broad, thick-haired snout contained rows of merciless teeth. And stories from my childhood had emphasized the dragonbreath—hot enough to melt flesh from bone, or to ignite a field of dry grass with one exhalation.

This was what Nuaga wanted me to receive as her mark. I couldn't imagine saying yes.

"Storm! What are you waiting for?" Rock's deep voice called from somewhere within a stand of trees.

I straightened my shoulders and checked my sword. "Coming."

It was the last training round of the day—my turn to deal with an unexpected attack. It was easier to feel fierce when I was the one hiding in a hollow or around a bend, but bracing myself for a surprise melee made me tense to my bones.

I picked my way carefully along the path, a half mile of mostly wooded terrain where four of my colleagues were hiding, ready to challenge me. I hadn't gone a hundred paces when Rock barreled toward me.

His role was clear—unarmed attacker with brute strength. Rock was a vast expanse of muscle; in comparison, I was a dwarf. He knew he could best me at tests of strength, so my natural instinct was to move immediately to Neshu in the hope of outwitting and defeating him.

It worked—barely. As I gave the Great Cry, I felt as though I had already used all my strength—and three more surprise attackers remained hidden.

"I thought I was ready for you," he said, breaths heaving.

"You shouldn't have called out to me," I said. "It was easy to guess you were nearby."

Coast and Briar were next, accosting me from opposite sides of a small clearing. Their practice swords were drawn, and I drew mine as I quickly debated which to engage first.

They were both excellent swordsmen, but Coast was definitely the better—and also more than a head taller than I. I was able to disarm Briar and kick his sword into the undergrowth with a series of Neshu moves, but Coast engaged me quickly and efficiently, pressing his blade against my neck before I knew what had happened.

"You took your eyes off me when you kicked Briar's weapon," he said. "That was all the time I needed."

I rubbed my nose with the back of my hand. "You always beat me with the sword."

"Not always," Coast said. "Not when you're paying attention."

I looked at Briar, but, as usual, he didn't offer eye contact. It was as though talking to people were physically painful for him.

"You're fast," I said to him. "And good. Maybe be prepared for Neshu combat next time?"

He nodded, but his face was knotted into a frown. "*S'da.*"

Coast clapped Briar on the shoulder. "Let's see if we can down some pheasants while there's still light."

I watched them go, angry at my defeat and wondering if Briar spoke more when he was alone with Coast. Still seething, I turned toward the heavily wooded rise of ground that held my final hidden enemy. I gave myself a few more seconds to catch my breath before heading into the trees.

Forest came at me silently, like a panther. I assumed a defensive posture and reached over my shoulder for the wooden dagger sheathed in my breastplate as soon as I saw the practice blade in his hand. He danced lithely to my left, avoiding my block and lunging headfirst into my stomach. I fell backward and he landed on top of me.

I cried out and used a swift cut with my knife arm to knock the blade from his hand. He countered by slamming both my arms into the ground and pinning them with his knees. The dagger fell from my grasp, but I was able to use my leg to knock Forest off-balance, and moments later we were wrestling on the ground, neither getting the better of the other.

Until suddenly he had me pinned. His forearm was tight against my neck and his nose was inches from mine.

"Surrender," he said.

"No."

I struggled to twist from his grasp, but the advantage was his. Determined, I snaked one arm free and used the heel of my palm beneath his jaw, shoving his head up and back in an effort to dislodge his hold.

"Storm, stop. You're beat."

"Not . . . beat." I kept shoving.

"If this were real, you'd be dead. My blade's right here."

He loosened his grip as he reached for the dagger, and I growled and flipped him over, landing hard on top of him. He went limp, and for several seconds my body rose and fell with his breathing. Every inch of my skin awoke, feeling his heat and the strength of his muscles beneath me.

I lifted my head and met his gaze, and the brown-gold of his eyes arrested me. I'd never noticed the depth of their color before.

"Storm. Get off me."

I rolled onto the ground, melting with embarrassment I couldn't show, and reached for my dagger. "Sorry. I should've stopped."

"It won't be the same with a real enemy," Forest said. "It's hard to say what would happen if we really wanted to kill each other."

I stood and resheathed my dagger and couldn't seem to make myself look at Forest. "True."

"Ready to head back?"

"Ready."

We walked mostly in silence, catching our breath. I couldn't find words to speak, anyway—I felt as though I had thrust my heart at him in full view, and there was no way to take it back.

And yet he hadn't seen, because he hadn't expected to see.

Great God, where had these feelings come from? I would have to stamp them out the way I would an errant campfire.

If only I knew how.

———

The last hold of summer slackened, and as the falling season approached, the nights grew chillier. As the sun set on Oradon, we were given heavier blankets and leather, fur-lined cloaks from the supply wagon. The coffers of the high king surely ran deep, to provide so well for his army.

First watch was mine that night. I hurried to my post, my hand sweaty on the hilt of my sword.

Quiet settled around me as the others disappeared into their tents.

River was last to go, banking the fire before crawling into the tent he shared with Sedge. I wondered how he could stand it.

It couldn't have been more than half an hour later when sudden darkness enveloped me, and I stood once more inside a waking dream. Soundlessly, Nuaga stepped forward.

"Nuaga." I spoke her name as boldly as I could.

She stopped several paces from me and lowered her face to the level of mine; she was huge and magnificent and real. She was also undeniably *familiar*. As though I had known her a long time.

Time grows short. Release me and receive my mark.

"You've said that before," I said, "but I don't understand."

Do you carry my Lament *in your heart?*

"Yes." I'd had it memorized for days. "But I still don't understand what you're asking of me."

A long, hollow sound, like a sigh, escaped her. *The* Lament *contains the words you will need to wake the dragons.*

"I don't understand." Remorse wound its way through me, and I couldn't account for it. Was this the magic of T'Gonnen rising up within me, or was it my own heart, finally opening to Nuaga? I thought of the baby dragon and its slaughtered mother. I thought of how Nuaga seemed sure I was worthy of her mark.

Yet what had I done to be worthy, other than to accidentally wake her by taking the dragon powder?

Nuaga seemed to be waiting for me to say something. I licked my lips and chose my words with care. "Teach me."

Behold.

Her eyes caught mine before I could look away. Once again, I was drawn in, as through a thousand doorways.

Darkness swirled around me like a living thing. I stood, nearly blind, my feet submerged in a warm, soft substance that felt like it was breathing. When I tried to lift a foot, it wouldn't move. As my eyes adjusted to the darkness, I saw that I was surrounded by a low wall over which I could barely see. It seemed like a stall of some sort. A pen.

A nest.

The swirling ooze pulled at my feet, irresistible and comforting, and I found I suddenly wanted nothing more than to sink into it and sleep. Slowly, I became aware of dark, hulking masses huddled around me—silent forms that breathed along with the muck at my feet, sinking into their own nests of undulating goo.

Dragons. Dozens of them. Their eyes were luminous in the dark, so that I was surrounded by pairs of blue and red and deep purple orbs that alternately gazed steadily and blinked sleepily. Voices ricocheted across cavern walls that I couldn't see.

We will rise again.

What if no one wakes the she-king Nuaga?

She will awake.

And who will pen her Lament?

Rest easy. It is already penned, and in the hands of Mennek the Lesser.

What human would dare to sacrifice for us? This last dragon moved toward me as if I weren't standing there. *It is without hope that I go to my rest.*

Peace, Solara. When he comes, he will bear her mark, and all will be well.

The dragon Solara continued toward me, oblivious to my presence, as though I were invisible. I tried to move out of her way, but the muck pulled me down, down, even as she stretched her great form over me, ready to crush me to the bottom of her nest.

"No!" I cried. "Stop!"

"Storm?"

I gasped forcefully and found myself kneeling in the dark near my post. The dragons were gone.

"I'm here." I didn't even know who I was talking to.

"What happened?" Jasper approached, weapon in hand.

I swallowed the dryness in my mouth. "It's nothing, sir. I'm sorry."

"Why did you yell?"

"I . . ." Sounds of others approaching caught my ear, and I felt utterly stupid. "A wild beast. It . . . caught me off guard. I'm sorry."

Jasper nodded; I could barely see his face in the darkness. "Better to rouse us for nothing than to let us sleep when danger is near."

I felt even smaller in the face of his mercy. "Thank you. Yes, sir."

Jasper and the others shuffled back to their tents, and I was left alone in the wake of magnificence unlike any I had ever seen. These, then, were the dragons Nuaga wanted me to call forth—intelligent and dangerous, beautiful and terrifying.

I chose not to fear them.

———— · ————

The rest of the week was a grueling blur, during which Jasper did everything he could to hone us for what lay ahead. He also reminded us daily what Tan Vey's victory would mean for our people—the slaughter of surplus citizens, the ruining of women, the murder of children. His words held fire and fear and turned my heart toward my family at home. Would Jasper's plan truly be the means of protecting those we loved? Or did our salvation lie in the dragons?

Every day, I thought of my brother, safe at home and oblivious to the danger I had taken his place to face. How long would he stay safe? I imagined the expression of uncomprehending terror on his face as nomads rushed toward him—eyes cold, weapons raised to kill—and my heart knotted with fear.

More and more, I felt as though the fate of those I loved best lay not in the hands of the high king's army, but in mine.

The cooler edge to the air made the long days more bearable, and in the evenings the fire brought more comfort. Outside its glowing circle, the night air held none of the late summer warmth it had a short while ago.

Nuaga didn't appear again, though every night I dreamed of dragons waking from their slumber and rising from their secret chambers. And every morning when I awoke, I was filled with a renewed zeal for the dragons that was hard to contain.

On the night before Oradon, I crawled into my tent and lit the lamp I'd hung from the crossbeam, hoping to capture a few minutes of study before joining the others around the fire. I had just unrolled Dalen's scroll when Forest lifted the flap and slipped inside.

"I was wondering why you had a lamp in here," he said, frowning at the scroll. "What are you reading?"

I'd apparently done an excellent job reading in secret. I was ready to offer a vague answer, but then I caught the expression on Forest's face—open, earnest. As though his question were born from friendship instead of curiosity.

"*The Lament of Nuaga,*" I said.

"Why?"

I lowered my voice to a near-whisper. "I have something to tell you." And it struck me that I should have, perhaps, told him sooner.

"Go on." He sat on his blanket and waited while I turned to face him.

"I started hearing Nuaga's voice in my dreams after we arrived at Grigsbane," I said. "And then she began appearing to me."

Forest's expression was flat. "You've seen a dragon."

"Yes."

"Where, exactly?"

"They're waking dreams," I said. "It's like she's taking me somewhere else, but I'm not really there."

"And you're sure you're not actually dreaming?"

"I'm sure." I watched the skepticism growing on his face. "She shows me things, Forest. And she talks to me. She wants me to learn this *Lament* and wake the other dragons. I've memorized it."

"Why you, though? Why would she arbitrarily choose you?"

"It's the powder," I said.

"For your pigeon toes?"

I cringed, hating the lie. "Yes. The woman I bought it from warned me that I might have dreams. But I never thought she meant anything like this."

He seemed, for a few moments, to withdraw into his own thoughts. "I don't know, Storm."

My stomach tightened. "I'm not lying."

"I didn't say you were."

"But you don't believe me."

"Great God, Storm, you're telling me you've been talking to a dragon."

I swallowed the indignation that was creeping up my throat. "Yes. Because I thought you'd listen."

"I *am* listening. But—" He sighed. "A *dragon*."

"I thought you'd believe me." I fought to keep the wobble from my voice.

Forest studied me, as though assessing my sanity. "You might've given me too much credit."

"My mistake."

I returned to my scroll, breathing through the hard lump in my throat.

"I'm sorry, *s'da?*" Forest said. "I don't know what to say."

I closed my eyes and opened them again. "Let's see if the meat is cooked." I rolled the scroll and shoved a million emotions deep beneath my breastbone.

And wished I hadn't told Forest anything.

We joined the others at the fire. Cedar was busy cutting chunks from the wild boar he'd knifed earlier—the best kill of the week—and throwing the steaming meat into bowls. Forest and I each grabbed a bowl; we were headed toward the fire when I saw Dalen standing off by himself. I slapped Forest on the back—boy code for "I'm leaving but I'll be back"—and joined Dalen.

"Why are you standing here?" I asked.

He shrugged. "Sedge said I always grab the food before everyone else. I'm waiting my turn."

"Oh." Now wasn't the time to tell him not to take Sedge seriously. "Can I ask you something?"

"As long as you're not asking for my share of meat."

"Nothing so awful," I said. "I was wondering if you thought maybe there's more to the *Lament* than what you gave me."

He frowned. "Why would there be more?"

"It feels cut off. Like there should be another stanza, at least."

"Onen is a common name in Ytel. It means 'not one.'"

"Not one?"

"As in, becoming a father to many sons. That's why a lot of mothers give their boys this name."

"But why does the *Lament* end with it?"

"It's a general call for someone to step forward and answer Nuaga's beckoning."

I thought for a moment. "A general call."

"Yes. Why does it sound wrong to you?"

"I'm a poet. I would never end something like that. It breaks the rhythm."

He hesitated. "Some people believe there's more. But I don't."

My heart quickened. "Why do some people believe it?"

"Like you said. They think it sounds cut off." He motioned toward the fire with his chin. "Kendel thinks there's more. It's the one thing we disagree on."

"But it would be easy enough to find out, wouldn't it? You said yourself that the original *Lament* is in the Archives at the commune."

"It's not like you can walk in there and look at whatever you want," Dalen said. "I've heard tales of people who traveled days to get there and were turned away. And some people don't even believe the commune exists anymore."

"But you do."

"Always have. My great-grandfather stayed there for three nights when he was a young man. But they wouldn't let him inside the Archives."

"So no one can be sure the *Lament* is actually there."

"I'm sure," Dalen said softly. "Mennek was the first keeper of the dragon writings and relics after the dragons went to sleep. Legend has it his daughter is the one who wrote the *Lament*."

My heart thrilled; the dragons Nuaga showed me had mentioned Mennek, and I believed Dalen's story. "Well, I hate to disagree with you, but I think part of it's missing."

"That gives you and Kendel something to talk about."

Not that Kendel talked much. "I think it's probably safe for you to grab some meat now."

Dalen smiled wryly. "If there's any left."

We walked to the fire and I handed him a bowl. There was plenty of wild boar, and Cedar filled Dalen's bowl while I sat farther from Forest than I normally did.

"Winter falls faster in the north," Forest said through a mouthful. "It will affect everyone's ability to fight."

"The nomads are used to the cold," Dalen said, sitting beside me. "We're the ones who will feel it."

"The cold does fall faster, but it isn't that much greater." Jasper stood by the edge of the fire. "Not until you go far beyond the borders of the outlying tribes."

"Well, that's something." Dalen scooted closer to me to make room, and Jasper sat on the other side of him, a mug of ale balanced between his hands.

In the beginning, something had always shifted when Jasper was nearby. Leadership set him apart, as it had set apart everyone else in authority in the training camp. Now, after all these days together, Jasper mostly felt like one of us, and the awkward hesitation when he wanted to join us at the fire had faded.

He seemed pensive, though. All day, I'd noticed his gaze drifting to the north, looking for another message from the outpost. But none had come.

"Commander Beldan and I have planned something special for tomorrow, to test how well you've honed your skills," Jasper said, breaking into my thoughts.

"What could be more special than roasted field rat?" Mandrake said, and several boys laughed.

Jasper offered one of his rare smiles. "We'll do a series of rope pulls with our strongest climbers, and some three-man melees with practice swords. We'll also have a Neshu match among the officers. The captains have motivated their companies for the first three weeks by telling them that their best men will be invited to a small tournament this Oradon. They'll be bringing more ale."

At that, a cheer went up. After it had died down, Jasper continued.

"For the sword fights, we'll have River, Briar, and Flint on team one, and Forest, Coast, and Kendel on team two. Everyone else on the rope pull, except you, Storm. You're our Neshu fighter."

I almost dropped my mug. "But . . ."

"I drew the lot for judging instead of fighting," Jasper said. "I want you to fight in my place."

"I'm honored, Commander," I said.

"You're a natural," Jasper said. "I'll bet money on you myself."

Rock slapped me on the back. "I'd place my coin on you any day."

"To our rising Storm!" Mandrake raised his mug.

"Rising Storm!" and "Stormrise!" came the answering calls.

I wanted to smile and swagger a bit, the way I thought I ought to. But visions of the entire mass of boys and men watching me spar with military officers made my insides quiver. The expression on my face was probably closer to a grimace than a grin.

"There will be two Neshu matches, and the winners from each

will fight for a prize of fifteen coin and a bottle of spirits." Jasper's
eyes glinted in the firelight. He seemed truly eager to create this
final diversion for us.

"What happens if I lose?" My voice cracked halfway through
the question, making me sound like I had the confidence of a dead
dog.

"You won't lose," Jasper said. "That's why I've chosen you."

I bowed my head, a silent thank-you. His certainty that I wouldn't
fail left me without words.

"Jasper thinks highly of you," Forest said later, as we were preparing to go to sleep.

"I don't know." Things felt stiff between us, and for the first time
I didn't feel like talking with him. I lay on my back and pulled my
blanket up to my shoulders.

"Um. About the dragon."

"What about it?"

"It's not that I don't believe you. Exactly."

I sighed. "I'd never make something like this up."

For a while, Forest was quiet. Then he said, "It could be visions
caused by that powder, couldn't it?"

"I suppose."

"But you don't think so."

I rolled to face him, though it was dark. "I never believed dragons were real, same as you. If I had a rational explanation, I'd offer
it. All I know is—I've met a dragon and she's chosen me."

"Chosen you for . . . what?"

"To wake the dragons. She says it's the only way to save Ylanda."

He was silent for another little while before he spoke. "You sound
crazy. You know that."

I didn't answer.

"If you have another dream, will you tell me?" he asked.

Something in me softened. "Yes."

"And if these dreams keep happening, you'll tell Jasper?"

"I don't know. If you don't believe me, why should he?"

"I want to believe you, Storm. It's just . . ."

I rolled onto my back. "*S'da.*"

More silence. "Are you afraid of dying?"

"No," I said. "I think I'm just afraid of the pain that will come first."

"Yes," Forest said. "That."

I closed my eyes and wondered if Jasper truly thought highly of me. Hadn't that been what I'd been striving for? Becoming Jasper's equal—perhaps surpassing him—would surely restore the honor Papa had lost by not having a mentally sound son to march off to war. For Papa, for my brother, I would do anything.

And a small, quiet corner of my heart whispered that the honor would be mine as well.

13

Forest fell asleep immediately, but I lay awake for a long time, unable to quiet my thoughts. The sense that I was being watched dawned gradually, until I sat up in a rush, blanket clenched in my fists.

"Nuaga?" I whispered.

Rain.

Her voice was so powerful inside my head that I jumped. I took a calming breath, reminding myself that she was visiting in a dream, not in the flesh. Then I closed my eyes. Immediately, I was drawn into the waking-dream state that had become so familiar, my true body as lost to me as if I were sleeping. Nuaga stepped forward, and for a moment I fought the desire to claw myself free from her.

This was a *dragon*. With *teeth*. And breath that could melt flesh.

At first, I couldn't move. Couldn't speak. The reality of what she was—what she could *do*—stole my ability to think beyond it. Nuaga was beautiful and terrifying. Magnificent and awful.

Yet she had become so much a part of me that I couldn't allow fear to render me powerless. I had spent days memorizing and studying the *Lament,* and my heart burned to understand more.

I met her gaze.

Nuaga drew her face near mine. Her expression was so human that my breath stuttered in my throat. She was almost . . . smiling.

Do you fear me?

"Only sometimes."

She regarded me for a few moments. *Do you understand my Lament now?*

"I still have questions."

Tell it to me.

Faltering at first, then growing steadier, I recited the *Lament*. When I finished, Nuaga was silent. Her breaths came slowly and evenly, and I tried to imagine what it would feel like for her to turn that breath toward me with the intent of melting my flesh. I waited, but still she said nothing.

She seemed, for the first time, uncertain. Perplexed.

"Nuaga?"

Something is missing . . .

"Tell me what's missing."

Her gaze was sad. *The words you will need to awaken the dragons. And the need for sacrifice.*

Sacrifice?

"Meaning what, exactly?"

The greatest dragon magic is only released through sacrifice, such as T'Gonnen's own life. And the dragon-waking words will speak for themselves.

"Why can't you just tell me?"

The sadness in her eyes deepened. *I did not write them; I spoke magic over my beloved scribe so that she could imbue the words with my power. The minds of the slumbering dragons are intertwined; if the waking words were in my mind all along, they would have long ago disturbed the ages-long sleep.*

"So I must bring these words to the dragons."

Yes. If you don't, there is no hope for Ylanda.

"But why?" I whispered. "How can there be no other hope?"

Her eyes grew large and transparent, as they had done before, and drew me somewhere else. This time, I didn't close my eyes or brace myself—I simply stood tall and waited while the scene settled around me.

You have a willing heart, Rain L'nahn. You deserve to know us.

I stood in what seemed to be a temple carved of stone. The walls were lined with gemstones the size of a man's head, each one giving off as much light as a small sun. T'Gonnen, high king of the dragon clan, stood beside Nuaga, his mate. Beside them stood four mighty offspring, two males and two females. Their sheer majesty gripped me, and I stepped backward, my boots scraping on the rough-hewn floor.

T'Gonnen's voice rang like thunder. "Nuaga and I have cleansed the land and guarded the people who are now the kingdom of Ylanda, and you are called to the same. This is your land. Your people."

The young dragons bowed their heads in reverence to T'Gonnen. Fierce affection welled inside me—a father's love for his children. I pressed my hand to my heart and held my breath, waiting to see what came next.

The high king and she-king stepped back, revealing a gem larger than the others, set into the center of the front wall. It pulsed and glowed a deep crimson, and the dragon offspring turned their heads toward it. I, too, was drawn to the brilliant light, like a moth to a lantern. My eyes were dazzled, and in my momentary blindness, I was pulled into the gemstone, weightless as air.

Landscapes shifted, time rolled backward. I watched, awe-stricken, as the Great God fashioned his dragons, breathing a thousand years or more of life into each one. People believed they were immortal—they were revered and sometimes worshipped. Their magic was coveted, collected. I watched farmers gathering dragon dung, a prized fertilizer that created such bounty that during times of drought, there was enough food. The smallest bits of a dragon—a scale, a piece of claw, a hair—were collected and treasured, and the dragons were happy to share. Truly, they were the most magical of all the Great God's creations.

Once more, a burst of light blinded me, and when it subsided, I stood again in the shadows of the temple, a mere cat's throw from Nuaga and her family.

"Always remember that you are revered," T'Gonnen said to his children. "But never take it for granted."

The room tilted and swirled, and I found myself standing near the edge of a rise of ground over a deep hollow. The sky darkened, and I watched a dragon give birth to her young. Somehow, I understood that she was at her most vulnerable, the heat of her breath temporarily lost as she transferred her magic to her dragonling.

I knew this place—I had been here before. Fear gripped my heart as I saw the band of men appear over the opposite rise, their swords already drawn.

"No!" I cried, cupping my hands around my mouth. "Save yourself! Take your baby and go!"

But no one heard me. The men rushed her, as I knew they would, killing her and nearly strangling the baby before stealing it away. I wept as they carved the mother dragon's body and divided portions among themselves, gorging on the ill-gotten magic.

Not nomads. Men of Ylanda, who had turned on the dragons for their own gain.

I sank to my knees in despair as the earth tilted and spun once more. This time, I knelt just outside a clearing in a deep forest, where at least half a dozen dragons had gathered.

"Our catacombs are nearly complete," the largest male said. "We will at least have a safe place to give birth and guard our young."

"But Stonewall is rising," said another, "a testament to the people's loss of faith in us."

"Yes," said the first, "and in its shadow, a black-market trade between those who seek to prosper by selling our magic and the nomads who crave it."

"The best we can do is to protect our young." A glorious female spoke this time, her voice much like Nuaga's. "Buckets overflowing with shed scales and bundles of fur sell for a decent price, but a freshly born dragonling, delivered alive? There is no comparison."

"We are like fugitives in our own land," the first dragon said.

"For now," the female said. "But T'Gonnen will set things right."

The scene swirled away like paper on the wind. I now stood on a high mountaintop, though it overlooked not an earthly vista, but a vast, swirling tapestry of light and color that shifted and changed before my eyes.

First the attacks began. Dragons were forced to protect their young and to seek out those who were selling their magic to the nomads. Those who had once revered them now feared them instead. Stonewall stood as a marker of Ylanda's defiance and pride.

I felt the dragons' indignation, and their misery. I felt the keen sting of betrayal, the silent pain of resignation.

T'Gonnen rose up before me, magnificent and terrifying. I watched the *Lament* unfold before me, and I doubled over with sobbing as T'Gonnen breathed his last upon the ramparts of Stonewall.

Every scale, every tooth, every talon was pulled and peeled and cut from his body. His eyes. His heart. The segments of his spine.

And when I saw them dismember the sacs of his manhood, a surge of heat tore through me. The very maleness of T'Gonnen was what had stolen my monthly bleed and deepened my voice.

I watched his body topple to the outside of the wall, where his remaining bones and whatever else was left of him were scavenged by the nomads. I continued to weep as Nuaga and the other dragons sank into the quiet darkness of their catacombs to be long forgotten.

A cold wind whipped me, forcing shivers from me as I folded my arms around myself. I was swept up again, blinded in the rush of wind and light and shadow. When my feet hit solid ground, I opened my eyes to find myself once more in the temple of stone, but this time, it was empty, the gemstones dark. I gazed into the shadowed space, imagining the dragons gathering there to pay homage to the Great God. But the emptiness of the chamber brought more tears; I wiped them from my face with both hands.

"I want to wake them, Nuaga." My voice, wet with crying, echoed in the hollow space.

The temple shifted, and I moved through layers of light and motion until I once again stood before Nuaga. Her eyes rested on me with new expectancy.

Will you release me?

"Why did you not appear before now?" I whispered.

Those who have awakened me before responded with fear and loathing. You are the first one who has willingly listened. Her eyes grew wide. *Will you release me?*

The longing of my heart burst forth with such fervor I could hardly contain it. "Yes."

Nuaga lowered her head so that her face was inches from mine. *Now?*

My words were mere breath. "Yes."

She stepped back, and suddenly I was inside my tent, my hands still clutching my blanket. With fierce purpose, I reached for my dagger and clutched it to my breast as I slipped outside. Soft as a breeze, I sank to my knees and, without stopping to think, sliced the blade into my palm. Gritting my teeth against the pain that bloomed as the blood swelled to the surface, I tipped my hand toward the ground. My blood dripped soundlessly into the dirt, though I imagined it was sizzling with the heat of a dragon's breath.

Rain.

Nuaga was before me again, wreathed in the shadows of a waking dream. I met her gaze, caught between fear and euphoria.

"The others," I said. "They won't be in any danger?"

Without a word, she lowered her head and, before I had time to react, reached with her long tongue and licked my bleeding hand. Warmth spread through my hand and up my arm.

No. Do you release me, Rain L'nahn?

"Yes. I release you."

Her countenance shifted from dark to light, from sunset to sunrise. A sound like music leaped from her throat, and when she bent her face to mine, I didn't shrink.

And are you willing to make a great sacrifice?

I thought of Tan Vey's bloodthirsty soldiers, and of my precious family, whose lives meant more to me than my own. If the *Lament* called for me to sacrifice myself, what of it? My willingness to die for them had resided in my heart since the day I donned my brother's clothing and cut my hair.

"I'm willing to do whatever it takes," I said.

And yet the Lament *is mysteriously lacking the words you need.*

Then revelation—and joy—welled up within me. "You can come to me now, yes?"

Yes. I can rise from the catacombs now.

"And you can move faster than any person ever could?"

I have three times the legs and twelve times the strength of a man. She smiled. *Or a girl.*

"Take me to the Commune of Mennek," I said. "The original *Lament* is there—I'm sure of it. I think some verses are missing."

Mennek. She said the name as though it drummed up an ancient memory. Then she raised her great head and looked down at me. *I will take you there. And if you are successful, be prepared to receive my mark. Once you do, you will be one with the dragons. Your loyalty will lie forever with us.*

How could I be loyal to the dragons *and* the high king's army?

Was Nuaga asking me to abandon Jasper and the others and follow her orders instead?

I wanted to do what was right. Part of me ached to follow Nuaga to the farthest reaches of the known world. Part of me clung fiercely to the honor I wanted to bring my family by serving the high king.

Could I do both?

The high king's army will not succeed without the dragons' intervention, she said softly.

I summoned the courage to ask the question that would reveal my true heart. "If I wake the dragons, will Ylanda truly be saved? Will my family be safe?"

The only hope for safety lies with the dragons. Without them, there is only death.

I raised my chin. "Then I will wake them."

I will hold you to that, Rain L'nahn.

Were Nuaga's words true? Would our army not prevail without the dragons' help?

Without *my* help?

Her eyes glimmered as she faded once more into darkness, and I found myself kneeling outside my tent, alone. My hand no longer hurt, and when I tentatively ran my fingers along the surface of my palm, it felt smooth and whole, as though no blade had ever pierced it.

Heart pounding, I climbed into the tent and rolled onto my side upon my blanket. Nuaga's words curled into the corners of my mind, echoing until they faded: *I will hold you to that, Rain L'nahn.*

What in the name of the Great God had I unleashed?

◆———◆———◆

I woke in the chill of morning, almost face-to-face with Forest. In the tent-shadowed light, he looked younger, except for the scruff of beard that had been growing all week.

I rubbed my palm across my cheek and beneath my nose. My skin felt a bit fuzzier, perhaps, but no one had said anything. Probably it was my imagination.

Which was fine. I didn't want a beard.

I watched him as he slept, my heart knotted by the battle within it. He wasn't mine to long for, yet I wanted to trace his cheeks, his jaw, his lips with my fingertips. I wanted to press my ear to his chest and listen to the beating of his heart.

Jealousy tore through me like wildfire. The thought of sharing Forest with my sister was unspeakable.

Not sharing—*relinquishing.*

I forced the ungenerous thoughts from my mind, reminding myself that the Great God had destined Forest for either my sister or death. And he had destined me to honor my family—and *save* them—not as myself, but as a soldier in the high king's army.

Almost, I woke Forest, wanting so much to tell him about my visit with Nuaga, in the hope that he would believe me. Instead, I blew him a soundless kiss and left the tent.

After morning warm-ups and breakfast, I excused myself and made my way back to our tent, empty cup in my hand. I gathered my dirty shirt and socks, as well as the extra shirt I wore on laundry day. I had just ducked out of the tent when Forest approached.

"Most of the others are washing shirts only," he said. "They say our britches won't dry before the other soldiers arrive."

"Hadn't thought of that."

"Something wrong?"

I frowned. "No. I just . . . need to be alone for a while."

"Nervous?"

Ugh. The Neshu match. "Yes. I'll be downstream a way. Can we talk later, though? I spoke with Nuaga last night."

Forest's expression was guarded. "*S'da.*"

"Thank you. And please don't tell anyone where I'm going."

He clapped me on the shoulder, yet another boy behavior I had become used to. "I won't say a word."

I headed across the field toward the creek. This would probably be my last opportunity to wash anything, and we'd all have to be content in our filth and stink. But while the air still held enough warmth, I intended to clean myself as well as my clothing.

Our bucket of soap sat at the edge of the field, more than half empty. I took my cup and scooped it full, then headed downstream. The trees thickened a bit in that direction, and the water curved eastward. My hope was that I would be able to find a private spot where I would feel safe.

I fought my way through thick underbrush in order to follow the stream around a bend that, with the trees' help, hid me from view. The day was warming quickly, one of those unusual days in early falling season when the sun tried bravely to elongate the summer. I swatted at a hornet with my fistful of shirts as I stepped onto a broad, flat expanse of the bank between two tree roots. Checking once more to be sure I was alone, I peeled off my shirt and unwound the ratty strips from my torso. I wrinkled my nose at the smell, which didn't even seem like it could come from me. Perhaps the dragon powder had affected that, too.

Quickly, I pulled the extra shirt over my head, relishing the freedom of my breasts beneath the scratchy fabric. Then I pulled off my boots and socks and stepped out of my britches, which I hung on a branch, leaving them unwashed as Forest had suggested. I felt almost giddy as I took the cup of soap and the stinky length of fabric to the water's edge and began to scrub.

After I'd washed away the stink, I looped the strips of fabric over some low branches, checked again that no one was approaching, and slipped out of my shirt and undergarment. I grabbed the cup of soap and waded waist-deep into the stream, until my toes sank into the soft, cool bottom.

I bathed with relish, knowing it would be my last bath for a long time. I scrubbed my hair clean and washed the grime from my face. The soap was pungent and earthy, and my skin sang with the sweetness of simply being clean.

I didn't linger, though I dearly wished I could. After a final rinse, I dragged myself from the water and reached for the strips of cloth. Then I stopped. It might feel better, I thought, if I let my strips dry a while before rewrapping myself. The thought of the damp strips around my torso after a few minutes of delicious freedom was too much. So I pulled the long shirt over my head and stepped into one of my undergarments, making sure I was well covered before taking my clothing into the stream to wash it.

The sound of babbling water just beyond the deep where I stood almost completely masked the distant sound of voices and laughter upstream. Trails of soap—and someone's errant undergarment— swirled by, clearly showing me the advantage of washing upstream.

It was no matter, though. The sheer decadence of complete privacy, and the freedom to allow my body to breathe for a while, was worth the disadvantage.

I washed my clothing as quickly as I could. When I'd wrung as much water from the garments as possible, I slung them over my arm and waded back to the bank. There was no sunlight here, so I would have to carry the clean clothes out to the field where everyone else spread out their things to dry. I looked around for somewhere mud-free to toss the shirts and other things while I rebound myself. The leafy, twisted undergrowth grew thicker several strides away from where I stood.

I tossed my shirts first. They cleared the mud and landed directly on the dry, clean undergrowth, disturbing a hornet in the process. I twisted the clean socks and undergarment together and tossed them onto the shirts. One of the socks slipped free, half-landing in the dirt. Quickly, I found a long stick and used it to pick up the sock and poke it farther on top of the leafy covering.

From everywhere and nowhere, hornets filled the air around me. I cried out as they attacked, their burning stings piercing my neck, my arms, my shoulders. Blindly, arms flailing, I turned and ran into the water, the hot sound of their buzzing in my ears as they stung. I plunged myself into the water, writhing as the insects caught beneath my shirt continued to sting me. When I had no more breath left, I came up for air. The swarm was gone.

Tears hot in my eyes, I pulled off my shirt and plucked the remaining hornets from my already-swelling chest and abdomen. Then I turned the sopping-wet shirt inside out and shook it frantically, getting rid of every last hornet. As they landed on the surface of the water, I slapped them with the shirt.

Finally it was silent. The pain of a thousand fires wracked my body. With great effort, I lifted my wet shirt from the water, unable to wring it, and turned toward the bank.

Forest stood at the edge of the water, staring at me with a face of stone.

14

F orest." I could barely move my mouth; my bottom lip was swollen from a sting just beneath it.

"Great God." He kept staring, his mouth working shapes without words.

I folded my arms across my breasts. "Help." I sank to my knees in the water.

"What *are* you?" Confusion mingled with disbelief on his face. He stood, arms by his sides, unmoving.

My pulse rang in my ears, and everything around me began to swim. I reached for the shirt, which was starting to float slowly away. I missed it.

Forest jumped into action, pulling off his boots and wading into the water toward me. "Hornets?"

"Yes," I said, cringing at the pain in my lip.

He grabbed the shirt and laid it gingerly across my shoulders. Then he offered his arm, gaze averted. I wrapped my hands around it and leaned on him, but the pain was too great, and I stumbled, my legs buckling beneath me. Forest caught me under the arms and half-dragged, half-carried me to the bank, where I collapsed onto my back.

He threw the wet shirt over my breasts and sat beside me. "You're lucky I came looking for you."

"Not so lucky."

I tried to read his face, but it was too guarded. The initial shock had been replaced by something more controlled. Like a wall had gone up between us.

"I'll make some mud," he said.

I closed my eyes, pain throbbing through me from every place that had been stung. I wanted to fold myself and hide my femaleness, but it hurt too much to move. So I waited while Forest did whatever he was doing, until finally he sat by my side. Then I opened my eyes.

"I'm sorry," I whispered.

Forest was busy scraping bits of what looked like a gnarled root into a sloppy patch of mud. "This will help with the swelling."

"Forest—"

"Stop."

I nodded, my eyes stinging with tears. He had every right to go straight to Jasper and tell him the truth about me. Maybe that was what he would do, in the end. I wouldn't blame him.

"You're going to have to sit up," he said. "Each sting needs to be covered, and then you'll have to let it dry. It shouldn't take long."

He helped me sit, and I held the wet shirt feebly to my chest. I couldn't look at him.

Gently, he took the shirt from me. "I won't look."

I didn't see how that was possible. At least two of the stings were on my torso, and my left armpit was throbbing, too. But I didn't fight him. I was a compliant statue, sitting still until he needed me to raise my arm or tilt my head.

The mud was cool against the heat of my skin, the hard knots at each sting mark momentarily soothed by Forest's touch, which was softer than I would have imagined. I was too numb to be embarrassed while he treated the stings on my torso and under my arm. When he'd dealt with all the stings he could find on the top half of me, he helped me stand so he could check my legs.

"You must've gotten into the water quickly. Most of the stings are on your upper body."

It was the first he'd spoken since he started smearing the mud on me. I stared at the top of his head as he examined the front of my legs and my feet, closing my eyes as he found the sting just below the curve of my buttocks. It was even more awkward than the armpit had been.

He stepped around to the front of me and, with his thumb, coated the sting beneath my swollen lip with mud, never quite looking at me the whole time. When he'd finished, he rested his eyes on mine.

"You'll have to stand there until the mud dries. I'll keep watch."

He walked away before I could summon the courage to thank him. I turned my head in time to see him disappear around the bend of the stream, just beyond the trees. A buzzing insect swooped across the water, and I gasped before I realized it was only a lacefly. Even so, my heart wouldn't stop pounding.

I stood there, completely exposed, for what felt like an entire day. The mud dried against my skin, bringing more comfort than I'd imagined. Every time I moved even a little, though, I ached. And whenever I heard a distant shout or round of laughter, it took every bit of my Neshu control not to jump into the water and hide.

Finally, Forest returned. I waited while he gave my body a quick look-over. Without a word, he retrieved my strips of cloth from the tree branches and brought them to me.

"This is your disguise?" He waited for my nod. "Do you need help?"

I shook my head and grabbed the strips from him, unable to bear another second of my nakedness. He turned his back, and I struggled to bind myself with the still-damp strips. I should have asked for his help, and probably I still could have—but I wouldn't allow myself to. He had done enough already.

I made the bindings as tight as I could bear, but they didn't feel secure enough. The stings on my arms were swollen, making them ache with every movement, and my armpit throbbed where the top edge of the binding pressed against the sting. I secured the binding as well as I could.

"I'm finished."

Forest turned around and assessed me briefly before picking up my shirt and giving it several shakes. He handed it to me, watching as I pulled it gingerly over my head and eased my arms through the sleeves. Then he reached to pick up something from the bank. As he approached me, I saw that it was my discarded hair tie. He stood behind me and pulled my hair into a bun, taking as much care as I might've done myself. When he was finished, he stood behind me, not moving.

"I've been thinking what to do," he said. "They'll arrest you and charge you as a thief without a trial."

"Yes." I barely rasped the word.

"I could bring you some supplies—enough for a few days. You could find your way to Grigsbane and present yourself as who you really are. I'll tell Jasper that you've deserted, and they'll never find you, because they won't be looking for a girl."

My throat was tight, and I couldn't speak. He was offering more than I deserved, but his words were cold. There was nothing I could say.

He came from behind and stood where we could face each other. "But I think you must have your reasons for doing this. So if you want me to keep your secret, I will."

I stared at him, not even certain that I'd heard him correctly. "You would do that?"

"I would."

My mouth opened on its own, wanting to say more, but no words were sufficient. I knew he was waiting for me to make a choice—to take the path that would be easier for both of us, or to accept his offer to partner with my deception, putting himself at almost equal risk.

"I don't want to make things harder for you," I said.

"It's your choice, Storm." He winced, as though suddenly the name didn't fit.

Of course it didn't.

"I . . . want to stay," I said. "I have to stay."

He nodded once, as though the whole thing were settled. "Go rest. I'm going to see if I can find some wild *tenepa*. It's past blooming season, but it's the leaves I'll need, anyway. It'll help draw the venom out and reduce the swelling."

"Thank you." I swallowed away the grateful tears that wanted to spill. "I don't know . . . I can't think of a way to . . ."

"I think you'd do the same for me."

I waited for him to smile, or for any kind of softening of his countenance. But the bland, controlled expression stayed in place, and Forest was carefully hidden behind it.

He walked away without another word. Slowly, I retrieved my wet clothes and my boots, which I stepped into without too much difficulty. Then I made my way across the field back to camp, a dull throb pulsing through my limbs with every beat of my heart. The dried mud on my face was tight, and my lip felt the size of a melon. If I could just rest for a while inside my tent, the pain of the stings would surely settle, and the swelling reduce.

I spread my clothes on the grass not far from the tents, figuring I wouldn't feel like walking all the way back to where everyone else's clothes were drying. It wasn't until I had sprawled onto the blanket inside my tent that I remembered the Neshu match. My spirits, which were already low, plummeted further. With the way I was feeling, there was no chance I would succeed against any Neshu opponent. Even the thought of crossing my arms and making the initial bow made me wilt.

I lay for what felt like a long time, listening to the sounds outside and catching snatches of conversation about the upcoming competitions. Soon I heard the arrival of the soldiers from Grigsbane, and the called greetings among officers and friends alike. There seemed to be a lightness in the camp, a sense of holiday. If that had been Jasper's intention, he'd succeeded.

Drowsiness had begun to worm its way through me by the time the tent flap parted and Forest ducked inside, a steaming cup in his hand. I sat up, stifling a groan.

"Drink this," he said, offering the cup. "There was nothing to sweeten it with, so it's fairly bitter."

I took the cup and sniffed the steam—it had a sour, earthy smell. I sipped it, grimacing as I swallowed.

"I warned you," Forest said.

"It's not bad," I lied. "Thank you."

"If you finish the whole cup, it should work quickly," Forest said. "But if you need more later, I have enough *tenepa* leaves for another cup or two."

"That's very kind, Forest." His knowledge of medicinal plants amazed me—I didn't know of much beyond Tenema's abundant *avila*.

He rose on one knee, ready to leave. "Do you want me to tell

Commander Jasper that he needs to find someone else for the Ne-shu match?"

I tightened my hands around the mug, then loosened them because it was so hot. "No. I'll be fine."

Forest stared at me for a few seconds, looking as though he might say something else. But he simply nodded. "*S'da.*"

I watched the tent flap fall behind him and stared at it. Earlier, I had longed to touch his face, to offer him my very female heart. Now that he'd found out the truth, I felt exposed and false, and it was obvious what he thought of me.

No matter. I owed him my life, and I would do my best to deserve it.

———————

The soldiers stood in a large ring in the middle of the field of drill. To the west, the earth had been dug up and trampled by the rope pulls, which proved a fairly matched level of skill among the different units. I watched Jasper stride to the center of the circle, my stomach in knots, my torso aching from the pressure of the bindings against the stings. I had washed the mud from my face and limbs, and, thanks to Forest's tea, the swelling had gone down considerably.

"Are you sure about this?" Forest asked.

"I'm sure." I clenched and unclenched my hands and took a long, cool breath.

Masterful control, Papa would say. *From a distance, no one would guess you were a girl.*

Would they guess that I had been stung at least a dozen times, though? That my movements would be restricted not only by tight bindings, but by the pain and swelling?

"Captain Lisbet and Storm L'nahn to the center!" Jasper called.

I made my way to the center, amid a chorus of shouts that occasionally included my name. Dalen, I knew, had placed money on my winning, which didn't help me relax.

Lisbet stood a head and a half taller. Papa would have reminded me that height didn't matter—that I could learn to read any enemy and anticipate his moves, and that eight or ten inches would not make a difference in my ability to knock someone down.

This is for you, Papa.

The crowd quieted as Captain Lisbet and I assumed the first stance. We bowed and then took the requisite time to size each other up. The slight curl to his upper lip told me that he considered me an easy defeat—and also that his overconfidence would ultimately be his weakness.

We assumed the second stance. I kept my face serene, hiding the discomfort I was already feeling beneath my bindings as I straightened my back. Seconds slid by. I breathed.

We engaged, both of us easily anticipating the other. I matched him move for move, blocked him with the speed Papa had always praised me for, and was quick with my knife hand. He was a worthy opponent, forcing me to think fast to keep a beat ahead of him. If it weren't for the pain, I would have finished him quickly.

I felt myself slowing sooner than I had ever slowed before. My chest heaved, and, as we circled each other, my concentration frayed. Each breath compressed the stings beneath my bindings, and each heartbeat pulsed pain into them. It wasn't debilitating, but it was distracting.

Quiet your breathing, Rain, I heard Papa say. I steeled myself against the discomfort and exhaled slowly, a thin stream through my dry lips. Then I redoubled my efforts, determined not to let my weakness show. Lisbet matched me, his stride long, his knife arm deadly. If this had been a true enemy, I could not have allowed myself any hesitation or lack of effort. When I saw my opening, I gave the Great Cry and dealt him the blow that sent him onto his back.

Cheers erupted as I helped him up and faced him. The sneer was no longer on his face.

"As the sun rises," he said, bowing.

I returned his bow. "So it sets."

My unit members were jubilant as I returned to their ranks, cheering and slapping me on the back to the point where Forest intervened by slinging his arm around my shoulders and offering me water. My legs collapsed under me, and I sat hard upon the ground.

Forest squatted, still holding the cup of water. "How are you?"

"Fine." I took the water and gulped half of it down. My entire body ached.

"That was amazing." Forest wasn't quite looking at me, something it seemed I'd have to get used to.

"Neshu is my strength," I said.

"But you were attacked by hornets a few hours ago, and—"

I pressed my mouth into a hard line, mentally completing the sentence he'd cut off: "—you're a girl." Already he was measuring my ability by the fact that I wasn't male.

The second match was ready to begin. I watched the contenders—Captain L'narah and Commander Beldan—face each other and assume the first stance. They were equal in size and stature, and I tried to guess which would be the faster and which the stronger.

Within seconds, it was clear that Commander Beldan's skill far surpassed the other's. His moves were perfect, seamless. It took less than two minutes for him to defeat his rival.

I stared as the fighters bowed to each other. "He's good," I said to Forest.

"You're better."

Under normal circumstances, I would have faced this opponent with confidence. My limbs were sore, and the stings beneath my bindings must have become irritated, because my entire torso throbbed and itched.

"A five-minute rest until the final round!" Jasper called.

I glanced at Captain Beldan; he was smiling and chatting lightly with several others. I didn't think he needed a single minute of rest.

"Can you do this?" Forest asked.

I didn't think I could. "Yes."

I drank the rest of my water, then rose and stretched, wincing at the pain. Jasper called us to the center, and I straightened my shoulders.

As I walked toward my opponent, a wave of dizziness swept over me. I paused, closing my eyes momentarily while the sensation passed. When I opened my eyes, Jasper was standing in front of me.

"Something wrong?" he asked.

I breathed out slowly. "No, sir. I'll be fine."

"You're not hurt, are you?"

"No." Was this lying? "Just a hornet sting or two."

For a moment, Jasper looked unsure. Then he stepped aside and let me approach my opponent.

We bowed and assumed the first stance. Like everyone else in the camp, Commander Beldan was taller than I. There wasn't a trace of smugness or overconfidence on his face; only the calm, centered expression that spoke of his Neshu mastery.

I felt uncomfortably warm, and my pulse pounded in my temples. If any sign of discomfort showed on my face, Commander Beldan didn't react to it. He met my gaze coolly as we assumed the second stance.

At first, I was ahead of him. I felt the power of having the upper hand and paced myself to keep him from realizing it. But by the time we were circling each other for the second round, my head had started to swim again, and I suddenly found it difficult to breathe. Twice, he blocked my knife arm when I should have easily circumvented him. Twice, I stumbled when I should have been nimble.

The blow to my chest came at the same time another wave of dizziness washed over me. I staggered, knowing exactly what I needed to do in order to recover.

I couldn't do it. My opponent's face tilted and swirled as I fell to the ground.

15

I awoke to a steady jostling, my face pressed against someone's chest. For a breath or two, I couldn't remember where I was or why someone was carrying me. Then it rushed back, and I opened my eyes and looked up to see Forest. His face was grim.

"I'm fine," I managed.

He didn't answer. When we got to our tent, he lowered me carefully to my feet and helped me inside. I waited while he shook out and respread my blanket, and then I lay gingerly on my back.

"Stay there," Forest said. "I'll make more *tenepa* tea."

He left, and I lay in the dim tent and thought only of the shame of my defeat. The stings beneath my bindings were angry and hot, and a dull ache throbbed in my head. I didn't try to stop the tears that burned their way down my cheeks. Might as well let them out now, so they'd be spent by the time Forest returned.

He appeared more quickly than I had hoped, steaming tea in his hand. I sat up—slowly—and reached for the tea.

"I should have given you more of this," he said. "Your body is struggling with the venom of nineteen stings."

I looked up from my sip of tea. "Nineteen?"

"I counted." He averted his eyes, and I was once again reminded of how hard this must have been for him.

"Thank you for . . . rescuing me."

"Jasper wanted to examine you, but I stopped him," Forest said. "I told him I'd already started giving you the tea. It was hard to convince him."

The enormity of what Forest was saying struck me. "If you hadn't intervened, they . . ."

"Would have discovered the truth."

I lowered my eyes. "Thank you."

"You don't have to keep thanking me." There was no warmth in his expression, though. No hint of the friendship we'd forged, boy to boy. When he spoke, his words were carefully measured, the way one might speak to a stranger.

I didn't know what else to say. I set the tea down and lowered myself to my side.

"I'll be back later with more tea," he said.

I nodded, and he left without another word. I drank my tea and rested my head, wishing I could unwind the bindings.

Later, when he brought supper and more tea, he merely set it down and lifted the flap to leave again.

"Wait," I said.

He frowned. "I can't stay. Jasper is planning on visiting you, so make sure you're . . . presentable."

I watched him leave, and then I stared at my food, wondering how I would ever swallow any of it, knowing that Jasper was coming. If I had fallen in his estimation, I wouldn't be able to bear it.

Stormrise, they'd shouted. It seemed laughable now.

I had barely finished eating when Jasper lifted the corner of the tent flap. "Storm?"

"Yes, sir." My voice cracked.

"May I come in?"

It felt strange for him to ask so politely, when normally I had to obey his commands without question. I gestured with my hand, and he entered and sat on Forest's blanket.

"How are you feeling?"

"Better," I said. "Thank you, sir."

"You should have said something about the hornet attack."

"I'm sorry." I didn't know where to look. "I thought I would be fine."

"Nineteen stings," Jasper said.

Heat rose to my cheeks. "Apparently."

"I don't think you realize what you've overcome here."

"Forest took care of the stings and brewed me a tea."

"I know," Jasper said. "But nineteen stings! Nine or ten would put down even the strongest man."

Unease wove its way through me. "I was foolish."

"Perhaps," Jasper said. "But I'm amazed at your constitution. You won your first match, and probably would have won the second if you hadn't been stung."

"Thank you." But the sinking feeling in my stomach continued to grow. I shouldn't have been able to withstand the stings. And the only reason I could think of for my added strength was the dragon powder.

Yet another layer of deception I'd have to hide behind.

"Don't let your performance today make you feel any less," Jasper said. "You've all worked hard, and your training shows. It speaks well of you."

"It speaks well of your command, sir."

His mouth tightened, as though my compliment tasted bitter. "It speaks well of my father, who trained me."

"Is he a grandmaster?"

"Was." The word sounded like dust. "He died with the special Neshu unit at Stonewall."

"Oh." I lowered my eyes. "I'm sorry."

"It is what it is." He let out a long sigh. "I was going to suggest you see Captain Lisbet, who has healer training, but you seem well enough."

My heart quickened. "I am. Forest knew just what to do."

"I've already commended him." He reached into his pocket. "This came for you at Grigsbane. Lisbet brought it."

He handed me a sealed, folded parchment. Even in the dimness of the tent, I recognized Papa's bold handwriting: *Storm L'nahn*. My heart tried to crawl up my throat as I closed my hand around the letter.

"Thank you."

He was silent for a moment that stretched to near-awkward proportions. "You can join the men at the campfires tonight, if you're feeling up to it. The others aren't leaving until morning, and there's extra ale."

"I might do that. Thank you." Papa's letter burned hot in my hand.

"I'm glad you're well," Jasper said, rising. "And next time you're attacked by a horde of stinging insects, let me know, *s'da?*"

His smile warmed me as he left, but all I could think of was the letter. I pressed it to my lips, imagining I could smell the soap on Papa's hands. He'd addressed the letter to Storm—did this mean he accepted what I'd done? Or had he merely written my brother's name because he had no choice? I stuck my thumb beneath the fold to break the seal, but then I stopped. If Papa's words were laced with shame, lamenting my deception and asking me to return to Grigsbane so that he could take my place, I wouldn't be able to bear it. Not now, with the throbbing hornet stings and lost Neshu match weighing on me.

I tucked the letter carefully beneath my folded blanket. It could wait.

———————

I took care of my personal business in the latrine tent, where I was certain no hornets' nests lay hidden. Then I grabbed an ale and joined Forest, Dalen, Rock, and River around a fire.

Everything felt strange. Not because of sympathy—everyone seemed to have his own tale to tell of stinging things and losing Neshu matches—but because Forest looked at me differently, if he looked at all.

Of course he would. I didn't blame him. But I hated it. It felt like every word, every gesture I made, was suspect.

Not a boy. Not a boy. As though Forest's knowledge of this made it obvious to everyone else.

Rock's singing kept me by the fire, his smooth, deep voice rounding the sharp edges of my day. Even if others were laughing or speaking, he kept singing, as though it were as important as the air traveling in and out of his lungs. I hung on every note, grateful for the gift he didn't realize he was giving.

But Papa's letter pulled at my heart until I couldn't bear it. I said good night well before the others were ready for sleep and headed to my tent. I thought of Nuaga, making her way toward the camp. My heart was heavy with the thought that if she arrived tonight, I would be unable to meet her. Though Forest's tea had helped considerably, the hornet stings throbbed with each movement.

"Nuaga," I breathed. "I'm hurt."

Too many heartbeats passed. Then, steady and clear, her words came.

I know. The power of T'Gonnen will restore you.

Relief trickled through me, easing the tension from my muscles and even lessening the pain of the hornet stings. "When will you be here?"

Tomorrow night.

So. I had one day to prepare myself to meet her face-to-face.

I lit the lantern on the crossbeam and retrieved Papa's letter from beneath the blanket. For a few moments, I held it, stroking his writing with my thumb. Then I broke the seal, unfolded the parchment, and read.

Dearest of My Heart,

After several days of not knowing what to do, I traveled to Grigsbane, only to learn that you had been sent off somewhere else. I am writing now in the hope that these words will reach you, for I fear they may be the last I will ever be able to share with you.

Once the shock of your departure wore off, I realized that your decision reflected your character and what I would expect of you. I am terrified for your safety, but I am proud of you.

In your letter, you mentioned receiving the medicine by mistake all those years ago. It pains me to think you have grown up with a misunderstanding of what happened that night. The healer arrived with enough medicine for only one of you, it's true. At the time, you seemed much sicker than your brother. Your mother and I were reluctant to choose one child over another, so we told the healer to make the final judgment. He came out of the room and told us he had given the medicine to our son, since we already had another daughter. After he left, we discovered that Willow had placed the son's cap on your head, a little game we had caught her at before. We have never told your sister about her role in this, as we didn't wish to burden her.

In his decision to honor an only son, the healer gave the medicine to you instead of your brother, who was not wearing the son's cap. Had he received the medicine, his fever would not have gone so terribly high, leading to the fits and eventually the damage.

Might the same have happened to you if you hadn't received the medicine? We will never know. But I trust the Great God's will, and I am thankful for your health and strength. I did not want you to march to war questioning your value. It is greater than you know.

All my love always,
Papa

I read the letter three times before the tears began to fall. I read it again as they streamed down my face, my breath coming in short, gasping sobs.

My parents hadn't chosen Storm over me. They had given that choice to someone else.

It didn't lessen the pain of knowing that my receiving the medicine had led to Storm's condition, but it did make me feel, for the first time, that I wasn't an afterthought—a mere third child who took the medicine that might've saved her brother's mind.

When I had drunk my fill of the words, I tore the letter between the second and third paragraphs. The first part I folded up small and tucked deep into my pocket. The rest I tore into tiny bits, which I gathered and rubbed into the dirt beneath my blanket.

"Thank you, Papa," I whispered. I blew out the lantern and lay in the darkness, my heart more satisfied than it had ever been.

It seemed a long time before Forest came to the tent. I was going to pretend to be asleep, to make things easier for him. But when I heard him gathering up his blankets, I rolled onto my back.

"What are you doing?" I asked.

"Sleeping in Jasper's tent," he said. "It'd be better if I didn't disturb you while your stings are healing."

I let him go without saying another word, feeling the death of our friendship like the point of a blade in my heart.

Before the sun had fully crept up, the visiting soldiers marched south, their cheerful farewells and huzzahs incongruous with the gravity of what was now our daily lives. They left behind a team of horses to draw our supply wagon to Chancory.

"If no news arrives today, we'll march out first thing in the morning," Jasper said as we ate a cold breakfast. "The silence makes me uneasy."

I knotted my toes inside my boots, his words leaving an ominous echo in my breast. The faces of my fellow soldiers reflected the same uncertainty that danced in my own heart. Except for Sedge, whose expression was almost arrogant. As though he feared nothing.

Jasper turned his face toward me. "How are your stings?"

"Better." They still throbbed and were starting to itch, but Forest's *tenepa* tea had worked wonders. That, and the power of T'Gonnen coursing through me.

"We need you, Storm," Jasper said. "If I could give you time to rest, I would."

"I don't need time to rest."

Jasper's slow nod expressed his approval. We finished our last few bites and rose to make our way one final time to the ropes. Sedge maneuvered himself so that he was walking beside me.

"Jasper doesn't pick favorites, midget."

"So?"

"So stop pretending the stings don't hurt, just to make the rest of us look weak."

"I didn't say they didn't hurt."

"You said enough."

I ran my tongue over my teeth in an effort to stem the hot words that wanted to shoot out. "I'm not going to fight with you."

He stepped in front of me, forcing me to stop. "You're not half the man you pretend you are."

"If you're the model of manhood around here, I'd rather be a girl."

His fist flew at me a fraction of a second too late; I blocked him, throwing my weight against my knife arm to shove him away.

"What's wrong with you?" My dragon-deepened voice gave power to my words. "Does it feel good to push around the only person who's shorter than you?"

He pushed back, his eyes glaring into mine. "Maybe I don't like your face."

"Is there a problem?" Jasper hovered over Sedge's shoulder.

"No problem here," I said, my eyes still on Sedge.

"Nothing here at all." Sedge turned and continued walking toward the ropes.

I gathered my courage and looked Jasper in the eye. "I'm sorry, sir. He won't stop baiting me."

"Stop taking the bait," Jasper said.

He walked away without another word, and I headed toward the ropes, my face burning with a heated mixture of anger and shame.

Hours later, I stood at the edge of the field wearing my leather breastplate and carrying a short, back-sheathed dagger. We'd practiced throwing the daggers, building accuracy for both combat and hunting, and we'd sparred with wooden ones, learning to incorporate weapons with Neshu moves. Apparently today would be different.

The breastplate was uncomfortable on top of my bindings and the healing hornet stings, but it made me confident that I looked like everyone else, and I would fight like everyone else, too. If I lived for even a single day of this mission, that would be a victory.

Jasper lined us up fifty or so paces from a crudely constructed, life-sized doll mounted to a wooden frame. It had a face painted in rich, black ink, so that it seemed to be staring at us from across the field.

"It's one thing to spar with each other," Jasper said. "But it's another to go face-to-face with an enemy who wants to kill you. Today, you will learn not to fear killing your enemy."

I glanced at Forest, who stood beside me, but his new habit of not quite looking at me made it impossible to catch his eye. So I stared instead at the stuffed soldier.

"There is no room for hesitation in combat," Jasper continued, "and no room for mercy. If the enemy is coming at you, you must attack. If the enemy falters, you must attack. If the enemy turns from you and runs away, you must attack. And if he falls, wounded, you must finish the job. He'll have a face, like yours. He will be a son or a husband or a brother or a father, or all of those things. But to you, he must become nothing."

The silence was heavy as Jasper paused to let his words sink in. I glanced at the others around me, their faces creased against the afternoon sun. They looked hardened.

Ready.

"When you're not on a battlefield, but in a corridor of the palace or alone in a stand of trees, it becomes even harder to face an enemy without hesitating. It's you or him. Live or die. Today, you will learn to live."

I continued to stare at the ink-faced soldier as Jasper walked across the field and took his place behind the doll, explaining how he would push it forward as we engaged it, offering as much resistance as he could and making sure the false soldier didn't topple backward. He then asked for a volunteer to go first.

I stepped forward.

Across the field, my eyes met Jasper's, and I once again read approval there. I breathed it as though it were air.

The moment didn't last long. "Listen well, soldier," Jasper said. "The enemy before you has one goal—to kill you quickly. Draw your dagger on my mark. Then I want you to charge, and I want you to yell until your guts spew and you're spitting blood. I want you to stab your enemy until you're sure he's dead. Do you hear me?"

"Yes, sir!" I said.

"I said, *do you hear me?*"

"Yes, sir!"

"You call that a yell? Tell me again!"

"Yes, sir!" My voice sounded octaves too high, even with its deepening.

"Again! Again!"

I yes-sirred until the words lost meaning. Then, heart pounding, I drew my dagger on Jasper's mark and waited for his order.

"Charge!" he yelled.

I ran toward the stuffed soldier, fingers tight around the hilt of my dagger. The staring face drew nearer, expressionless, vapid— nothing like a real person's face. I imagined hordes of nomads storming Stonewall and killing our men. I imagined them combing the countryside on their way to the capital, killing anyone in their path. I imagined that the not-real soldier I was closing in on meant to run his knife clean through my heart.

I gave a Great Cry and plunged my dagger into his chest.

Jasper leaned into the doll from behind, and the force of his resistance caused me to stagger a bit. I hesitated, then pulled out the dagger.

"If this were a real battle, you'd be *dead!*" Jasper yelled. "Don't stand there, soldier!"

I gritted my teeth and stabbed my soldier again, a sort of grunt escaping my mouth.

"He's murdered your family!" Jasper yelled. "It's you or him! How badly do you want to live?"

I stabbed a few more times, without making a sound. Jasper put his hand on my shoulder, stopping me.

"Go back in line," he said. "Find your anger."

I fought the weight of shame as I ran lightly back to the others while Cedar stepped forward to take his turn. How was I supposed to summon anger from thin air? I watched as Cedar attacked the doll and felt somewhat better when he received a similar speech from Jasper.

A creeping sense of doubt curled through me as I watched each man before me attack the stuffed soldier with his knife and his hoarse yells. I tried to imagine it was a true melee, and that each man fought to his death. But as my turn grew closer, I didn't feel much more capable of murderous rage than I had the first time. And I knew with sinking certainty that if I couldn't accomplish this, I really would fall quickly at the hands of the enemy.

An honorless death, swift and brutal.

"Next!" Jasper's voice was ragged from yelling. I stepped forward, my eyes on the now-battered target, and waited for Jasper's command. Then I drew my dagger and ran.

Within those fifty paces, I conjured a sudden and jarring vision of my family dying at the hands of enemy soldiers, their anguished cries silenced forever, their blood soaking the ground by the fence around our home. My eyes burned into the stuffed soldier as I raised my dagger. I didn't see a drawn-on face anymore; I saw Sedge's face.

"Die!" I yelled, stabbing the face. I pulled my dagger free and stabbed again and again, neck, chest, stomach. I yelled until my throat burned hot and gave way, until I coughed dry heaves and fell against the shredded soldier, hand curling around the buried dagger, strength spent.

"Well done, soldier," Jasper said when he reached me. "You found your anger."

My hand shook as I pulled my dagger out and resheathed it. It wasn't anger that had motivated my attack. It was hatred.

Was this what I had become?

"Thank you," I said. But this time, I didn't mean it.

———

I lay alone in my tent, ears straining for the slightest sound of Nuaga's approach. But my eyes grew heavy, and I soon fell into dreamless sleep.

In the blackest of night, I awoke, knowing without hearing a sound that Nuaga was waiting for me. My boots were already on my feet, so all I had to do was grab my cloak and slip quietly outside and away from the other tents.

My heart pounded with such force I was certain it would awaken everyone.

"Where are you?" I mouthed.

Among the trees.

Rock stood on guard duty, too close for comfort. I waited until he turned his back and walked several paces in the other direction; then I crept lightly toward the trees, my eyes pulling at the darkness, searching for Nuaga.

She stepped forward—even in the dark, I could see that her fierce beauty was ten times what it had seemed. She opened her mouth and spoke real words—teeth and tongue, sound and syllable. "Rain L'nahn."

"Nuaga."

Her face shone when I said her name, as though she hadn't heard it spoken aloud for a long time. She held her head just so, appraising me. "Thank you for releasing me."

I met her gaze and did not feel afraid. "You are . . . breathtaking."

Joy radiated from her eyes, so palpable I was certain I felt its throbbing warmth. "Are you ready to ride?"

For several seconds, I didn't respond. Tentatively, I stepped forward and reached my hand toward the thick coat of fur just behind her ear. The moment my fingers brushed it, a warm peace settled within me, fear trickling from me like water. How much harder could it be to mount a dragon than it was to mount a barebacked donkey?

I took one deep breath. Then I grabbed fistfuls of her pelt and swung myself onto her broad neck.

16

S he took off so quickly that I gasped and threw myself forward onto the base of her head, burying my face and throwing my arms wide, grasping her long fur with as much strength as I could muster. Her body undulated beneath me as she half-glided, half-ran across terrain I could not see, both for the darkness and for how swiftly she bore me.

The night wind stole my breath whenever I lifted my head, so I kept it pressed to her neck, her warmth seeping into me and keeping me from shivering. It was like no ride I'd ever imagined—swifter than any horse and so fluid that it seemed her six mighty legs barely touched the ground. Exhilaration and a wild giddiness left no room for terror, and I reveled in the strength and majesty of the creature who had become less fearsome the moment I mounted her.

I felt safe. And free. And utterly invincible.

Too soon, we reached the base of a gently sloping knoll, and she came to a stop. I slid from her neck, my pulse still racing from the joy of the ride.

"The power of the dragons is strong here," she said, "but I fear things have changed since the days of Mennek. I will wait here."

I nodded and looked up. Lights shone at the top of the knoll, which didn't seem so great a climb as I made my way toward them. I reached into the leather pouch at my belt and felt for the writing instruments I'd tucked inside for easy access, my boots soft as cat's whiskers in the grass. The night was clear, starlight and a bit of moon helping me along my way. Now that the thrill of riding Nuaga had passed, the fear of being discovered grasped at me, making every errant sound suspect. Leaving Jasper and the others was no small thing. I felt as though I had severed myself from a living entity—a special unit of the high king's army, to which I'd pledged my life and service.

The penalty for deserting was death. I knew my value, and part of me hoped that Jasper would make an exception. But I couldn't risk it. I'd simply have to make it back to camp before morning light. That way, no one would ever know I'd gone.

I pressed on, eventually reaching a broad clearing. From there, it was easy enough to move quickly across the tended expanse. The lanterns—or torches—glowed at intervals, welcoming me.

I was fairly out of breath by the time I reached what was certainly the wall surrounding the commune. It was made of rough stone and about shoulder-high, with a sputtering oil lamp hanging every several paces. Clearly it wasn't meant for keeping out intruders, but would it be wise for me to enter by the gate?

I couldn't risk it. Taking a small running leap, I hoisted myself over the top of the wall and landed in a squat on the inside. Once I was certain I hadn't been seen, I picked my way carefully toward the cluster of low buildings that seemed to grow from the earth itself.

Each structure was identical—a wide dome with a thatched roof and windows that were merely thin rectangles covered with translucent glass that would let in light but not a view. This worked in my favor as I crept past dome after dome, until I came to the end of the row and entered what seemed to be the heart of the commune, consisting of three structures. The one in the center was clearly a small temple to the Great God, its door propped open for access at all times, its outer walls set with an intricate mosaic of dragons and warriors. I didn't draw too near, as lanterns glowed on either side of the door, casting a bright light I wanted to avoid.

The structures on either side of the temple were similar to the domes that sat in the circle enclosing them, except they were oblong instead of round, and much larger. Both sat in darkness; neither seemed a likely place for the Archives.

I walked between the temple and the dome on its right to see what lay behind. My breath caught as I saw the form of a dragon rise up in the darkness—a glorious, lifelike sculpture, rearing on its hind legs and arching its neck toward the sky. Its mane was full and flowing, and my heart whispered that this was the fierce T'Gonnen, whose magic I swallowed every night.

"Nuaga," I whispered. "Your mate is honored here."

Silence met me, and I tore my gaze from the statue and looked instead beneath it, where a stone stairway led into darkness. I scanned the area to make sure I was still alone. Then I unsheathed my dagger and crept down, my back sliding against the wall at one side. At the bottom, a substantial door was faintly lit by a tiny oil lamp on either side. Carved into the door was a single word: *Archives.*

I ran my fingers lightly over the carving, a thrill rushing through me. I grabbed the iron handle and pushed.

It was locked.

I pulled instead, but the door didn't budge. I leaned my forehead against the rough wood and willed myself to think of a way to break in without creating a lot of noise.

"Who's down there?"

The voice shot through me like an arrow, and I lifted my head and swung around, dagger poised and ready. The steps were too steep to see anything but a pair of boots and what looked like the hem of a skirt.

"Is that you, Naden?"

I tightened my grip on the dagger and backed against the door. Maybe she'd give up and go away if I remained perfectly still.

"Naden?" Her boots made soft shuffling noises as she descended the stairs.

In one swift move, I sheathed my dagger and assumed the second stance, figuring I'd rather be discovered without a weapon. I tensed as the woman neared the bottom, her boots stopping suddenly as her eyes met mine.

"Dragon's blood, who are you?"

"A seeker."

She looked me up and down, her brow furrowed. "You're a soldier."

"I only want to read something."

"In the middle of the night?" She took one more step, now standing three from the bottom. "I hear deserters are executed on sight."

I raised my chin. "Are you in charge of the Archives?"

"What if I am?"

"I've come to read *The Lament of Nuaga.*"

Her eyebrows lifted. "We've seen the smoke from your fires. Why are you here?"

"We're training for a mission."

She eyed me for several moments. "Your second stance is very practiced, but still discernible by a master."

I couldn't mask my surprise. "You're a master?"

"Not officially. Do I look like a man to you?"

I bowed and said nothing, sure that silence would be better at this point. The not-a-Neshu-master descended the final three steps and stood facing me, lamplight dancing across the fine lines on her face. She must have been at least sixty, though she carried herself like a much younger—and stronger—woman.

"We are a peaceful commune," she finally said.

"I come in peace."

"You come fully armed in the dead of night, wearing a breastplate."

She had a point. "Will you let me in?"

She narrowed her eyes. "Do you have a name?"

"Storm."

"You're not from Province Ytel."

"No."

For an eternity of seconds, we stared wordlessly at each other. Then something in her posture shifted, as though she sought to look taller.

"I can't let you in," she said. "You'll have to come with me."

My heart sank. I didn't want to fight her—she wasn't my enemy. But I needed to get inside the Archives, and she was in my way.

I let my shoulders sag, hoping to look defeated. As she reached for me, I knocked her arm with an uppercut, catching her off guard. She sprang into the second stance, but I already had the advantage of surprise and slammed her against the wall in three swift moves.

Before she could recover, I grabbed her head and knocked it against the stone. She slid to the ground like a sack of buttons.

My heart hammered against my skull as I pressed two fingers to her neck to check her pulse. Hands shaking, I searched her until I found a long key inside a pocket, attached to a chain hanging from her belt. I pushed it into the lock and opened the door before kneeling by the woman's side and returning the key to her pocket. I would not be branded a thief as well as an assailant.

I couldn't leave her lying there. Still stunned by how quickly I had decided to attack her, I took her by the boots and dragged her through the open doorway. As soon as she was sufficiently out of the way, I pushed the door shut.

A single oil lamp hung on the back wall, casting just enough light for me to find my footing as I crossed the small room, its ceiling so low I felt my head would brush it at any moment. Beside the lamp hung a wire basket that held a bundle of thin sticks. I pulled one free, then used it to light the row of smaller lamps on the rough wooden table in the middle of the room. My gaze flicked to the motionless woman as I blew out the flame, unease prodding me like unwelcome fingers.

"I'm sorry," I whispered.

I took a pair of silk gloves from an oblong dish on the table and slipped them on, assuming they were needed to protect ancient documents. Then I turned to the rows of scrolls along the wall behind me, tucked into individual alcoves of carved stone. A quick scan told me that these were historical scrolls, arranged by year. The opposite wall held a similar array of scrolls, but upon a closer look, I saw sections labeled *Words of the Great God* and *Dragon Lore*.

My heart pounded as I moved toward them. So many alcoves. So many scrolls.

And then I saw it. A long, marble-faced drawer spanning the width of the alcoves, bearing an aged plaque that read, *Legacy of Nuaga and the Dragon Clan*. I ran my gloved fingers across its surface, and a tingling warmth coursed through my hands and up my arms.

The drawer was heavy and unwieldy, but it opened without resistance. I stood for several breaths staring at its contents. On beds of silk in individual compartments, enormous teeth, iridescent scales, and braided lengths of golden and white and fiery-red hair rested in silent splendor. I sucked in a breath, marveling at the perfect condition and palpable power of these artifacts.

I could *feel* them. Like a vibration in my veins and chest.

The scroll lay in the center of the drawer. I hesitated, fingers hovering, before lifting it from its nest of silk and bringing it to the table. Slowly, I unrolled the parchment and placed stone weights on its upper corners. I didn't allow myself to look at the writing until the scroll lay flat and I had adjusted the lamps so that I could see clearly.

The woman groaned softly; I looked over my shoulder to see her still lying where I'd left her. I didn't have much time. Taking a great breath, I began to read, each word exactly as I had learned it, each stanza in place.

Until.

My heart beat furiously as I came to what had been "Where is Onen?" and saw more.

So much more.

> Where is one not loath to answer
> Brave Nuaga?
> Willing sacrifice to offer,
> Selfless, like T'Gonnen.

> She who knows the pain of parting
> Knows its power.
> Deep beneath the Hold in caverns,
> Waiting to awaken.

> Through the ages, sons from fathers,
> All Ylanda
> Waits in safety for the Dragons
> Once again to join them.

> Breath of Dragon, searing, cleansing,
> Necessary.
> Bear the mark and bring your boldness
> To the sleeping Dragons.

Call to them with words predestined
Over ages
In the ancient tongue of Dragons—
S'danta lo ylanda.

If the line of kings is severed
Then the Dragons
Ever will belong to those who
Snuff Ylanda's bloodline.

Destined to command and lead them—
Dragon she-king,
Through her mark, the bearer's presence
Satisfies the calling.

Wake, O Dragons! Do not tarry!
Save your people.
Let us usher in the reign of
Loyal, brave Nuaga.

There was nobody named Onen. Dalen's copy of the *Lament* had
come from a partial manuscript, which must have been torn in the
middle of the word "not." And so it had been passed down for who
knew how long, with the rest of the *Lament* lost to those who believed
it. Perhaps for generations.

Except for Tan Vey. He obviously knew the full *Lament* and had
united the northern tribes with the intent of claiming not only the
kingdom of Ylanda, but also the dragons.

How much time had I wasted because I didn't have the knowledge I needed to trust Nuaga? To answer her call?

I looked up to check on the woman again, but she wasn't there.
My blood iced—she'd gone for help, and I hadn't heard her leave. I
needed to be quick.

I scrambled about the room, searching for something—
anything—to write on. Finally, in desperation, I unrolled a fairly recent history scroll and tore off a section at the end, whispering apologies

to the Great God. I dug my writing tools from my cloak pocket, created a quick ink from my inkstick and spittle, and set to copying the remainder of the *Lament*.

> Willing sacrifice to offer,
> Selfless, like T'Gonnen.

There it was—the call for sacrifice. I chewed my lip as I wrote, my heart pounding. For Papa and Storm and Mama and Willow, I would do this. If waking the dragons meant that they—and thousands of others—would live, then I had no need to shrink from my own death.

I reached the fourth new stanza.

> Breath of Dragon, searing, cleansing,
> Necessary.

My hand trembled as I copied the words. This was what Nuaga wanted. Needed. The mark of the dragon.

My own flesh.

> Bear the mark and bring your boldness
> To the sleeping Dragons.

Without the mark of Nuaga's breath, I would not be able to wake the dragons. She knew that—and now I knew it, too.

S'danta lo ylanda.

Hadn't Dalen once told me that "*ylanda*" meant "dragon"? What did the rest mean? Was this all it would take to wake the dragons and save my high king and my kingdom?

That, and the burning of my flesh?

"Nuaga, I'm ready. I'll receive your mark." I hurried to finish the last few words, my strokes rushed and uneven. "I'm saying yes. Please answer me."

Rain. Her voice coursed through me like a warm breeze.

"I'll receive your mark. I'll wake the dragons."

I never doubted you would.

"I'm here," I said. "I'm coming." I let my hurried ink strokes dry as I rolled up the *Lament* and placed it in its drawer, then returned the silk gloves to their dish.

Sudden voices at the door arrested me, and I froze as I reached for my copy of the verses.

"He's still here, as I said he would be." The woman's words were laced with pain.

A middle-aged man, his face creased with sleep marks, pushed past her and strode toward me. "You. Step away from the table."

I stepped away and assumed the first stance.

The man reached inside the neckline of his sleep gown and pulled out an amulet that seemed familiar. He held it in his fingers— tentatively, as though he feared it—and I remembered the amulets in Madam S'dora's shop. And the one around Kendel's neck. Holding the amulet at eye level, he grabbed my arm with his other hand and held fast. At first, nothing happened, and I forced myself to be still. Then the amulet glowed a deep orange, as though lit from within. The man cried out, letting the amulet fall and bounce against his clothing.

"Out! Out!" He gestured wildly to the woman as he staggered backward. "He's *filled* with T'Gonnen's magic!"

Before I could react, they were both out the door, which slammed heavily behind them. The silence that followed was punctuated by the resounding click of the lock.

17

I roared my frustration as I ran to the door and beat it with my fists. How could I have been so slow?

"You can't keep me here!" I yelled, knowing it was futile. "I'm a soldier in the high king's army!"

Silence met me.

I paced, the cramped room adding to my agitation. There had to be some way to break the door down. I took stock—dagger, sword, bare fists. None of them would be useful. I scanned the room for something heavy and sharp, but I only found a willow broom and a feather duster.

We are a peaceful commune, she had said. Clearly.

"Nuaga, I'm trapped."

Move away from the door.

Her words were forceful—jarring. I backed away, bumping into the table and moving around it as the door began to shudder. I watched, half excited, half terrified, as the door crackled, then ignited, then burst into flames, the heat forcing me back against the far wall.

Run, Rain!

I had no idea where to run, but I soon saw that the door had been completely incinerated, its remains reduced to glowing embers scattered on the earth floor. I grabbed my copy of the new verses and shoved it into my pocket as I ran through the smoldering doorway.

Screams pierced my ears as I took the steps two by two. When I reached the top, Nuaga stood there in all her magnificence. The warmth of her breath reached me as she lowered her face and met my gaze with an expression of joy so fierce that I almost laughed out loud. I swung my leg around her neck as though I had done it a thousand times. As I found my balance, she took off, all muscle and sinew and fathomless strength. She wove through the commune, then took a soaring leap over the wall, landing as lightly on the other side as though she weighed no more than a handful of pebbles.

I closed my eyes and hung on, with no idea where she was taking me. When she came to a stop some minutes later, I released my white-fisted hold and slid from her neck, landing lightly on the ground.

She'd brought me to some sort of hollow, with trees that grew above its sloped walls like a canopy. Though it was dark, her eyes were glowing, and I could see her face clearly.

"Well?"

"Why did they lock me in?" I asked.

"Either because they feared you, or because they coveted the magic inside you. Perhaps both." She watched me, waiting.

"I have the missing verses." I dug the parchment from my pocket and read, the words tingling on my tongue.

Nuaga closed her eyes, soaking in the words like a lullaby. When I finished, she opened her eyes.

"You have half of what you need. Words to wake them by."

"*S'danta lo ylanda*. What does it mean?"

"'Release the power of the dragons.'"

Just as Dalen had said—our very kingdom was named for the dragons.

"*S'danta lo ylanda*," I whispered.

"Yes."

"And . . . the other half?"

"Your sacrifice, Rain L'nahn. Selfless and timely, like T'Gonnen's. You will know when the time comes. And so will I."

I wanted to ask her how it was possible to give my life *before* waking the dragons, but I swallowed the question, figuring it was better to know as little about my own death as possible.

She moved nearer. "It's time."

I rolled the parchment—slowly. Even more slowly, I tucked it back into my pocket. Then I met her gaze.

She waited. She would not bestow the pain without my consent.

"Nuaga . . ."

Flesh-melting breath. The mark of a dragon. My heart withered inside me.

She dipped her face near mine. "Trust that you are worthy, Rain L'nahn."

I'd spent a lifetime feeling unworthy. Could I now believe otherwise?

My breaths came fast and shallow; every muscle in my body tensed, begging me to run away. Why was it easier to face death in combat than it was to face voluntary pain?

Great God, help me.

"Choose the place of your marking," Nuaga said.

Terror rushed through me like a cold wind. Which part of my body could I willingly sacrifice? I didn't want to offer my hands, which I would need to fight, or my face, for fear that the breath would blind me.

In the quiet of the hollow, I slipped, shivering, from my cloak and shirt, and unwound the strips that bound me. Then I turned around and offered my bare back to Nuaga.

At least I wouldn't have to watch.

"I'm ready." I closed my eyes, a million tremors quaking through me as I braced myself for the pain.

It came not as a blast, but as a subtle, intense heat that, at first, felt comforting. In mere seconds, though, Nuaga's breath became so hot that the pain was exquisite. Unbearable.

I threw back my head and yelled, falling to my knees as wordless agony engulfed me. Instinctively, I folded into myself, clawing the dirt with impotent fingers, screaming until my voice was stripped of sound.

Screaming, until everything went blissfully black.

——— · ———

I opened my eyes to the deep gray of predawn. I lay on the grass, my shirt draped over me as though someone had thoughtfully covered me.

"Nuaga?"

I sat up, memories of the pain surfacing like an explosion in my mind. Cautiously, I rolled first one shoulder, then the other. Nothing hurt. I reached my right hand over the opposite shoulder and brushed my fingertips across my back. It felt marked and uneven, but it was smooth and dry, as though the wound had occurred weeks ago. When I stood and twisted at the waist to test it, I felt some tingling and soreness.

But that was all.

Dazed, I rewrapped my bindings and dressed quickly. I felt certain that Nuaga was nearby, watching. Our connection felt deeper, more intimate.

"Where are you?" I whispered.

She appeared not far away and came to my side in a fluid move that added to her majesty. "I felt you awaken."

Of course she had. "Nuaga, the man in the Archives wore an amulet. It glowed orange when he touched me."

"Dragon blood," Nuaga said. "It heats to burning in the presence of dragon power."

So Dalen was right—Kendel's amulet really did contain dragon blood. The physical contact we'd made during Neshu rounds must have been too brief to ignite it.

"I have to get back to camp." Already the sky was lighter than I had hoped.

"Has your body rested enough?"

"Yes." I felt surprisingly refreshed.

"Then let us leave this place."

I mounted her easily. Her power thrummed through me, uniting and resonating with the magic of T'Gonnen in my veins. Like water in a stream, she bore me across the miles, and when we reached the outskirts of camp, she folded her legs so I could slide easily down. I landed, and she swung her head around to face me.

"The dragons will know you now, and will awaken at your voice."

It was as though a new heart beat within me—the heart of a dragon. I felt large and mighty, buzzing with the magic of T'Gonnen. In a rush, I wanted nothing more than to go with Nuaga and wake the dragons. To ride her into the midst of the enemy and feel the weight of her feet crushing them.

"Let's go now," I whispered.

She regarded me for what felt like eternity. "You are one with our clan now. But is your loyalty complete?"

"Yes," I said, and the fire of dragons burned within me.

"Yet love for a man is embedded in your heart. Perhaps he will be your downfall when your time comes."

I sucked in a breath. "It's nothing."

"His name swims through your dreams. His face is always in your thoughts."

"He's betrothed to my sister," I said. "And that's the end of it."

Nuaga nodded her head slowly, like a ship riding the swell and dip of the sea. "Time is short. It will be better spent if I run ahead while your men march north. I can travel unseen when I bear no rider, and I will scout faster and farther than any man ever could. I will find Tan Vey's army and determine our safest route to the dragons."

"You would hide from them?" I couldn't imagine it.

"One dragon cannot take on an entire army," Nuaga said.

"I want to go with you." Desperation welled up in me. Or perhaps it was the passion of T'Gonnen, roaring through the dragon magic in my blood.

"Take this time to teach the others to trust me."

I laid my hand on her neck, unwilling to part from her. "*S'da*."

"As long as the power of T'Gonnen flows within you, you will hear my voice. When you call, I will answer."

She brushed my face with her mighty ear before speeding away, swift as a gale. I watched her for a breath or two, longing to wrap my arms once again around her neck. Then I turned and jogged the short distance back to camp.

Almost immediately, I saw Jasper and the others, less than a hundred paces away, standing as though made of stone.

Staring.

At first, I thought they were staring at me. But I as drew near, I saw that their gazes went beyond me. I looked over my shoulder in time to see Nuaga disappear into the morning mist.

They had seen her.

Dalen spoke first. "Nuaga."

The terror of the men around me was palpable. I focused on

Jasper, waiting for him to speak. He finally tore his gaze from the horizon and fixed it on me.

"What were you doing that far from camp?"

I glanced at Forest, but he wasn't looking at me. "I . . . wasn't deserting, sir."

"I didn't suggest you were."

Heat flooded my cheeks. Jasper once again lifted his gaze across the grove, searching. I turned, a mixture of hope and dread sifting through me. But Nuaga was gone.

"It was right behind you." Rock's voice cut through my reverie. "Didn't you hear anything?"

I read the faces of the soldiers around me and knew they weren't ready to hear my story. How could I convince them to trust Nuaga in the wake of such fear?

"No," I said.

The silence that followed pressed against me with a weight that stole my breath. Even Dalen and Kendel, who believed in the dragons, looked at me warily.

Jasper was the first to break the spell. "We don't have time to debate this. It's time to march."

"But, sir, it was to the north, directly in our path," Flint said.

"It could still be close by," Cedar said.

"It may have been a trick of the enemy," Jasper said. "We have to press on."

Everyone began to go about their business, slowly at first, and then more naturally. Dalen caught my eye, his expression a mixture of awe and worry.

"I'm sure it was Nuaga," he said in an undertone. "Didn't you notice her at all?"

I pressed my mouth shut and offered a short nod. Dalen looked like he wanted to say more, but I frowned and shook my head. Now was definitely not the time to discuss Nuaga's return.

Light rain stung my face as I struck my tent and loaded it into the wagon where the others had already piled theirs. I hurried to join them in a loose formation in front of the wagon, which Flint had won the coin toss for driving for the day. My fur-lined cloak hung extra long over my shoulders, accentuating my short stature.

Nuaga, I mind-spoke. *They fear you.*

I rolled my head from side to side, stretching out the night's stiff-ness. For the first time since riding to the Archives, my thoughts turned to our army and the fact that no messenger had arrived, though we'd kept our fire burning late in case someone needed to find his way in the dark.

No one spoke of what the silence might mean, just as no one spoke of Nuaga. Fear stilled everyone's tongue and hung like a vapor among us as we set off.

We marched all day, stopping only once for a quarter of an hour to rest and drink some water. No one spoke of the dragon. And no one but Dalen seemed willing to exchange more than half a dozen words with me. Including Forest.

But he had other reasons as well.

Nuaga stayed out of sight, but I felt her within me, a tangible presence that knotted me with the desire to call her forth and bathe in her majesty. To press my cheek into the warmth of her pelt.

To go with her to wake the dragons.

As night began to fall, we made camp on a wide expanse with thickly treed hillocks to the west. I stood behind Forest in the line by the provisions wagon that held the tents and blankets. These were community possessions now, and I forced myself to let go of the idea of having my own things in my own sleeping space.

Forest pulled a tent from the wagon and handed it to me, his eyes still not quite meeting mine. "Here you go."

My stomach folded in on itself. Clearly he meant to continue shar-ing a tent with Jasper. When he took two blankets and promptly dropped them, both of us bent to pick them up, and our heads cracked together.

"Dragon's blood, I can do it myself!" He grabbed the blankets and walked away without a backward glance.

The ache in my heart hurt worse than the throbbing of my head. I took my own blankets from the wagon and made sure no one saw the tears that clouded my vision.

We worked quickly to pitch our tents. Light rain tickled my face and hands, and as soon as the tent was secure, I tossed the blankets and my cloak inside to keep them dry. When I turned around, Jasper stood there, arms folded.

"A word," he said.

We walked a distance away from the others. Jasper looked over his shoulder before stopping to face me.

"What were you doing that far from camp this morning?"

I'd had all day to come up with an answer, but still the words teetered uncertainly on my lips.. "I didn't desert, sir," I said.

"I asked what you were doing."

It was hard to hold his gaze. "I'm sorry," I said. "I didn't realize how far I'd walked. I was up earlier than everyone else, and . . ." I raised my hands and let them fall.

"And you didn't see the dragon? Or hear anything?"

For a moment, I wanted to open my heart and tell him everything—about Nuaga and dragonbreath and the heart-wrenching story of T'Gonnen's sacrifice. Even as I stood there, the fiery strength of T'Gonnen rose up within me, and I could barely contain the words that clambered for release.

"I thought I saw something, yes," I said.

"A dragon?"

"It might've been." I bit my lip. "Do you believe it was a trick of the enemy?"

Jasper folded his arms. "It doesn't matter what I believe. Whatever it was brought with it the kind of fear that can paralyze men who need to pick up their weapons and fight."

"What if it really was a dragon?" I offered. "And what if she's loyal to Ylanda, just like the *Lament* says?"

"It's more likely to be a ploy of the enemy than a dragon coming to rescue us."

"I think maybe—"

"I can't afford to have my soldiers wandering off. If I find you've done so again, I'll consider it a desertion."

My mouth was sand. "Yes, sir."

Jasper clapped me on the shoulder. "I need you, Storm. Don't go soft on me."

"Never, sir. I'll never go soft."

He nodded and dropped his hand. I walked away feeling as

though I had told a thousand lies, and made my way to the water barrel to quench my dust-coated mouth. How did Nuaga expect me to
teach them to trust her? She had wooed me, dream by dream, visit
by visit, until I knew her. Even then, I had feared her for many days.
Now I had brought that fear upon my entire unit—and I didn't know
how to undo it.

Water ran down my chin as I gulped, wishing I had an answer.

———◆———

The rain that had been teasing us all day came and went as we built
a fire and huddled around it, eating twisted ropes of dried meat and
drinking the last of the ale. The wary glances and stilted conversation tossed my way told me what no one was actually saying—that
many thought that somehow my disappearance from camp had something to do with the dragon. Forest sat by me, as he usually did, but
his conversation was mostly directed at others. After a while, I decided to crawl into my tent and let the rest of them speak freely about
the dragon.

Probably that was what they needed to do. I couldn't blame them.

"I'll say good night," I said to no one in particular.

The night felt extra dark as I turned away from the bright flames
and headed toward my tent. I ducked inside and felt for the small
leather pouch that hung from my belt. My bag of dragon powder
filled the pouch almost halfway, leaving little room for much besides
the few coins beneath it and the writing things that lay on top. I'd
had to break my writing pen in half so it would fit.

The powder was bitter as always beneath my tongue, but I had
grown so accustomed to it that I didn't flinch. Mostly I was afraid of
running out of powder too soon. Meaning, before I died.

I shuddered as I tried once again to embrace the prospect of my
own death. Mostly I wondered if it would come swiftly, or if I would
linger in pain while my lifeblood drained from a gaping wound.

Great God. It was better not to think of it. I could at least find
comfort in knowing that I'd take my last breath saving the lives of
everyone I loved.

The evening's ale sloshed inside me, so I ventured out again to
make a final trip to the trees, thankful for the campfire that helped

me find my way in the rain-misted night. I had just finished my business and stepped from behind my chosen tree when Sedge's stocky form emerged from the darkness to my left, his face deeply shadowed.

I didn't want a confrontation. I nodded curtly and started to walk around him, but he cut in front of me, blocking my path.

"Why are you snooping around in the dark, midget?" he said.

"I was taking a piss."

"That so?" He stepped closer. "You sure you're not out here looking for dragons?"

I stiffened. "You afraid of dragons, Sedge?"

"I'm not afraid of anything." But a slight catch in his voice told me otherwise. "And I'm not the one dreaming about dragons."

My stomach dropped. "What are you talking about?"

"It's no secret," Sedge said.

"My dreams are none of your business." I tried to go around him again, but he stopped me with his arm.

"So, you admit it? You dreamed about the dragon and sneaked out to find it?" A note of fear in his words stole their accusatory edge.

His vulnerability caught me off guard. "That's ridiculous."

"Were you dragon hunting or not?"

"If you're looking for someone to blame your own fear on, you're looking at the wrong person."

"I have no fear. It can't touch me."

I remembered his visit to Madam S'dora's and stepped closer, weighing words on my tongue before I spoke them. "And where did you get this freedom from fear? How much did you pay for it?"

His jaw tightened as he stepped back. "You don't know what you're talking about. Stay away from me."

He disappeared quickly among the tents, and I stood in the dark allowing my heaving breaths to quiet. Dalen's betrayal shredded my spirit as if it were Mama's cabbage salad.

I'd been prepared to talk with Dalen about Nuaga—perhaps enlist his help in convincing Jasper and the others that we could trust her. But clearly, I couldn't trust Dalen to keep my words to himself. And any rumors that wove their way through our unit would be worse than my simply telling Jasper everything outright.

Oh, Nuaga. How can I make them trust you?

It seemed a long time before she responded. *You cannot make them. You can only model your own trust in me.*

I sighed. That didn't seem much easier.

The rain fell harder as I slipped into my tent and tied the flap behind me.

18

The rain that had strengthened during the night grew even heavier as we ate a simple breakfast and broke camp. By the time we started off across the same, dull terrain, the clouds were emptying their bowels in sheets, the rain making dull thunking sounds on the wagon top and forcing our gazes downward. In no time, the ground had softened to mud. It sucked at my boots and slowed us down. When we stopped for a short afternoon rest, there was no way to sit without becoming soaked. Some of the soldiers sat anyway, but I didn't relish having a wet bottom for the rest of the day, so I stood and stretched my back and arms, wishing for nothing more than a warm fire.

For four solid days, the rain fell, bringing with it the colder air of the falling season, so that at night we were all eager to climb into our damp tents and burrow under our blankets. Every morning, our cloaks and clothes were still damp, and it was miserable stuffing my damp socks into my damp boots. My bones ached with the constant chill and wet, and I often found myself longing for the warmth of Nuaga's breath and wishing I could nestle into her.

Conversation was almost nonexistent, though I noticed Dalen and Kendel walked often together, heads bent against the rain and toward each other. I so needed their support in convincing the unit that the return of the dragons was a good thing—but I wasn't willing to trust Dalen in light of his betrayal of my secret. No one spoke of the dragon when I was nearby, and I had no idea what they might have been saying among themselves.

Teaching them to trust Nuaga felt impossible.

On the fourth evening, the rain slackened to a light mist. After our meager rations, I spread my wet cloak outside my tent; though it had no chance of drying, at least I would be slightly less damp during the night. I crawled into my tent with the lantern I always took from the supply wagon. It had been ages since I'd written anything, and I was aching to find the words that would help me express my growing need to be with Nuaga and what it meant to have the mark of her breath on my back.

I pulled a folded bit of parchment from my bag, along with the broken pen, the nubby inkstick, and a small stone well. I held the well in the palm of my hand and spat into it, rubbing the inkstick into the spittle until I was satisfied with the depth of color. The lantern light flickered and teased, but the parchment on my lap was fairly illuminated. I dipped my pen into the ink and scratched the first word.

Warrior, it said.

I stared at it, the shapes and angles poking at me, daring me to own it. Then I dipped my pen again and continued to write, the words spilling from my fingers in a hot torrent. I imagined Storm sitting at the foot of my bed while I wrote, as he often did.

Every word on the parchment was for him.

"How do you always manage to have a lantern?"

I hadn't noticed Forest lifting the tent flap. He held his rolled-up blankets under his arm.

"I borrow it," I said, every muscle tense.

"Ah." He cleared his throat. "Mind if I come back?"

My heart somersaulted. "Did Jasper kick you out?"

"Yes and no." He came in and started spreading out a blanket. "I couldn't keep using the stings as an excuse to avoid you. They've clearly healed."

"True."

He pulled off a boot. "I, uh, haven't really wanted to be around you."

"I know."

"And I needed a few days to get used to the idea of sharing my tent with a girl."

"It's been almost a week."

"That's a few days." He pulled off his other boot.

I set my pen and parchment aside. "I'm sorry. I know this is . . . awkward."

"You could say that."

It was hard to know where to look. I shoved the well and ink-stick into my pouch and folded the parchment.

"What are you writing?"

"It's nothing," I said. "I write poems sometimes."

"When you're not dressing like a boy?"

I pressed my lips together and forced myself to look at him. His expression wasn't accusatory, the way I had expected it to be. He had raised one eyebrow, and his eyes hinted that he was teasing.

"I'd just started my first boy-poem, but you interrupted me."

The hint of a smile lit his face, but it quickly faded. "I'm sorry for ignoring you. It's just . . . I thought I was friends with . . . someone named Storm. And then, there you were in the creek, and . . ." Color crept into his face.

I felt heat in my own cheeks. "It was a horrible moment for me, too."

"Who are you, really?"

"Rain L'nahn," I said. "I came in my brother's place."

"Why?"

I told him all about Storm and what the fever had done to him, and how the medicine had been given to me.

"I always believed my parents meant for my brother to receive the medicine, but a few days ago Jasper gave me a letter from my papa," I said. "He explained that it was the healer who made the decision, and that he gave the medicine to me because I was wearing the son's cap."

"Why were you wearing it?"

"Because—" Did I want to shed such a dark light on Willow? "My sister was little. Nobody saw her put the cap on me."

"Mistaken identity."

"Yes."

"How ironic." He said it matter-of-factly.

"I left at night," I said. "They never would have let me come. But my father was planning to come to Grigsbane with Storm, and I couldn't let him do that. If anything happened to him, my mother would be destitute. He couldn't even afford Willow's dowry until she turned nineteen, and if she knew that you were—" I stopped, mortified.

"Willow?"

I sighed. "Willow L'nahn. Your intended bride."

Forest studied me, his brow furrowed, his mouth slightly open. "Is there anything else I need to know? Like, you're betrothed to the high king, or you were actually sent here to murder me in my sleep?"

"If that were true, I'd have done it already."

It was Forest's turn to sigh. "I'm not even supposed to know her name, and now I find I've been sharing a tent with her sister."

"That sounds worse than it is."

"What's she like? Unless you'd rather not tell me."

I opened my mouth to sing my sister's praises, but a hard knot in my heart stopped me. Forest waited, the soft lantern light dancing on his face, softening the contours and creating an ache that had become familiar. "She's wonderful," I finally said, though the words felt like stones. "Beautiful, sensitive, eager to be married."

"Why?"

I shrugged. "Aren't most girls? Anyway, she's nineteen, so she feels like she's had to wait so long for what many of her friends already have."

"That's the only reason? She's tired of waiting?"

"It's hard being a girl. Waiting tables doesn't bring in much money, and not everyone has the funds to open a shop or eatery. There aren't many options."

"Unless, of course, you want to pull on some pants and run away to the army."

I folded my arms. "I can't tell if you're teasing or not."

"I'm teasing," he said. "I promise."

An easiness was growing between us that I'd been afraid to hope for. Worse than the sudden and embarrassing exposure of my femaleness had been my fear that I had forever destroyed our friendship.

"Do you forgive me?" I asked.

"I forgive you," Forest said. "But . . ."

I frowned. "But?"

"It'll be easier if we just keep pretending you're . . . who you say you are. It's taken me almost a week to make myself realize I've been with a girl all along without knowing it. So nothing's really changed. Right?"

"Right." I bit my lip. "I think I'll like having you for a brother-in-law." But my words rang hollow.

"Yes, we can sit around the supper table and talk about our days in the army together."

I laughed lightly. "Willow wouldn't allow it."

He grew serious. "Sometimes I worry that . . . well, that I won't make Willow happy. Or that I won't even like her."

"It's hard not to like my sister," I said softly. "And you're a wonderful person. I think she'll fall in love with you the moment she meets you."

Forest smiled. "From what you've said, I could be a warty old goat and she'd still fall in love with me."

"Not if you were a warty old goat, she wouldn't," I said. "Seriously."

"I know. You're being kind." For a moment, he looked uncomfortable again, but he hid it quickly. "Thank you."

I swore on T'Gonnen's bones that I wouldn't bring up my sister again.

"Is anyone going to attempt a fire?" I asked.

"Was that a challenge?"

I shrugged and raised my eyebrows. "Four solid days and nights in the rain? I'd call it desperation."

"Let's see what we can do."

I blew out the lantern and tucked the parchment away with my other writing things, my heart a strange mixture of warm and cold.

The fire turned out to be an impossibility, but the thirteen of us gathered anyway, by the paltry light of a few lanterns clustered together in the middle of the ring we sat in. Cedar was busy carving something, his curls escaping stubbornly from his bun, as always. Rock hummed softly, his deep voice gently comforting. And Coast and Briar were having a low conversation that seemed to consist of more words than either had spoken since we'd all met. Perhaps it was true that adversity had the power to draw out the best in us.

Jasper's expression was grim, but when he spoke, it was clear he was trying to keep our spirits from flagging.

"We've lost at least a day, on account of the rain," he said. "But we should reach Chancory tomorrow."

"The wagon's slowing us down," Flint said.

"As I knew it would," Jasper said. "But once we reach the outpost, we'll be able to move quickly from there without encumbrance."

No one mentioned the unspoken fear—that the days of silence meant something awful had happened. I saw the hollow looks in everyone's eyes and shoved my own trepidation deep inside my belly.

"At least we know this rain is slowing the enemy down as well as us," Mandrake said.

"We may well have news tomorrow," Jasper said.

"Whether we do or not, we'll get the job done." Mandrake's gaze swept around the circle, including each of us. "This is the best team I've ever been a part of."

"Agreed," Kendel said softly.

"Some news would help," Sedge said. "The silence doesn't bode well."

I rested my chin in my hand as I leaned on my bent knees. Nuaga had been scouting and running before us. Would she offer news that I could share? My desire to be with her had grown into an ache so deep that I sometimes despaired of having any peace until I was with her again. I longed for her as conversation rose and dipped around me.

"Here." Cedar handed me the small bit of wood he'd been working on. "It's not my best work."

I held it to the light of the lanterns. He'd carved a dragon, with six legs and a long neck that curved just so. It fit in the palm of my hand. I looked at him, unsure what to say.

He lowered his voice. "I know you saw it, and it didn't scare you. So I'm not going to let it scare me, either."

I closed my fingers around the gift. "Thank you. It's beautiful."

Cedar smiled. "Glad you think so."

I held the carving to my chest, my heart beating against it. This was the first sign that the men might, perhaps, learn to trust Nuaga after all. And I hadn't spoken a word to Cedar about her. I pushed the little dragon deep into my pocket.

Not much else was said, and our collective exhaustion made heading to our tents the best option. I fumbled in the dark for my dragon powder as Forest made himself comfortable beside me. After I'd taken the powder, I stretched out and pulled my blanket up to my armpits.

"Isn't it hard to sleep with those strips of cloth around your— around you?" he asked.

"I'm used to it."

He was silent for a few moments. "So, that dragon powder?"

My stomach tightened. "What about it?"

"Is it really because you're pigeon-toed?"

"No," I said. "It's not."

"Does it have something to do with . . . I'm not sure what I'm asking."

I drew a deep breath and told him everything—my trip with Willow to Madam S'dora's shop and my subsequent return, and everything Madam S'dora had told me about the dragon powder. I told him how well the powder seemed to be working, and how my voice had even lowered a bit, as Madam S'dora had said it might.

"My face feels a bit . . . hairier, too," I said.

"I haven't noticed anything."

"If you say so." I shifted onto my side. "There's one thing. When I was in the shop buying the powder, Sedge walked in. He was rude, and I . . . hit him. And I'm always afraid he's suddenly going to remember where he saw me before."

"Great God. Has he said anything?"

"The first time I met him, he thought he recognized me."

"How hard did you hit him?"

"I think I hit his pride harder," I said. "The fact that I hit him at all, being a girl."

I could practically hear Forest smiling in the dark. "Wish I could've seen it."

"It was over in a second."

"Honestly, I wouldn't worry too much," Forest said. "He's never going to suspect that the girl in the shop who hurt his pride is now a boy in his unit."

"I hope you're right," I said.

"I know I'm right." He was silent for a while; it seemed he was gathering his thoughts before he spoke. "So. This dragon."

"Yes."

"It's the same one you told me about?"

I told him about the trip to the Archives, receiving Nuaga's mark on my back, and her promise to find the safest route to the dragons. The longer I spoke, the less strange it all felt. When I was finished, I took a great breath.

"Do you believe me now?"

Forest didn't answer right away. "When I saw the dragon that morning, I . . ." He blew out a stream of air. "I was still angry. I didn't want to admit I might've seen proof that you weren't going mad."

"It's not easy to believe something like this."

"No. It's not." He was silent for a bit. "Do you feel safe when you're with her?"

"Yes," I said. "More than anything, I wanted to go with her. It's like she's part of me now, and I'm part of her. I'm not afraid anymore."

"Why don't you tell Jasper the truth?"

"I want to. But he's so . . . resistant. And it all goes back to the dragon powder. If I weren't taking it, none of this would be happening."

"And he can't know about the powder."

"Right," I said. "It's the reason Nuaga came to me, and the reason I can speak with her. And now that I've received her mark, I'm part of the dragon clan."

Forest's voice softened further. "What was it like, receiving her mark?"

"She was gentle." I didn't want him to know how horrible it had been.

"That's all? Gentle?"

"I'd rather not talk about it."

"*S'da*." He was silent for a moment. "You're really part of a dragon clan now?"

"Yes."

"When Nuaga returns, what will you do?"

"Whatever she needs me to."

"Even if Jasper says otherwise?"

I sighed. "Even then."

"Be careful, *s'da?*"

I nodded in the dark, though he couldn't see me. "I will."

He was silent for so long I thought he'd dozed off. Then he said, "Maybe we'll both make it home. Maybe you'll be my children's favorite aunt. Or uncle."

I giggled. It was the girliest sound I'd made in weeks. "I hope we do."

———————

Morning dawned cold but rain-free, and we packed quickly. All day, we traveled hard. A chill wind sprang up, and my face was soon numb from it. It seemed our marching hit an almost frantic pace as we pushed forward, yet I was grateful for my warm cloak. The temperature kept dropping.

Shortly before nightfall, the watchtowers of Chancory rose up, ragged against the blood-red sky. Relief that we'd have shelter for the night gave way to uneasiness as we drew nearer. The grounds were too quiet, the watchtowers unlit. We pressed on, the squeaking of our wagon wheels cutting through the silence.

I saw the glow first—the warmth of firelight reflecting from inside the arch of the entryway. We slowed, and Cedar, who was driving the wagon, pulled the team to a stop. Jasper held his hand out and took several steps forward, his boots hardly making a sound. I rested my hand on the hilt of my sword.

Watching.

Barely breathing.

I couldn't identify the *zing* until I saw the arrow embedded in Cedar's neck. He fell from the wagon with a solid thud.

19

The frozen horror of the moment erupted into frenzy as half a dozen soldiers poured from the archway, daggers drawn. I hesitated for too many heartbeats, unsure in the sudden confusion which weapon to draw.

Dagger.

Sword.

Dagger.

I reached over my shoulder and unsheathed my dagger, assuming the second stance as Forest and several others lunged to attack. A second arrow whizzed over my head, and I looked up to see the lone archer restringing his bow. Heart in my teeth, I shifted my grip on the dagger, ready to throw. In the next breath, one of the nomad fighters kicked my dagger from my hand. I spun to engage him, my Neshu training taking over, sure as a heartbeat. He came at me fluidly, his dagger like a fang, slicing the air as he danced toward me. I countermoved, my knife arm arcing up—and missing. I spun and ducked, avoiding his second lunge by a hair's breadth and reestablishing my balance before he turned to engage me a third time. As he came in for the kill, I gave a Great Cry and brought both arms up under his knife arm. He didn't drop the dagger, but he faltered enough so that I was able to kick him in the chest. As he staggered backward, River ran at him, stabbing downward as I looked up to find the archer in the tower. He was just drawing his bow when Jasper took several running steps forward and threw his dagger. It shot through the air and landed square in the nomad's chest. He toppled like a sack of grain to the earth, and silence fell.

Seven nomads lay dead. Along with Cedar, Mandrake had also taken an arrow, his lifeless body sprawled facedown in the muck.

My knees felt like water, and I sank heavily to them. Someone handed me my dagger; I looked up to see Dalen, his face bloodied from a slash across his cheekbone.

"It's only a scratch," he said, his eyes blank.

"Weapons ready," Jasper said. "Let's make sure no one else is inside."

I rose, a strange numbness creeping through me as I followed Jasper and the others through the archway into the outpost. Minutes ago, we had been thirteen; now we were eleven.

The arrow could as easily have struck me, and then where would Nuaga have placed her hope? It shook me to my core to imagine that so much might depend on whether I lived or died.

We walked through the stone archway, its gate long rusted away, and stared. The charred remains of wooden structures lay smoldering, a hint of smoke still acrid on the breeze. My heart sank.

"Clearly those seven were left here to guard the plunder," Jasper said, his voice strong and steady, as though two of our men hadn't died minutes ago. "They didn't expect any challenge, or there would have been more of them."

And yet they'd fought us one-to-two, hoping the archer would give them an advantage.

Jasper scanned our faces, then frowned. "Where's Sedge?"

"I'm here." Sedge appeared through the archway, looking hesitant.

I tried not to watch him as he made his way toward us. His normal saunter was gone, and for a moment I thought the loss of our men had affected him.

"Where were you?" Jasper asked.

Sedge raised his chin, his mouth a tight line. "I was . . . out there, sir."

"Out there . . . where?"

"I . . . lost my dagger."

It struck me like a falling tree, and it seemed to strike Jasper, too. Sedge had hidden instead of fighting.

The word "coward" hung in the air, unspoken.

"First combat is always hardest," Jasper said. "Let's move on."

We fanned out and searched the watchtowers and adjoining stone structures, the roofs of which had long ceased to be sound. Other than a cluster of lit lanterns and the nomads' piles of bedding and provisions, we found nothing else. No nomads, no dead bodies.

"Maybe they took them prisoner," Forest said as we returned to the open area.

I looked at the burned-out buildings. "But why? Jasper says they kill everyone in their path."

"Meat." Jasper's voice was raw. "It keeps their men easily fed."

The horror of his words coiled around me, but I only stared, unable to feel their full impact. Jasper walked past us as we gathered in the failing light, waiting for his next order.

"We'll bring the wagon inside and double our watch," Jasper said. "We'll regroup, bury our dead, and head north as soon as possible."

Forest rested his hand on my shoulder as we moved to follow Jasper's orders. "Do you need a moment?"

"No." My very bones trembled as I forced myself to keep moving. Forced myself not to feel anything.

I slipped my hand into my pocket and wrapped my fingers around the little dragon until its edges dug into my flesh. I imagined I could feel the warmth of Cedar's hand on it, and an unearthly wail threatened to escape my throat and pierce the sullen air.

I clamped my mouth shut and buried my anguish deep within my breast. Death had always been an inevitability, and I couldn't allow it to undo me. The surge of tears that flowed cold down my face was the only release I allowed myself. I set my jaw and swiped them away.

The supply wagon held enough dry firewood for one decent blaze. The promise of warmth staved the weariness threatening to claim me, and I gladly helped carry loads of wood to the center of our circle of tents, which we'd set up as far from the burned-out buildings as possible. My eyes were ever skirting the lengths of the wall that surrounded us, searching with every heartbeat for Nuaga.

Have you found the safest route? I asked. *Will you be here soon?*

Nuaga's words felt like music. *I have much news. Look for me after the sun has risen.*

I've failed. Only four trusted you, and now one of those is dead. My heart pounded as I waited for her to answer.

Let them trust you, Rain L'nahn. If they do, then whatever you trust, so will they.

I closed my eyes and drew a long breath that I was sure carried her scent. How could I tell her that allowing the men to see her when I had just parted from her had done nothing but fuel suspicion—and fear?

I dumped my final armful onto the pile at the same time Dalen dumped his, causing several of our sticks to collide and tumble back down.

"Sorry," he said, and it took me an extra heartbeat to realize he was talking about the logs.

"Are you?" I pushed past him and walked quickly away from the log pile.

"Storm." Dalen matched me step for step. "It's not what you think."

If he'd said this a day ago, I would have lashed out. Blamed him for not keeping a secret. But in the wake of sudden death, being angry with Dalen no longer seemed worth it.

"I trusted you," I said softly.

Dalen glanced over his shoulder. "It was Sedge, *s'da?* He gave me a hard time, tricked me into telling him what I knew about you."

"You're blaming *him* for your inability to keep your word?"

"No, I—" He gulped. "*S'da.* I shouldn't have told him."

I steeled myself against the crescendo of emotion within me and took a slow breath. "That's right. You shouldn't have."

"I'm sorry. Really."

He looked pathetic standing in the fading light with shame in his eyes. I knew Sedge well enough to imagine how he could easily have abused Dalen into telling him anything he wanted to know.

"It's forgotten," I said.

"I didn't think he'd tell anyone. Honestly."

"Here." I reached into my pocket and pulled out the scroll. "Thanks for letting me have it."

"You're finished with it?"

"I memorized it."

Dalen's mouth dropped a bit as he took the scroll. "That's impressive."

"I'm a poet. Words come easily."

"It's still impressive," he said, tucking the scroll into his pocket. Then he trudged away, and I turned my sight once again to the nearly dark sky.

"Be safe, Nuaga," I whispered.

And my heart longed for her coming.

———————

The wood, kept dry in the wagons during all the rain, ignited quickly, offering a bit of relief to the somber mood in our camp. I added my wet cloak to the dozen already spread out near the blaze. Soon the damp stench of drying soldiers mingled with the scent of stew cooking in large pots at the edge of the bonfire.

I wrinkled my nose. "Anyone could smell us from miles away."

"It'll strike terror in their hearts," Forest said.

"Storm?" Kendel stood beside me, his eyes on mine. "A moment?" His voice cracked.

I nodded and followed him a few steps from the fire, answering Forest's questioning glance with a shrug.

"Dalen says you believe in the dragons."

"I do." I kept my voice even.

"I've never met anyone from outside Ytel who's believed."

"What do you want to ask me, Kendel?"

He drew an audible breath. "Do you believe that Nuaga has returned?"

"Yes."

"Are you . . ." His gaze drifted to his feet, and he kicked at a stone. "Does she speak to you?"

"Show me your amulet."

He hesitated a moment, then pulled the amulet from beneath his breastplate. As he held it, I wrapped my hand around his wrist. I waited three breaths. Four. Faintly, the amulet began to glow orange. Kendel's eyes grew round as the glow became brighter, and I released his wrist.

He dropped the amulet and clapped his hand on my shoulder, gripping me solidly. "You're Onen."

"No." I didn't feel like explaining. "But I've received Nuaga's mark."

Kendel's mouth formed a soundless O as he let his hand drop. "Dragon's blood. Have you?"

"Yes. She wanted me to help the others trust her, but I've failed. How do you teach someone to trust something they fear—or that they don't even believe in?"

"I trust her. And you."

"Thank you, Kendel." It felt good, this show of solidarity. "I wish Jasper would say the same."

"Talk to him."

"I've already tried."

Kendel's gaze was more direct than I'd ever seen it. "Maybe you should try again."

We stood for a few moments in silence. Then we made our way back to the fire, and I settled beside Forest and offered him a subtle expression to let him know I'd tell him later what Kendel had said. When the soup was ready, we lined up for our steaming bowls and settled back around the fire to warm our bellies. The salty broth, laden with turnips, carrots, and dried fish from the stores in the tower, was a feast on my tongue.

Jasper scraped the last bit of soup into his mouth, then wiped his hands on his britches and asked for our attention. My stomach tightened.

"Tomorrow at first light, we'll bury our dead and burn the enemy corpses." He spoke as though they were less than human, and I remembered the hatred with which I'd stabbed the stuffed doll. "The last news I had was that the high king's army was conducting a series of small attacks on Tan Vey's southern flank to distract and slow them down. Ultimately, they want to engage the enemy just south of Ylanda City, to hold them at bay as long as possible. In the days that have passed, though, we have no way of knowing what has happened."

Silence met him. I gazed again into the night sky, my heart thrusting itself against my ribs. If I could scout, I'd be able to meet Nuaga some distance from camp, which would be so much better than the risk of terrifying everyone if they happened to see her.

"Our goal remains to rescue the high king before Tan Vey breaks through our forces and takes the capital," Jasper continued. He swept his gaze across our firelit faces. "The nomads have had to deal with the rain, as we have. That may work to our advantage—but we're still dealing with unknowns. Kendel, Forest, and Rock, I want you to track for a mile in all directions in the morning. Despite the rain, you may find evidence of the route Tan Vey's men followed after they took the outpost—and whether they've brought our men with them."

I was disappointed that Jasper hadn't asked me to track; I was small and fast, and he knew it. The sinking feeling that Nuaga's appearance—and the discovery that I'd been outside of camp—had affected his ability to trust me crept through my stomach.

"First thing tomorrow morning, I'm going to scout to the north," Jasper said. "I'll be back well after dark—sooner if I can. With the information I've brought, we'll leave first thing the following morning for Ylanda City."

"With due respect, why you, sir?" River asked. "Any of us would be willing to scout for you."

"Because I want to take the responsibility," Jasper said. "And because I'm fastest."

It wasn't true. He was by far the greatest Neshu fighter I'd ever met, with the possible exception of Papa, but I was faster on my feet. And Jasper knew it.

He ended by laying out the night's double watch and suggesting we bank the fire sooner than later. Conversation buzzed low around me, but I was miles from it. I waited until Jasper wasn't talking with anyone else; then I rose and stood beside him.

"Sir."

He looked up. "Yes?"

"A word."

My heart tumbled in all directions as he lit the lamp sitting at his feet and rose. He made a small motion with the lamp for me to follow him outside the fire's light to the wall near the entryway. I walked several paces behind him, my eyes on the back of his head, reminding myself that I had earned my place in this special unit and that Jasper had seen value in me, even if he now had doubts.

"I'd like you to send me to scout," I said.

Jasper's face was a map of hard lines. "I've made it clear why I want to go myself."

"I know," I said. "But I'm smallest and fastest. I want to do this."

"Storm, it's no secret that most of the men in this unit believe you have something to do with that dragon's appearance, no matter how I try to convince them that it was surely some ruse of the enemy."

"What does their belief have to do with my willingness to scout?"

"I'm going. End of discussion."

Anger tightened my words. "Forgive me, but I think you're foolish to go."

"Noted." Jasper's gaze was unwavering, his voice even.

"There's a fine line between strength and stubbornness," I said. "If you choose to cross that line and put your men in jeopardy by risking your life, then let it be said that at least one of us tried to stop you."

His mouth opened as though he had a quick retort, but he didn't say anything. Instead, he let out a long, slow breath. "It's true you're our fastest."

"Thank you."

He hesitated. "You call it stubbornness, but you have no idea what you're talking about." I waited, not daring to speak while he made his decision. "*S'da,*" he finally said. "You can leave before dawn for the farthest point north of the plateau. Get there and back as quickly as you can."

My skin tingled. "Yes, sir."

He placed his lamp in a niche in the wall, then pulled his master copy of the map from a long leather tube and unrolled it. "You've studied this," he said. "Five miles east, across the stretch of Nevora Plateau but before you reach Fingerling Forest, is a ridge overlooking the Plains of Seeking. Ylanda City sits high on a hill, visible from a long distance. From the ridge, Tweezer Pass will sit to your right— there." His finger traced the route. "Our army is hoping to stop them at the pass. If they haven't engaged them yet—or if they've failed—Tan Vey will have moved on toward the capital from there. You'll have an excellent vantage point from the ridge. I need a report of the enemy's progress and the likelihood of a clear path to Ylanda City."

I nodded, my chest swelling with the trust Jasper was placing in me. "I understand."

He handed me the map. "Tell me if you have any questions."

I didn't need to look, but I looked anyway for a moment or two. Then I handed him the map.

"No questions."

"Be careful. We need you, Storm."

It wasn't the first time he'd said it, but this time he looked so uncertain and every bit the young man he was. Not that much older than me.

"Thank you for letting me do this," I said.

He nodded. "Sometimes it's hard to know what's right."

"You're a good leader."

Jasper tightened his lips. "It's my first command. And the only reason I'm here is because my father isn't."

"The men trust you," I said.

He straightened. "I'm sorry. I don't know why I said that."

"It helps to say things."

"You're different, Storm," Jasper said. "You know how to listen. It will serve you well."

If only you knew how different I am. "Thank you, sir."

"You'll need to leave before first light."

"You can count on me."

"I know," Jasper said.

I bowed my head and turned to go.

"Storm." He waited while I turned around to face him. "Thank you."

I nodded and headed back to the fire, determined to surpass Jasper's expectations. Forest met my eye.

"What was that about?" he asked.

"I told him I wanted to scout in the morning," I said.

"You just . . . told him?"

"It took a little convincing."

His jaw tightened, as though words were getting stuck. "How do you *do* that?"

"Do what?"

"Walk up to Jasper and tell him what you want." He lowered his voice. "Is it because . . . ?" He shot a glance at my chest.

I went cold, then hot inside. "Are you kidding?"

"No. I mean—"

"It's clear what you mean." I rose, my throat hot with unspoken anger. "I need to get to sleep."

I walked to our tent, my heart stinging. I didn't know which was worse—Forest being more amazed by my skill after he'd learned I was a girl, or his assumption that Jasper had said yes to me because of my hidden feminine wiles.

When he came into the tent a short while later, I pretended I was asleep.

20

In the tired darkness of predawn, I slipped from my tent. No one but the watchmen was awake—Sedge and River stood at the archway as I prepared for my journey. I had never felt so full of energy and life. It was as though the very heart of T'Gonnen beat within my chest.

Forest and the other trackers were up and preparing for their own missions as I started out, but I didn't bother to wave to him. I tucked the water skin into the inner pocket of my cloak along with the strips of dried meat that were already in there. Drawing my cloak closed against the morning chill, I jogged through the archway and across the clearing to the tree line, which I hugged until it thinned and disappeared. From that point, I was fully exposed, since the land had flattened into farmland, its fields muddy and empty now that the harvest had passed. I skirted along the edges of farms, running quickly to gain as much coverless ground as I could before the sun rose. Already the horizon glowed with a hint of gray.

I'm coming, Nuaga.

Beyond every outcrop or cluster of trees, I expected to see her. Longed to see her.

Yet the miles rolled on and the sun rose, quiet and warm on the right side of my face—and Nuaga was nowhere in sight. The increasing rise and unevenness of the ground tired my legs, and I slowed my pace and sipped from my water skin. The air was cool, but I was sweating beneath my breastplate. As I drew near what I hoped was the apex of my climb, I slowed, taking broader steps and feeling apprehensive. I sank to my knees and crawled the last bit, to keep my profile low against the noon sky.

As I reached the top, the plains spilling before me, my eyes fell on the land below, at the mouth of Tweezer Pass. And my heart shrank.

Stretched before me as far as I could see in both directions, bodies of soldiers lay twisted and morbid where they had fallen. A profound stillness rested over the battlefield, except for, here and there, clusters of carrion birds rising and falling. I pressed my hands over my mouth and stared.

"No," I whispered.

"We could have stopped them, Rain L'nahn."

I turned to see Nuaga beside me, her head lowered, her eyes on the mass of death below us. I knew then that she had tested me—that this unspeakable carnage was something I had to discover on my own.

Horror squeezed my heart, and I had a sudden urge to find someone—anyone—who had survived. I scanned the edge of the cliff until I found a way down that wasn't a sheer drop. Flat on my stomach, I half slid, half backward-crawled my way down the twisting, uneven ridge, dread washing over me in waves. I continued on for at least an hour, not knowing when I'd reached the bottom, until my feet suddenly dangled in open air and I fell the last several feet, landing on my back.

I lay panting for several seconds, grateful I hadn't hurt myself. Then, slowly, I rose and turned around.

The nearest corpse lay not twenty paces away, and the stench of death was heavy in the air. I walked with leaden feet to the edge of the carnage. That's when I saw the broken remains of what must have been a small village, tucked into the hollow at the side of the pass, a dozen or so thatched roofs standing haphazardly or lying on their sides, and everything so trampled that it was barely recognizable as having ever been an organized habitation.

As I stared slack-mouthed, clear shapes took form among the chaos. Leathery bare feet, rotting in the sunlight. A man draped over the back of a broken wagon, his head partially severed. A woman and two children, facedown in the mud, their bodies crushed.

This wasn't like the sudden loss of Cedar and Mandrake in the heat of combat. This was the brutal death of innocent people who would never wake to see another sunrise, their eyes forever staring, forever darkened.

I fell to my knees and retched in the dirt. Afterward, head still bowed, I caught my breath, a slight breeze cooling the sweat that had broken out on the back of my neck. When I looked up, the scene shook me a second time, and I fought a wave of dizziness. I closed my eyes and covered my mouth and nose against the stench that rose with every breath of wind.

"Nuaga," I cried through my hands. "Nuaga, I need you."

In a smattering of seconds, she was there.

"You have not seen death like this before." Her words were gentle—if that were even possible.

"I'm a warrior," I said. "I should be able to look at this and . . . and . . ."

"The warrior who is not moved by death has lost his soul."

Her words lay upon me like a summer blanket. I cupped my eyes with my hands and squinted at the jagged hills in the distance, at the highest point of which stood Ylanda City, our capital. "How far north have they since marched?"

She was silent for many breaths. "They are not marching north."

"The capital is to the north," I said.

"They are not marching to the capital."

I stared. "Why not?"

"Because the high king is not there."

Her words spun inside my head. "But . . . of course he's there. Our mission is to rescue him."

"He is not there, Rain L'nahn. But he still needs to be rescued. Will you ride with me?"

I pulled myself out of my stupor and threaded my fingers through her warm fur. Then I mounted, and she took off across the plain like a streaking arrow. I hugged her close and closed my eyes against the wind. The taste of bile was bitter on my tongue, and I fought the ever-rising horror of what I had seen. I would never be able to wash away the crumpled bodies, the empty faces, the forever-stilled agony of their final breaths.

This was what war looked like. This was what I had signed up for. And in its wake, I wondered—feared—what my own death would be like.

Let it be swift, Great God. And let it be hidden, where no one will see my rotting flesh.

Nuaga sped across open fields and scaled rocky outcroppings as though it were child's play. No horse could have moved so swiftly; no soldier could have kept up. She came to a smooth and sudden stop almost before I realized we'd stopped moving. Sensing that she was waiting for me to dismount, I released my viselike hold and slid from her neck, landing lightly on the ground.

I stood near the edge of a ragged cliff overlooking the sweeping expanse of the Plains of Seeking. The wind was cold on my cheeks, and I squinted into it and gazed at the vista below. A dark mass moved slowly toward the northwest—an army so great I couldn't count them. They marched in even rows, their supply wagons matching their remarkable pace. The wind carried the faint sound of their drums to my ears.

Then I saw, at the back of their formation, several rows of men in different uniforms, chains dipping and swaying between them, wrist to wrist. Ylanda soldiers.

Prisoners.

"Will they—" My voice caught, and I coughed. "Will they truly use them for food?"

"It is likely. When food is scarce, the nomad fighters believe in deriving strength from the flesh of enemy soldiers."

I fought another wave of nausea as I watched the prisoners marching. In my darkest dreams and deepest fears, I had never faced any thought so barbaric.

My voice sounded hollow, like an echo. "Where are they going?"

"To the High King's Hold."

I frowned. "Where's that?"

"Tan Vey and his soldiers know," Nuaga said. "Why doesn't a soldier of the high king's own army know?"

And it struck me. "Jasper knows. He said he would disclose the location once we'd rescued the high king from Ylanda City."

A long sigh—like a hiss—filled my ears. "Too much of the ancient knowledge has been lost."

"And yet the high king himself knew."

"The high king has drunk an elixir distilled from the brain of
T'Gonnen for many years, and the wisdom of the dragons has filled
his dreams. If the beliefs of those in Ytel weren't so disparaged—if
the people of Ylanda had paid attention instead of telling their
children the dragons were a myth—the dragons would already be
awake, and Tan Vey would have no hope of winning the kingdom
and commanding us."

"How far is the hold from here?" I asked.

"For men, a five-day march."

Five days. But Nuaga and I could get there faster.

"Jasper's waiting for my report. I have to fulfill my duty to him
first."

"That is your wish, not mine."

My heart twisted. "Will you wait for me?"

"I will wait."

"And . . . we'll go together?"

"I will take you there," she said, "but you alone must make the
willing sacrifice. You alone must bring your boldness to the sleeping
dragons."

"They're sleeping at the hold," I said, the revelation dawning like
sunrise.

"Yes," Nuaga said. "In catacombs beneath its foundation."

"And after I wake them?"

"I will take my rightful place as their she-king, and I will lead
them into battle. For they will not go forth without me."

I remembered, then, a line from the missing verses of the *Lament*:
Destined to command and lead them—Dragon she-king. So. I would
wake them, and she would lead them.

Nuaga and I were as one.

"And you'll show me where to go?"

"Yes. As long as you swallow the magic of T'Gonnen, you will
hear my voice." A rumble vibrated in her throat, imbued with joy I
could feel in my own breast. "And once the clan has awakened, you

will always hear my voice. All of our voices. And we will serve Ylanda once more."

I swallowed the dryness in my throat. The dragons *wanted* Ylanda to awaken and claim them, even though we'd turned our backs on them. "I don't understand any of this."

"No human has ever understood a dragon's loyalty."

Something larger than life itself welled inside me, and I felt I could take on Tan Vey's entire army single-handedly. "Let's go back."

I swung myself onto Nuaga's neck, and we rode, clan members, dragon-sisters, mighty as the wind, strong as the love of T'Gonnen for his mate.

The sun was heading toward the horizon when Nuaga brought me within a mile of the northern edge of the tree line. I pressed my face to her neck and gave her a squeeze before dismounting.

"I'll come as soon as I can," I whispered.

I walked lightly back to the outpost, my footfalls feeling strange after riding Nuaga. Jasper stood just outside the archway, his hand on the hilt of his sword. When he saw me, he did nothing but stare for what felt like a full minute.

"Storm." He looked me up and down. "Why are you back so soon?"

One thing at a time. "I have news." I watched his face, choosing my words with care. "I came upon the scene of battle. We were utterly destroyed, sir."

Jasper's expression didn't change; he simply waited, his eyebrows furrowed, to see what else I had to say. "And the enemy?"

"They are a huge force. And they've taken prisoners." I gave him a moment before continuing. "The remainder is marching northwest."

Jasper frowned. "Northwest?"

"To the High King's Hold."

For an awkward stretch, Jasper was silent. Then he stepped toward me, glancing over his shoulder into the outpost. My heart thrummed against my chest as he draped his arm around me and drew me away from the archway. When we had gone about thirty paces, he dropped his arm and faced me.

"The High King's Hold is one of the best-kept secrets of the royal

house of Ylanda. Only the royal family, their personal priests, and
those in command positions in the high king's army are aware of it.
To any passerby, it appears only an ancient ruin." He drew closer, his
eyes catching the firelight. "So you're going to tell me right now how
you know about it."

21

I hesitated, the moment too big for quick words. Telling the truth seemed suddenly terrifying.

"I'll ask you again," Jasper said. "How could you know this?"

I took a tremulous breath. "It has to do with dragons, sir."

Jasper jutted his jaw to the side, his mouth a compressed line. Other than that, his face was unreadable.

"You must be hungry," he finally said. "Let's get you some stew, and we'll talk inside where's it safer, s'da?"

I walked with him through the archway, the watchtowers like staring sentinels to either side. The interior of the outpost felt exposed, despite the high walls enclosing it, and I shivered. We approached a small fire that looked as though it had been made from debris from the burned buildings. He fished out the dregs of stew from the cookpot and slopped them into a bowl, which he handed to me. I took the bowl and followed him to his tent.

He held the flap and I ducked inside, cradling my bowl and gathering courage to say the words that needed to be spoken.

"One moment," he said, fumbling in his pocket for a flint.

Seconds later, a small lantern hanging from the cross poles cast its glow. In the flickering light, he looked older. Or perhaps that was the weight of worry on his face.

"You're going to tell me something I don't want to hear," he said.

"I didn't believe in the dragons, either. And then I met one."

He raised an eyebrow. "The morning you were caught outside camp?"

"Before then." I watched him closely, marking the practiced expression of patience on his face.

"Go on."

"You know of *The Lament of Nuaga?*"

"Not really."

"It speaks of the sacrifice of the great dragon T'Gonnen, and of the reawakening of his mate Nuaga." I gauged his response before continuing. "She's awake."

"Awake."

"Yes. She showed me the army and told me about the High King's Hold."

"She showed you . . . how?" His voice was thick with skepticism.

"For whatever reason, she's decided to reveal herself to me." I couldn't tell him about the dragon powder; that would lead to questions I couldn't answer. "I rode her to the—"

"You *rode* her?"

I tightened my hands around the bowl of stew. "Yes. That's how I was able to scout and return so quickly."

Jasper stared, his mouth working. "I can't believe this. Not any of it."

"I wouldn't lie to you."

"No. But perhaps you're lying to yourself. Seeing things that aren't there."

"You saw her. You *all* saw her. But you tried to make yourself believe her appearance was some sort of trick. It wasn't. She was there, and I was with her."

Jasper rubbed his jaw. Slowly. Methodically. "Assuming this is true, why would a dragon seek you out? I'd think it more likely that it would kill you."

"The dragons are loyal to Ylanda," I said. "They mean us no harm." I hesitated, then leaned forward. "I know this is hard to believe. It took me a long time to believe it myself. But I'm asking you to trust me." I sat back.

"What else has this . . . dragon . . . told you?"

"That Tan Vey is right—killing the high king will give him not only the kingdom, but also the service of the dragons. Nuaga doesn't wish to serve the nomads."

"So Tan Vey also knows about the High King's Hold."

"It seems so," I said. "His army is marching to the northwest."

"Perhaps a week away, then."

"It was a five-day march from where I saw them today."

"That will be four, come morning." He hadn't questioned my calculation.

"Sir," I said. "The dragons are sleeping in catacombs beneath the High King's Hold. Let me go with Nuaga to wake them. We can get there faster."

"You're asking me to let you leave your unit to ride a dragon to the hold so you can . . . wake more dragons?"

"Yes."

Jasper shook his head and, for a moment, looked like words failed him. Then he sighed. "You've brought helpful information about Tan Vey's troops. I'm grateful. But I'm not sending you on some . . . dragon's errand."

Desperation welled up. "Please, Commander Jasper. Let me do this."

"You'll travel with your unit to the hold, as planned. If, when we get there, we discover there's a dragon waiting for you . . . I won't stop you."

"There's not enough time," I said. "I can get there faster with Nuaga."

"Yesterday we lost two men," Jasper said. "Those who remain are soldiers in the high king's army, under my command. We're a unit, and no man leaves that unit."

I opened my mouth to speak, but he cut me off.

"No man."

I looked into my bowl. "Understood, sir."

"We'll leave at first light for the High King's Hold," Jasper said. "Please don't speak of this to anyone."

"I won't."

"Thank you, Storm. You've done well."

His expression didn't match the words of praise. I nodded and slipped from the tent, my heart in my feet. There were no tears as I made my way to the fire with my bowl of stew, though—only Jasper's words, tumbling through my brain over and over.

No man leaves that unit. No man.
I wasn't a man.

———————

Forest and the other trackers still hadn't returned when I dragged myself into my tent several hours later. Darkness had barely fallen, but my body begged for sleep. I'd requested third watch, which would not only ensure that I'd be awakened three hours before dawn but also give me the perfect opportunity to slip away.

In the silence of the tent, visions of the battlefield crept into my brain, raw and unrelenting. Dead, staring faces . . . trampled bodies . . . the sickening scent of rotting flesh.

I rolled onto my side and sobbed out the pain of the last two days. Cedar and Mandrake, the battlefield of corpses, the dead children in the mud. I wept until my throat ached and snot ran into my mouth. When I had nothing left, I wiped my face on my blanket and hiccuped my way to sleep.

Some time later, I awoke to the sound of Forest taking off his boots. I lay still, not wanting him to know he'd disturbed me. But he leaned over in the darkness, his face near mine, his voice a whisper.

"Storm?"

"I'm awake." My face felt sticky.

"I wanted to say I'm sorry. For what I said."

"All you see is a girl. Like nothing else could possibly be true about me."

"That's not it." His voice was gravelly. "I just wonder why I'm here sometimes. I feel like an imposter. And when Jasper let you do exactly what you asked . . . I don't know. I was jealous."

Something like satisfaction settled in my belly. "You're not an imposter. And I forgive you."

"I was worried about you all day."

My breath stilled. "You were worried?"

"Well, yes." He moved away, and in a few seconds I heard him fussing with his blankets. "What did you find? Anything?"

I hesitated. "I saw the battlefield. Thousands of dead soldiers and a small village in ruins."

"Was there any sign of Tan Vey's army?"

"Yes. A huge force." I rolled onto my back and folded my arms beneath my head. "They took prisoners, too. A hundred or two of our men."

For a few moments, Forest lay in heavy silence. "What's Jasper going to do?"

"I don't know. I gave him some information that I apparently wasn't supposed to have, and he . . . I'm not supposed to talk about it."

"You know I'd never tell anyone anything you said, don't you?" Forest said.

"I know that." And I did.

"Do you have feelings for him?"

My heart faltered. "Why do you say that?"

I heard Forest settle himself onto the ground and pull his blanket up. "I see the way you look at him."

"I don't look at him any certain way."

"Yes, you do," Forest said. "Probably he can't see it because he's not expecting it. He doesn't know you're—anyway. Be careful with that."

My mouth was dry as dust. "It's not like that, Forest. I admire him and I want to exceed his expectations of me. That's all you see." My breath felt shallow. "I'm not here to give my heart to anyone. I'm here to fight for the high king."

"I know why you're here," Forest said. "I'm only telling you to be careful."

His voice was gentler than I'd heard it. Tender. Confusion washed over me, and I was overwhelmed with a desire to tell him how much more his esteem meant than Jasper's. But I brushed it away and forced my next words to sound casual and unaffected.

"If he knew what I really was, he'd have me arrested."

"There's no one to arrest you out here."

"Then he'd kill me himself," I said. "I'm not stupid."

My words must have come out more harshly than I'd intended, because Forest let out a long, slow breath and went silent. I started to think he had fallen asleep.

"I shouldn't have said anything." His words fell like stones.

I lay for a while, my heart aching dully. Waves of longing gave way to the piercing knowledge that I had hurt Forest somehow, which sent a sinking feeling to my stomach. I kept listening for the low, even breathing that meant he was asleep, but it never came.

"Did you find anything today?" I said into the silence.

Forest moved; he must have been turning toward me. "Nothing. It was a long day of nothing."

"I'm sorry," I said.

"Sounds like your day was harder than mine."

His kindness broke me. In a rush, I told him the details of my day. It poured out of me in a flood of words and emotion—the broken bodies, the horror of so much death spread out like a grisly sea, riding upon Nuaga's back to spy upon Tan Vey's army, my decision to return to Jasper even though Nuaga wanted to leave immediately. He listened without interruption, without judgment. The longer I spoke, the faster the words tumbled and the greater the trembling inside me. When I'd told him everything, I took a deep breath.

"Thanks for listening."

In the darkness, his fingertips brushed my palm, and he curled his hand around mine. "I'm with you. Whatever happens, *s'da?*"

His touch felt so reassuring—and stole my breath. "Tan Vey's army will reach the hold in four days, which gives us barely enough time to get there first. But the only way to protect the high king at this point is to wake the dragons—and I'm the only one who can do that."

"And you've explained this to Jasper."

"Yes. But he won't release me."

"And you think he's wrong."

"Nuaga and I could get there in a day. I'm sure of it."

"How much powder do you have left?"

I wrinkled my brow. "Plenty, why?"

"If it takes us four days to get there, you'll still be able to talk with her when we arrive, right? It might not be the fastest way, but it does give you time to help Jasper see reason about the dragons."

"True."

Forest was silent for a bit, his thumb stroking my hand and sending shivers up my arm. "You're planning something, aren't you?"

"I might be."

"I won't try to stop you."

I sighed. "It would be better if you didn't know. You've already risked so much, keeping my secret."

"It's nothing. Just . . . be careful."

I nodded in the dark, though he couldn't see me. "I will."

My hand remained in his as he fell asleep, and as drowsiness claimed me, I was comforted by the fact that I'd found, in the midst of so much difficulty, the best friend I'd ever had. And the greatest love I would ever know.

"Storm."

River's voice on the outside of the tent cut through my sleep like a blade. I grabbed my boots and ducked outside, ready to take his post.

"See you at dawn," he whispered, and shuffled to his own tent.

I dressed quickly, grateful for the warm cloak. Coast, who was taking this watch with me, met me at the archway. He nodded, then adjusted his breastplate and leaned against the arch on the opposite side. I was certain he'd never taken me seriously, even after all these weeks. Maybe it was my smooth face. Now that everyone had stopped shaving, his face was swathed in a thick beard that crept around the edges of his jaw.

I'd still beaten him at Neshu, though. Every time.

I stayed at my post until the stars told me nearly three hours had passed. The night was still dark, but the horizon bore a hint of paled black. I took a slow breath to still my racing heart.

"I need to piss," I said.

Coast inclined his head, and I turned from him and made my way along the outside of the stone wall. I followed it to the end of the far tower and turned left as though meaning to relieve myself on the side. When I had gone another twenty paces, I stopped, my ears straining for the sound of footsteps, though I knew Coast wouldn't leave his post.

Not yet, anyway. I wondered how long it would take him to suspect that I wasn't coming back.

Nuaga, I mind-spoke. *I'm here.*

I'm waiting.

I knew she was hidden among the near trees as surely as I knew my own location. Her warmth, her scent, the strength of her legs as they bore her mighty weight—my heart and spirit were imbued with every part of her.

Dragon-sisters. United by the power of T'Gonnen.

I tensed my legs, ready to run.

The faintest crack of a dry twig sent a cold rush up my spine. I froze, pressing my back against the stone and listening.

There. Another sound, faint but unmistakable.

Barely breathing, I drew my dagger, then inched along the wall and around the tower toward the front. As I rounded the curve of the tower, a figure, facing the other way, loomed suddenly before me. I stifled a gasp and stepped back, fear gripping me so hard that, for a moment, I couldn't move.

I held my breath. He hadn't seen me.

If I ran, I might get away unseen. But where there was one enemy soldier, there were others. How many were there? Surely Coast would see them and sound the alarm.

But all was silent.

I took two steps toward the soldier, whose back was still facing me. He wore a hefty breastplate of braided leather with long sleeves of fur covering his arms. A thick coil of braided hair hung down his back.

This wasn't like a Neshu match at all. This was killing, plain and simple.

Seconds passed. My life or his. My men's lives or his.

I thought of stabbing the stuffed doll over and over, raw hatred spilling from me like vomit. I thought of the many times Jasper had drilled into us that our enemies must become faceless. That there was no room for mercy on the battlefield.

This was no battlefield. And yet, this was war.

Great God, forgive me.

With all the strength in me, I grabbed his braids and yanked his head back. Before he had time to yell, I drew my dagger across his neck.

Like slicing a cucumber.

He fell soundlessly at my feet. My blade, dark with his blood, dropped from my hand like a stone, and I staggered back, breaths coming too fast, too shallow.

"Nuaga." It was more like a gasp than a word. "Nuaga, help."

Her voice came, sharp and commanding. *Come to me. Come away from death.*

I shook my head clear and picked up my dagger, wiping it on the grass without looking directly at it. My hand trembled as I closed it around the hilt, holding the blade before me as I crept around the body and peered through the blackness. Sure enough, the dark shapes of enemy soldiers moved silently, taking positions in a wide arc outside the entrance to the outpost.

My heart lurched. They must have killed Coast and were now merely waiting for the light to attack the rest of the men inside. My men. Who had no idea they were surrounded by the enemy.

Rain L'nahn!

I took several steps backward, fear and indecision momentarily weakening me. Then I turned and ran toward the trees, not slowing until I reached the outer edge. I crashed through undergrowth and saplings and came to a stumbling stop at Nuaga's feet.

"Nomads," I said between heaving breaths. "Surrounding the outpost."

"There is nothing more you could have done," Nuaga said.

"I have to warn them."

Nuaga cocked her head. "You have fulfilled your duty to your commander. Your duty to Kingdom Ylanda looms larger."

I balled my hands into fists. Was *this* the sacrifice I would have to make? Knowing that Jasper and the others would face certain death at the hands of an unknown number of soldiers I might have warned them about? Letting myself believe that their loss would serve the greater good?

T'Gonnen hadn't sacrificed others. He'd sacrificed himself.

"I can't leave them, Nuaga."

She studied me, and understanding deeper than time filled her eyes. "Then I will do as you ask. We are sisters, you and I."

A moment of dread gripped me. Was this reckless? Would I die, and would the chance for Ylanda's salvation die with me?

I swung myself onto Nuaga's neck. I couldn't save the high king without first saving the men marching to his rescue.

Her gait was smooth and rapid, and the air stung my face as I squinted into it. The sky had changed from velvet to downy gray, and I smelled the smoke of the morning fire as we approached from the northern side. Nuaga took a running leap over the wall—higher than I had dreamed she could possibly jump—and landed neatly among the burned-out buildings. My heart squeezed within me as I saw my men milling about, fastening cloaks and warming their hands by the small blaze. River had just led the horses to an open patch of grass to graze.

"We're under attack!" I yelled as Nuaga veered toward our row of tents and came to a stop. "Arm yourselves!"

Heads turned and eyes grew wide as I slid from Nuaga's back and ran toward them. In the same instant, a deafening roar shattered the morning air as a mass of nomad soldiers poured through the archway, swords drawn. For several panicked heartbeats, nothing around me felt real. Forest shouted something, and the tumult of battle erupted around me. I drew my sword and tried to make sense of the chaos. For the second time that morning, terror rooted me to the ground as though I were a tree. An ancient stone. I watched Forest's blanket roll fall and his cloak slide to the ground as he released its clasp, freeing himself to fight.

Cloak. I had to get it off. I couldn't fight like this.

But I still couldn't move.

Rain.

Someone screamed, and the clash of metal against metal brought me to my senses. I was reaching for the clasp of my cloak when one of the nomads pushed through the fighting, coming right at me. I drew my sword a second too late, then twisted to my left to avoid the blade that swiped so close to my side I felt it graze my ear. In an instant, Forest cut in front of me and sliced his blade beneath the soldier's arm. I kicked the soldier in the neck as he swung around to attack Forest. He fell backward, and Forest plunged his sword into the man's throat.

The earth tilted and spun. Faces and bodies blurred before me, and I couldn't tell friend from foe. It was a maelstrom of color and movement and terror, and I couldn't find my bearings.

There were too many enemy soldiers. Too many.

I tightened my grip on my sword.

Lead them, Rain.

In a movement so swift and powerful it took my breath away, Nuaga swept in, disrupting the battle and trampling whatever lay in her path. Then she raised her head to the sky and bellowed. It was like no sound I had ever heard—like thunder and storm and the cry of a man in distress. The horses screamed and ran free.

"Run!" I shouted to Dalen and River. "Toward the back of the outpost!"

Frantically, I looked for others. Already enemy soldiers were dropping their swords and scrambling to get out of Nuaga's way, but many were still fighting. Nuaga opened her mouth and breathed on the campfire; it erupted into an enormous tongue of flame that licked heavenward and ignited the rotted timbers of the tower roofs, even as arrows pierced her neck and back. Many nomads fell screaming, their bodies aflame.

"Run!" I yelled to Briar.

I turned to see Sedge already running, and Kendel, too, though he limped. He stumbled to his knees as Dalen and Flint came up on either side of him, pulling him up and half-dragging him between them. Forest called my name as he ran, looking over his shoulder and slowing down when he saw that I wasn't running, too.

Because I had just seen Jasper fall near the edge of the flames.

"Storm!" Forest called again as Nuaga sent out a second blast of hot air, this time toward the wooden stable.

Rain! Go!

"Run!" I called to Forest, desperate for him to reach safety. "I'm right behind you!"

I ran toward Jasper instead. Toward the chaos.

Toward death.

Jasper lay on the ground, his sword knocked from his hand, the enemy soldier bearing down as if the fire weren't inches from them. I yelled and sprinted toward them, kicking the blade from the enemy's hand a half-second before it made contact with Jasper. He retrieved the weapon and was on me in a moment, our blades cracking together with such force that I was almost knocked from my feet.

Within several heaved breaths, I could tell that my skill, compared to his, was lacking. In a moment of clarity, I shifted my focus to Neshu and, giving a Great Cry, used my sword to knock his knife arm off course. Then I kicked the sword from his hand and dropped my own.

Undaunted, he drew his dagger from his back at the same time I drew mine. There was no time to center my breathing, no time to assess anything. There was only the choice between my death and his.

He came at me quickly, and I parried just as Jasper rose up with a fierce growl and threw himself onto my attacker. I dove forward as the two landed hard in the dirt, yelling myself hoarse as I came at the enemy soldier's throat with my dagger.

Stuffed soldier.

Living man.

Slicing cucumbers.

My dagger dripping with blood, I turned to Jasper, who was rolling slowly onto his side, his face a grimace of pain.

"Get up!" I yelled.

He tried but fell back.

"Get up!"

I reached my arm around him, tucking myself under his armpit, and pulled him to his feet with a strength I didn't know I had. He staggered, leaning heavily on me, as I made my way toward our escape. The fire's heat made it hard to breathe, and when Jasper stumbled to his knees, I knew we weren't going to make it.

Through the smoke, Nuaga appeared by our side, arrows sprouting from her like branches. She swung her head around and gave Jasper a nudge while I strained to pull him onto her back, which was slick with her blood—I had to pull two arrows out to make room for Jasper. We were barely secure when a nomad soldier yelled and thrust his sword deep into Nuaga's side. She extended her neck and roared with a sound that surely curled mountaintops as she trampled the soldier underfoot. Then, in a flash, she turned and bore us swiftly away.

22

I closed my eyes and held tightly to Jasper, who lay splayed across the base of Nuaga's neck. The sounds of the roaring blaze dimmed, and when Nuaga stopped, I opened my eyes.

Forest and the others stood scattered before the back wall of the outpost. As Nuaga raised her head, they moved quickly out of her way.

The warmth of her neck grew beneath my grasp as she opened her maw and breathed on the stones of the wall. I tightened my grip on Jasper's arm as I watched the stone glow red and melt, until a portion of the wall had tumbled away in a pile of smoking debris. Nuaga stepped back and allowed the others to exit before following them through. She stopped several paces away from the wall.

"Take him," she said.

I slid from her back, then reached up and eased Jasper down. He landed heavily, leaning on Nuaga more than relying on his own legs. The others, except for Kendel, stood in a ragged cluster, staring. River and Sedge. Dalen and Flint. Briar and Forest. Kendel sat with his forehead resting on his bent knees.

Rock was missing.

I swallowed. "This is Nuaga."

Jasper fell heavily to one knee. I went down with him, supporting him with one arm.

"What hurts?" I asked.

"Broken ribs." Jasper's voice was jagged as the edge of a bone.

"Can you walk?"

He looked up, his face dark. "What . . . just happened?"

For a terrifying moment, I believed he was accusing me of something. But then I read utter disbelief and confusion in his eyes.

"You were saved by a dragon, sir."

"We were all saved," Dalen said.

"That dragon almost killed us." Sedge. Paragon of bravery.

"No, she didn't," I said.

Jasper's grip on my shoulder tightened. "The dragon rescued us."

"You didn't feel that hot breath blasting toward you, singeing the hair in your nostrils!" Sedge's words were laced with panic.

"You didn't seem to mind when he used his breath to get us through the wall," Flint said.

"She," I said. "Nuaga is a she-dragon."

If their stares could have become more horrified, they did. I left Jasper's side and moved to Nuaga, where the hilt of the enemy sword protruded from between her front and middle legs. I grabbed it with both hands.

"I have to pull it out," I said softly.

She nodded once. I steeled myself, then withdrew the sword in one steady motion. Nuaga shuddered as it came free, and I stepped back, prepared for a torrent of blood. Only a thick ooze formed at the site of the wound, though, bubbling up slowly and running down her side as though it were honey instead of blood.

I reached for the nearest arrow, embedded low in her neck, but she stepped back.

"Those are nothing," she said.

I looked at the others, who stood staring. Briar actually moved backward.

But not Dalen.

"Nuaga is the mate of T'Gonnen. I know all about her."

At this, Nuaga dipped her head in Dalen's direction. He beamed, his face a mixture of rapture and terror.

"I must go on with her alone," I said to Jasper, "as I told you before."

I saw the struggle on Jasper's face—pain, indecision.

No, Rain.

Nuaga's mind-speak caught me off guard. There was something

in her voice I'd never heard before. Unease crept through me as I turned to face her.

"No?"

I'm hurt and unable to bear you.

"Then we will walk together."

That will accomplish nothing. Stay with your men. See that they escort you safely to the hold. I will meet you there.

Panic stabbed me. *We're supposed to do this together.*

Rain L'nahn. I felt the gentle admonishment in her words. *If I do not allow myself to heal, how can I lead the dragons into battle? You have known the swiftness of dragon healing—your own flesh bears witness. By the time you arrive, I will be well.*

I knew the wisdom of her words, but every inch of bone in my body ached to go with her. *We'll move as fast as we can.*

As will I. And, Rain? She lowered her face, bringing her eyes directly across from mine. *Remember that we are dragon-sisters. You are a she-king in your own right.*

"Why is it staring at him? We should kill it when it's not looking." Sedge's voice was barely audible, but I spun to face him, quick as a Neshu kick.

"One word from me and she will silence you where you stand."

Sedge's mouth hung open, and then it snapped shut. He folded his arms, his expression dark.

I knelt beside Jasper, who was still on his knees. "Nuaga is hurt and unable to bear my weight."

"I never said you could go."

Kendel suddenly slumped over, and I saw for the first time that his right pant leg was soaked with blood. Flint and Dalen rushed to his side, stretching out his legs and slapping his cheek as they called his name.

"Dragon's teeth, he's lost a lot of blood," Flint said.

"Don't worry about me." Kendel's words were fuzzy. Weak.

"We can stop the bleeding," Dalen said.

But Kendel's face was pale, and he didn't respond. I stared helplessly as Dalen tore at Kendel's pants in a frantic effort to expose the lethal groin wound.

"How can I tie it off?" Dalen sounded frantic. "It's up too high. Someone help me."

But Flint laid a hand on his shoulder. "It's too late, Dalen. He's already bled too much."

"It's not too late," Dalen said, his voice cracking. "Kendel. Kendel, stay with me."

But Kendel didn't stay. He breathed twice more, then stilled, his eyes fixed on unseen eternity. Dalen dropped his head onto Kendel's chest. I pressed my hand to my mouth, my heart railing against this fresh loss.

No.

Not Kendel. Not Rock.

Not anyone else. Please, Great God.

Nuaga nudged me with her snout. *I must go.*

I nodded, unable to speak in the wake of fresh grief. Nuaga circled soundlessly away from us, respectful of our moment of loss.

Let the others know that I will guide you as my healing allows, she said as she departed.

I watched her go, and my heart yearned to be with her. Then I looked again at Kendel. Briar had stretched his lifeless arms out, palms up toward the Great God, and was closing Kendel's eyes with his thumb. Dalen stood several paces away with his back to us. I looked through the hole in the wall to the smoke rising from our recent battle. Somewhere among the fallen lay Rock, whose melodies had soothed me many nights by the fire.

I sucked in cold air and tried to breathe out the weight of grief. But it had become a part of me, and all I could do was push through it.

I returned my attention to Jasper, who breathed heavily through his teeth. Quietly, Forest knelt at his other side and helped support him.

"What did she say?" Jasper asked.

"That she'll meet me at the hold," I said. "And to let you know that her voice will guide me."

"We need to move," Jasper said to everyone. He struggled to rise, and Forest and I helped him.

"Move where?" Sedge said. "For all we know, there are more soldiers out there."

"Up." Jasper gestured with his head. "We'll skirt the base of the knoll and head northwest."

Forest and I helped Jasper to his feet. I started to walk with him, but he pulled his arm from around my shoulders and straightened, the effort apparent on his face. "I'm fine."

He wasn't, but I nodded and continued on with Forest. I couldn't bear to look at Kendel's body as we passed it.

It took us about ten minutes to reach the base of the knoll. From there, the ground began to rise steeply, and we stumbled and staggered to the edge of a precipice and looked down.

Jasper stood tall, his knife arm cradling his torso. His gaze swept the rolling plain below, across which I had scouted just yesterday.

"This dragon. Nuaga," he said.

"Yes."

"She wants you to . . . wake more dragons." His voice was tight—whether with pain or frustration, I couldn't tell. Probably both.

"Yes."

"Did you see the fear in those men's eyes?" Jasper's voice had lowered to a sharp hiss. "What bond do you have with that thing? What unspeakable magic do you possess that would enable you to . . . to communicate with a monster like that?"

I stared at him and breathed, afraid that if I let my words out too soon, they would ignite and burn him where he stood. Finally I dared to speak.

"Nuaga pursued me for reasons of her own." I couldn't tell him anything more.

"And you feel confident that she means you no harm?"

"I do. She has never brought me harm."

"And she won't bring us harm, either?"

"No. She won't."

Jasper was silent for bit. "You said you can communicate with her. Can she at least let us know if there is danger ahead?"

"She will do that for us."

Jasper let out a sigh, long and slow. "I've watched you grow into a formidable warrior. I don't pretend to understand any of this. But . . . I'm ready to listen."

My heart danced. "Are you?"

"If you say the dragon speaks to you, I believe you," Jasper said. "And for reasons unknown, you seem to trust it."

I wanted to tell him I'd received Nuaga's mark—that I was part of the clan of dragons and trusted her as I trusted my own papa. But the mark lay concealed beneath bindings I couldn't let Jasper see.

"I trust her with my life," I said. "And I believe her heart is for Ylanda and our high king."

Jasper looked at me with such intensity that I feared he had, perhaps, decided I was insane. But he nodded and said, "I believe you." Slowly, he turned around and looked at the others for what felt like a very long time.

I held my breath.

"We'll make with haste northwest, to the High King's Hold," he finally said, "an ancient site unknown to you."

"I thought we were going to rescue the high king from Ylanda City," River said.

"He's not there." Jasper's gaze flicked to me for half a heartbeat.

"Why?" Sedge asked.

"Because he chose to seek refuge at the hold instead." Jasper's tone was firm. "Our goal is to arrive before Tan Vey's army, and to deliver Storm safely to the dragon. If there's any danger ahead, the dragon will let us know. If for any reason Storm is unable to accomplish his task, the rest of us will remove the high king from the hold as we trained to do."

"And then what? Take down an entire army?" The scorn in Sedge's voice was unmistakable.

"Our mission has always been to rescue the high king," Jasper said, "or die trying."

"What is this . . . dragon task?" Flint asked.

Jasper looked as though he were tasting the words before he spoke them. "Storm is going to wake the dragons."

"Wake more dragons?" Sedge sounded incredulous. "Are you serious?"

"Regardless of what each of us believes, it's Tan Vey's belief that killing the high king and his family will give him not only the kingdom but also the allegiance of the dragons as well. The dragon has proved she means us no harm, and if there's any chance that these dragons will help us, we're foolish not to try."

Sedge looked like he wanted to argue, but he clamped his mouth shut and turned away from Jasper.

"We'll discuss details once we've reached the hold," Jasper said. "We need to move out."

"The way is longer if we continue on high ground," River said.

"We are few," I said. "We can move fast." I glanced at Jasper's arm encircling his ribs, knowing well that he would not be able to move fast.

Jasper drew back his shoulders. "Let's go."

A slight hesitation among the men made me fear dissension. But then, one by one, they started moving quickly up the path. Forest gave me an encouraging nod, and I set off with the rest, satisfied with Jasper's trust in me.

For hours, we scrambled up inclines and slid down narrow passages and half-jogged, half-staggered across long stretches of open ground, the dark trees of Fingerling Forest always drawing nearer. By midafternoon, it was clear that Jasper was flagging, our pace hampered by his inability to move as quickly as the rest of us. No one approached him or dared to suggest that we slow down. His face was twisted in a grim expression that spoke of unabated pain.

Finally he stumbled to his knees, then sank the rest of the way to the ground, his head bowed.

I called to those ahead of us to stop and ran to Jasper's side.

"Lie down. We can rest here," I said softly.

He shook his head. "We may be pursued."

"Just for a short while," I said.

He nodded, and his head sank lower. I rose and gestured for Forest to come close. I didn't want to risk making it sound like I was giving orders.

"He's in a lot of pain," I said quietly. "He needs to rest a bit, but we also need to make sure we find a source of water, and perhaps some herbs or roots that will help ease his pain."

Forest turned to the others. "Jasper needs rest. We'll take a break here." Then he turned to me. "Will you help me find some rag root?"

I smiled. "I knew you'd know what to look for."

We left the others and ducked into the trees that had been gradually thickening around us. Most of the leaves had dropped, and there wasn't much green growing beneath the trees, other than a tangle of nearly dead undergrowth and late falling-season brush gone to seed.

"How did you end up on the back of a dragon?" he asked as soon as we'd covered some distance.

"I left my post at the archway."

He stopped and stared at me. "That was your plan?"

"Nuaga was waiting for me. Jasper wouldn't listen, and I knew I had to do it on my own."

"And you saw the soldiers and came back to warn us?"

"Yes." I hesitated. "I murdered one."

Forest frowned. "Murdered?"

"He never knew I was behind him. If he'd discovered me, I wouldn't have been able to bring Nuaga to rescue you."

Forest was quiet for a bit. "When we get to the hold, will Nuaga keep you safe?"

"She hasn't said so."

"Because if you're planning on being some sort of martyr . . ."

I started walking. "I have to wake the dragons, Forest. No matter what."

He fell into step beside me. Moments later, when a dead branch caught him in the face, he pulled it free and threw it at a tree with such force that it broke.

I stared at him, but he continued to push into a thick cluster of trees as though nothing had happened.

"Let's find that rag root," he said.

"What does it look like?"

"It's actually not a root at all," Forest said. "It's a lichen. Look on the tree trunks, close to the bottom. It's usually a reddish-brown color, but it turns gray in the winter."

"So, somewhere in the middle of those two colors?"

"Probably."

We searched in silence for a few minutes. I found some lichen, but Forest said it wasn't rag root. Minutes later, he called out with a note of triumph.

"I found some," he said. "Come look at it. We'll need more than this."

I joined him at the base of a knobby tree, and he pointed out the ruffled, shelflike growth near the bottom. "It's more gray than red, but it still has a hint of color. So this is what you need to look for."

I marveled as I watched him delicately cut the rag root from the tree with the tip of his dagger. "How do you know so much about these things?"

"It's what I love best." The wistfulness in his voice grew an edge that sounded bitter. "I've always wanted to be a healer, but my father wouldn't hear of it." He reached for the small leather bag at his side and tipped the rag root into it.

"Why not?"

"Not good enough for an only son," Forest said. "He wants me to be a grandmaster."

"Do you want that?"

"No." He smiled wryly. "You and Jasper are the only ones I know who are good enough for that."

"You're an excellent Neshu fighter," I said.

He gestured to the base of the tree. "But I'm better at this."

"You're brilliant." My heart twisted as I chose my next words. "Willow will love this about you."

He didn't answer. Instead, he rose and pointed to a thicker stand of trees. "More trees like this are growing right here."

I followed him, feeling a bit put off. "Did I say something wrong?"

"No." He stepped on a swath of dead brush to help me walk over it. "Careful, there are thorns under there."

We lapsed into silence as we ducked around the bases of the trees, looking for more rag root. I glanced at him more than once, but he kept his gaze firmly on the work before him. It was as though he'd forgotten I was there.

I sighed and circled around the next tree, searching for the odd lichens and seeing nothing. I moved to a larger tree and began the process again. Almost immediately, my gaze fell on a thick shelf of what I hoped was rag root.

"I think I've found some." I flipped my cloak off my shoulder and unsheathed my dagger.

"Wait." Forest's footfalls crunched in the underbrush as he made his way toward me. "Let me see."

I pointed. "There."

"That's it," he said. "Well done."

"So, I cut it off at the base?" I asked, dagger poised.

"Yes, as close to the bark as you can," Forest said. "Be careful not to cut into the fleshy part, or it'll ooze and lose potency."

I started to cut, but he placed his hand on mine, stopping me. "Straight down," he said. "Not angled."

But he didn't remove his hand, and I was suddenly breathless. I stared at his hand, our hands, and couldn't find any words.

"Rain." He said my name softly, like an evening breeze. Like the warmth of sunlight splayed across my bed in the early morning.

My real name.

My heart pounded in my teeth, in my temples, and still I stared at his hand. Then, slowly, he curled his fingers around mine, and I let the dagger slide to the ground.

"Look at me. Please."

I looked, and his eyes were blazing with something I had never seen. I held my breath.

"I don't want to marry your sister," he said. "I could never feel for her—for anyone—what I feel for you."

A moment of disbelief shifted to exquisite joy. "Forest . . ."

"We may never make it home," he said. "We may not even live until tomorrow. But even if we do—if we survive and somehow find our way back to our lives and families—I'm promised to your sister. And to break that promise—"

"Would dishonor both of our families," I said. "And destroy my sister."

"Yes."

My expanding soul shrank back, curling in on itself like a leaf succumbing to flames. I couldn't have Forest, and he couldn't have me.

Not now. Not ever.

He laced his fingers through mine, sending hot shivers up my arms and into my stomach. "I don't want to die out here. But when I think about dying, it seems easier than facing a life without you."

"I . . ." Words threatened to strangle me. "Let's not talk about dying."

"No." He drew my hand near and pressed his mouth to it. The warmth of his lips on my skin radiated through me as he closed his eyes, holding my hand captive as though he would never let go. A single tear escaped from beneath one eyelid, tracking down his face like the path of a shooting star.

Everything ached—my heart, my bones, my breath. I felt the loss of him as though he had died before my eyes. As though he and I were one being instead of two, and he had been cut from me, the blood gushing freely from the wound.

He opened his eyes and lowered my hand. "I won't say anything again."

Gently, I extricated my fingers from his and curled my hand around his tear-wet cheek. With my thumb, I wiped away the tear. "*S'da.*"

I wanted time to stop. I wanted to stay there, drowning in his eyes and forever living in a moment when nothing could take him from me. But I let my hand fall away.

"Forest! Storm! Are you alive or dead out there?" It sounded like River, but the distance and the rushing of my pulse in my ears made it hard to be sure.

"We should hurry," I said, still holding his gaze.

Forest nodded, then turned his head in the direction we'd come. "We're fine. Heading back," he called.

I retrieved my dagger and removed the rag root from the tree the way Forest had shown me. I didn't let him see the tears gathering in my eyes and spilling over despite my struggle to keep them in.

"I can't fit the rest into my pouch," he said. "Do you have room in yours?"

"I should." My dragon powder and the last bits of dried meat in my leather bag left half of it still empty.

I reached for the bag at my belt without feeling it. Looking down, I felt again for the bag, but my fingertips brushed only the frayed ends of the leather thongs that had once attached it to my belt.

The bag—and my dragon powder—was gone.

23

No." I pressed my hand flat against my belt where the pouch should've been, like I was stemming a flow of blood.

"What's wrong?"

I forced myself to look at Forest despite my teary eyes. "My pouch is gone."

"Not to worry," Forest said. "I'll carry the rest in my hand and give it—" His jaw dropped. "The powder."

I pressed my fingers to my lips. "What will I do?"

"Surely you won't suddenly start bleeding."

"It's not that," I said. "I won't be able to hear Nuaga."

Forest's brow knitted. "You're sure?"

"Yes. I'm sure."

"We'll figure it out."

I nodded and followed him to the clearing, not at all sure that I'd be able to figure anything out. By the time we reached the others, I had mustered a hard exterior and shoved every conceivable emotion beneath it—fear, desperation, worry. And a broken heart. That, too.

Jasper lay on his back, his breastplate beside him. Someone had taken it off to alleviate the pressure on his ribs, and I wished I had thought of that myself.

Forest opened his fingers and showed the rag root to Jasper. "This will help."

I held Jasper's head while Forest squeezed the thick contents of one of the rag roots beneath Jasper's tongue.

"Let it sit under there and swallow it gradually," Forest said as Jasper righted his head. "It'll ease your pain."

Jasper shuddered. "It's bitter." His words were thick as he attempted to hold his tongue in place.

"I know," Forest said. "That'll fade."

"Two of his lower ribs are broken," Briar said, "and there's a bruise that's causing some swelling. I removed his breastplate to make him more comfortable, but it would help if we could bind him somehow, to keep the broken bones from rubbing together beneath the leather." It was the most words I'd ever heard him speak all together.

Jasper raised a hand. "The night will be cold enough without someone sacrificing his shirt for my comfort. I'll be fine."

"I agree with Briar," Forest said. "If we each took just a portion of—"

"No one is sacrificing for me." Jasper's words seemed stronger; perhaps the rag root was helping already. "Half of you aren't wearing cloaks, and those who are will have to share. I'll be fine."

Several others attempted to argue with him, but he quelled it all with a shake of his head. I stood silent and guilty, knowing that the fabric strips around my own chest would be put to better use around Jasper's. But that wasn't an option.

We pressed on for the rest of the day, veering twice off our chosen path in the hope that we'd find water. Both times we were wrong, and by sunset, the back of my throat burned with thirst. Several of the men had lost their water skins along with their cloaks, and I had shared mine with Forest until it was empty.

The silvery-gray trees of Fingerling Forest stretched before us to the west and north, whispering of shelter and the warmth of a campfire. This "finger," one of the twisting expanses of trees that gave the forest its name, meandered in the same general direction as our march. The wood was ancient—older, it was said, than Ylanda itself. Older, perhaps, than the dragons.

I watched Jasper closely, tensing every time he stumbled, slowing my pace to match his whenever he flagged. Beads of sweat from his brow had long begun to track down the sides of his face, and pain was etched around his eyes and in the tightness of his mouth. I wasn't sure how much longer he would last.

As the light faded and the temperature dropped, we made our way down a narrow embankment that gradually rose toward the edge of the forest. Gleeful shouts from the men ahead of me were the first positive sound I'd heard all day.

"There's a spring trickling from the rock ahead!" Dalen called.

Relief washed over me as I made my way forward, walking purposefully slowly to stay by Jasper's side. Forest walked on his other.

"Give me your skin," I said. "I'll fill it."

I expected him to fight, but instead, he reached for the skin at his side, grimacing and struggling until Forest intervened, taking the skin and handing it to me.

Nuaga. I'd waited all day, to give her time to heal. *Is there any danger on the path before us?*

Your way is clear. Her words felt weak, as though speaking tired her.

I swallowed a wave of despair. *I've lost the dragon powder. I've lost T'Gonnen.*

The silence was long, and I began to fear that our link had already been severed. I took my place in line by the spring, which was a thin stream but better than nothing. Jasper sank to the ground, the first groan escaping his lips that I'd heard all day. When Nuaga spoke again, I jumped.

How?

It must have happened during the battle. My pouch was cut from my belt.

More silence. Then, *In the back, Rain.*

What? My heart pounded. *Nuaga, what?*

"Storm." Forest's hand was on my shoulder. "Are you going to fill the skins?"

I pulled myself back to the moment at hand and stepped toward the spring, holding Jasper's skin, and then my own, beneath it. I tilted my head and opened my mouth beneath the stream of water, swallowing until I was satisfied. The wind was cold on my face where the water had dribbled and splashed, and I shivered.

I moved to give Jasper his water skin, but I'd only taken a few steps when Sedge grabbed it from my hand and blocked me with his arm.

"Give someone else a chance to win favor, *s'da?*"

Anger coursed through me like molten bronze. "We could all be

lying dead at the outpost right now, and all you can think of is winning the commander's favor?"

"I'm not the one walking by his side and filling his water skin,
am I?"

"You're *jealous*?"

"Of a midget? No. I'd just like to show Jasper that he's got other
men he can count on, besides his pet."

His *pet*?

I opened my mouth to say something more, but Forest's hand
closed on my shoulder. "Leave it," he whispered.

I clenched my teeth until they ached, the shadow of Forest's whisper dancing in my ear and sending waves of warmth through me.

"We need to decide where to camp," Sedge said to no one in particular. "Jasper can't make it much farther."

"I'll scout ahead," I said, taking off before anyone had a chance
to answer. A quick jog and a few minutes alone would do me much
good. I didn't know how to tell Jasper that I wouldn't be able to speak
with Nuaga anymore. Or that I had no idea how to find my way to
the sleeping dragons without her.

Fingerling Forest spread out before me like a welcoming hug. It
didn't take me long to find a spot that afforded enough space for us
to sleep beneath the trees while still having room to build a fire. With
not much light left to guide me, I hurried back to the others.

"There's a perfect campsite ahead," I said. "It's not far."

"Let's go." Jasper's voice was rough.

I stuck my mouth once more under the spring, swallowing lovely
mouthfuls of cold water. Then I followed Forest and Sedge, who supported Jasper on either side. He hung heavily on to both of their
shoulders, and their pace was so slow that I feared full darkness would
fall before we'd be able to make camp. I approached them from Forest's side.

"We'll run ahead and start gathering wood," I said.

Jasper barely nodded. River and Flint went off to hunt for whatever they could manage to see, while Dalen, Briar, and I gathered
sticks and branches. By the time Forest and Sedge arrived with Jasper, we had cleared a large circle of earth and begun to heap kindling
in the center.

Jasper groaned as Forest and Sedge eased him onto the ground, and then he lay flat on his back. Briar knelt at his side, palpating gently.

"If I push the bones together, it may hurt less," I heard him say.

I crept forward, horrified to see how white Jasper's face looked in the near-darkness. Behind me, someone kindled the fire, and the feeble light gave Jasper's face a false tinge of color.

"Do it," he said to Briar.

I bit my lip as I watched Briar manipulate the bones beneath Jasper's flesh, prodding them and guiding them so that the broken edges would meet. After a minute or two, he stopped and looked at Jasper.

"How does that feel?"

"Better." But he spoke through clenched teeth.

"Here's some more rag root," Forest said. "This will take the edge off."

"He needs to keep these bones still," Briar said. "If we strip his shirt—"

"He'll have nothing to keep him warm," Forest said. "He threw off his cloak like half the rest of us. What good is it lessening his pain if he dies of exposure?"

I walked away, turning toward the growing blaze and holding my hands to its warmth. And knowing beyond a whisper of doubt that I had to provide Jasper with the bindings he needed.

River and Flint returned with one fat hare and two opossums. I cleaned and gutted the hare because I couldn't bear to look at the opossums. Then I sat with the hare meat speared on a stick, roasting it over the fire, while others took care of the rest of the meat. Jasper sat beside me, looking a bit more comfortable now that the rag root had taken effect.

"Have you heard from Nuaga?" he asked.

I nodded, unspoken words thick in my throat. "Yes. She says the way before us is clear."

"Anything else?"

I couldn't bear to tell him the painful truth—that I would not be able to speak with her and had no idea how to find the sleeping dragons. "No."

"I don't think I can make it," he said softly. "I could bear the pain, but I can't move fast enough. We'll never make it there before Tan Vey's army if I'm dragging us down."

I didn't know what to say. He was right.

"I always thought there was something different about you," Jasper went on. "I've never seen anyone work so hard to overcome obstacles, or fight Neshu with the skill of someone much older." He shifted his weight, grunting a little. "When you first told me about the dragons, I couldn't let myself believe you. I've always thought they were a myth. But I should have set that aside. You have strength and integrity, and I should've known to trust you." He sucked his lips between his teeth and let his gaze fall.

I should have thrilled at his words, secure in the knowledge that he viewed me as his equal. Now all I could think was how I had earned the trust of my commander when, the entire time, I had been living a lie.

"You're a good leader," I said. "I'm honored to be part of this unit."

He shook his head, dismissing my words. "I shouldn't even be here. I should be dead."

I frowned. "Why?"

Jasper seemed to struggle with the words, and his gaze rested somewhere far away. "I was part of the special Neshu unit that died at Stonewall. I should have been there with them, training. But my father and I fought, and he sent me to Grigsbane and went in my place. When he was killed with everyone else, I was given his command post in the training camp. I don't deserve to be here."

His regret was so palpable that my chest ached. "You do deserve it," I said softly. "You've proven yourself a hundred times over."

"Maybe that's what I've been doing all along—trying to prove myself. This unit was my idea. It all falls on me."

"You're a good leader," I repeated. "And the past is . . . past."

He looked at me then, but there was no flicker of hope or relief in his eyes. "At first light, you can leave—you and the others. I'll follow behind at my own pace. You can meet me afterward."

"No! You can't travel by yourself, wounded."

"It's my decision, Storm. I'm holding you back. If you can wake the dragons and end this madness, then I want to give you the best possible chance of succeeding."

My stomach was in a million knots. How would I be able to do this without Nuaga's help?

"I'll do my best," I said.

"I know you will."

"When will you tell the others?"

"In the morning. No need to discourage them tonight." He grimaced. "I need to lie down."

"Let me help you."

"No. I'll bear my own pain."

He eased himself down, his face contorted with the effort to brace himself against the pain. Once he'd stretched onto his back, his chest heaved. I watched as River brought his own blanket—the only one any of us carried—and laid it over Jasper, who didn't protest.

My heart wept for him.

"You're burning that side," Forest said, sitting next to me.

I refocused my attention on the sizzling hare, turning the stick. "Sorry. I'll pay attention."

But my mind was on what I needed to do next.

The meat was greasy and bland without the salt it desperately needed. It was also barely enough to take the edge off our hunger. But the fire was warm, and at least we were alive. Dalen, River, and Forest fashioned a torch and walked back to the spring with our skins, to refill them for the morning. I was relieved when they returned, bearing the filled skins and no bad tidings.

I pulled Dalen aside after taking my skin from Forest. He looked at me questioningly, and I pressed the slip of parchment into his hand.

"This is the rest of the *Lament*," I said.

Dalen, wide-eyed, read the verses. When he'd finished, he looked at me. "Where did you get this?"

"Nuaga took me to the Archives and I copied it. You can keep it."

"I . . . are you sure?" He waited for my nod. "So there was never anyone named Onen."

"No."

"I can't believe these verses were lost for so long."

"Yes." I hesitated. "The dragons are sleeping in catacombs beneath the hold, and Nuaga is going to meet me there."

His eyes were still wide. "Why are you telling me this?"

"Because . . ." My throat tightened. "Kendel told me you didn't think I trusted you. And for a while, I didn't. But you taught me to believe, and I know I have your support."

"You do. And Kendel—" His voice broke. "He supported you, too."

"I know."

Dalen held up the parchment. "Thanks for this."

"Thank *you,* Dalen. For everything you've taught me."

"Don't say it that way," Dalen said. "You make it sound like you don't expect to live through whatever comes next."

I smiled and clapped him on the shoulder and didn't tell him I expected to die.

We returned to the fire. Jasper caught my eye, gave me a slight nod, and then requested everyone's attention.

"We all have different ideas about this dragon. I've decided to place my trust in Storm and his relationship with Nuaga. I'm asking each of you, right now, to place your trust in Storm, too. And if you're unable to do that, then place it in me, because I'm the one making this decision."

No one said anything, but I could feel the underlying tension. Our group was split—those who trusted Nuaga and me, and those who didn't.

"I'm placing Storm's safety on the same level as the high king's. See that no one stops him from waking the dragons."

Unspoken words crackled around the fire. Respect for Jasper was surely the one thing keeping some of the men from questioning me or expressing their dismay.

"I'm with Storm." Dalen's words were more confident than I'd ever heard them. "I've believed all my life that the dragons would return. I trust them."

"I trust them, too." Forest, quiet and strong.

"You all saw how the dragon came to our rescue this morning," Jasper said. "There's no denying that her loyalty is with the high king and not Tan Vey. Bear that in mind as you wrestle with your fears."

He offered no further explanation, and aside from a few wary glances, I received no challenge from the others—not even Sedge. My heart was heavy, though. Without the dragon powder, my chance of succeeding was greatly diminished. I had counted on Nuaga's guidance. What if I were unable to find the catacombs on my own?

Dear Great God, what then?

The wind at our backs grew colder, and soon those of us who still wore cloaks were sharing with those who'd dropped theirs during battle. Forest and I sat shoulder to shoulder by the fire, my cloak wrapped as far as it would go around both of us, which was barely. I felt every breath he took, and when he spoke, his voice buzzed through my bones.

I wouldn't let myself make eye contact with him. I was certain that if anyone caught even a glimpse of our looking at each other, they would know.

Flint was in the middle of a long, bawdy tale that embarrassed me. It was as good a time as any for me to excuse myself under the pretext of needing to pee. I counted the faces around the fire—seven. Then I slid from beneath the cloak and tucked it fully around Forest.

"I'll be back," I said.

The darkness was thick behind the trees. I found a wide trunk far back enough to make me feel covered, but not so far as to swallow me in complete blackness. I stood still, barely breathing, listening for the sound of someone else making his way into the woods. All was quiet, except the thin whistle of wind through nearly bare branches.

I removed my breastplate and laid it gently at the base of the tree. Then, shivering, I untucked my shirt, revolted by the smell of my filthy body. I fumbled with the knot of my bindings. My fingers were cold and stiff, but soon I was able to loosen it, and, working quickly, I unwrapped the strips of cloth. They hadn't been removed for so long that when my fingertips brushed against my bare flesh, it felt strange and tingly.

That, and I smelled even worse now, as though the bindings had trapped my unwashed stench and held it captive until this moment. I wished I could offer Jasper something clean, but we were all of us disgusting, so it didn't matter. Defying the cold, I lifted my shirt and held it beneath my chin to keep it out of the way as I unwrapped the last bit, which was scrunched up in my armpits. While I worked, I silently rehearsed my story about having worn an extra shirt for warmth, and how I'd been embarrassed to admit it.

The last length of fabric fell free as I heard a crunch and looked up to see the light of a small flame held aloft. Sedge's shadowed face loomed behind it, his mouth a dark cavern of surprise.

"Great God." He grabbed me by the neck and slammed me against the tree.

24

Sedge's fingers tightened around my throat, his eyes boring into my breasts as though he couldn't look away. When he finally looked at me, his words were thick.

"I knew there was something about you," he said. "Something . . . wrong."

I swallowed with difficulty. "Nothing's *wrong*."

His shocked stare formed itself into a leer. "You've kept these under wraps all this time? But it wasn't much effort, was it? They're no more than a handful."

"Stop." My voice was ragged beneath the pressure of Sedge's hand. "I only wanted to give the bindings to Jasper."

"Is that so?" He moved his face closer; I could smell the greasy opossum on his breath. "And you think that makes everything better, midget? You're a woman. Not even that—you're a *girl*. You deserve the first dagger that pierces your heart."

I was shivering violently, from the cold and from the horror of being so utterly exposed. One word to Jasper would condemn me. Unless Sedge decided to take justice into his own hands.

"Aren't you going to beg me to keep your secret?" he purred.

"No."

He loosened his hold on my neck—not completely, but enough that I could breathe. Enough that I thought I might have a chance to fight him off. It wouldn't keep my secret, but at least I would have the dignity of confessing to Jasper myself.

He dropped the small torch he'd fashioned from a stick and some animal fat, crushing it to darkness beneath his boot. Then he stepped forward, pressing into me, his rough hand cupping my breast, kneading it like dough. "My silence is easy to buy. Give me what I want—whenever I want it—and I keep your secret, *s'da*?"

Revulsion washed through me, and I wanted to claw and kick myself free from his lascivious touch. But I stayed frozen, waiting for the right moment.

"Well, midget?"

He pressed closer, wedging me between the tree and his unyielding body. His other hand found my other breast; I pushed my back into the tree as hard as I could in an effort to move away from his grasp, the rough stroke of his thumbs. He moved in for a kiss, his mouth open. I turned my face.

"You don't like the unshaven face, little bitch? We don't have to k—" He stopped as though someone had plugged his throat with tar. Then, suddenly, he grabbed my face in his hand, squeezing my cheeks together and forcing my chin to tilt up, toward his face. "Little bitch," he whispered.

And I remembered when he'd called me that once before.

"It was you," he said, his grasp tightening. "In the shop. It was *you.*"

I couldn't respond; he was squeezing my face too tightly. He released me, shoving my head into the tree.

"Talking to dragons, dressing like a man—what were you buying that day?"

"I could ask you the same."

He backhanded my cheek so hard that I saw stars. "You'll ask me *nothing.* You disgraced me in front of that old hag."

I tasted blood. My pulse raged in my ears, making me feel almost dizzy. But by releasing me, Sedge had given me the chance I'd waited for. He came at me again, reaching for my neck. In one swift motion, I moved from second to third stance and kicked him in the chest. He staggered back just enough to lose his bearings, and I leaped forward and kicked him in the throat, giving a Great Cry so long and loud that it shredded my voice.

He fell, gasping and gagging, and I assumed the second stance again, knife arm ready. Flickering torchlight reached through the trees, and the heavy crunch of boots moved rapidly closer.

"What happened?" someone shouted.

I looked up, breathing rapidly. Forest's face was the first one I saw, his expression confused and fearful.

"Sedge attacked me." My voice was ragged.

"Why?" River asked, coming up swiftly behind Forest, sword in his hand.

I looked at Sedge, who was on all fours, still coughing. Then I scanned the faces in the flickering torchlight—River, Dalen, Briar. Forest.

I opened my mouth and closed it again.

Sedge made a sound like he was trying to talk. I brought my foot down hard on his shoulder, causing him to fall flat.

I would not allow him to steal my moment.

"Because he discovered my secret." My pulse rammed against my temples, and a fierce trembling seized me.

They all waited, staring. Uncertain. Forest was stone-still, an unbreathing statue.

"I'm a girl."

Someone snorted. Forest remained frozen.

"Is this a joke?" River's words were strained.

I closed my eyes, unable to bear Forest's reaction. In one swift motion, I grabbed the hem of my shirt and lifted it high, exposing my breasts—my girlhood, my secret—to everyone standing there. When I was sure they had all seen clearly, I let the fabric fall, my face hot.

Utter silence fell around me.

Sedge grabbed my arm. "The bitch attacked me when I threatened to tell everyone."

"He's lying! He tried to make me buy his silence by—"

Sedge twisted my arm behind my back, the pain stealing my words. "Your accusations mean nothing. You're a *walking lie*."

Everyone else was staring at me with different degrees of horror. Everyone except Forest, whose expression bore more pain than I wanted to see.

I looked away.

Sedge tightened his grasp. "Jasper has lost his pet." He pulled me along through the trees, the others following quietly. My shirt hung loose and flapping in the cold wind, and I shivered so violently that I began to ache. Sedge didn't release me until we reached Jasper, who lay on his back near the fire. He tossed me forward so roughly that I stumbled to my knees before hastening back to my feet, hugging myself against the cold.

Jasper rose slowly . . . so slowly. I saw the effort it took, the grim lines of pain on his face. The others circled us, silent, watchful. Forest stood closest, his jaw tight.

"You want to know what I found hiding in the woods, Jasper?" Sedge moved to my side. "This."

He tried to yank my shirt up, but I knocked him away. "I'll tell him myself." I raised my chin and met Jasper's eyes. "I lied to you, Commander. I'm sorry."

It was ten thousand times harder to stand in the light of the fire and expose myself to him. If I hesitated, Sedge would lunge for me again. So I lifted my shirt quickly and let it fall.

Jasper stared, his face so taut I swore I saw it twitching in the firelight. No one moved; no one spoke. Finally, he rubbed the palm of his hand across his mouth, pressing it there for a few moments before letting it drop. When he spoke, his words were ice.

"Who are you?"

I forced myself to look him in the eye. "Rain L'nahn."

"Rain."

"It all makes sense, doesn't it?" Sedge's words were ugly with anger. "The way she never took her shirt off—her secret ways—"

"Hold your tongue, soldier." Never had I heard such barely contained rage in Jasper's voice. His eyes still piercing mine, he took a step toward me. "Explain yourself."

It was more than I had hoped for, but his unyielding expression told me that my words would not sway his heart, no matter what I said. "Storm is my twin brother. I took his place because he's a simpleton and would never have survived." I swallowed hard. "My father was ready to take his place. I couldn't let him die and leave our family destitute."

"Did it not occur to you, *Rain,* that, by disobeying the high king's law and impersonating a man, you would bring them only dishonor?"

My teeth chattered in the cold. "I . . . f-figured I would die on the battlefield. My father would only have known that I f-fought for the high king and brought my family honor."

Jasper's steps toward me were painful to watch. His effort to portray strength he didn't have made him look wildly determined. He stopped inches from me, so that I had to tilt my head back to maintain eye contact. Perhaps he expected me to lower my eyes, but I didn't. I'd met his gaze for weeks as a soldier—I would continue to meet it now.

"I believed in you," he said in a thin voice meant only for my ears. "I gave you opportunities to excel. I let you drag me onto the back of a dragon. And I've told my men to lead you safely to meet a dragon for a mission I still don't understand." Several tight breaths escaped his lips, as though he were reining in a torrent of emotion. "I trusted you."

Everything I had admired about Jasper faded like mist. Had he truly devalued everything I'd done simply because I wasn't a man? "You can still trust me."

"No," he said. "I can't." He turned and walked toward the fire. When he reached it, he faced me again and raised his voice. "What you've done is punishable by death."

The cold that had already set my body to shivering turned to ice in my veins. I hugged myself against the wind, aware of the shuffling around me, the stares of my fellow soldiers, who surely felt as betrayed as Jasper.

A more pronounced movement caught my eye, and I looked to see Forest stepping forward. Panic ripped through me, and as soon as he glanced at me, I shook my head—a tight, subtle movement that begged him not to speak.

Begged him not to implicate himself in my guilt.

"Sir," he said. "We have no army. No tribunal. And our only hope is for Storm to—"

"*Rain.*" Jasper's voice was a growl. "And we're not placing our hope in a girl."

Forest looked like he was going to say more, but a flick of his eyes toward me gave me another opportunity to beg him silently not to speak. He compressed his lips and lowered his gaze.

The injustice of Jasper's words raked my insides, and I didn't try to hide the anger from my voice. "I'm the same person I was five minutes ago. The same soldier who trained with the others and found her strength and saved your life by dragging you onto a dragon's back. Am I suddenly nothing?"

My sharp, quick breaths were the only sound aside from the snapping of the fire. Jasper was stone-still, his face unreadable.

He looked at no one in particular. "Bind her." Then he turned his back toward me and lowered himself to the ground in front of the campfire.

At first, nobody moved. Then Sedge said, "I'll do it," and disappeared into the trees.

No one else seemed quite sure what to do. Flint and Briar simply walked to the fire and sat down to warm themselves. River and Dalen stood awkwardly together, not speaking, not really looking at me. Dalen's face, especially, reflected deep dismay. Nobody reacted further.

Except Forest, who walked purposefully toward me, removing my cloak from his shoulders as he walked. He draped the cloak over me and fastened it.

"I'm sorry," he said, forming his words so softly that the wind nearly carried them away.

"Say nothing," I whispered.

He gestured vaguely to my chest. "Why . . . ?"

"So Jasper could have the bindings for his ribs."

He gazed at me with tenderness and pain and feelings I had no words for. Then he gave the slightest nod and turned away. I pulled the cloak tightly around myself, burrowing into its warmth. When I looked up, River and Dalen were both watching me. I lifted my chin, determined not to feel shame. To my surprise, each of them offered a slight bow before turning to face the fire.

A flicker of hope warmed my heart. Perhaps Forest wasn't the only one who didn't see me as something less.

Sedge returned moments later, my dirty strips of cloth piled in his hands. He removed my sword and grabbed my arm more roughly than he needed to. I responded instinctively by assuming a defensive stance and raising my knife arm to knock loose his grasp. I stopped myself as quickly as I'd started, but he tightened his grip and pulled me to him.

"Not this time, bitch. Your game is over."

He yanked my arm behind my back, and I willingly offered the other one, to avoid more conflict. He knotted my wrists together with a length of the cloth, ripping it off and tossing the remainder of the fabric beside me. Then he walked to the edge of the fire and started a low conversation with Flint.

I lowered myself to the ground and bowed my head. The cloak was warm, but I would have liked to be near the fire, to connect with this group that I'd worked so hard to be a valuable part of.

Exposed, my value was lost.

Without a word, Forest retrieved the remaining strips of cloth from my side and approached Jasper, who still sat silently staring at the flames. Forest laid the strips beside him.

"She took them off so you could have them," he said. "I'll bind you, if you'd like."

Jasper looked at the crumpled pile, then returned his gaze to the fire. "No."

Forest stood for a few moments more, waiting, perhaps, for Jasper to say something else. But he didn't, and Forest walked away. I drew my knees up and rested my forehead on them, despair wrapping itself around me like a snake.

Nuaga. I am found out.

I closed my eyes and crawled inside the memory of her voice, listening with an intensity that made my heart patter.

Rain.

It was a mere whisper. Hardly a breath.

Relief rushed through me—the dragon powder hadn't worn off yet.

Sleep.

I didn't know how I could possibly sleep, cast off from the group and away from the fire's warmth. And I didn't know how much longer the remaining magic would be active inside me.

My sigh, long and tremulous, was captured by the wind. "I'll try."

But I had never felt so wide awake.

25

The night grew colder, and everyone huddled near the fire, warming their hands and sharing cloaks—except for Forest, who had none. I didn't dare move nearer to the blaze, though the wind chafed my face and I shivered despite the fur lining of my cloak.

I was a pariah in the dark. Tossed aside because I was a girl.

A low, intense conversation grew among the men. I couldn't quite hear their words, but I was certain they were talking about me. As I surreptitiously scooted a bit closer, River eased Jasper's shirt over his head. Forest took the remaining strips of my binding and began to wrap them around Jasper's torso.

For a brief moment, my heart warmed. But then I caught words that, a few minutes earlier, the wind had carried away.

"There's no place for her here," Jasper said. "I don't even have the words to—ugh!"

"Sorry," Forest muttered. "I need to make it tight enough to keep the bones set."

"I'm with Jasper," Sedge said. "What she's done isn't natural. What kind of girl would tell a lie like that?"

"It's beyond the fact that she lied to us," Jasper said. "She's broken the law and dishonored our high king."

"She also saved your life," Dalen said.

"That's not the point."

"We've lost five men," River said. "Is it worth it to condemn someone else to death?"

"I agree," Dalen said. "We need her."

I almost smiled. Their support meant so much.

"I say toss her into the fire and be done with it," Sedge said.

"Lay a hand on her, and I'll toss you in after her." Forest's voice. Low and menacing, like I'd never heard it before.

I held my breath. Nobody responded right away.

"Why are you so interested in saving her?" Sedge asked. "So you can take a piece of her when everyone's asleep?"

Forest lunged so quickly that Sedge didn't see it coming. He recovered quickly, and within seconds, they were wrestling dangerously close to the fire, with the others shouting and jumping out of the way.

I rose to my knees, desperate to see what was happening. Forest was quick, able to recover his advantage the moment he lost it, but Sedge was strong, overpowering Forest whenever he had a moment's lead. They writhed and clawed like animals, Forest eventually gaining the upper hand and slamming Sedge's head hard to the ground.

Jasper's voice rose above the din. "Stop this. Stop it *now*."

Dalen and River pulled on Forest while Briar and Flint pulled on Sedge, tearing them from each other and standing between them to keep them from reengaging. The commotion dwindled to silence.

"No one touches her," Jasper said. "And no one decides what to do with her except me. She's my responsibility. My liability."

This was too much. "Commander." I rose unsteadily. "I'm *not* your liability. Or anyone else's. I deceived you and you're angry, but don't dehumanize me. Let me prove that my worth is what it has always been. Nothing has changed."

Jasper's words had jagged edges. "*Everything* has changed." He looked away. "You've broken the high king's law, and are therefore in my custody as a thief. You will not speak again unless you're spoken to."

I stood in the cold, stunned by his unwillingness to even consider my words. Then I folded myself onto the ground and was silent—not because I was a girl, but because Jasper was right: I'd pretended to be a boy, which made me a thief. I was at his mercy.

"How do you know she won't call that dragon down on us while we sleep?" Sedge said.

"The dragon saved my life," Jasper said. "Saved all of our lives. Enough of this fighting."

"We can't just leave her here to die," Forest said. He was still breathing heavily.

"I'd already decided to travel behind the rest of you," Jasper said. "I'll stay and guard her until you return."

Silence fell, and I guessed that everyone else was grappling with not wanting to leave Jasper behind, while knowing they had little choice.

"Nobody but Storm can wake the dragons," Dalen said. "We need him. Her."

"How can you know that? *Believe* that?" Flint asked.

"It's in *The Lament of Nuaga*. I can read it to you, if you like." He glanced at Jasper, who gave an almost-imperceptible nod.

One by one, the men sat as Dalen read Nuaga's *Lament* from his scroll. I closed my eyes and let the words wash over me, so familiar now. When he finished, no one spoke.

"There's more," Dalen finally said. "Several verses that I never knew existed, until Storm ran off to the Archives and copied them. And they explain a lot."

"She went where?" Jasper's words were hollow, as though he were resigned to learning about every possible secret I'd kept.

"To the Archives, several miles west of our training camp," Dalen said.

"You knew she was going to run off?" Flint asked.

"No, she told me about it recently."

"Where are those verses?" Jasper asked.

Dalen dug the parchment from his pocket and read.

> "Where is one not loath to answer
> Brave Nuaga?
> Willing sacrifice to offer,
> Selfless, like T'Gonnen.

> "She who knows the pain of parting
> Knows its power.
> Deep beneath the Hold in caverns,
> Waiting to awaken.

"Through the ages, sons from fathers,
All Ylanda
Waits in safety for the Dragons
Once again to join them.

"Breath of Dragon, searing, cleansing,
Necessary.
Bear the mark and bring your boldness
To the sleeping Dragons.

"Call to them with words predestined
Over ages
In the ancient tongue of Dragons—
S'danta lo ylanda.

"If the line of kings is severed
Then the Dragons
Ever will belong to those who
Snuff Ylanda's bloodline.

"Destined to command and lead them—
Dragon she-king,
Through her mark, the bearer's presence
Satisfies the calling.

"Wake, O Dragons! Do not tarry!
Save your people.
Let us usher in the reign of
Loyal, brave Nuaga."

"Killing the high king would sever the royal bloodline," Briar offered.

"How did Tan Vey even know about the hold?" Flint asked.

"The nomads obviously know our history," Jasper said.

Sedge threw something into the fire. "What does any of this have to do with . . . *her*?"

"She's the one who's answered Nuaga," Dalen said.

"Where is one not loath to answer
Brave Nuaga?
Willing sacrifice to offer,
Selfless, like T'Gonnen."

"There it is," Sedge said. "She needs to die."

"Agreed." It was soft, but it sounded like Flint.

"How do we know she's the one, though?" River asked. "Why would a dragon choose her over anyone else?"

"Because she was swallowing a powder every night that had dragon magic in it," Forest said.

A cry tried to escape my throat; I choked it back.

"She told you this?" Jasper said.

"She did."

"What powder? Why?" Jasper.

Forest glanced at me for the briefest instant. "For her own reasons. But I saw her swallowing it every night. And she told me about the dragon's speaking to her weeks ago."

"And you said nothing?"

"What could I say? It wasn't my secret to give away."

Every string of my heart knotted. *Please don't say more. Please don't implicate yourself.*

For a while, no one said anything. Someone threw a stick into the fire; Briar took a swig from his skin. It was Jasper who broke the silence.

"It seems that, if Rain has been swallowing dragon magic, she's the only one who can do this."

"No, she's not." Sedge's voice cut through me like a hot blade. "I can do it."

Muttering broke out, and a disbelieving laugh or two. But Sedge's face remained serious, his eyes locked on Jasper.

"Explain," Jasper said.

Sedge reached into his own pouch and pulled out the small bottle I'd seen once before. "Dragonsweat. I've been using it for at least a year now."

More disbelieving laughter broke out, but Jasper's face was stone. So was Forest's.

"Dragon . . . sweat?"

"That's what the old hag called it," Sedge said. "It's . . . oily. For all I know, that's all it is. Oil."

"What makes you think you can wake dragons with it?" Forest asked.

Sedge shrugged. "I may have had a couple of dreams. I didn't take them seriously."

I stared until the firelight burned my eyes. Sedge had dreamed of Nuaga?

"You've seen this dragon in your dreams?"

"I don't know if it was the same dragon or not. Like I said, I didn't take it seriously. Or maybe it's because I only use a bit of the oil every day, to make it last. Maybe it's not strong enough that way."

"What's the oil for?" Jasper asked.

For the first time since I'd known him, Sedge looked sheepish. "Courage. Strength. Stamina in bed. Things that are important to a man."

I could hardly believe my ears. Sedge, with all his piggishness and posturing, relied on Madam S'dora's oily potion to make him into the man he wanted to be. Which wasn't a very nice sort of man at all.

"What will happen if you use a lot of the oil at once? Or all of it?"

"I don't know. But I'm guessing it might be strong enough for me to wake the dragons—whatever that means."

"It means exactly that," Dalen said. "It's not some sort of euphemism."

"Are you willing to risk it, Sedge?" Jasper asked.

"No!" I cried out without thinking. "Not him!"

Several sets of eyes turned my way, including Forest's. Jasper and Sedge did not acknowledge me.

"I'll do it," Sedge said, as though I hadn't spoken.

"Nuaga hasn't been talking to you, though, has she?" Dalen said. "You can't just show up without understanding—"

"I'll use the oil and she can tell me what to do. If some stupid girl can wake these dragons, I can do it."

"You can leave at first light," Jasper said. "Same plan as before, except you'll be the one to lead the way."

My spirits sagged to the ground and pulled my heart to my feet. Not only had I been bound and outcast, I had been replaced by Sedge.

"What about the girl?" Briar's voice.

Jasper gave me a long, dispassionate look before turning his face toward the others. "If we survive this, I'll deal with her myself."

His words were final. Everyone else must've thought so, too, because no further conversation ensued. Awkwardly, I eased myself onto my side and tried to get comfortable. It was nearly impossible, though, with my hands tied behind my back. By the time I found a position that didn't make my arm fall asleep, my cloak had shifted off my exposed shoulder, leaving me shivering again.

If only I could find a way to unknot my bound hands. I didn't shrink from the thought of running off on my own, but it would be stupid to try with my hands tied behind my back. For a while, I tried twisting and pulling, hoping that somehow the fabric would stretch or tear. I tried until I was panting with the effort, but Sedge had done his work well; the knotted strips didn't budge.

I gave up. Wearily, I determined I'd try once more in the morning to make Jasper see reason, though my hope of success was small.

I closed my eyes and despaired of ever falling asleep.

Rain.

Nuaga's voice was clear as a spring-fed brook and sang through my dream like music. I stood on a windswept plain, and Nuaga's words danced around me, echoing through clouds and off hilltops, first near, then far.

Rain. You are slipping away.

"I'm right here." But the gale sucked the sound from my words.

I'm waiting.

I searched the sky, the ground, the hilltops, but I could not see her. Our connection was dissolving, and I couldn't stop it. The wind spun around me like twirling skirts, like spinning wool, like a whirlpool. The earth beneath me sank, until I stood at the bottom of a basin. I reached up.

"Nuaga. Can you hear me?"

Climb, Rain. In the back, where no one can see.

"What?"

The sky grew darker and darker, until I stood in complete black-ness, the storm raging above me, the last words of Nuaga carried on its tail.

. . . where no one can see . . .

I gasped myself awake. The fire had burned low, and somehow my cloak was once again wrapped around me. I felt strangely hot and my heart was racing. My mouth ached for the comfort of the pow-der beneath my tongue.

I lay still, breathing through the uneasiness, feeling more alone than I'd ever felt. It looked like everyone else was asleep, though I guessed that Jasper must have assigned someone to keep watch.

"Rain."

The voice was soft—mere breath—and behind me, but I knew it right away. I twisted my head to the left and met Forest's eyes in the low glimmer of remaining firelight.

"What are—"

He pressed his finger to my lips. "Sit up."

He helped me do so, and a sudden swipe from his blade released me from the knotted strips. Heart pounding, I rubbed my wrists and waited while Forest bent to retrieve something.

"Here." He handed me my breastplate. "Took me a while to find it back there."

I took it, not fully comprehending what he wanted me to do. Nu-aga's voice still whispered in my memory, and my heart ached to hear her again.

"Is your water skin full?" Forest whispered in my ear. I nodded, and he lowered his voice further. "Now's your chance to leave. This is third watch, which gives us about three hours until dawn."

"Us? But—"

"Us."

"You're leaving your watch?"

"Yes. It's you or them—and I choose you."

A thrill ran up my spine. Without a word, I donned my breast-plate, making sure my dagger was in the attached sheath, and arranged my cloak over it. Then I sheathed my sword, which Forest had also retrieved for me.

"You don't have to come," I whispered.

"I would never let you do this alone."

He cupped his hand around my cheek, and, for a breath or two, warmth from his touch surged into my heart and lightened the darkness inside me. In the next instant, we moved quickly away from the camp and into the cover of night, the sound of our footfalls lost in the never-ending whine of the wind.

26

We jogged across open ground, our speed hampered only by the darkness. As the wind had increased during the day, so had the clouds. Now they obscured whatever light the stars may have offered us. Twice, I fell headlong, tripping as I stepped into an unseen hollow. When I felt like I couldn't go any farther, Forest guided me beneath the canopy of the trees, where we stopped.

"How long do you think we've been running?" I said through heavy breaths as I reached for my water skin.

"At least an hour," Forest said. "We can talk freely now."

I nodded, then tipped the water skin to my mouth and drank just enough to take the edge from my thirst. I handed the skin to Forest and he did the same.

"Thank you." I wanted to say more, but suddenly words wouldn't come.

"I couldn't let Jasper do that to you," Forest said. "I've known you as both Storm and Rain, and you're the same person. I wanted to tell them that."

"I was so afraid you'd say something."

"I almost did. But I might've ended up with my hands bound, too, and then I wouldn't have been able to help you escape."

I sighed. "I've lost contact with Nuaga. If we make it to the hold, I'm on my own."

"But she'll be there, right?"

"Yes, but I won't be able to talk with her. I have no idea how to find the catacombs."

"Well, Nuaga knows you," Forest said. "You've been in contact with her for weeks. Just because you can't hear her anymore doesn't mean she's going to abandon you."

"I know. But I don't know how she'll be able to guide me if I can't hear her."

"We have to try, *s'da*? The alternative is doing nothing." He reached out and squeezed my hand. "Let's go."

Fingerling Forest grew ever thicker to the west. We stayed just beneath its outer edge, where traveling was easier but still somewhat sheltered from the wind. The tangled branches were mostly bare, scratching and clacking above us like dry bones. Beneath our feet, layers of dead leaves crunched and swished as we moved swiftly through them.

We traveled until the sky changed from purple to dull gray and the wind had died to a gentle, intermittent gusting. Our training had given us the endurance to keep moving without rest, but the same would be true for Sedge and the others. So we kept going.

When the sky was fully light, we veered away from the forest's edge and crossed a small stream, then stopped to drink and refill the skin. From that point, the terrain began a steady, gradual climb, so we soon stopped on a flat rock to give ourselves a bit of rest.

Forest lay on his back, shielding his eyes with his forearm. "Are you ready to tell me about the mark?"

"Why does it bother you?"

"Because I don't understand it. How did she do it, exactly?"

"Dragonbreath. We've talked about it before, with Dalen."

"Refresh my memory."

I bit my lip. "Receiving a dragonbreath was required, so the dragons will know me. Nuaga let me choose where I wanted her to breathe on me."

Forest lifted his arm and looked at me. "Wait. She *breathed* on you?"

"Yes."

"As in, melted your flesh?"

I shivered, remembering. "Yes."

He rolled onto his side, his expression incredulous. "You let her burn you, Rain?"

"It's almost completely healed already. There's no pain." *I am the dragon-sister of Nuaga.*

"But there *was* pain, surely!"

"Yes. I passed out."

He sat up. "Show me."

I hesitated, then bent my head forward. "A little may be showing."

He moved so that he sat behind me. I thrilled to the light touch of his fingers, moving my shirt aside, stroking my ruined flesh.

"This . . . doesn't hurt?"

"No."

He withdrew his fingers and lay on his back beside me. "Was this the sacrifice mentioned in those verses?"

I wanted to tell him yes, or that I didn't know. I lowered my eyes.

"Rain?"

I met his gaze. "I'm prepared to make whatever sacrifice is necessary."

"You're willing to die."

"We're all willing to die," I said. "Or we wouldn't be here."

"I know," he said. "But this isn't the same as fighting on a battlefield. It's . . . a complete unknown."

"If I do nothing, there's no hope," I said. "What would you do in my place?"

"I—" His whole body seemed to sag. "I don't know."

My heart hitched a beat. "That's not true."

"Yes, it is." Forest's words were matter-of-fact. "I don't think I would've gotten past the dragonbreath part."

"You would have, if you were the one who'd woken Nuaga," I said.

"Maybe."

I was torn between wanting to either reassure him or kick him. "I guess I have more faith in you than you have in yourself."

"I've never been enough, that's all. Not the son my father had hoped for."

I stared at him without speaking, without breathing. He was an only son—a father's honor and pride. How could he—how could *any* boy—feel this way?

"You're more than enough," I said.

He rolled onto his back again. For a while, he was silent, and I stared into the distance wishing I could say a thousand beautiful words to let him know what he meant to me.

After a while, he sat up, his expression grim. "Sedge and the others will have started by now. Can you keep going?"

"I can."

"We'll have to sleep at some point, but not yet. Let's cover some more ground."

We traveled until hunger forced us to stop. Nothing but a strip of dried fruit lay in the bottom of Forest's pouch, and my pouch was gone. We split the fruit, which didn't begin to satisfy our hunger.

"It's as good a time as any to get some sleep," Forest said. "You rest, and I'll find us some food."

I didn't argue. Sleep claimed me almost immediately, and when I awoke, the scent of roasted meat curled through my nose and into my rumbling stomach.

"What did you find?" I asked, sitting up.

"A hare," Forest said. "Enough to fill us for a while."

The saltless meat was a feast in my mouth. We picked the bones clean, and then Forest lay down for a short sleep while I kept watch. I rested my dagger on the ground and stretched out my legs, listening for the smallest sound of pursuit. None came.

I woke Forest after about an hour. We did our best to hide the traces of our small campsite, but it wouldn't make much difference, anyway, since Sedge and the others knew which way we were headed. Forest and I stood for several minutes, studying the horizon, considering.

"I'm not exactly certain," he finally said. "If we bear too far to the north, we risk encountering Tan Vey's troops. But if we travel too far west, we may miss the hold altogether, and have to backtrack and waste time."

"I don't know," I said. "The forest recedes the farther we go, which makes it harder to judge." A nudging in my heart, like the memory of Nuaga's presence, grew so strong that I had to speak. "This way." I motioned with my head and began to walk.

"You're sure?" Forest fell into step beside me.

"I am." And I was.

We pressed on through the day, covering more ground than I thought possible. At dusk, we came upon the near banks of Lake Lehara. I stood at the edge of the water and gazed at the mountain on the other side. The pass through which Tan Vey's army would come was visible, a day's march or more around the lake on this side. There was no sign of them, though, and no sound of a chase behind us.

Everything was, in fact, eerily still. The wind had died, and the clouds rolled back as the sky darkened, opening us to colder air and the first hint of stars.

"Let's get a small fire going while there's still light," Forest said. "I'll hunt."

A splash sounded in the water, and then another. "We can fish," I said.

"Without bait?"

I smiled. "You start the fire. I'll fish."

Forest raised an eyebrow. "If you say so."

I raised my eyebrows in return. Once he'd begun to gather sticks for the fire, I removed my cloak, boots, and socks. The ground was cold and unyielding beneath my feet, and I shivered as I stepped out of my pants as well.

It wouldn't be wise to have wet clothing during a cold night.

I took a deep Neshu cleansing breath to steel myself against the bite of the water. Then I stepped in, gooseflesh spreading across my legs as I waded in up to my knees. I stood perfectly still, the way Papa had taught me. And I waited.

The first fish nibbled at my toes, as I knew it would. But I was too slow, and it slithered from my grasp. I swallowed my frustration and waited for the water to still. When I looked up, Forest was watching me, his arms full of wood.

"You're crazy, Rain L'nahn!" he called.

I nodded and returned to my fishing.

It was almost completely dark by the time I brought two fat, flopping fish to the newly lit fire. I tossed them to the dirt and pulled my cloak over my shoulders as I sat with my bare feet to the blaze, drying them.

"I take it back," Forest said as he grabbed the first fish. "You're not crazy. You're amazing."

There was plenty of fish for supper. Forest stored the rest in his pouch, so that we would have something to eat in the morning.

"I'll take the first watch," he said.

I nodded, unable to ignore the weariness that had crept into every corner of me. The night was cold, though the wind had blown itself out in favor of clear skies with stars that twinkled into infinity. I fell asleep gazing at them.

When I opened my eyes, Forest's fingers were brushing my cheek, his face inches from mine. My heart tumbled into my throat, and I lay there, savoring his touch, aching for what could never be.

"I hated to wake you," he said softly. "You look so beautiful."

No one except Papa had ever called me beautiful. I wanted to rest in the warmth of Forest's gaze, to *feel* beautiful. To abandon myself to what my heart desired more than anything.

But I couldn't.

We couldn't.

"Willow is more beautiful than I am," I said.

Forest's fingers stopped moving. His face hardened, and his hand fell away from my face. "I'll never love her, Rain."

His words pierced me, not only because my heart wanted what his did, but because I had destroyed my sister's dearest dream by stealing the heart of her betrothed.

I sat up and scooted subtly away from him. "We may not survive. Let's not think about what life will be like if we do, *s'da?*"

He nodded and folded his arms around himself, shivering.

"Take my cloak," I said, reaching for the clasp.

"No. I'll sleep near the fire."

"Please, Forest."

But he refused and rolled onto his side, facing away from the fire. I waited until he was asleep—then, gently, I laid my cloak over him and sat with my back nestled against his.

The fire warmed my tears as they slipped down my face.

We set out again before it was fully light, traveling fast, speaking little. Bright sunlight took the edge off the cold air, but there was nothing to take the edge off my hunger. By late afternoon, the morning's meal of cold fish had long worn off, and we couldn't afford to waste time fishing in such an uncovered area. I knew Forest had to be feeling it as keenly as I was.

All day, we'd followed the curve of the lake. Now the land rose sharply to our left, and the shoreline that had afforded us such easy passage was quickly disappearing.

"We're better off with a higher vantage point, anyway," Forest said. "We'll be able to see Tan Vey's army from up high."

"And they'll be able to see us," I said.

"Not if we're careful," Forest said. "Let's climb now before it becomes impossible."

By the time we reached the high ground, my legs were wobbly from lack of nourishment. We sat beneath an overhang to catch our breath and sip some water.

"No sign of an army," I said.

Forest wiped his mouth on his sleeve. "We should have easily beat them here, for how fast we've traveled. But we'll need to keep a sharp watch."

I leaned against the rocky earth and closed my eyes. With my stomach gnawing this fiercely, I didn't know how I would be able to be sharp about anything.

We continued on, and as the sun drew near to setting, the hold loomed before us. It was built directly into the base of a steep hill, its stone face imposing and impenetrable. From where we stood, it seemed little more than a part of the hill, with no windows or ramparts to distinguish it.

"It looks abandoned," Forest said.

"It's supposed to look that way." I tried to imagine a horde of sleeping dragons beneath the hold. Then I tried to imagine waking them.

"It's too far to go the rest of the way now," Forest said. "We need to find shelter for the night. Somewhere warm, because we can't risk a fire this close to the hold."

I knew he was right, but my spirits sank. No food and no fire— how would we wake the next morning with any semblance of strength?

Nuaga, I mind-spoke. *I'm here. Can you see me?*

But silence met me, as I knew it would.

About an hour later, we had a stroke of fortune. In a crevice of a hillock, Forest discovered a hollowed-out depression that was almost like a cave, except it was shallow and small with no sign that it led anywhere farther underground. At least two-thirds of it was covered by an overhanging of rock, and the space reached back far enough to create a perfect shelter.

"We can build a small fire in here, if we need to," I said. "Let's gather as much kindling as we can."

It wasn't easy to find wood, since trees were thinner up here, but we came up with enough armloads of brush and twigs that, if we were careful, we could use to create a small blaze. I cleared out as much debris as I could from the hollow.

The first stars were winking to life as we crawled inside. Forest laid a pile of bulbous, gnarled roots on the ground in front of us.

I wrinkled my nose. "What's that?"

"*Ptanyan,*" Forest said. "It's a wild tuber, spicy and a little sweet. It'll fill our bellies for a while."

"It doesn't look edible."

"It will." He took his dagger and shaved off the dirty, hairy coating of the *ptanyan,* leaving behind wet, purplish things that looked like twisted fingers.

I was too hungry to care, though, and I bit into one so aggressively that I coughed at its pungency. "Spicy and sweet, you said!"

"More spicy than sweet," Forest said. "I didn't think you'd taste it if I made it sound horrible."

It wasn't horrible at all, once I got used to the peppery-earthy taste. When we'd eaten every morsel, my hunger was strangely satiated, and my fingers were stained purple. We each sipped some water, careful to save enough for morning, in case we couldn't risk refilling our skin.

The night grew dark above us, and the cold of the rock at our backs soon seeped through even the warm cloak, which I'd spread behind us. Neither of us was willing to sleep in a breastplate in this small space, despite any added warmth it might offer. We couldn't afford to wake up stiff and unrested.

"I'll make a fire," Forest said.

In no time, he'd coaxed a small blaze from the sticks and brush, and our little hollow felt suddenly cozy and safe. He crawled outside to make sure the firelight wasn't visible.

"We're facing away from the hold," he said when he returned. "The small bit of light peeking out doesn't pose a threat."

I sighed with relief. The fire was small, but it was warm and comforting, and I didn't want to extinguish it. Forest sat beside me, and I offered half the cloak, which I had unconsciously wrapped around myself in his absence. He hesitated, and I frowned.

"We need to survive," I said. "That means staying warm."

"Rain, if you only knew . . ."

I met his eyes in the firelight, and they burned with a different kind of fire. "Knew what?" I whispered.

His mouth found mine, a tentative brush of his lips that stole my breath and sent a rush of heat through me like I had never before felt. Then his hands curled around my face, and he deepened the kiss until I thought I would drown in it.

His breath was warm on my mouth when he drew back, and all I could think about was how I had no idea what I was doing—no idea if I had kissed him properly.

"I love you." He spoke the words against my lips. "Whatever happens next doesn't change that."

Somehow my arms were around him, pulling him madly closer as he crushed my lips to his. Our mouths opened, and we melted together as though we were never meant to be two separate beings. Something wild and desperate tore loose inside me, and I lost myself in his kisses, in the tangle of our legs, in the warmth of his hands sliding down my back and finding my skin beneath my shirt.

The cold, the army, the dragons—everything slipped away like faded dreams. Here, in the warmth of Forest's arms, in the only moments we might ever have together, was where I wanted to be. Needed to be.

"So this is why you didn't mind sharing a tent with her?"

I thrust myself away from Forest and looked up. Sedge stood in the entryway of the hollow, firelight gleaming on his sword.

27

Forest and I scrambled to our feet. Sedge broadened his stance, blocking our exit. His eyes were wild, his mouth sucking in air as though he'd gone rabid. My pulse beat a sharp warning in my temples.

"You made good time," Forest said.

"I ran ahead of the others," Sedge said, his gaze resting on me. "She doesn't need you anymore."

"Who doesn't?" I eyed my sword, which was lying in its scabbard at the back of the hollow, next to Forest's.

"The dragon." He took a step forward. "You're nothing but an imposter. A *girl*." He spat on the ground.

"I have a job to do," I said. "What you think doesn't matter."

"It does matter." A tremor underscored his words, and I couldn't account for it. "I'm going to save Ylanda. Not you."

"This isn't about you," Forest said. "Stand down."

Sedge swung his gaze to Forest. "You're no better than she is. You should have seen Jasper's face when he realized you'd abandoned your post and gone with her."

"You're the reason I did," Forest said.

"Seems to me you have your own reasons," Sedge said. "Is she good and tight, or has she been around the town?"

I lunged for my sword, but Forest was faster, swinging to face Sedge, weapon drawn. In one smooth movement, Sedge thrust his sword into Forest's shoulder. I cried out as a torrent of red bloomed across Forest's shirt.

"Stay out of this," Sedge said. "It's between the bitch and me."

I pointed my sword at Sedge. "I've never been afraid of you."

"Maybe you should have been."

"Stop this!" I stepped forward, weapon poised, forcing him backward out of the hollow.

"Jasper should've taken care of you right away," Sedge said.

Our blades engaged twice, three times, but I was off my mark. Sedge knocked the sword from my grasp with his blade, a look of triumph spreading across his face.

I gave a Great Cry, and taking only a heartbeat to find the correct stance, I shifted my balance and kicked his sword from his grasp. He cursed and crouched to face me, initiating the second stance, back straight, eyes spewing hatred that belied his control.

"You have no advantage," he breathed. "I have the power of T'Gonnen."

My heart railed against his words, but I didn't allow him to throw my concentration. I remembered, now, what I'd heard him say about the oil he'd purchased from Madam S'dora. How it made him courageous. How much of the oil had he used?

"I don't fight with borrowed courage," I said.

Sedge's rage was barely contained. We engaged, matching each other move for move until my first falter, which he took advantage of with a fast uppercut to my chin. I staggered backward, scrambling to regain my balance and concentration, but he came at me again, blocking my next three moves and pushing me farther from the entrance to the hollow.

I regrouped and steadied my breathing, forcing myself into the calm required for effective Neshu technique. Almost, I could see Papa smiling and nodding his approval, his words of encouragement flowing through me, steadying me.

For a while, I had the advantage, effectively blocking a double palm thrust and a well-placed kick. The heat of combat now fully engaging me, I moved from defense to offense, striking at Sedge with every opportunity. Finally he miscalculated, and I initiated a carefully timed two-part move with my knife arm. His block caught me by surprise, but I used my weight to push him off-balance again, one of the tricks Papa had taught me. Immediately, I saw I had regained my advantage as Sedge stumbled slightly backward.

For half a moment, he stopped, shaking his head. Papa's words coursed through me: *The hesitation of an enemy should be the moment of your victory.* I waited one heartbeat too long.

My hesitation cost me, just as Papa had always warned. Sedge gave a Great Cry and brought me to my knees with his knife arm and foot, in a move I knew well and should have been able to avoid. But instead of ending the match honorably, he unsheathed his dagger and came at me with bloodlust in his eyes.

With a fierce yell, Forest flew at Sedge, knocking him backward with such force that I heard the wind as it was knocked from Sedge's chest. Forest was on top of him in a moment, dagger raised, ready to strike.

"No!" I rushed to their side. "Don't kill him!"

"He meant to kill you." Forest held the dagger at Sedge's neck. "He deserves the same."

"Forest, no! Please."

For a moment, Forest breathed hard and stared at Sedge's bulging eyes. Then he dropped his dagger and punched Sedge in the face—twice, three times, more times than I could count—until Sedge lay motionless.

Then Forest slumped and fell onto his wounded shoulder.

I sank to my knees at Forest's side. His breathing came in great, sharp gasps, and he clutched his hand over his shoulder.

"Let me see," I said.

"It's not too bad." But he winced as I lifted his blood-soaked shirt.

"We have to stop the bleeding." My voice trembled. "I need to take your shirt off."

A fresh torrent of blood poured forth as I eased the shirt over his head, then used my dagger to slice it in half. I wadded up half the fabric and pressed it to the gash on Forest's shoulder. He grunted, his mouth clenched tightly.

"I'm sorry," I whispered.

"Bind him." Forest's eyes were closed. "He'll wake, and he'll only attack you again."

"I have to take care of you first," I said.

He shuddered, and I realized how cold the air was, how completely alone I was with a bleeding man I'd have given my life for and an unconscious man who had tried to kill me. Mama's warm kitchen and my walk with Willow to the shops of Nandel seemed a thousand lifetimes away. I pressed with both palms on the wound, willing it to stop bleeding.

When the flow had slowed considerably, I tore the remainder of the shirt into strips and bound the wound. Supporting as much of his weight as I could manage, I helped Forest back to the hollow and covered him with my cloak. Then I returned to Sedge, who lay unmoving on his back, his face battered and bloodied. I fought a surge of revulsion as I scrambled to figure out how I could bind him.

All I could think to use was his belt. I unfastened it and struggled to remove it, shifting him first to one side, then to the other, until the belt came free. Then I laid him on his side and drew his arms behind his back, wrapping the belt around and around his wrists and forearms and securing it as best as I could, my fingers stiff with cold.

He was strong, though, and unnaturally bold because of the oil. I couldn't be sure if the belt would hold. When I'd made it as tight as I could, I felt around in the dark until I found Sedge's leather pouch. Heart pounding, I opened it, removing the dried meat and figs and reaching in to find what I really needed—the bottle of oil. I thrilled when my fingers touched its smooth surface, and I pulled it out and held it up to the stars.

Empty.

My heart sank, but I took the bottle and replaced it in the pouch, along with the food, and attached the pouch to my own belt. Of course Sedge had used all the oil—he had come to wake the dragons and wanted to be sure he was successful. It was empty, but it was all I had. Perhaps the traces of oil left inside would be enough to connect me with Nuaga when I needed her. It would have to do.

I removed Sedge's boots and took his sword and dagger as well. The boots I threw into the hollow, and I buried the weapons to one side, covering the spot with as much brush and rock as I could find. Satisfied that there was nothing more I could do, I crawled into the hollow, where Forest lay by the dying fire. I tended the blaze, building it up so that its heat soon filled the space and stopped my shivering.

I sat beside Forest, whose eyes were still closed.

"How's the pain?"

"Fine."

I lifted the cloak to check the makeshift bandages. No red had yet seeped through, which meant the blood was thickening as I'd hoped. I replaced the cloak.

"Rain." Forest's voice was gravel. "We can't stay here with him."

I stroked his forehead. "I've bound him and taken his weapons. And his food."

"You should have let me kill him."

"No," I said. "He's slathered himself with dragonsweat. It's beyond what he can handle."

"You should have let me kill him," Forest said again.

But I wasn't going to argue. I kissed Forest's cheek and said nothing.

"I don't regret tonight," he said.

At first, I thought he had changed his mind about not killing Sedge. But then I saw the way he was looking at me, and I knew that wasn't what he meant at all.

I nodded, not trusting myself to say the right words—to say that, if I died tomorrow, I would die knowing what it felt like to be loved by him, despite everything. And that if I *did* die, it would be the only way to erase our kisses. And the honor we had stolen.

"Great God damn you!" The shout rang out, forceful and angry. "Damn you both!"

The corner of Forest's mouth twitched. "Guess he woke up."

I closed my hand around the hilt of my dagger. "I'll go."

Sedge continued yelling his outrage to the night as I approached. He was on his knees, thrashing and twisting wildly in an attempt to loose his hands from the belt. When he finally saw me, he staggered to his feet.

"I should have killed you when I had the chance," he said.

He'd barely uttered the words when I lunged forward and kicked him to his knees. Then I shoved him to the ground and straddled him, my dagger at his throat.

"You have no weapons, and I've taken your food as well as your boots. You can either lie out here and freeze, or you can come into the hollow with us and survive the night. But if you try anything at all, I'll slit your throat."

"The others are on their way," Sedge said. "You'll pay for your crime."

I pressed harder with the tip of my dagger. "Which is it? Out here, or in there?"

"You don't scare me."

"You don't scare me, either."

Sedge tightened his jaw and said nothing. His left eye was swollen shut, and drying blood coated the entire left side of his face. His chest heaved, and he swallowed loudly.

"Which is it?" I said.

"Dragon's blood," he muttered.

"Is that your answer?"

"I guess you've turned the tables, little bitch."

I took that as a yes. I kept my dagger pointed at his neck as I got off him. "We have a common enemy, Sedge. You'd do well to remember that."

"I have nothing in common with you."

I moved the dagger away so that he could get up. "No sudden moves."

For a moment, his face grew hollow. "It's too much," he said in a strangled whisper.

"What is?"

But he shook his head, and the next moment, his obnoxious bluster had returned. "You'll pay in the end. Not me."

I kept my dagger pointed at his neck as we walked to the hollow. At the entrance, I motioned with my head for him to duck in and to the left, on the opposite side of the fire from Forest.

"Over there," I said, pointing to the farthest corner. "Against the wall."

"Afraid you won't be able to resist me?"

I slammed him against the embankment. "Actually, I'm afraid I might kill you in my sleep."

The look in his eyes was a strange mixture of loathing and respect. Or had I imagined that? No matter. I was finished with him. Finished feeling less than human because I wasn't a man. Finished worrying about things that were no more than a distraction from what I had to do.

"This isn't a good idea," Forest said as I settled beside him.

"We're all on the same side whether we want to be or not," I said, my words coming out more harshly than I meant them to.

The tension crackled around the fire as though it were a blaze of its own. I sat, rigid and alert, for hours, determined to protect Forest and make sure Sedge didn't do anything stupid. I cupped my hand around the pouch holding the food and bottle of oil and pushed aside the creeping thought that I had stolen it.

It didn't matter. I needed to wake the dragons, and Sedge had tried to kill me. This wasn't the time to worry about shades of right and wrong.

My eyes opened suddenly—I must have dozed off. Horrified, I grabbed for my dagger and squinted in the dim light cast by the dying embers at Sedge, who was snoring lightly. Then I laid my hand gently on Forest's chest. He slept quietly, his breathing even.

I had no idea how long I'd slept, but the night felt fairly spent, and I was wide awake. I stretched my legs and, with another glance at Sedge, slid as soundlessly as I could from our shelter.

The cold air whipped me immediately into a state of higher awareness, and I hugged myself and made my way to the nearest trees. Shivering, I climbed up toward the edge of the high rise we'd been traveling along, the lake's shores far below. The sky was still dark, but a slight fading of night's black curtain had crept almost imperceptibly across the horizon, and I knew that morning was near.

As I approached the highest point, I heard, quiet and distant, the splash of small waves as they lapped the shore. It was a cold, lonely sound, and I shuddered.

And then I heard something else.

Soft but distinct, the sound of metal on stone—the long, scraping whine of a whetting wheel. My breath caught in my throat, and I strained to listen more carefully.

There it was. The faint cracking of axes on wood. And the clatter of metal on metal.

I ran to the top of the ridge and gazed below, and my mouth dropped open in dismay. Below me, spread across the plain leading to the hold, the orange dots of a dozen campfires pierced the predawn darkness. And spread among them were the dark shapes of what had to be the tents and supplies of the army we'd been rushing to beat.

Tan Vey and his nomads were already here. And their camp blocked my way to the hold.

28

It didn't seem possible that Tan Vey's army could have beaten us to the hold. Had we miscalculated so horribly?

I gazed again at the sheer number of tents dotting the darkened landscape. And my heart shriveled within me.

I would have to leave at once, while I still had the cover of darkness. Alone.

I crept back to the hollow, where Sedge and Forest slept. Careful not to make a sound, I retrieved my breastplate and sword, laying them outside the hollow so I could don them without waking the others. Then, soft as silk, I took my cloak from where it lay across Forest's chest. I hated doing it, but I would need it more than he did.

He didn't stir. I touched the back of my hand to his brow and felt no fever, which gave me a measure of peace. I took the strips of dried meat from Sedge's pouch and laid them next to Forest. With a final glance at Sedge, I backed out of the hollow. I sheathed my sword, then walked several paces away to finish dressing. Sedge's pouch hung from my belt, the empty oil bottle tucked inside.

Already the protection of darkness had begun to betray me, as it was now light enough to see without stumbling. I stood for a minute or so at the top of the rise, gazing at the army camp below and assessing how best to approach the hold unseen. Then I turned and made my way toward a thin cover of trees, hoping my chosen path wouldn't veer too far from the hold—or too close to the army camp. Without the sun to guide me, it was hard to know which direction I was moving in.

"Rain."

I turned, my heart in my throat, to see Forest behind me, breathing heavily. "Go back."

"You can't go alone."

"Tan Vey's army is camped below," I said. "I'm not even sure how I'll make it past without being seen. There's no reason for two of us to attempt it."

"You need me to cover for you."

"You don't even have a shirt. And you're wounded!"

"I'm fine."

"Forest—"

"It's not my fighting arm, *s'da*? If I didn't think I could defend you, I wouldn't be here."

I planted my fists on my hips. "I'm willing to sacrifice myself. But not *you*."

"And I'm not willing to sacrifice you, either. I told you before that I'd never let you do this alone. I mean it." He stepped close and lifted my chin with his fingers. "I love you. I'm coming with you."

His kiss was soft as spring and warm as summer. I looked into his eyes and knew I couldn't turn him away.

"You're sure you can fight?"

"I'm sure."

"What about Sedge?" I asked.

"He can fend for himself."

I felt a twinge of guilt for leaving him unarmed, despite his wretchedness. "But he's bound."

"If he's determined enough to be free of that belt, he'll find a way," Forest said. "It's leather, not metal."

"Fine," I said. "But not like this."

I unsheathed my dagger and slipped the cloak from my shoulders. Piercing the seam between the outer leather and inner fur, I sliced the two layers apart, so that, when I was finished, I had what was essentially two cloaks. I draped the outer layer over Forest's shoulders and hooked it closed, then made a slit in each side for his arms, with a smaller slit behind his right shoulder for his dagger. Finally, with a strip cut from the end of my half of the cloak, I fastened the leather shell around his waist.

"Bare arms, but it's better than a bare torso," I said.

"I didn't know you were a seamstress on top of everything else."

"One of my finest skills." I threw the fur lining over my shoulders and, with nothing to fasten it, held it closed with my left hand, to keep my knife hand rested and free. "Let's go."

We moved as quickly as we could. Forest was noticeably slower, and I soon began to worry that he would falter before we'd made it safely to the hold.

"How are you?" I asked for at least the third time.

"I'm fine." The same thing he'd answered each time.

By the time the sun had fully risen, we'd reached the last easy cover of trees before the open plain that stretched in front of the hold—and the horde of soldiers occupying it. From here, we could easily hear the sounds from the army camp—the sharpening of blades, the shouting of orders, the sounds of hammering.

"What are they building?" I whispered.

Forest listened for a moment. "Catapults, I'd guess."

I closed my eyes. How would we get past an entire army?

"From the sound of things, they're getting ready to make their move," Forest said.

"We'll need to cut around to the southwest and circle back," I said. "How's your shoulder?"

He shrugged. "Sore. I'm fine."

I shoved aside my growing worry. "Let's head to the lower ground and go as far as we can."

It wasn't much of a plan, but neither of us knew what to expect from the terrain as we moved forward, other than the fact that the expanse was flat and clear ahead, and completely blocked by Tan Vey's army.

So we pressed on.

By the time we'd reached a small, rocky outcrop that gave us cover, we knew we'd come to the end of the easy part. Between where we crouched and the hold, there was little to hide us, unless we swung even farther to the southwest.

We couldn't do that, though. We were running out of time.

"Our only choice is to keep as much distance as we can between us and their southern flank," I said. "It looks like a stream or small river is running toward the lake . . . there." I pointed. "We can head for the edge of that tree line and approach the hold from that side."

"Let's do it."

We ducked along the back of the ridge until it was no longer high enough to cover us. An empty plain stretched before us, leaving the hold in full view.

"I shouldn't have fallen asleep," I said. "This would have been easier at night."

"And you'd be so exhausted that you wouldn't be able to fight off a moth."

I knew he was right. But I couldn't tell him how terrified I was to run across the open ground.

"On three," I said, dropping my cloak so it wouldn't hinder me.

"Rain." Forest touched my arm. "No matter what happens, keep going. Don't stop."

I knew what he meant, but I couldn't admit it to myself. I formed what I hoped was an encouraging smile.

"We'll make it."

He nodded. "We'll make it."

I took a breath and counted. Then, heart blazing within me, I ran. It felt as though ten thousand eyes would descend upon me at any moment as I pushed myself to run faster than I ever had. Breaths came sharp and cold, and the sound of my footfalls pounded in my ears like drumbeats, calling attention to me. I hazarded a glance over my shoulder and saw that Forest was far behind me.

Too far. He was flagging. Far worse than I had expected.

No matter what happens, keep going. Don't stop.

But already I was slowing down, glancing first at the army to my right, then over my shoulder, then at the army again, losing time, losing ground.

Then I saw something that gripped my entire body with such horror that I stumbled and lost my footing. In a shallow pit in the open field, with chains around her neck, Nuaga lay with her head lifted as far as her restraints allowed her, watching me. For several petrified seconds, I stood gaping, unable to make sense of what I saw.

How had they overpowered her? How would I wake the dragons without her?

And how could she then lead them into battle?

I recovered and started to run again, though thick dread clouded my heart. A great bellow cracked through the morning air, and my heart rejoiced—Nuaga was creating a distraction so that we could cross the open field, despite her chains. Moans of dismay rose up from the troops as she continued to keen, swinging her head back and forth so that the chains rattled mightily.

With new confidence, I quickened my pace, running until I'd made it safely to the side of the hold. I flattened myself in a depression at the base of the knoll into which the hold was built. Peering out, I saw Forest still running, barely more than halfway across. I bit my lip and willed him to run faster.

Nuaga gave a final cry, then fell silent. Another outcry issued forth from Tan Vey's army, one that could only mean that the captive dragon had been once again subdued.

Forest was still running. I pressed a fist to my mouth, holding back the terror that he would be seen. If only her distraction had lasted another minute or two. I watched him, silently willing him to hurry, and in those moments, nothing mattered more than his safety.

Then, as Forest drew ever nearer, Nuaga's words burned in my memory: *Love for a man is embedded in your heart. Perhaps he will be your downfall when your time comes.*

My insides twisted. She'd been right to warn me. I couldn't allow my love for Forest to stand in the way of whatever was required of me right here, right now.

"Forest," I whispered.

He made it, staggering to a stop and dropping to his knees beside me. I scooted over, and he lay on his back, panting.

"You made it," I said.

He nodded, unable to speak. His face, swathed in sweat, looked too pale. Clumsily, I removed the skin from my cloak pocket and offered it to him.

He raised his head and drank a few swallows, then lay back down. "Just a bit dizzy." He closed his eyes.

I crawled to his feet and lifted them onto my lap. "This should help. Be still a moment."

"I'm fine," Forest said, still breathing hard. "What's next?"

"Did you see Nuaga?"

"No. Where?"

"In a pit on the field." I fought to keep my voice from trembling. "She's in chains."

"Great God. Is that what that awful sound was?"

"Yes. I don't know how I'm going to find the entrance to the catacombs without her."

"We'll figure it out."

"There's more." Despair clutched at me, tightening my throat. "She needs to lead the dragons into battle. Tan Vey must know that, too."

For the first time, Forest looked truly worried. "We'll figure it out," he said again.

But it was clear his hope had faltered, same as mine.

I cupped my hand over my eyes and looked up at the hold. From here, its girth and height were impressive, though it had the appearance of being old and abandoned, tucked into the hillock like a relic from another era. As I looked, I saw movement on a high balcony and a glint of metal in the light of the rising sun.

"There." I pointed, forgetting that Forest's eyes were closed. "Soldiers."

Forest sat up, swinging his feet off my lap. "The high king must not have expected the enemy to know where he was. Even if he brought a hundred soldiers, it won't be enough to fight off this attack."

"There must be provisions inside, though," I said. "If they lay siege—"

"This will be no siege," Forest said. "They're going to storm the hold and bring it down."

I gazed across the field at the mammoth catapults that stood in a long row, a few of them not quite complete. Then I noticed a pavilion off to one side, its canopy festooned with black and red banners. Beneath it stood several men who looked important—commanders? Generals?

One of them stepped from beneath the pavilion and faced the catapults, arms crossed, a mass of braided hair hanging down his back. He gestured sharply to the other men, speaking words I couldn't hear. The others bowed and made their way toward the catapults. He watched them for a few moments before returning to the pavilion.

My chest tightened. "Tan Vey," I whispered.

"Where?"

"There. Beneath the pavilion."

We watched him, words silenced in our throats. Here was the man who had single-handedly united the nomads and initiated the invasion. He knew our history, he knew of the dragons, and he had come to claim what he thought was his for the taking.

"Not on my watch," I said.

I reached into the pouch at my waist and pulled out Sedge's oil bottle. *Please work.* I pulled the stopper out and tipped the bottle into my palm, tapping it repeatedly in the hope that even the smallest drop might come out.

There it was. A smudge of oil on my palm—hardly anything, but enough to feel when I ran my fingertip through it.

I took my oily palm and rubbed it into my neck, over the warmth of my pulsing veins and in the hollow where my shoulder blades met.

Please work. Please.

But only silence met me. The oil wasn't working.

I replaced the stopper and shoved the useless bottle into the pouch. "The catacombs must be accessible from inside the hold," I said. "I have to find a way in."

"Those soldiers on the balcony aren't going to know that you're not an enemy soldier," Forest said.

He was right. Once more, I gazed along the weatherworn stone surface of the hold. But there was nary a window, nor any hint that anything lay hidden behind that ancient wall.

No visible way in.

A long note sounded from a deep horn, followed by answering notes from other horns. Whatever signal this was, I knew it meant I didn't have much time.

Then Nuaga's words, which hadn't made sense before, returned to me: *Climb, Rain. In the back, where no one can see.*

"We need to climb the knoll," I said.

"You're sure?"

"Yes." I frowned. "Can you make it?"

"Yes. Let's go."

We picked our way over the rocks that made up the foot of the knoll. The sound of rushing water tickled my ears, and as Forest and I climbed over a ridge to mount the next level of the knoll, I saw why—the rocks and earth ended suddenly in a drop-off so severe that it made my head swim. Below, a raging waterfall threw a fine mist into the morning air.

"Great God," Forest muttered.

I shrugged, acting more confident than I felt. "A good natural defense. Are you sure you're up for the climb?"

He nodded, and we pressed on.

The gentle rise of ground quickly gave way to a steep, treacherous climb that made it obvious why the hold had been built here. Grateful for the strength in my arms due to Jasper's relentless training, I pulled myself up over rocky outcrops and navigated steeper areas without slipping. We were about halfway up when Nuaga's bellows echoed from the plain. I stopped, listening. There was something frantic in her tone. A warning.

"What is it?" Forest called from somewhere behind me.

"I don't know."

I turned to look at him, dismay creeping through me when I saw how far he'd fallen behind. Nuaga's cries became more insistent as I continued to climb. Were the nomads torturing her? Or was she trying to tell me I'd gone the wrong way?

"Midget!"

I froze, the familiarity of Sedge's voice piercing me. Then I turned and saw him not far below where Forest stood clinging to a sharp ridge of earth and rock. Forest reached over his shoulder for his dagger, pain spreading across his face like a storm.

Nuaga's last cry was still fading when I saw what it was she surely had been trying to warn me about. Scrambling up the rocky incline with an agility that defied belief were two nomad soldiers, their hair in tied-back, thick coils, their teeth clamped onto the hilts of long daggers. One headed toward Sedge, the other toward Forest.

Sedge was unarmed. Forest was wounded. For one agonizing second, I stood, torn.

"Midget!" Sedge was scrambling now, trying to outclimb the

nomad that was quickly gaining on him. "I have what you need! I can hear her!"

I started back down the knoll, rocks sliding beneath my boots. Forest had found better footing and was holding his dagger in a defensive position, his eyes on the nomad coming toward him.

"Forest!" I called.

"I've got this. Go."

I unsheathed my own dagger and clamped it in my teeth as I made my way down the slope toward Sedge. The nomad was closing in fast as Sedge backed his way up the slope. I slid to his side moments before the enemy soldier was close enough to strike.

"Climb!" I yelled.

The nomad lunged at me, nimble and deadly, a growl in his throat rising to a guttural cry as he struck. I was ready with my own blade and diverted his strike, enjoying the advantage of higher ground.

But he was quick, and he soon swung again, his footing more secure, his attack stronger. I blocked him a second time, then shifted my stance and gave a Great Cry, moving fluidly into the third stance of Neshu. In three swift moves, I disarmed him and knocked him to his knees. He yelled and pulled a second, thinner blade from inside his boot, but I was faster.

I had found my anger.

My hatred.

I kicked the blade from his hand and plunged my dagger into the hollow of his neck. The vivid red of the blood that spurted and gushed and sprayed my hand made me stagger. Made white spots flash across my vision.

Made me sway as I pulled the blade from his neck.

"Dragon's blood, get up here!" Sedge's words were frantic.

I looked up to see him scrambling up the knoll toward its pinnacle. Forest yelled, and the clash of metal brought me fully awake again. The nomad had engaged him on a particularly steep part of the slope, though Forest had the upper ground.

Then my heart grew dark as I saw two more nomads climbing toward him.

No.

Nuaga's words seared my heart: *Perhaps he will be your downfall when your time comes.*

No. No. No.

This couldn't be my sacrifice.

Not Forest.

Dear Great God, no.

There was no time to fight for him. No chance to save him.

I had to choose the dragons over Forest.

With a heaving sob, I picked up the dead man's dagger, turned once again toward the top of the slope—toward Sedge, toward Nuaga—and started to climb.

29

I reached the summit and Sedge pulled me the rest of the way up.
The moment his hands grabbed mine, I felt a surge of familiar
warmth and the brush of words against the silent reaches of my mind.

Nuaga.

I turned, trying to find Forest, but I saw only more dark shapes
climbing the knoll. How had so many of them spotted us?

Sedge grabbed my shoulders and turned me to face him. His expression was grim. Determined.

"All night," he breathed. "All night, I ran in my dreams to the top
of this knoll. And all I could understand was five words—'T'Gonnen,'
'High King's Hold,' and 'Rain.' And the vision, over and over, of having my flesh burned with dragonbreath."

"Nuaga's mark."

"I could never do that. I don't have that kind of courage."

Like a man possessed, he tore off his breastplate and shirt, tossing them to the ground. For only a second, an expression like revulsion crossed his face. Then he wrapped his arms around me and
pressed me to his chest.

My first instinct was to scream. But the heavy scent of the oil, and
the slipperiness of it against my cheek, brought me to my senses. Desperate for Nuaga's help, I willed my arms around Sedge and pressed
myself into his body.

Rain!

My heart did an ecstatic leap. *Nuaga! Show me where to go!*

Sedge cried out as if in pain. "Your words are in my head!"

I shushed him.

Climb the rest of the hill and veer to your left, along a narrow out-cropping too small for a dragon's claws. Follow it until you reach a slope that leads to a flat area concealed from view. The entrance to the cata-combs will be under your feet.

"The sacrifice . . ."

Is complete.

Her words pierced my soul. I thought of Forest fighting alone on the hillside against three enemy soldiers, and how I had left him to die so that others would live. My heart threatened to shatter within me, and I remembered words from the *Lament* that hadn't struck me before: *She who knows the pain of parting knows its power.*

T'Gonnen's sacrifice wasn't merely his own life—it was forever parting from his beloved mate. He had chosen Ylanda over Nuaga.

I dug my nails into Sedge's back. "You're in chains. Can you not free yourself?"

I cannot.

"Is there no hope?"

You are a she-king in your own right, Rain L'nahn.

Her words rang in my breast—words she had spoken to me before. And I knew what was to be.

We were dragon-sisters, Nuaga and I.

I would lead the dragons into battle in her stead.

"I'm coming," I said.

I extricated myself from Sedge and faced the highest point of the rounded peak, where the hefty stone wall of the hold seemed to grow from the very earth. I picked up the dagger I had dropped and handed it to Sedge.

"Watch my back," I said.

He nodded and took the dagger. I climbed the hill, my breaths coming in short gasps, my body strangely numb. Sedge was a few steps behind me struggling into his breastplate as we walked, his breathing loud in my ears. The outcropping was obscured by tangled brush, and I almost missed it. I followed it to the left, its length never-ending, its width so narrow that my boots felt too big. When I reached the slope, I was engulfed by the fear that I had come to the wrong place.

"There's a doorway here somewhere," I said. "In the ground."

"There," Sedge said, gesturing toward a tangle of half-dead vines that stretched across the expanse of earth as though they'd climbed there.

I fell to my knees and began to pull at the vines. Sedge knelt beside me, slashing the curling stems with his dagger so that I could pull them up more easily, faster. Every second felt like a day as we worked at the vines, but soon our efforts were rewarded. Beneath the remaining bits of stick and leaf, a slab of marble lay fitted into the earth.

A door.

Sounds of horns and shouting from the army below increased, carried on the wind. Was it the noise of attack? Between the wind and the pounding of my heart, I couldn't be sure. I only knew I needed to open that door.

The surface was smooth, untouched by the ravages of time and weather. On one side, two great brass hinges were affixed, so I dug my fingers beneath the opposite side and lifted.

It opened easily. Of course it did. There was no need for a lock or other barrier—who in their right mind would willingly walk into the catacombs where mighty dragons slept?

"As soon as I'm inside, close the door," I said.

I lowered myself through the trapdoor. Cut into the inner wall of the stone were deep slats—a steep ladder that would not in any way be easy to climb down. Darkness closed around me as I fitted one foot, then the other, into slat after slat, hand under hand, foot after foot.

At first, the stone was cold beneath my fingers. But after a minute or two, the air and the stone and everything around me was wrapped in a warmth that felt as though it had a life of its own.

The warmth of dragons.

The darkness was so complete that I could see nothing—not my hands in front of me, not the passage above me through which I'd already climbed. Looking down wasn't an option; the only way I could keep my nerve was not to think about the distance beneath me.

Only step after step. Hand under hand.

The air became thicker, infused with the stillness of a dream and the buzz of vibrant, powerful life. The dark became less so with each step, until finally the tunnel was lit with a faint, almost-not-there, orangey-red glow. Enough to see by, but barely.

Then, suddenly, my foot couldn't find another slot. After a few panic-filled moments, I braced myself and let go. The fall was short, and I landed on my feet in a chamber so large it felt like a world in itself. Around me, the faintly orange darkness swirled like living mist.

Same as the dream.

Creeping forward, I stepped into a large, oval depression, where tendrils of the swirling mist wrapped around my ankles and caressed my legs. The sensation was warm and familiar, like a hint of something I knew. My boots sank softly in shallow muck that, when I stood still, seemed to breathe.

As my eyes grew accustomed to the ruddy light, I could see a large archway that opened into a chamber beyond. I walked through it into what seemed to be a sort of honeycomb, branching out in three directions like a maze, with walls low enough for me to see over. Within each enclosure lay a dark, hulking shape, the orangey-red light emanating weakly from each one and the dark tendrils swirling, swirling around them.

I stared at the hulking masses sleeping before me. The salvation of Ylanda. The promised army.

All along, I'd worried I wouldn't be able to wake them. That I would somehow stand mute and powerless in their presence, unable to do anything. But as I stood there, the thickness of their power curled into me with every breath, a familiar feeling that I recognized from every dream, every conversation, with Nuaga.

I'd been forever marked by her—a clanmate of the dragons. They would know me, because the mate of T'Gonnen had left her mark on me. Fear faded like a dying storm.

A deep, bone-jarring thud echoed through the catacombs. I tensed, thinking at first that it was the dragons and wondering if I might be trampled to death. A second thud rang out, and a wave of dread tore through me.

It was the sound of boulders slamming into the hold. The enemy had unleashed its catapults.

I had to wake the dragons *now*.

I moved toward the closest one. It was at least a third bigger than

Nuaga, its scales a deep red, the mane around its face long and majestic. A male dragon.

Another thud reverberated through the catacombs. And another. Tiny stones and debris rained from the ceiling. I stepped toward the dragon and placed my hand, fingers splayed, on his neck.

Everything inside me went utterly still. Like a blanket of snow over the heat of summer.

Another thud rocked the catacombs. I stared at the dragon's eye, willing it to open, and terrified of what it would look like when it did.

The thudding increased, and so did the swirling vapor, rolling into a frenzy around the dragons, around me.

I took a great breath. "*S'danta lo ylanda.*"

The dragon's eye opened.

I met its gaze, willing myself to keep my hand where it was and not to shrink. He blinked once, twice. Then, slowly, he lifted his head and turned it directly toward me. I stepped backward. The swirling mist rose higher, thinner.

Dragon-waker.

His words knifed into my brain with palpable presence, and I winced at their force. Then I raised my chin, confident.

"Yes."

Across the catacombs, in competition with the thudding of the stones from the catapults, the dragons stirred. Great heads rose on sleek necks, and hundreds of eyes caught the light of the mist as it dissipated.

The dragon I had laid my hand on still stared at me. He arched his neck so that his face was directly before mine. This time, when he spoke, it wasn't inside my head.

"Show me the mark of Nuaga," he said.

I removed my breastplate and laid it beside me, then turned around and lifted my shirt. When I felt he had gazed long enough at my ruined back, I let the shirt fall and turned to face him.

"The hold is under attack. The nomads seek to kill the high king and claim the dragons."

His face brightened into what looked very much like a smile. "But we are awake now."

All at once, the words of the dragons coursed through my head and through the catacombs as they called to one another, relaying the message and preparing to move forth.

But how? I felt suddenly vulnerable, unable to withstand a dragon stampede. I retrieved my breastplate and pulled it on, the power of T'Gonnen pulsing through me, rising with every breath.

Then I grabbed the red dragon's mane and pulled myself onto his neck—an immense neck, harder to navigate than Nuaga's. With all the strength still in me, I swung up and mounted, holding fast.

"Where is the mighty Nuaga?" the dragon asked.

"I am Nuaga's dragon-sister. I will lead you into battle."

A rumbling of wordless exclamation cascaded through the chamber, rising in intensity. I tightened my grip and sat tall.

"We rise!" the red dragon cried. "We rise!"

In a tumult greater than that of any storm, the dragons arose as one, moving forward through the catacombs, breaking down the walls that once separated their sleeping areas, trampling the abandoned beds and broken pieces of stone in their headlong rush through the caverns.

The noise was so thunderous, so deafening, that my ears ached and I couldn't hear the sound of my own scream. The dragons surged forward as support posts cracked and chunks of ceiling fell. I pressed my cheek to the dragon's pelt and wrapped my arms around him, breathing in centuries-old dust and the heady scent of dragon as we lumbered forward through the dark. All around me was chaos and heat and the newly woken power of the dragons, which coursed through me like a living thing, calling my heart to their purpose. Moments before it happened, I knew we were going to break free—and I didn't know if I would survive it. The very earth cracked open above us, breaking into a million pieces as the dragons tore up from the catacombs, bellowing with arched necks and open maws, majestic and terrible as they trampled up and over the crumbling ground toward the enemy.

I raised my head as daylight momentarily blinded me. All around me, a sea of dragons surged forward toward rows of nomad soldiers that seemed, in comparison, minuscule. Inconsequential.

Screams of terror rose above the cacophony of the dragons as they bore down upon the army, trampling the catapults and the men as though they were mere dust and breathing their heated breath toward those who tried to flee. I rode at the right flank, passing Nuaga in her chains and veering toward a wave of soldiers who had broken formation and were running out of the path of the oncoming dragons. I tightened my legs around my dragon's neck and sat tall, the fierceness of the clan raging in my veins. Rain L'nahn, sister-dragon to Nuaga, she-king in her own right.

My dragon slowed as it cut a path of heated breath before it, felling the soldiers seeking to escape. I closed my eyes, unwilling to watch them melt and burn before my eyes. We trampled them underfoot as we turned, then, to join the surge of dragons that closed in on the bulk of Tan Vey's army, allowing them no escape.

The prisoners! I mind-spoke.

Without hesitation, my dragon turned and headed toward the rows of terrified Ylanda soldiers, shackled together and tripping over each other as they tried to escape. We swung around them, cutting them off from the advancing dragons.

"Retreat to the west!" I called. "The dragons are for Ylanda!"

They stared as though I were a dragon myself. Then, as if of one mind, they gathered their wits and began to move. My dragon and I held our ground until they were well on their way. As we turned to rejoin the throng, I looked up and saw Tan Vey's pavilion in flames.

A roar of satisfaction left my throat as my dragon reared his neck and we returned to the heat of battle. By now, Tan Vey's army was a cowering mass of nomads who had dropped their weapons, desperate to outrun Nuaga's army. Jasper's words burned in my memory: *If the enemy turns from you and runs away, you must attack . . . he must become nothing.*

"In the name of Nuaga!" I cried. "Onward, for Ylanda!"

The triumph of the dragons was almost complete. We were slowing now, crushing already-dead nomads and searching the perimeter for any who had found a way to break through. The stench of scorched flesh was acrid in my nostrils as we headed toward a small band of nomads seeking to escape. My dragon's breath burst forth as he slowed to a near-stop for better aim. I sat tall, and this time I didn't close my eyes.

Sharply and suddenly, something grabbed my leg, and I fell, landing forcefully on the dirt.

I rolled quickly and drew my sword. Two enemy soldiers were
upon me almost before I'd jumped to my feet. I moved quickly from
the second to the third stance and kicked the first soldier's sword from
his hand before swinging to engage the second. Our swords met with
a clash that sent a shock up my arm. He was swift and deadly, and I
danced away from the sweep of his blade while keeping the other soldier in my view.

If death came now, it wouldn't matter. The dragons were free.
The kingdom would be saved.

And yet I wanted to live.

I cried out and came at my attacker with renewed vigor, dragon
power hot in my blood. We were evenly matched strike for strike,
until I feinted and turned on him with Neshu footwork, gaining an
advantage and striking a killing blow. I turned before he hit the
ground to engage the other soldier, who had regained his weapon
and was bearing down on me, a guttural roar in his throat. Immediately, I sensed his prowess with the sword and knew I was out-
matched. Each move I made was defensive; each step I took was
backward. My breaths came in raw gasps as I tried to gain the upper
hand.

The dragons continued to clamor and rumble forth, the sound
muffled and distant in the heat of my own battle. I'd lost my focus,
intent on the panicked countermoves that kept me alive.

Papa, help.

I reached deep inside for my centeredness, past the thudding of
my heart and the fear of death. I found the second stance, parried
my enemy's next blow, and then shifted my weight, twisting in a perfect arc and kicking him in the chest. He staggered, and I disarmed
him with a move Papa would have been proud of. I kicked the sword
out of our path as the soldier unsheathed his dagger. I dropped my
own sword and pulled the dagger from its sheath on the back of my
breastplate.

This was a fight I could win.

My opponent matched my Neshu stance, and we circled twice before engaging, our daggers poised. He was good, and his knife arm

deadly—but I was better. It didn't take long for him to make a misstep, and when he hesitated, I did not.

My Great Cry was almost lost amid the tumult of the dragons, and as my enemy landed hard on his back, I lunged toward him, finishing him quickly with my dagger. Breaths ragged, vision dotty, I raised my dagger and spun, scanning to see if anyone else was coming at me.

But I stood alone among the dead.

Rain. Nuaga's voice, strong inside my head now that the dragons were awake, drew me, and I turned and ran toward the pit where she was chained. Around her lay the charred remains of those who had guarded her earlier. As the dragons thundered over the remaining catapults, I jumped onto Nuaga's back, surveying the seven chains around her neck, thicker than any chain I'd seen.

The passion of T'Gonnen rose within my breast, and my hands burned with a heat that couldn't be contained. From the first chain, I took a link in each hand and pulled, a Great Cry ushering from my throat unlike any I'd ever given. The metal gave way as though it were fresh cream, the chains falling to the sides of the pit with a dull clatter. I did the same for the remaining chains, pulling them apart as if they were grass necklaces, until the last one fell from Nuaga's neck and she stepped out.

"My wounds have healed, dragon-sister," she said. "My breath is hot again."

I slid from her back so that she could take her place with the others, her glorious bellows joining theirs. The last catapult toppled before my eyes as Nuaga raced across the death-strewn field toward the mighty dragon army, taking her place as their she-king in command.

For several heartbeats, I watched her. Then I turned my gaze to the hold, to survey its damage. A dark shape moved up the left side, clambering over a broken area where the stones were jagged and torn. Heavy boots, braided armor, a thick cluster of coiled hair hanging down his back.

Tan Vey.

I stared, disbelieving. Then, the weight of dragon power still heavy upon me, I ran to the hold and climbed as though I were a spider, the strength of my hands to grasp the stone beyond what I could comprehend. I bypassed the balcony to avoid being seen by anyone inside who might think me the enemy and continued climbing until I'd reached the roof.

I drew my dagger and waited.

He appeared moments later over the broken edge of the hold, hoisting himself up and over and rising quickly to his feet—he was no taller than Sedge. I assumed the second stance and met his gaze as he looked up. A flash of surprise flickered across his face before it hardened into an unfeeling mask.

"Are you the dragon-waker?" His words were clipped. Gruff.

I narrowed my eyes. "I'm the dragon-sister of Nuaga."

A slow smile grew across his mouth. "You're a boy."

"No," I said. "I'm a girl."

I raised my dagger and moved fluidly into the third stance. He matched me, his own dagger almost twice the length of mine. We circled each other, and he eyed me as though I were of little consequence.

"The high king's life belongs to me," he said. "You're a minor distraction."

"It's over," I said.

"It's only begun."

His first move was swift as lightning; I matched him and countered. Three more times he came at me, measured and precise, his dagger swiping close. And three times I blocked him. I switched to the offensive, dancing to his left and incorporating a series of moves I had perfected under Jasper's training. Tan Vey was fast, though, and he matched and outsmarted me, nearly knocking the dagger from my grasp.

I recovered and came at him again, this time thrusting my knife arm sharply upward against his wrist, so that his dagger clattered to the stone. Without missing a beat, he pulled something from his belt and tore it open with his teeth. He tipped whatever was inside it into his mouth and chewed as though it were made of leather. He grimaced and swallowed noisily, his gaze never leaving mine.

Within seconds, his eyes bulged, glowing fiery orange and gold, and his lips grew deep red, stretching and curling into an inhuman snarl. I stepped back, too stunned to react. He took a great, rattling breath and exhaled. Dragonbreath exploded from his mouth toward my face. I ducked and rolled away, barely avoiding the stream of deadly heat.

He threw back his head and bellowed, his voice a strange mixture of dragon and man. "I am Ylanda's high king!"

Whatever dragon magic he'd swallowed would give him the advantage he needed to enter the hold and kill everyone inside it. And I was the only one who could stop him.

The power of T'Gonnen still raged within me. I drew myself up and gave it free rein; it coursed through me like a second stream of blood, and I felt my own breath grow hot, deep in my lungs.

Tan Vey lunged toward me, dragonbreath streaming from his mouth. I leaped higher than I should have been able to and landed safely out of his aim. I turned on him and breathed my own heated breath; it tore from my lungs and savaged the air before me. Tan Vey twisted out of its path, lithe and limber as a dragon.

I assumed the third stance and came at him again, my breath coiled within me, ready to strike. Tan Vey rose up, his head thrown back, blood trickling from the corners of his eyes. He roared, a mixture of anger and anguish, and then he threw his breath at me again.

Its heat singed my hair as I danced out of the way, sending my own breath toward him. He rolled to the side, bellowing as my breath swept over his left flank. When he rose, his face was livid, striped with blood and misshapen by a mouth that was too big. Driven by power that was greater than he could bear, he attacked with a series of Neshu moves so rapid that my responses flagged, and he caught me in the chest with a kick so powerful that I flew backward and landed hard. He inhaled noisily, ready to finish me with a final breath, but I jumped to my feet and roared my own breath at him, causing him to leap and twist out of the way, his dragonbreath shooting harmlessly upward.

He landed near the edge of the roof, his entire body visibly trembling. I drew another breath, but before I could exhale, he threw back his head and screamed, blood gushing from his eyes and nose. He staggered, then fell backward off the roof, his scream slicing the air until, suddenly, it stopped.

I walked to the edge of the roof. Tan Vey's body lay among the rubble where the dragons and I had arisen through the catacombs. I stared at the broken form of the man who had been undone by his lust for the dragons' power. Then I drank in the scene of the dragons' triumph, pressing my hands over my mouth as I stared at the carnage, the utter destruction of the enemy who had sought to destroy our kingdom.

For several crowded heartbeats, I remained one with the spirit of T'Gonnen, high king of dragons, as he exulted over the victory of his clan, the faithfulness of his mate . . . the return of the dragons to Ylanda. The heat of my breath, the length of my fangs, the flowing beauty of my mane—I felt it all, breathed it all, as though my flesh and bones were dragon-shaped. I bellowed, and it was a deep and resonant sound, imbued with the strength of the dragon who had sacrificed himself for this very moment.

The voice of T'Gonnen.

In a rush, the power faded, and I felt suddenly small and spent. I fell to my knees, arms dropping to my sides. And I closed my eyes.

From across the field came Nuaga's answering cry. Then the entire clan joined in, keening and bellowing in a glorious tumult. I opened my eyes and gazed at their magnificence . . . their utter beauty.

We will bring news of the victory to Ylanda City, dragon-sister!

I smiled, Nuaga's voice sweet and familiar inside my head. As one, the dragons turned toward our capital to the north, moving with such grace and majesty that my throat ached.

An unearthly silence fell. Below me, stretched across the plain, lay the broken remains of what had been a mighty army from the north. Nothing moved; no hint of life rose from the battlefield.

I breathed in, long and deep, and let out a shuddering sigh.

"Rain."

Battle-ready, I leaped to my feet and turned around, landing in the second stance. Jasper stood at the other end of the rooftop, blood trailing down his face from a gash across his brow. He extended his hands, palms up.

"Jasper." I stared at him, not moving.

"Who . . . what . . . was that?"

"Tan Vey."

He approached me cautiously, as though I might suddenly leap from the hold. When he reached the edge, he gazed blank-faced at the devastation below.

"Dragons . . . ?"

I nodded. "I woke them."

He stared at the carnage, his face contorting with emotion I couldn't name. Slowly, he turned to me. "I'm sorry. I—" He pressed his lips together.

"You were angry."

"I let anger cloud my judgment," he said. "Everything you accomplished—it had nothing to do with being a man or not. I'm . . . sorry."

A weight, hard and unyielding, lifted from my heart. "I forgive you."

"The bindings you offered," he continued. "They made a difference. It's hard to explain, but my bones started to heal more quickly than they should have. The pain is nothing more than a dull ache now."

"Dragon magic," I whispered.

"I believe you." He smiled. "Thank you."

It was the moment I'd dreamed of for weeks—Jasper's complete acceptance of me as a girl-warrior. But my heart was black with the loss of the man who had loved me best, and the knowledge that I had chosen Ylanda's survival over his.

"Jasper!"

I turned to see River, and then Briar, leap onto the rooftop.

"How did you find me?" I asked Jasper, overwhelmed to see the living, breathing faces of my friends.

"We set off shortly after Sedge," Jasper said. "We were right behind him when he went to your aid, and right behind the nomads that meant to stop you."

"But how—"

Words froze in my throat as Forest stepped onto the roof.

30

Dalen stepped up just behind him, supporting him with one arm. I could barely breathe.

"Forest."

I ran to him, heedless of the others, my chest heaving with silent sobs. He opened his good arm to me, and I slid into it as he wrapped it around me. Beneath his half-open leather shell, his wound was slick with fresh blood.

"I left you," I said, my voice breaking. "I had to leave you."

"Jasper and the others arrived," Forest said. "They outnumbered us by one, but we took care of them."

I suddenly became aware of the silence around us and extricated myself from Forest's embrace. Reality rushed back with painful precision—we had both survived, and we would return to the lives that awaited us.

"You're a hero, Rain," Forest said softly.

"No." I didn't want that title.

Distant shouts wafted on the breeze, likely some of the high king's men, emerging to inspect the damage. And probably wondering what in the universe had happened.

"It's time you were presented to the high king," Jasper said. "Forest is right—you *are* a hero."

"Sedge helped me." Even now, I wanted to choke on his name. "Where is he?"

The silence that met me answered more loudly than words. I looked at Jasper.

"I saw him fall," he said. "I don't know if he survived."

We made our way off the rooftop to the peak of the knoll and started down. I stopped short when I saw Sedge lying on the ground, his head on Flint's lap.

I knelt by Sedge, who coughed blood as he looked up at me. Blood saturated his shirt and the edges of his breastplate where a blade had pierced through his armpit.

"Thank you," I whispered.

He shook his head. "Don't thank me."

The revulsion I'd always felt for him melted into sorrow. In his piteous, last gasps of life, he couldn't see his own redemption.

"I couldn't have done it without you," I said.

"The dragon magic. It was—" He grimaced, his body shuddering. "Too much. I wanted to be . . . strong."

"Your strength helped save our kingdom."

"It wasn't my strength. I'm a coward." He coughed again, throaty and deep. "I'm sorry, s'da?"

Was this the same boy who had done nothing but abuse me since the day we'd met? Had these moments of dying brought a glimpse of his heart the way it looked before it turned dark?

How young he looked. And sad.

"I forgive you," I said.

"I wanted the glory," he said, "and you got it."

"No . . ."

He closed his eyes and drew a gurgling breath. When he spoke, his words were mostly air. "Turns out you were a better man than I was."

Utter stillness replaced the spasms of pain across his face. Forest's hand was warm on my shoulder as I drew in a long breath and made my peace with the boy who had meant me nothing but harm—until the very end, when he had given me exactly what I needed.

"Peaceful rest," I whispered.

We scrambled down the hill, bearing Sedge's body. When we reached the bottom, we laid him out on the ground, face and palms up, toward the Great God, who would bear his spirit home. Later, we would see that he was properly buried. For now, we left him and made our way to the front of the damaged hold, where several men were standing on the balcony taking in the view of the devastation and talking in loud voices. When they saw us, they stopped, staring down at us as though we were shades that had risen from the bodies of the dead.

Jasper cupped his hands around his mouth. "I'm Commander Dane of the high king's army." He gestured to me. "And this is Storm L'nahn, who woke the dragons and saved Ylanda."

My stomach dropped to my toes. He had introduced me as the boy he knew I wasn't.

We waited while two of the men disappeared from view. I shot a glance at Forest, whose expression was grim with the pain of his wound. He didn't look at me, and it was just as well. Whenever his eyes met mine, the ache in my heart was unbearable.

Two men, dressed in the canary-yellow livery of the high king's household, appeared from somewhere around the bend of the hold's right half-tower. We stood at attention, our training kicking in and presenting us, I hoped, as the loyal soldiers we were.

"Where is the rest of your army?" the taller man asked.

"We were a special unit of thirteen," Jasper said. "We're all that remain."

The tall man turned to me. "And you? You claim to have awakened the dragons?"

"Yes." The word felt like a speck of dust.

"The high king wishes to see you," the other man said. "All of you."

We followed them down a hidden stairway of five or six deep steps that led to a ponderous door fashioned not from wood, but from vertical, wrought-iron rods thicker than my wrist, so close together I could barely see through them and four layers deep. We entered and waited while the tall man slid five heavy bars in place across the door, locking us in.

I wasn't sure why, at this point, he felt the need to secure the door. Perhaps it was simply habit.

We walked through a narrow tunnel, lit at intervals by oil lamps set into crevices in the wall. A second, four-layer-thick iron door sat at the end, and we walked through it and up a curving flight of stairs, then through another passageway that opened to a set of heavy wooden doors.

The tall man stood before the doors. "When you enter, simply bow and wait for His Majesty to address you."

My palms were wet and I was breathing too loudly. The doors opened soundlessly, and we stepped inside a large, tapestry-hung room that was more opulent than I would have imagined possible. The high king sat on a long, low bench against the back wall, robed in traditional red and gold. Even seated, he seemed remarkably tall, with broad shoulders and a long, sloping nose. He wore a thin silver circlet on his head, and his hair hung well past his shoulders. His expression seemed practiced, as though he had no intention of showing us what he was feeling.

But I saw it in his eyes—awe. The high king of our great kingdom could not comprehend what had happened.

My legs trembled beneath me as I bowed low and waited for him to speak.

"Which of you claims to have awakened the dragons?" His voice was deep and thin, as though he hadn't spoken in a long time.

I placed my hand on my racing heart and bowed my head. "I did, Your Majesty."

"Come." He waited as I approached, my footsteps faltering. "So you are he, the dragon-waker I had long ceased believing in."

"I—" The storm in my breast rose to a fevered pitch. I couldn't accept his honor as someone I wasn't. "I am *she,* Your Majesty. Not he."

His eyes widened and he rose slowly to his feet. "You're . . . a *woman?*"

"Yes." I sank to my knees. "I deceived my commander and everyone else. They're all innocent." A small lie to make up for my much larger one. My parting gift to Forest.

The chamber fairly crackled in the silence, everyone waiting with me for the high king's response. I had begun to tremble so violently that I sat back on my feet and pressed my hands against the cool stone floor. When the high king spoke again, my heart seized.

"You willfully defied the law, knowing its consequences?"

"I did."

"And yet the Great God chose to show you favor."

I opened my mouth and closed it again. The high king seemed to be speaking more to himself than to me.

"Your Majesty." Forest stepped forward, hand cradling his wound. "What Rain has said is only partially true."

My heart clenched within me. *No! Don't implicate yourself!*

"I discovered her deception some weeks ago and remained silent," Forest continued. "I'm complicit." He looked at me, his eyes bathed in sorrow. "There's no life for me without you," he said softly.

Jasper cleared his throat. "What she hasn't told you, Your Majesty, is that she also single-handedly defeated Tan Vey on the roof of your hold. I saw the very end of it—he looked as though he were under the influence of some sort of . . . dragon magic."

The high king looked at me. "Is this true?"

"Yes, Your Majesty. Tan Vey swallowed something that gave him dragon power."

"How . . . how did he end up on the roof? How did he escape the dragons?"

"I saw him climbing up," I said. "He must have run from his post when the dragons broke free."

"No one in here would have survived, had he gotten past Rain," Jasper said.

"And I wouldn't have made it to the dragons if it weren't for the rest of my unit," I said. "They fought off the soldiers who would have stopped me from entering the catacombs. Truly, I didn't accomplish this alone."

The high king made a temple with his hands and pressed his forefingers to his lips. For several moments, he seemed overcome. "The only power greater than myself is our Great God, who saw fit to return us to the care of his dragons. I dare not question his method of bringing us this unexpected salvation." He reached his hand to me. "Rise."

I must have looked unable to do so, because suddenly Jasper was there, taking my arm and helping me to my feet. I steadied myself and gazed at the high king.

"What is your full name?"

"Rain L'nahn," I said.

"Rain L'nahn, you have served your high king and your kingdom, and you have done what no one before you has dreamed of doing. I offer you a hero's honor and my personal blessing."

I clapped my hand over my mouth before realizing I had done so. "Thank you," I whispered through my fingers.

"The Great God has seen fit to bless our kingdom with deliverance through a means I would never have foreseen," the high king said. "All of you standing here were part of that. You have my clemency and my deepest appreciation."

I closed my eyes as a grateful tear sneaked its way down my cheek.

31

Almost four weeks later, I stood outside the double doors to the high king's Majestic Hall, adorned in the traditional white and gold tunic of an honored soldier, my hair hanging free. Forest stood beside me, with Jasper in front, both wearing the same tunics, Jasper's with a thick purple braid across his shoulders, signifying his rank. The others stood behind us.

I had barely seen them since our arrival at the palace three days earlier, after nearly two weeks of slow travel from the hold. The room I'd been assigned was separate from the others, down a long, ornate hallway with complete privacy. It didn't feel like a demotion, though; it felt like an honor. I'd received the gift of my life and the high king's blessing, but I was very much a girl again. Or perhaps a woman.

And I didn't mind.

"I wish this were over with." My voice, once deepened by the dragon powder, sounded normal again.

"So do I." Forest didn't look at me. But in the past month, I'd grown used to it.

"I wrote home," I said, desperate to break the silence. "As soon as we arrived. But the messengers are running extra slow, they say. I'm afraid I may get there before my letter does."

"I wrote home, too." His voiced hitched on the final word, and he pressed his mouth shut, his eyes still not meeting mine.

I sighed. "Forest . . ."

"There's nothing more to say, *s'da?*"

"Will you at least let me thank you?" I fought to keep my voice from wobbling. "When you found out the truth about me, you didn't treat me differently. I wanted to be a soldier instead of staying home and getting married and sewing things. And you embraced me for who I was. I didn't think that was possible."

Forest's gaze had the depth of a thousand oceans. "You're easy to embrace," he said softly.

The doors opened, and we were ushered into the presence of the high king. I blinked, my eyes dazzled by the reflection of sunlight from the walls of the Majestic Hall, which were overlaid with gold. The ceiling, also gilded, soared to such a height that looking up made me dizzy. Standing to either side of the roped-off pathway, thousands of citizens stood packed together like fish at market, waiting for a glimpse of the girl who had awakened the dragons.

I focused on the high king instead of the ogling masses. We walked slowly, as we'd been instructed, though I wished I could run.

Has the high king honored you yet?

I smiled at the sound of Nuaga's voice, which I could now hear freely. *I'm walking toward him now. Don't distract me.*

Her laughter bubbled through my head. *Does he know we're coming?*

I'm sure he does.

Nuaga's words were infused with joy. *We'll talk later, Rain L'nahn.*

When finally we stood before the high king, the hall quieted into a deep hush. He spoke at length, telling the tale of his time in the hold, the despair of believing the kingdom would fall to the nomads, and the story of my arrival and how I had awakened the dragons and led Tan Vey to his death. His ringing voice was the only sound in the chamber, as though everyone had decided not to breathe until he finished.

Once the story had been told, he asked us to turn around and face the crowd. "These men—and this woman—are the last standing soldiers of their unit. Together, they made it possible for the dragons to be awakened and our kingdom to be saved. I offer them all my eternal honor."

My face grew hot as applause and cheering erupted, and it grew hotter still when the high king laid his hand on my shoulder and bade everyone be quiet.

"To this woman alone, I give highest honors, and name her Rain L'nahn Ylanda, Dragon-Waker."

At this, the applause and cheering doubled, as I tried desperately to grasp what the high king had just said. Ylanda? Had he given me his own surname? Confusion washed over me as he turned me to face him and addressed me with a softer voice.

"It is my wish to grant you a position here," he said, "and bestow upon you whatever your heart desires. Ask, and it is yours."

I felt breathless—overcome by this outpouring of his kindness. What could I possibly ask? The aching desire of my heart was for Forest, but I couldn't ask for him, even if the high king himself paved the way.

Wouldn't ask.

"I only wish to go home," I said. "And . . . perhaps to repay my father the dowry money he entrusted to me."

The high king smiled. "So it shall be, Rain L'nahn Ylanda—this, and tenfold." He repeated my request to the waiting crowd, who cheered yet again.

I waited until the tumult quieted, and then I summoned my courage. "Your Majesty," I said. "My other desire is to become a Neshu grandmaster—to train both boys and girls in this ancient and sacred martial art. I wondered if . . . if you . . ."

"If I would lift the ban on women participating in our Neshu traditions?"

I raised my eyes to his and swore I saw a twinkle there—the last thing I expected. "Yes."

The high king pressed his hands together, fingertip to fingertip. "You have already shaken the foundations of long-held beliefs about what women can do. Considering your contribution to the kingdom of Ylanda and Commander Dane's commendation of your skills, I can think of no better use for your talents. You have my permission *and* my blessing to become a grandmaster."

This time, there were a few moments of silence before the crowd applauded, as if they weren't sure how to receive his words. As the clapping increased, I bowed low before my high king, words failing me.

When I rose, I was unable to contain my smile. "Thank you."

Color and movement suddenly filled the tall, narrow windows on both sides of the hall, and a collective gasp rang out as shadows darkened the sunlight. I looked up to see dragons lined up outside both rows of windows, their majestic necks arched proudly. My heart swelled as I searched for Nuaga among them, but I couldn't find her for the sheer number of them.

The high king raised his arms and shouted, "We welcome you, dragons! And we thank you!"

After a slight hesitation, the crowd echoed his words, raising their arms and shouting their welcome and thanks to the mighty dragons, who bowed their heads in acknowledgment. I was proud to be counted as one of their clan.

Proud and humbled.

But I was relieved when we were dismissed.

Three smart rows of the high king's guard led us down a wide, gilded hallway to a small banquet room festooned with colorful silk banners. The high king's chair at the head of the table stood waiting, and I took my assigned place to the left of it. Jasper sat on my right. When I tried to meet Forest's gaze across the table, he looked pointedly at Dalen, who sat beside him.

"I'll miss the food here," Dalen said, eyeing the steaming dishes as servants laid them on the table. "Especially the sauces."

River laughed. "I pity your wife."

I looked at Jasper, who was running his finger along the edge of his goblet. "Will you be happy here?"

"I'm honored that His Majesty wants me," Jasper said. "And I still don't understand why you don't want to be in my elite Neshu unit. You deserve the honor more than I do."

I raised an eyebrow. "You don't mind girls who fight Neshu after all?"

For a moment, he looked sheepish. "I can't imagine there are many girls like you."

There will be, once I start training them. "You didn't answer my question."

As Jasper opened his mouth, the high king entered with his son, the crown prince. We all rose, but he waved us back to our seats as he made his way to the head of the table.

"You've changed the world, Rain L'nahn," Jasper whispered as we sat.

I smiled, his words warming me like a sunrise.

The high king took his seat and raised his goblet. "One final feast with the woman—and the men—who saved our kingdom. Today is a fine day to be high king of Ylanda!"

We raised our goblets and cried, "Ylanda!" The *avila* liqueur was rich and smooth in my mouth, some of the finest from Tenema's distilleries. A taste of home.

It was where I longed to be.

———

I stood beside the golden carriage in the fading light of dusk. True to his word, the high king had filled a chest with ten times the amount of money Papa had given me, as well as a trunk filled with beautiful silks and linens, enough for Mama to sew a lifetime of clothing. The gifts were packed in the carriage, along with a smaller trunk of personal items the high king had given me—mostly clothing, but also an exquisite dagger, which meant more than any other gift.

"Rain."

My heart melted at the sound of Forest's voice. I turned to him, arranging my face in what I hoped was a convincing smile.

"Ready for our journey?" I asked.

"I'm not coming," he said.

My smile fell. "What do you mean?"

"I'm going to ride with River as far as Grigsbane, and I'll pick up my donkey from my uncle's and ride home from there."

"But . . . we live so close to each other, and—"

"Rain." He stepped close and cupped my face in his hands. "There's no point in drawing out the pain. Every moment I'm with you reminds me that I can't have you. We have to let go. Say goodbye."

Tears I'd promised myself I wouldn't allow to fall defied me, spilling into Forest's hands. "I know, but . . ."

"I'll be good to your sister. I'll try to make her happy."

"She'll love you for it." I could barely choke the words out.

We kissed, and I clung to him, burying myself in his warmth and the sweet taste of his mouth. I wanted to linger, but, with a will greater than I thought I had, I untangled myself from him.

"I'll always love you," I said.

He took my hand and pressed his lips to it, blinking back tears. Then he turned abruptly and disappeared into the shadows.

My heart was colder than the wind.

32

The low wall around my parents' house looked as it always had. As the royal carriage pulled up to the gate, I scanned the yard and the windows of my house, my heart fluttering incessantly. The door opened, and Mama stood gaping at the carriage. She didn't see me inside.

"Mama!" I jumped from the carriage, not bothering to wait for the driver to assist me.

Mama's eyes grew round and her mouth opened wide in a perfect O. She reached her arms toward me as I ran, finally catching me in a hug.

"What is this? What is this, my sweet girl?" And then she was sobbing into my neck, and all I could do was hold her until she settled.

She pulled back and looked at me, her expression one of complete disbelief—and unfettered joy. "How can this be?"

"Did you not receive my letter?"

"No, there was no letter." She wiped her cheek with her palm. "What carriage is this? Oh, my precious Rain."

"It's the high king's," I said. "Where's Papa?"

"The high king's? But—oh, Papa!"

I followed the trajectory of her eyes to see Papa standing there, one hand pressed against his mouth.

"I'm home, Papa," I said.

"You . . . did not fight with the army, after all?"

"I did fight," I said. "I will tell you everything." I gestured to the carriage, where the driver was already unloading the first trunk. "Gifts for you and Mama."

But he walked toward me with thunderous love in his eyes and caught me in the kind of hug I'd known since I was a tiny girl. "*You are my gift, Rain L'nahn. I never expected to see you again.*"

I nestled against his chest and pretended I didn't feel the vibrations of his silent sobs. He kissed the top of my head and released me. His eyes were wet with tears.

"You look strong," he said. "Hardened."

"I am."

"You have much to tell us." Papa's words were breathless.

"I do. Let's get the trunks first, *s'da?*"

Together with the driver, we moved the three trunks into the house. Storm stumbled sleepy-eyed from his bedroom and stared at me with his mouth hanging open.

"You back, Rain?"

"I'm back." I held out my arms for a hug.

He shuffled across the floor and wrapped me in his strong man-arms. "I kept waiting for you at the gate, but Mama and Papa told me to stop."

"I'm glad you obeyed them."

"No, Rain." He withdrew his arms and looked at me with an expression that transcended his limitations. "I knew you'd come home."

I glanced at Papa, whose eyes still glistened with tears. Then I rose on tiptoe and kissed Storm soundly on the cheek. "Thank you for believing."

We sat together at the table. Mama bustled to prepare some *t'gallah* and hot tea, and I suddenly realized my sister wasn't there.

"Where's Willow?" I asked.

"Serving tea to her future mother-in-law," Papa said.

My heart sank. Forest's letter to his parents had apparently arrived. "I see."

"We're thankful for her sake that she had the chance of a second betrothal," Mama said.

I stopped breathing. "A second betrothal?"

"Word came that the entire army had been decimated, with no hope of survivors," Papa said. "When Willow heard the news, she consented to marry Bird Tanner."

My mind scrambled. "The old widower?"

"Not old," Mama said. "He's barely forty."

Ancient. "But her betrothed—" I stopped. How could I even begin to tell them about Forest?

Papa cocked his head. "What is it?"

"He's not dead."

"You *know* him?" Mama asked.

"Yes."

Papa laced his fingers together. "Tell us everything."

I started at the beginning and told them. But I felt separated from my own voice, my heart dancing and aching and somersaulting while I spoke.

She's betrothed to someone else. He's free.

I didn't speak of my love for Forest. I had no idea what he would tell his parents about me—or even *if* he would tell them.

But he was all I could think of.

"Forest had every intention of honoring the betrothal," I said, though the words felt bitter on my tongue.

"There was no way to know he would come home," Papa said. "We will talk with your sister tonight and decide what should be done."

My heart tangled into an unspeakable knot, and I didn't have the courage to ask if she would be obligated to honor her former arrangement. I only nodded and offered the best smile I could muster.

Storm grabbed my hand. "Were you brave, Rain? Were you a good soldier?"

"I was brave," I said.

"Braver than me?"

I squeezed his hand, thankful for its warmth and strength in mine. Thankful that he was there, safe and whole. "I thought of you every day, Storm," I said. "You *made* me brave."

His smile lit the room. "That's what twins are for."

Willow dropped her teapot when she walked in the door two hours later and saw me sitting there. I rose to greet her, and she threw her arms around my neck and buried her face in my shoulder, weeping.

I told her everything that had happened in the last three months, except about my love for Forest. She listened, wide-eyed, as Mama held her hand and Papa drank in my words all over again, as though he hadn't heard them before.

"So his parents had to tell him he no longer had a bride waiting," Willow said after I'd finished.

"I'm sure they didn't word it like that." Actually, I was sure that, in the joy of their reunion, it was the last thing on their minds.

Willow pulled her hand from Mama's and wrung her own two together. "Papa, have we dishonored his family?"

"The betrothal was honorably broken," Papa said. "But now that we know the truth, what is the honorable thing to do?"

I held my breath as I watched a flurry of emotion scuttle across Willow's face. She had never wanted to marry the old widower, and I had come home and handed her the perfect excuse not to.

"Bird came home just before tea was over," Willow said. "It was only the second time we've been in the same room together, and . . ." She lowered her eyes. "I like the way he looked at me."

"Your betrothal is valid, daughter," Papa said. "We need do nothing to change it, if you feel that's where honor lies."

"I . . ." Willow looked up, and her cheeks were rosy pink. "Is he handsome, Rain?"

I dug my nails into the palms of my hands. "He's pleasant enough to look at. And he's kind." And a hundred other wonderful things, if she would dare to think beyond his appearance.

Willow chewed her bottom lip and sighed. "I've waited so long to be married. I don't think I want to start over again with another betrothal."

"That has nothing to do with honor," Mama said.

"No, but . . ." Willow looked at me. "You know this boy. Would he feel dishonored to learn I hadn't waited for him?"

I swallowed. "No, he wouldn't."

The room was silent as Willow weighed whatever was important to her. Even in a state of confusion, she was beautiful, and her desire to do the right thing made her even more so.

Forest might never love her, but she would certainly love him.

"I think I should honor my betrothal to Bird," Willow said.

My heart burst from its cage with a jubilant song only I could hear. I hid my smile and said nothing.

"It's settled, then," Papa said.

Willow turned to me, her expression softened by relief. "He's a good man, and not so very old, even if he does walk with a cane. I think you'll like him."

"I'm sure I will."

She reached forward and squeezed my arm with both hands. "Everything's turned out so well, sister!"

Oh, Willow. If only you knew.

For four days, with every breath, every heartbeat, I thought of him. At night, I hugged my pillow and ached for him. In my dreams, his name was on my lips. I couldn't speak of him, couldn't allow myself to hope. No one but Forest knew of my love for him—my agony was my own.

On the morning of the fifth day, Papa and I finished breakfast and prepared to go to our favorite sparring spot to begin my Neshu master training. I opened the front door, calling for Papa as I walked into the cold sunshine.

Forest stood at the gate.

The sky, the trees, the clucking of the chickens—everything ceased to exist. I stared at Forest, my breaths coming in short white puffs in the morning air.

Papa emerged, his eyes on Forest. "Who's this, coming so early?"

I ran to the gate, my gaze never falling from Forest. When I reached him, I stopped, gasping for breath, my hands curled around the top of the gate.

"Forest."

"I woke up while it was still dark," he said, "and got an early start."

"Did you?"

"Are you going to let me in?"

"Oh." I fumbled at the latch like a scattered child. "Yes."

"Rain, is this a friend of yours?" Papa had reached us, Storm two steps behind him.

"Yes," I said, stepping aside as the gate swung open and Forest walked through. "This is Forest, whom I told you about."

Forest bowed, hand on his chest. "I'm honored to meet you."

"And this is my brother Storm," I said.

"Storm." Forest smiled. "You look so like your sister."

Storm grinned. "Except she's a girl."

"Rain has spoken highly of you," Papa said. "Won't you have some tea to warm you?"

"I—" Forest glanced at me. "Yes. Thank you."

Something in Papa's face changed—a knowing sort of look that made warmth rush through me. "I'll go ask my wife to prepare it. Come with me, Storm."

Forest waited until Papa and Storm had reached the house. Then he took my hands in his—they were as cold as my own.

"I had to come," he said. "My parents told me they returned Willow's dowry to your father, and that they'd help me find another suitable match. But I said I'd already found one."

"You said that?"

"Yes." He drew my hands to his chest. "I want to talk to your father. I'm not asking for a dowry. Only you."

My smile was so wide that my cheeks ached. "Do you think maybe you should ask me first?"

He smiled back. "If you insist." He wrapped his arms around me and pressed his forehead to mine. "Will you be my wife, Rain L'nahn Ylanda?"

I slipped my arms around his waist and brushed his lips with mine. "Yes." Because he loved me for who I was. And because, in a million lifetimes, I would never find anyone to replace him.

We kissed until we were breathless, until everything except the taste and touch and warmth of him lost meaning. When we finally drew apart, I looked up to see my parents standing in the doorway, their arms around each other. They were smiling.

"Ready for some tea?" Mama called.

I smiled and waved. Then, hand in hand, Forest and I walked toward the warmth of Mama's kitchen and the hope of Papa's blessing.

Together. As we were meant to be.

ACKNOWLEDGMENTS

The publication of this book was preceded by fourteen years of writing and growing and dreaming and writing some more. Throughout my journey, I've been blessed by encouragement and help and insight from countless people (on so many projects), and *Stormrise* is the end result. Each of you has touched this story without knowing it.

Endless thanks to my agent, Danielle Burby, whose enthusiasm and undying belief in me, coupled with her sharp editorial eye, have sustained me and pushed me to heights I wouldn't have reached without her. Thanks also to my talented editor, Elayne Becker, whose incredible vision for *Stormrise* made it what it is today. And, of course, huge thanks to the entire Tor Teen team who have made this book a reality.

To those who read: Maggie Boehme, whose input I could never do without and whose reaction to this story made me believe like never before; Rain Czine, whose enthusiasm for an early draft lit a fire beneath me that never went out (and also whose name I stole for my own Rain); Adam Heine, whose world-building prowess I need almost as much as oxygen; Courtney Karmiller, whose top-notch editorial notes and in-person encouragement were invaluable; Constance Lopez, who read the draft twice in a row simply because she wanted to (love you!); Ellen Oden, who helped me discover Rain's authenticity; Rena Rossner, with whom I've shared a long, twisty, writerly journey (congratulations, dear one!); Peter Salomon, who wasn't afraid to admit my story made him cry; and Mónica Bustamante

Wagner, who was the first person to tell me that Forest needed more fleshing out (I should have listened then)—thank you all so much!

To my personal cheerleaders: Rachel Boehme, who has been continual light and joy along the way; my parents, Janet and Mockie Schafer, whose never-ending chorus of *YOU CAN DO THIS* still rings in my ears; and Jamie Soranno, my sister and the best friend a gal could ask for, who makes me feel like I could do absolutely anything—your support and encouragement mean the world to me.

To Jake O'Brien, who came up with the original title for this novel. It may not have stuck, but you're still my hero for it!

To my blog readers and the online writing community: Those of you who have known me as Authoress for more than a decade have been a constant source of encouragement, solidarity, and accountability. Thank you all for being part of my journey!

To Jonathan, Maggie, Rachel, Spencer, and Molly, who grew up watching me pursue an invisible dream: Thank you for who you are. I love you.

To my husband Eric: You've been there from the beginning. From my darkest low points to the giddy heights of dreams fulfilled, you have been my champion. That, and you taught me to laugh at my badly written, incredibly dorky dialogue—and never to write it that way again. You are, and always will be, the love of my life.

To Jesus Christ, my Lord and Savior: The glory is yours.

*I can do all things through Him
who strengthens me.*
—PHILIPPIANS 4:13

ABOUT THE AUTHOR

JILLIAN BOEHME is known to the online writing community as Authoress, hostess of *Miss Snark's First Victim,* a blog for aspiring authors. In real life, she holds a degree in music education, sings with the Nashville Symphony Chorus, and homeschools her remaining youngster-at-home. She's still crazy in love with her husband of more than thirty years and is happy to be surrounded by family and friends amid the rolling knolls of Middle Tennessee.